P9-DNQ-864

CAROLINA
GOLD

**Center Point
Large Print**

Also by Dorothy Love and available from Center Point Large Print:

A Respectable Actress
Mrs. Lee and Mrs. Gray

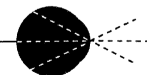

CAROLINA GOLD

Dorothy Love

CENTER POINT LARGE PRINT
THORNDIKE, MAINE

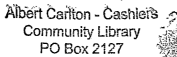

The text of this Large Print edition is unabridged.
In other aspects, this book may vary
from the original edition.
Printed in the United States of America
on permanent paper.
Set in 16-point Times New Roman type.

ISBN: 978-1-68324-275-8

Library of Congress Cataloging-in-Publication Data

Names: Love, Dorothy, 1949– author.
Title: Carolina gold / Dorothy Love.
Description: Center Point Large Print edition. | Thorndike, Maine :
Center Point Large Print, 2017.
Identifiers: LCCN 2016048755 | ISBN 9781683242758
    (hardcover : alk. paper)
Subjects: LCSH: Women plantation owners—Fiction. | Reconstruction
(U.S. history, 1865–1877)—South Carolina—Fiction. | Large type
books. | GSAFD: Christian fiction. | Historical fiction.
Classification: LCC PS3562.O8387 C37 2017 | DDC 813/.54—dc23
LC record available at https://lccn.loc.gov/2016048755

Dedicated to the memory of
Elizabeth Waties Allston Pringle
(1845–1921),
whose remarkable life and work
inspired this novel

From the collections of the
South Carolina Historical Society

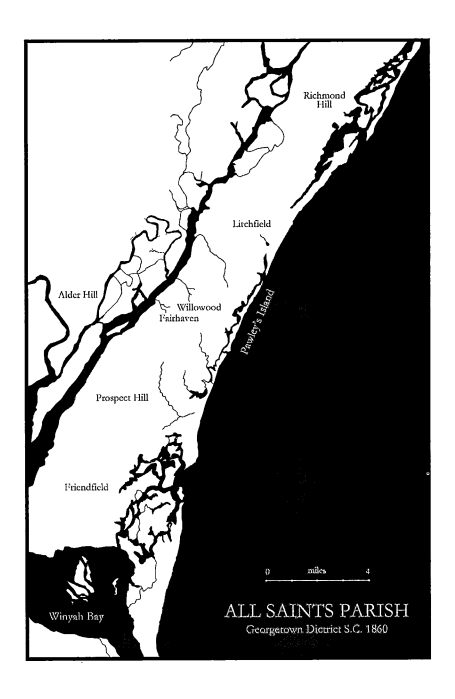

Richmond
Hill

Litchfield

Alder Hill

Willowood
Fairhaven

Pawley's Island

Prospect Hill

Friendfield

0   miles   4

Winyah Bay

ALL SAINTS PARISH
Georgetown District S.C. 1860

CAROLINA
GOLD

There is in every true woman's heart a spark of heavenly fire . . . which kindles up and beams and blazes in the dark hour of adversity.
WASHINGTON IRVING

One

Charleston, South Carolina
3 March 1868

In a quiet alcove off the hotel lobby, Charlotte Fraser perched on a worn horsehair chair, nursing a cup of lukewarm tea. A wind-driven freshet lashed the windows and roiled the bruise-colored sky, sending the pedestrians along Chalmers Street scurrying for shelter, jostling one another amid a sea of black umbrellas.

She glanced at the clock mounted on the wall above the polished mahogany reception desk and pressed a hand to her midsection to quell her nerves. An hour remained before her appointment with her father's lawyer. She had anticipated the meeting for weeks with equal measures of hope and dread, her happiness at the prospect

11

of returning home to the river tempered by fear of what she would find waiting for her. In the war's crushing aftermath, Fortune had cast her powerful eye upon all of the Lowcountry and passed on by.

A black carriage shiny with rain executed a wide turn onto Meeting Street, the harness rattling as the conveyance halted beneath the porte cochere. The hotel door opened on a gust of wind and rain that guttered the lamps still burning against the afternoon gloom. A young man wearing a rain-splotched cape escorted his lady to the reception desk. He signed the register, then bent to his companion and whispered into her ear. An endearment perhaps. Or a secret.

"Every family has its secrets. And its regrets." Charlotte set down her cup. Such strange words from Papa, who had been widely respected for his forthright manner. At the time, she'd had a strong feeling he was trying to tell her something important. Now the memory pinged inside her head like a knife against glass, prickling her skin. But perhaps such talk was merely the product of the laudanum clouding his brain during his final hours.

For weeks following his funeral, Charlotte's natural optimism lay trapped beneath a cloak of sorrow and she could feel little but the jagged edges of her grief. Now it had softened into something less painful. Acceptance, if not yet peace. And, as the indignities brought on by

Reconstruction multiplied, gratitude that death had spared him yet another cruel irony. As former slaves wrestled with the implications of their freedom, their masters were mired in poverty that made their own futures just as uncertain.

Despite her personal hardships, Charlotte was relieved that slavery had ended. At twenty-three she was too young and too inexperienced to assume responsibility for the welfare of so many others. During long nights when sleep eluded her and her problems crowded in, she sometimes doubted whether she could look after herself.

When the clock chimed the three-quarter hour, she gathered her cloak, reticule, and umbrella and crossed the hotel lobby, the sound of her footfalls lost in the thick carpet.

The doorman, a stocky red-haired man of uncertain years, touched the brim of his hat. "Shall I find a carriage for you, Miss Fraser?"

"Thank you, but it isn't necessary. I'm going to my lawyer's office just down the street."

He peered through the leaded-glass door. "Rain's slacking off some, but the walk will feel like miles in this damp."

She fished a coin from her bag. "Will you see that my trunks are delivered to the steamship office right away?"

"Certainly." He pocketed the coin and held the door open for her. "Take care you don't get a chill, miss."

She threw her cloak over her stiff crepe mourning dress, stepped from beneath the hotel's protective awning, and hurried down the street, rain thumping onto the stretched silk of her umbrella. Meeting Street hummed with carriages and drays, freight wagons and pedestrians headed in a dozen different directions. A buggy carrying a dark-skinned woman in a pink-plumed hat raced past, the wheels splashing dirty water onto the side-walk. At the corner of Meeting and Broad, a Yankee officer stood chatting with two burly Negro men smoking cheroots. Charlotte picked her way along the slick cobblestones, past the remnants of burned-out buildings and the rubble of crumbled chimneys, feeling estranged from a city she knew like the back of her hand.

As long as Papa was alive, she'd felt connected to every street and lane, every shop and church spire, every secret garden beckoning from the narrow shadowed alleys. Now everything had been upended. Nobody was where they were supposed to be and she was floating, adrift in a strange new world with no one to guide her.

She dodged a group of noisy boys emerging from a bookshop and gathered her skirts to avoid the dirty water splashing from the wheels of another passing carriage. Beneath the sheltering awning of a confectioner's shop, two women watched her progress along the street, their faces drawn into identical disapproving frowns. No doubt they thought it inappropriate for a young woman to walk on the street unescorted. She lifted her chin and met the older women's gazes as she passed. If they knew the purpose of her visit to the lawyer, perhaps they'd be even further scandalized.

At the law office, she made her way up the steps and rang the bell.

Mr. Crowley, a wizened man with a bulbous nose and a fringe of white hair, opened the door. "Miss Fraser. Right on time, I see. Do come in."

She left her dripping umbrella in the brass stand in the anteroom, crossed the bare wooden floor, and took the seat he indicated. She folded her hands in her lap and waited while he settled him-self and thumbed through the pile of documents littering his desk.

Through the window she watched people and conveyances making their way along the street, ghostlike in the oyster-colored light of the waning afternoon. Down the block a lantern struggled against the gloom, casting a shining path on the rain-varnished cobblestones. Music from a partially opened window across the street filtered into the chilly office. Somebody practicing Chopin.

She felt a prick of loss. According to their neighbors, the Federals had destroyed her piano on one of their wartime raids up the Waccamaw River. Probably everything else as well. Since the war's end, the difficulties of travel and her father's prolonged illness had prevented her from learning firsthand whether anything was left of Fairhaven Plantation.

"Well, Mr. Crowley?" Charlotte consulted the ornate wall clock behind his desk. Captain Arthur's steamship, *Resolute*, traveled from Charleston to Georgetown only on Wednesdays and Saturdays. She meant to be aboard for tomorrow morning's departure. If she could ever get an answer from the lawyer. "What about my father's will?"

Without looking up, he raised one finger. Wait.

She tamped down her growing impatience. Waiting was about all she had been able to do since Papa's death. That and worrying about how she would make her way in the world alone. Now that the war was lost and all the bondsmen were free, the rice trade that had provided her with a comfortable life was in danger of disappearing altogether. She was trained for nothing else.

At last Mr. Crowley looked up, wire spectacles sliding down his nose. "The will has been entered into the record and duly recognized by the court." He paged through a file, a frown creasing his forehead.

"But?"

"I'd feel much better if your father had provided a copy of the grant to his barony." He studied her over the top of his spectacles. "You're certain he left no other papers behind?"

"No, none." She felt a jolt of panic. "Does that pose a problem?"

"I hope not. There's a new law on the books that provides for testimony regarding lost wills and deeds and such, but if you've never seen such a document, then you can hardly swear to its existence in court."

"No, I suppose not."

"Now that the Yankees have taken over, they can seize whatever they want in the name of Reconstruction." He snorted. "Reconstruction, my eye. Theft is more like it." He leaned forward, both palms pressed to his desk, and blew out a long breath. "Lacking proof of your father's grant just makes it that much easier for them. Frankly I'm surprised he left no record behind. He seemed like a man who left little to chance. But I suppose we all have our shortcomings."

Charlotte toyed with the clasp on her reticule. As a small child she had thought Papa the perfect embodiment of wisdom, intelligence, and prudence. A man without shortcomings. Only occasionally had she glimpsed moments in which he seemed lost to time and place, standing apart and alone, an unreadable expression in his dark eyes. She still revered him as the finest man in Carolina, the only man in the world in whom she had absolute faith and confidence. Learning of such a grave oversight had come as a shock.

She met the lawyer's calm gaze. "I don't know why the Yankees would want my land now. According to everything I've heard, they just about destroyed every plantation on the Waccamaw—and the Pee Dee too."

"Exactly. And sentiment aside, I can't fathom what a lovely young woman such as yourself would want with such a ruin."

"You've seen it, then? You've been to Fairhaven?"

"No, but all I've done since the war ended is work with the other rice planters, and the story is the same all over. I'm sure it's no surprise to you that the Yankees and the freed slaves have stolen everything. Right down to the linens off the beds at Mrs. Allston's place."

"Yes, I heard about that. Papa said it was a blessing Governor Allston passed on before that sad day came. Chicora Wood meant so much to him."

Mr. Crowley nodded. "I can't imagine that your plantation has fared any better."

She swallowed the knot in her throat. In his last months, Papa had spoken of little else but the bewildering loss that had stunned the entire Confederacy. Following General Lee's surrender, everyone hoped the worst was over. No one realized that the future under Yankee occupation would become a tragedy all its own.

Mr. Crowley leaned back in his chair, causing it to squeak. "While I was looking into your father's will, Gabriel Titus over at the bank told me you'd applied for credit."

"That's right. To buy rice seeds. And whatever else I need to make Fairhaven profitable again."

He shook his head. "Forgive me, Miss Fraser, but if an experienced planter like Ben Allston can't make a go of it, what makes you think you can?"

"Because I have no choice. The plantation and our summer cottage on Pawley's Island are all I have left in the world."

"You'd be better off to sell both of them and get yourself a nice little room here in town. Or better yet, find yourself a stable gentleman and settle down."

Charlotte bit back a tart reply. More than a quarter million Southern men had been lost to the war, and many who survived had come home maimed in body or spirit or both, missing limbs and their fortunes. Just who in the world did Mr. Crowley think she could marry? "Mr. Titus told me that no one is interested in paying a fair price for Fairhaven or for Pelican Cottage. It would be quite impossible to sell even if I wanted to."

"Did Titus lend you the money?"

"He agreed to a mortgage on Fairhaven. Out of respect for my father."

"And what happens if you can't repay the loan?"

"I have a year before it comes due. And I

expect to earn a bit of money writing articles for the *New York Enterprise*."

"My word." He inclined his head, and his thick spectacles caught the light. "I had no idea you harbored journalistic ambitions. Or that you had the training for such an undertaking."

"I'm not formally trained, but I can write a clear sentence and I know the Lowcountry as well as anyone."

"Good gravy, woman. You think Yankees care about anything that goes on down here? They did all they could to destroy us."

"The editor, Mr. Sawyer, seems to think his readers will be interested. I sent an inquiry last month and he has just replied, offering to pay ten dollars for each article. If I can write one a month, I'll at least earn enough to keep the taxes paid. And if my rice crop comes in, I can repay the bank loan too."

"If, if, if." The lawyer sighed and glanced out the rain-smudged window. "I know how much that property means to you, but as your attorney and as your father's friend, I still say the city life is more suitable for a young lady. Charleston is coming to life again. Folks are starting to rebuild. My wife tells me the St. Cecelia Society is already planning to hold two balls next year. But you surely know that."

"I've had neither time nor inclination to pay attention to the social scene of late."

"Still, going to a dance sounds more proper than wading around knee-deep in that foul-smelling muck, praying for rice to sprout."

"I suppose." As a young girl attending Madame Giraud's boarding school, she'd loved the noise and gaiety of Charleston. Race Week, picnics at White Point, lectures and plays and dances provided welcome diversions from the monotony of lectures and recitations. Yet even then she had longed for quiet days in the country, trailing after Papa and learning everything he could teach her about the cultivation of rice. They loved all the same things—books, music, dogs and horses, and growing the special kind of rice called Carolina Gold. Even if she had money to burn, Charleston society held little appeal for her now. She wanted only to go home to Fairhaven, to pick up the pieces of her shattered world. To make it whole again.

Mr. Crowley leaned forward, his piercing gaze holding hers. "You're still a young woman. You ought to find a suitable husband."

"Thank you for your advice." She opened her reticule and slid a check across the desk. "This should cover your fee."

"Now you're offended, and I didn't mean anything by it. I hate to see you get your hopes up only to be disappointed when you find out how bad things are up on the river." He picked up the check and handed it back to her. "Your father was a good friend and I'm mourning him too.

I'm not about to take money from his only daughter at a time like this."

"I . . . thank you. I'm sure it will be put to good use." She rose. "I must go. I'm booked aboard the *Resolute*. I should check to see that my things have been delivered to the pier."

"I see. And what if the news here today had been different? What if I hadn't been able to find your father's will?"

"I'd have gone anyway, for one last ride around the fields. Lettice Hadley wrote last week that she and Mr. Hadley have returned to Alder Hill. She's invited me to go riding with her as soon as I'm settled."

"I'm glad of that. But the way I hear it, Charles Hadley is in a bad way and has been ever since the war. It isn't likely he'll be of much help."

"Mrs. Hadley says the Magills are returning to Richmond Hill even though it's in shambles too. She says the bank is holding the Magill sons responsible for an enormous debt their father incurred buying slaves, and they owe money to the Georgetown stores as well."

"I wouldn't know about that, but you'd best stay away from John Magill's boys. The whole family has a bad reputation among the Negroes."

"Yes. Papa often said he was the worst plantation owner in the entire Lowcountry. One cannot starve workers half to death. It's not right, and it's bad business as well."

"True enough. It's no wonder they hated him." He paused to polish his spectacles. "From what I hear, there's still some occasional unrest on the river. I'd hate for you to get caught up in it."

"I imagine most of the Magills' bondsmen are gone by now or working in Georgetown."

"Just the same, you stay away from Richmond Hill." He escorted her to the door and retrieved her umbrella. "For what it's worth, I hope you succeed in restoring Fairhaven. I enjoyed many happy visits there in the old days."

"I intend to do my best."

"Please call on me anytime you're in Charleston. I want to know how you're getting on."

"You're very kind. But I don't expect I'll make the trip too often. I'm not much of a sailor, and sixty miles is a very long way by land." She drew on her gloves. "I intend to live simply, Mr. Crowley."

"There's nothing simple about growing rice."

"That's true. I meant that I'm sure I'll find everything I need in Georgetown and will have little need to travel to Charleston."

He held the door open for her. "It's damp out there. I'd lend you my carriage for the ride to the pier. If I had one."

Bitterness tinged his words. Charlotte nodded in sympathy. All across the South, as part of an attempt to cripple the Confederacy, the lawless Federals had stolen or killed as much livestock as possible. Lettice Hadley had been lucky indeed to have her horses spared.

"Good-bye, Mr. Crowley. And thank you again." With a final wave to the lawyer, she opened her umbrella and hurried toward the pier.

At the steamship office she checked on her baggage, then peered out the office window at the red-and-white steamship rocking gently on the Cooper River. Beyond the breakwater, the Atlantic was a dull sheet of gray.

Outside on the docks, draymen came and went with wagons bearing wooden cargo crates. Other passengers, Northerners mostly, judging from their speech, arrived and began boarding the steamship with bags, parcels, satchels, and umbrellas.

"Miss?" The agent approached, his hat pulled low against the gray mist, a mug of steaming coffee in his hand. "You'd best go aboard now and get settled for the night. We'll be putting out to sea at first light."

She joined the line of passengers waiting to board. The gangplank screeched and swayed beneath her feet as she reached the ship and handed the ship's master her ticket. He glanced at it and waved her aboard. "First room to starboard. It may be a bit noisy, but the ride will be smoother there if we hit bad weather."

"Are you expecting a storm, Captain?"

He shrugged and offered the slightest of smiles.

"It's March in the Atlantic, miss. Anything can happen."

Some years ago, the steamer *Nina* had left Georgetown bound for Nassau and was never heard from again. Lost in a storm, people said. Charlotte shivered and drew her cloak more tightly around her shoulders. The sooner she reached home, the better. She found her way to her quarters and went inside. Barely large enough for a narrow bed, a chair, and her trunks, the cabin at least had a small grimy window opened to let in the damp, chill air. She lit the lamp and set it on top of the larger trunk.

Darkness fell and the noise abated as the last of the cargo was stowed and passengers settled in for the evening. The murmur of voices from those on deck and the smell of cooked meat drifted on the cooling air. Charlotte nibbled on a bit of chocolate, remembering a trip up the Waccamaw with Papa—had it been only ten years ago? It seemed a lifetime. She rummaged in her bags for her writing paper and a pencil.

Aboard the steamer Resolute.
3 March 1868.

The spring I turned thirteen, Papa arranged a trip from our plantation to Charleston, sixty miles to the south, to celebrate my birthday. It was our first such outing since my mother died the year before, the yellow fever wringing the last breath from her slender body. Papa and I were left to mourn—and to assign a measure of blame, for Mama knew that to remain on the plantation in the summer posed the risk of fever. But Minty, one of her favorite house servants, was in the throes of a difficult birthing, and the doctor who customarily tended to such matters was nowhere to be found.

Mama insisted on staying behind until the babe was safely delivered. Though she never expressed an opinion contrary to Papa's, she saw herself as the savior of the more than three hundred slave women who lived at Fairhaven and her sacred duty that of preparing them for their freedom which surely would one day come. That she lost her own freedom, her very life, in pursuit of that ideal was not lost on Papa and me. But we carried on as best we could. There was rice to plant and to harvest and, when the time came, a birthday to mark.

And so, on a breezy Friday in March, Papa and I found ourselves steaming southward on the Island Queen. Upon disembarking we enjoyed dinner at the Mills House, a new production at the theater, and a shopping expedition along Meeting Street. In a milliner's window I spied a cunning little hat bedecked with blue ribbons and prevailed upon Papa to buy it for me.

"You are too young yet for flirting," he said when the milliner told me the ribbons trailing down my back were called flirtation ribbons.

I quite agreed with him then, for I couldn't imagine finding any man who would be as wonderful and handsome as Papa.

I wore my new hat on our trip home, standing with my father on the sooty deck as the steamer made its way into Winyah Bay and nudged the pier at Georgetown to discharge passengers and cargo. Since we had an hour's wait before continuing our journey up the Waccamaw River, Papa and I disembarked and crossed a rickety dock stacked high with casks of turpentine and resin and with lumber bound for Northern markets. Slaves hurried about like a colony of ants, moving cargo, directing drays and rigs. Steam whistles shrieked, drowning out the voices of the vendors stationed near the steamship office.

Arm in arm, Papa and I strolled past the courthouse and the bank, the newspaper office and the busy slave market. We bought fried pies from a pastry shop on the waterfront. Papa wiped a smudge of sugar from my nose and told me I was a lucky girl indeed to be living in the very heart of the Lowcountry.

Now everything has changed. I wonder whether I shall ever again feel so lucky.

Charlotte set aside her pencil. Perhaps she'd disembark in Georgetown and post her article for Mr. Sawyer's newspaper from there. The sooner she could start earning money, the better.

Standing on tiptoe, she peered out the small window. The ship's master strolled the deck smoking his pipe, watching a scrim of high clouds forming on the horizon. In the next cabin two women laughed. The ship's bell tolled the hour. Charlotte stepped out of her dress and draped it over the edge of the narrow bed. There was no basin for washing up, only a small pitcher of lukewarm water and a single tin cup. She unpinned her hair, dabbed at her face with her handkerchief, and crawled into the narrow bunk.

Despite her trepidation at what she would find upriver, she was filled with something like hope. Tomorrow—for better or worse—she would be home.

Two

From Georgetown, the *Resolute* steamed northward along the winding path of the Waccamaw, past cypress swamps, brown marshlands, and stands of magnolia, pine, and oak. Standing on the deck, Charlotte watched a flotilla of wood ducks bobbing near the bank and a pair of cooters sunning themselves on a sun-warmed log. Overhead an osprey traced lazy circles in the azure sky. She shaded her eyes and followed the bird's swooping movements, hoping to spot its nest. But the steamer changed course, following a sharp bend in the river, and she lost sight of the osprey as they approached Calais, the first of several plantations belonging to Papa's friend William Alston. Next came Strawberry Hill, Friendfield, and Marietta.

Charlotte peered through the stands of cypress, hoping to catch a glimpse of the houses she had often visited as a girl. As the steamer continued past Bellefield and Prospect Hill, she spotted roofs, chimneys, and an occasional outbuilding still standing and felt slightly more hopeful. If her neighbors' homes had survived the Yankees' predations, perhaps her own had too.

A young woman wearing a brown cotton frock and a feathered leghorn hat came to stand beside Charlotte at the rail. She couldn't have been much older than sixteen, but she had a vibrancy about her that seemed to shimmer in the humid air. Certainly she was the kind of girl men noticed. She nodded to Charlotte and waved one dainty hand toward the ruins of a white house visible through the newly leafed trees. "It makes me heartsick to look at it. Remember how beautiful it used to be?"

Charlotte nodded.

"Are you going home?" The young girl fished an apple from her bag and polished it on her sleeve, her eyes bright with curiosity, and took a dainty bite.

"If there's anything left of it. I haven't been back since the war ended."

The girl stopped chewing. "Mercy. Who has been taking care of it all this time?"

"A couple of men who belonged to my father looked after it for a time after the war. But they left sometime last fall, just as my father's health worsened. He was too ill to travel, and I had no one to look after him, so I couldn't go."

"I'm sorry. I shouldn't have asked so many questions. I'm Josie Clifton. My family owns Oakwood Hall."

"How do you do? I'm Charlotte Fraser. Fairhaven."

"Oh, I do hope you find your house in good repair. Ours is barely standing, but my father says we must occupy it to keep it out of the hands of the Negroes and the Yankees. He says the Yankees are looking for any excuse to declare the property abandoned and hand it over to the Negroes. Our friend Mr. Kirk is heading back to his place in the pinelands, and supposedly his niece, Patsy, is coming to keep house for him. At least there will be somebody my age to talk to." Josie heaved a dramatic sigh. "I swear, if we don't return to some sort of social life soon, I shall go mad."

"Many of us are still in mourning."

Josie nodded. "Our family is too. But honestly, what good does it do? The departed are still departed, no matter how deeply we grieve. And I simply detest not having any entertainments to look forward to."

In the soft sunlight filtering through the black-laced canopy of trees, the girl's face seemed devoid of any sign of hardship, as if the war had barely touched her. She reminded Charlotte of so many privileged young women she'd known in Charleston, with little purpose beyond having fun and snaring a suitable match. Josie ate another bite of apple. "Father says the Tuckers have invited a new minister to stay at Litchfield. He'll hold services at the chapel there and use it as a base for his sundry charitable endeavors."

"Another sign of life returning to normal."

"I suppose." The girl shrugged. "Did you know the Hadleys are back on the Pee Dee at Alder Hill?"

"Yes. Mrs. Hadley is meeting me at the landing."

"I feel sorry for her. Mr. Hadley is not well."

"So I hear."

A few more passengers appeared on deck. Josie moved closer to Charlotte and lowered her voice. "They say he has trouble with strong drink."

"Poor Lettice. I hope that's not true."

Josie shrugged. "They also say one of the Willowood heirs has turned up, intending to start up the rice fields again." Josie shook her head. "I don't care what Papa says. Rice growing is a lost cause, if you ask me."

"I hope you're wrong about that. I'm planning to restore Fairhaven and plant rice again."

"But where will you get enough workers? Papa tried to hire a few of our former slaves to help with our cotton and corn crops, but they don't seem all that interested."

"Perhaps I can find workers in Georgetown."

"Maybe." Josie Clifton regarded Charlotte from beneath the brim of her hat. "I don't remember seeing you around here."

"I enrolled at Madame Giraud's boarding school in Charleston when I was nine." She smiled at the younger woman. "I'm older than you. It's unlikely our paths would have crossed then."

32

"You are not that much older. I'll be seventeen in a few weeks. I've never been to boarding school. I'm sure I could not have abided being so far away from my parents."

"My cousin Della was a student at Madame Giraud's, and I wanted to go with her. After that I was home between terms and at Christmas. We spent summers on Pawley's Island."

Instinctively, Charlotte glanced over her shoulder. Pelican Cottage, her own little paradise at the edge of the sea, lay only four miles away as the crow flies. As soon as the rice was planted and growing, she would move to the island for the summer. Pawley's would do wonders to soothe her spirit.

The steamer slowed and bumped the pier. The passengers gathered their belongings and lined up along the ship's rail.

"We're home." Josie tossed her half-eaten apple into the river. "Perhaps I'll see you again some-time."

Charlotte joined Josie and the others waiting to disembark and searched the landing for Lettice Hadley. Soon she spotted her mother's oldest friend sitting atop a farm wagon, a pink ruffled parasol unfurled to ward off the sun. A uniformed black man held the reins. Not the most fashion-able conveyance, but the wagon was needed for ferrying Charlotte's belongings across the Waccamaw River and up the road to Fairhaven.

She waved and hurried down the slanted gangplank. Lettice's driver jumped down from the wagon and hurried over, a smile creasing his wrinkled face. "Miss Cha'lotte? Is that really you?"

"My word. Trim?"

"Yes'm. It's me all right. I'm still on this side o' the dirt."

"I never expected to see you again. Peter and Quash sent word to Papa that everyone had gone."

"Yes'm, that's about right."

"How are you, Trim? How are you getting on?"

"Well, I got me a wife now. Name's Florinda. Got a job in town. And I preach at the Negro church of a Sunday. Me and Florinda got ourselves a house and a team of oxen. But I hires out to Mrs. Hadley now and then, when Mr. Hadley is feeling poorly." He looked past her shoulder. "Them your things there on the dock?"

"Yes. The two trunks and those boxes of linens and kitchen supplies. And Mother's writing desk."

"I 'member that desk—set by the window that looked out on Miss Susan's garden. Used to see her there writing in her household books, back in them days."

"That's right. It's practically the only thing I have left of hers. Quash told Papa the Yankees destroyed her portrait." Her stomach clenched

34

at the memory. "Pure meanness, if you ask me."

"Yes'm, that's the truth. But it don't do no good studyin' over what's gone. We got to carry on till the good Lawd come to fetch us home."

Three loud blasts from the ship's whistle signaled its departure. The *Resolute* belched a cloud of steam and smoke and inched away from the landing. Charlotte thought of the plantations farther upriver—Springfield, Laurel Hill, Wachesaw. Were any of them left standing? Would the heir of Willowood—whoever he was—find that he too was master of a ruin? Charlotte swayed, suddenly dizzy from hunger, worry, and fatigue from her twelve-hour journey.

"Miss Cha'lotte?" Trim motioned to her. "Come on. Let me help you up on the wagon. You just sit and rest a spell while I look after your things."

He boosted her onto the rickety wagon seat and into Lettice's motherly, powder-scented embrace. "Oh, Charlotte. Dear girl, I am so happy you are back."

Mrs. Hadley held Charlotte at arm's length, and Charlotte saw the hollows beneath the woman's pale gray eyes, the wrinkles that had deepened around her generous mouth.

"You have no idea how lonely it has been here," Mrs. Hadley said. "We ourselves returned only a few months ago, and it feels like years. But Mr. Hadley won't hear of moving into Charleston or

35

even Georgetown. Though heaven knows that poor town has little to recommend it these days."

"I'm happy to see you too." Charlotte's empty stomach groaned, but she was thinking of something else entirely. "I can't wait to go riding. I've missed it so."

Mrs. Hadley's lips tightened. "Unfortunately we had to sell the blooded horses. All I'm left with is this old nag. He isn't much to look at, but he's indispensable these days."

"Oh, I am sorry. I know how you loved your horses."

Lettice stared out at the river. "The taxes came due in November, and they were much more than we thought. And the house is falling down and needs repairs. Stables too, so I suppose it's for the best. Charles wasn't able to look after the horses properly anyway, and most of the servants we counted upon have become completely unreliable, even when good money is offered. I do miss my little bay mare all the same. And I'm sorry to have promised you an outing. I should have told you about the horses before now. I know you were looking forward to a good long ride."

"I was. But it doesn't matter. I'm sure I'll be busy anyway until I get my house repaired and my rice planted."

Lettice fixed her with a firm gaze. "I'm all for restoring whatever you can, but you mustn't be too disappointed if things don't work out the way you hope."

"Things must work out. There is no other option." Charlotte patted the older woman's hand. "Thank you for going to the trouble of meeting me. Even the shortest trip these days seems a trial. And I am so happy to see you. Trim too. He was one of Papa's favorites."

"No trouble at all, my dear." Lettice sighed and watched Trim struggling to balance Charlotte's large trunk on his shoulders. "Now that the Negroes are free, I suppose we must do our part to see that they succeed. Trim at least is fairly dependable. I hire him whenever I can, and of course he is glad of the money."

Trim shoved the trunk and the desk onto the wagon next to the boxes. He climbed up and rattled the reins. They headed west down the dirt road.

"Now, I know you're anxious to get to Fairhaven," Lettice said, "but I knew you'd be famished, so I'm taking you to Alder Hill first. Florinda came this morning to prepare a light supper for us."

"Thank you. I am hungry."

"As soon as we heard you were coming back, Mr. Hadley sent March and Percy up to Fairhaven. They boarded up the broken windows and replaced the front door and cut down the weeds, but there wasn't time to do much else."

"Or money either, I expect. Thank you, Lettice. I will repay you as soon as I can."

"No hurry. We're doing all right."

Charlotte glanced at her mother's friend. Mrs. Hadley's threadbare shirtwaist and scuffed shoes told a different story. But perhaps pretending that nothing had changed was Lettice's way of coping with unimaginable loss.

"Percy says your kitchen is fairly intact, but the rest of the house . . ." Lettice's voice trailed away. "You mustn't be too upset when you see the state it's in."

"It's bad, then."

"Apparently. He reports the house is nearly bare of furnishings. I sent over a bed and a mattress for you and a set of linens. They're threadbare but clean. Oh, and a table and some chairs—odds and ends, I'm afraid, but serviceable enough."

"Thank you. I brought a few things with me, but I hadn't even thought about where to sit or sleep."

"You've had much too much on your mind of late."

"Yes."

"We were sorry to miss your dear father's funeral. Augusta Milton says it was well attended."

"It was. And Augusta was a great comfort to me. At least I'll have her for company on the beach this summer."

"I'm glad of that. She said his last days were peaceful."

"For the most part. Near the end he became confused, talking out of his head about secrets."

"No doubt the effects of the medicines."

"I suppose." Charlotte paused. "The evening he breathed his last, he seemed to gather strength."

"I've heard that's often the case."

"He suddenly raised himself in the bed and grasped my arm with more strength than I supposed he had. He spoke my name, clear as day, and then he said, 'The fire . . . the fire.' "

"Poor Francis. No doubt he was remembering the destruction in Charleston, back in sixty-one."

"I suppose." Charlotte chewed on her bottom lip. "But at the time I had the eerie feeling that it was more than just a deathbed memory. I felt he was trying to tell me something important." She shifted on the seat. "Lettice, did he ever mention anything about having papers associated with our land? Any official documents, anything like that?"

Lettice frowned. "Not that I recall. Why? Is something amiss?"

"The lawyer can't find proof that Papa ever filed for ownership of our barony."

"Oh, I'm sure he did, Charlotte. If he hadn't, surely the situation would have come to light before now. I wouldn't worry about it."

As they approached the ferry that would take them to Alder Hill, Trim slowed the wagon and guided it onto the flat, wide boat that once had carried tons of Carolina Gold rice down river. The boat settled on the water. Charlotte's breath caught as peace washed over her. This was the world she had shared with Papa, who often declared that an attachment to the Lowcountry was a bit like being in love. During her long absence, first at her Aunt Livinia's during the war and later in the house in Charleston that Papa had been forced to sell, she had suppressed her longing for the marshes and tidal creeks, the salt-scented air, but now she remembered exactly what he meant.

Now that she was almost home, she could hardly wait to get started. She began a mental inventory of Fairhaven as she had last seen it: twelve rice boats, a steam-powered threshing machine, two barns for oxen and horses. The cabins in the slave street, no longer necessary. How much, if anything, remained? If the cabins had been spared, perhaps she could salvage materials from them to repair the house. More than likely the pasture fences were down, the smokehouse too. And what of the rice-field trunks, the wooden gates that allowed the workers to flood the fields? After so long, they were bound to be in disrepair. All of it would have to be replaced at great cost.

The peace she'd felt just moments before turned to anger that roiled her stomach. From childhood she'd been taught that it was wrong to hate anyone, even an enemy. But how could any Southerner not hate the Northerners who had decimated every home and field in an effort to wipe the Confederacy off the face of the earth?

The two ferrymen guided the vessel to the dock and held it fast while Trim drove the wagon onto the lane and over a rickety wooden bridge that spanned a deep tidal creek. In another five minutes the smoke-blackened porch columns and boarded-up windows of Alder Hill came into view. Leaving Trim in charge of the horse and wagon, Lettice led the way up the sagging porch and into the parlor, where sunlight filtered weakly through limp linen curtains.

"Please, my dear, sit down," Lettice said. "I'll see to our supper. I'm sorry about the gloom. My husband prefers darkness these days. He says the light hurts his eyes."

Charlotte chose a chair upholstered in blue velvet and looked around the once-familiar room. In the old days, Mama and Lettice had spent hours here bent over their needlework or reading and talking while the men were out hunting and collecting ricebirds for dinner. The birds gathered by the thousands in the rice fields, a dark cloud against the pale sky, so small that even she could eat half a dozen at one sitting.

The wooden floor creaked as Lettice returned with a tray laden with biscuits, a plate of fried ham and potatoes, a pot of fig preserves, and a small cake dripping with caramel icing. Charlotte dug into her meal, grateful for every succulent bite. During the war when the Yankees blockaded the Southern ports and nearly starved them all to death, sugar and flour had become luxuries. At one time she had wondered whether she would ever again enjoy such simple pleasures.

Lettice ate quickly, her eyes darting toward the darkened staircase.

"Is Mr. Hadley at home?" Charlotte polished off the last crumbs of her cake and blotted her lips with her napkin. "Papa would have wanted me to pay my respects."

"Charles is sleeping." Weariness tinged Lettice's words. "He hasn't felt well these past days."

"I'm sorry. Another time, then. Please tell him I'm grateful for his help at Fairhaven."

"I will."

Something crashed overhead, and Lettice shot to her feet, spilling her lemonade onto the bare floor. "I don't mean to rush you, my dear, but the ferry is so unreliable these days—perhaps you should go. You don't want to be stranded on this side of the river in the dark."

She hurried to the door and called for Trim. "Miss Fraser is ready to go now."

She kissed both Charlotte's cheeks. "Trim will take good care of you. I must see to Charles."

Trim helped Charlotte onto the wagon seat. He

called to the horses and they set off again. From her perch on the wagon seat, Charlotte took in the sights and smells of home. On either side of the river, serpentine creeks crisscrossed the marshes in an endless pattern of blue and gold. The air was fresh from the sea, and the riverbank was covered in new green that in a few weeks' time would blossom with violets and blue jessamine.

They passed a family of Negro women casting their nets for herring, their children playing in the shafts of late-afternoon sunlight falling across the shallows. One of them called to Trim and he returned her greeting, tipping his hat as they passed.

When they reached the other side, they drove off the ferry, left the road, and turned up the long avenue of two-hundred-year-old oaks toward Fairhaven. Trim jumped down to open the gate and Charlotte's heart sped up. Here was home at last. Though long neglected, the climbing roses had survived; here and there, new leaves had stitched through the banks of wild jessamine, forming patches of green among the brown thorns.

They continued along the edge of the river past a narrow sand beach where she had played as a child. To the right was a sloping green lawn, now marred with burned-out patches, and the over-grown garden where neat rows of lettuce and asparagus had once thrived alongside roses and camellias. Charlotte peered through deepening shadows at the burned-out skeletons of her barns and stables, a falling-down shed missing its door. The little schoolhouse where her tutor, Miss Heyward, had taught her to read, the "chillun house" where the older slave women had tended babies, even the chicken coop had been reduced to rubble. Of course the livestock were long gone. As were Papa's prized peacocks who had ruled the yard with their showy feather displays and haunting calls.

Trim tethered the horses and jumped off the wagon. "You go on in, Miss Cha'lotte. I'll bring your things."

The front steps had been torn away. Skirting the gaping hole, Charlotte entered through the pantry steps and walked through the empty rooms assessing the damage. Not a shutter or sash was left intact. The mahogany woodwork around the windows and doors and the magnificent stair-case banister were gone. The grandfather clock that for all her life had stood on the stairway landing was gone. The zinc-lined water tank that supplied water for the bathroom, gone—along with the bathtub. In the musty parlor, dark rectangles on the faded cabbage-rose wallpaper marked the places where seascapes and family portraits had once hung.

She continued along the gritty hallway to her father's study, her steps echoing in the emptiness. She stepped through the wrecked doorway, overcome with memories of countless afternoons reading with Papa or sitting on his knee as he showed her how to make entries in his leather-bound account books. The delight he took in listening to her recitations. The birthday when he'd wrapped her present in a length of muslin and hidden it on a wide ledge high inside the fireplace where the chimney met the firebox. He had left clues all over the house, leading her at last to the exquisite porcelain doll she named Polly. She had slept with Polly every night until the girls at Madame Giraud's discovered what she was doing and made fun of her.

A fly buzzed about her head and she swatted it away as another memory surfaced. She'd been fifteen the day she returned from a visit to friends at Strawberry Hill to find Papa sitting alone in the study, the contents of his strongbox scattered across his desk. At her knock he'd scooped every-thing into the box and turned the brass key in the lock. He'd reassured her that nothing was wrong, but even now she remem-bered the look in his eyes, a look that told a different story.

She moved toward the windows, shards of glass crunching beneath her feet as she crossed the room. She ran a finger along the windowsill. Dirt daubers had built nests in the corners, and thick cobwebs hung from a shattered chandelier. In this room, too, rugs and paintings were missing. Only the remains of a woven rush rug lay crumpled in the corner. Her father's account books and papers, copies of his articles on rice cultivation, were torn and piled knee-deep in one corner. She picked up a couple of volumes and fanned the pages, reading random entries. It would take days to sort through it all, but the effort would be worthwhile if some proof of her ownership of the barony could be found. She tamped down a jolt of anger. What had Papa been thinking? Surely he had not intended to leave her in such a precarious position.

She moved to the library, surprised to discover a good number of books still lying on the shelves. But the spiders and the dirt daubers had been at work here too. Sighing, she went down the hall and crossed the short covered walkway to the kitchen. Mercifully the stove was still there, and the butter churn. A cracked platter. A creamware pitcher. A frying pan. A scarred table and three battered chairs, one with a broken seat. She looked around for a teakettle and settled for a battered tin pot that had been a childhood play-thing.

Trim came in with her trunks, and she directed him to her old bedroom on the second floor. He trudged up and down the stairs, huffing and puffing beneath his burden, until everything was in place. He placed her mother's writing desk in the library, then took out a blue bandanna and wiped his face. "Reckon tha's ever'thing, Miss Cha'lotte."

"Thank you, Trim."

He waved one hand toward the kitchen. "I expect you'll be needin' stove wood and some fresh water to see you through the night."

"Yes, please."

He shifted his stance and focused on a cobweb wafting from one corner. "For such chores, I usually gets a dollar."

"A—"

"I'm a free man now, entitled to charge for my work. I brung you here for Miz Hadley, but now I got to charge you for extrys."

She looked at him, confounded. In the old days, he would have gladly looked after her every need. But the old relationships had changed. A dollar for such minimal tasks seemed outrageous, but perhaps in this strange new world of equals it was the going rate.

Trim stood quietly, arms at his sides, looking as uncomfortable as she felt. Perhaps this new way of doing things was not easy for him either. In any case, she was too tired for argument.

"Fine. Please bring the wood and water. I'll get my bag."

When his chores were complete, she paid him and followed him outside. "I'm planning to seed that field closest to the road, Trim. I'll need at least a dozen men to get it planted and someone to oversee things."

"You way behind schedule, miss. The trunks in that field needs fixin'—they's rotted out, mostly. And the ground oughta been plowed and broke up las' month."

"I know that, but I couldn't get here any sooner. We'll simply have to work faster to make up for lost time. Now, can you find some men and see that my field is ready in time for planting next week or not?"

"Don' know. Tha's a tall order these days."

"Are any of Papa's men still around?"

Trim shook his head. "When the Yankee gunboats come up the river back in sixty-two, Aleck and Hector and Henry run off up north with a bunch of slaves from Richmond Hill. Ain't had no word of them this long time. Cinda and Molly run off back then too."

"So I heard." After the gunboats began their forays up the Waccamaw, Papa had moved her to her aunt Livinia's small farm eighty miles away. But he had stayed on at Fairhaven until the last possible moment to prepare for Sherman's arrival, leaving her and her aunt to manage the farm alone. Until then, her place in society had protected her from the rigors of manual labor. But the blockade and the predations of the Union army had left her no choice.

It hadn't been easy. Aunt Lavinia was old and

ill, and the bulk of the labor—planting, hoeing, laundry, and cooking—had fallen upon Charlotte's sixteen-year-old shoulders. But surviving years of hardship had shown her what she was capable of. How much she could endure.

Trim swatted at a water bug buzzing around his head. "They's a couple of Mast' Fraser's boatmen working down around Winyah these days. And his tailor come to our church las' Sunday."

"A tailor won't do me a bit of good. What about Thomas? Papa said he was the best carpenter in the Lowcountry. He can fix my broken trunks."

"Maybe. If I can find him."

"Tell the field hands I'll give them work on a contract and a share of the profits."

"Yes'm. I'll tell 'em. But I can't make no guarantees. Mast' Ben Allston over at Chicora Wood hired some freemen to plant his rice the year before las', but the men run off. I reckon they's plenty of black folks 'round here don't want to set foot on nobody's plantation. Not even this one."

He crossed the wide lawn to the wagon and drove away.

Charlotte rummaged in a box to find her tea caddy and a china cup. She brewed tea in the battered pan and took her cup out to the porch. Shafts of golden light slanted through the dark pines, casting long shadows across the avenue and the weathered cypress-shingled roofs of the slave cabins. In years past the slave street had pulsed with the sound of many voices and the aromas of woodsmoke, fried fish, and boiling field peas. Children played among the ancient trees while their mothers, home from their tasks in the fields or the house, swapped stories as they tended their own gardens of corn, tomatoes, collards, and okra. To outsiders those evenings might have presented a picture of perfect harmony. But even at her tender age, Charlotte had realized that beneath the calm facade ran a complicated undercurrent of loyalty and betrayal, affection and hatred, resistance and accommodation.

Of course, none of it mattered now. Everything was in ruins, and the planters were on the verge of bankruptcy—scarcely better off than the former slaves.

She sipped her tea and watched a blood-red sun sink into the mellow spring evening. Sunlight rippled through the ancient oaks and pines, the gold turning to fiery red as the sun went down on the river. But the specter of poverty and ruin cast a pall over everything.

Everyone living on the Waccamaw and the Pee Dee—blacks and whites alike—depended on rice cultivation for their livelihood. If other planters couldn't survive here, how on earth would she?

Three

Wearing a frayed poke bonnet she'd found hanging in the attic and a pair of her father's old boots, Charlotte stood shin deep in the flooded rice fields. With Trim's help and that of Thomas, she had managed to repair the rotted and broken trunks. Nine men with teams of oxen had plowed and trenched the fields and then planted twenty-five acres in seed that had been soaked and dried so it would float to the surface when the fields were flooded.

Yesterday at high tide Thomas and Trim had opened the trunks to flood the fields. In three days the men would return to drain the sprout flow. In the meantime, she had sent them to higher ground to plant potatoes, corn, collards, and peas.

She bent to rake a bit of trash from the water, her sore muscles protesting the unaccustomed activity. Every day she worked from sunrise until late afternoon, stopping only for a mid-morning breakfast of biscuits, bacon, and clabber. Day before yesterday she had dragged the wash kettle into the backyard at dawn, hauled water from the river, and made a fire to heat it. With a wooden paddle, she'd stirred lye soap into the hot water, laundered her petticoats and chemises, shirt-waists and skirts, sheets and tea towels, and spread it all on the back porch railing to dry. Now her hands were red and raw, her palms a mass of blisters from wielding the laundry paddle and the heavy rake.

And this was only the beginning. Once the rice germinated, the fields must be hoed and flooded twice more by the middle of July and the water changed when it became too stagnant.

The memory of the stench of standing water in the fields caused her nose to wrinkle. On a hot July day the fields stank worse than an outhouse. But by then she would be miles away on Pawley's Island, within sight and sound of the ocean. Away from the foul-smelling fields and the threat of the fever that had claimed her mother's life. Her hired men would be responsible for the hoeing, harvesting, and threshing. She would keep a close eye on everything, though, traveling by boat from the island to the fields just as her father had.

Voices sounded from the road. She left the fields, let down her skirts, and pushed through the garden gate, expecting to find the Hadleys waiting in the yard. In the six weeks since she'd returned to Fairhaven, Lettice and Charles had visited often, bringing eggs, milk, and the mail from Georgetown. Last week she'd received her first check from the *New York Enterprise*. Most of it would be set aside to retire her debt, but she intended to splurge on a few yards of linen fabric from Mr. Kaminski's store. She wasn't a skilled seamstress, but she could manage to cut and hem curtains. New curtains would make the house feel more like a real home.

"Is anybody here?" A small girl in a tattered dress held the hand of an even smaller one whose dirty face was streaked with tears. Both were barefoot and covered in angry red hatch marks, no doubt the result of a tangle with the briars and brambles that covered the riverbank.

Charlotte crossed the yard. "My goodness, what happened to you?"

"Our boat turned over," the younger one said. "And we got lost."

The older one, her cornflower-blue eyes wide, bobbed her head. "We wanted to surprise Papa. Now he'll be mad that we lost the rowboat."

Recalling her own childhood adventures on the broad, beautiful Waccamaw, Charlotte grinned. "I imagine he'll be so happy you are safe that he won't care at all about the boat."

"Yes, he will," the older one said. "He says we don't have any money now that the war is lost, and we can't afford to be wasteful."

"I see. But there's a good chance your boat will drift ashore somewhere and your papa can get it back."

"Not if somebody else finds it first. It's a really good boat."

"Why don't we go inside and get you cleaned up, and then we'll see about getting word to your papa." Charlotte bent to the older of the two. "What's your name?"

"Marie-Claire," the child said, with a French-accented roll of the *r*'s. "I'm nine. But my sister is only six. What's *your* name?"

"Charlotte." She turned to the younger. "And you are . . ."

"Anne-Louise," said the younger girl. "How old are you?"

"Oh, I'm ancient. Nearly twenty-four."

Anne-Louise giggled. "I'm hungry. Have you got any sweets?"

"No sweets, I'm afraid. But I have bread and butter. Will that do?"

Anne-Louise shrugged. "If that's all you've got. But I'd rather have cake."

Charlotte frowned. Where was the mother of these ragamuffins? And why had she not taught them better manners?

She led them into the house and helped them wash up before seating them at the kitchen table with plates of bread and butter. She put the kettle on for tea and took a cup from the cupboard. Through the window she saw two of the men she had hired cutting through the woods, hoes and rakes balanced on their shoulders, leading a skinny calf on a rope. Where on earth had it come from? And why had they abandoned their tasks in the garden?

She suddenly felt weary. Mr. Allston had been unable to win against the unwillingness of the freedmen. That she would have to fight them too, on top of her other difficulties, sapped her energy. She poured tea and carried it to the table, perching gingerly on the broken chair, which she had temporarily repaired with a board.

Marie-Claire finished her bread and butter, then picked up her plate and licked it clean.

Eyes wide, Anne-Louise reached over and yanked her sister's dark braid. "I'm telling Papa you were naughty."

"I don't care." Marie-Claire let her plate clatter onto the table. "I'll tell him it was your idea to take the rowboat."

"But it wasn't!" The younger girl's eyes filled.

"So? Papa believes anything I tell him. You know he does."

"Young ladies." Charlotte slapped her open palm on the table, rattling her teacup. "You will not behave this way while a guest in my house. Is that clear?"

"She started it," Marie-Claire said. "She shouldn't have pulled my hair."

"You aren't supposed to lick your plate," her sister retorted. "Papa said so."

The garden gate squeaked outside. Charlotte

looked through the window to see Trim coming through, his hoe balanced on his shoulder. Leaving the sisters to their argument, Charlotte went to meet him in the yard. "Trim. I didn't expect you to finish the planting so quickly."

"Well, Miss Cha'lotte, tha's just it. Mercury and Old Pete was feeling poorly and went off to home. Me and the rest got the corn and the collards planted, but we ain't got the p'tatoes in yet."

"Then why are you standing here? There's plenty of time before dark."

Trim leaned on his hoe and regarded her from beneath his hat brim. "Well, miss, when we signed the contrack, we thought Mercury and Old Pete would be helping. If we gots to do more work, then we gots to have more money."

Of course they must be paid, but the thought of her dwindling bank account made her stomach clench. "Oh, for goodness' sake. They won't be sick forever, will they? Perhaps they will come back tomorrow and help you finish the job. Surely they'll be back on Thursday to help drain the fields."

"Maybe." He shrugged. "Reckon I'll go on home myself, though. Florinda will have my dinner ready time I get there."

She folded her arms across her chest and glared at him. She might be young, but she was mistress of the plantation now, and it wouldn't do to let anyone take advantage—not even Trim. "If you walk off this land now, do not come back. I must have men I can depend on. You and the others made a promise to me, and I expect each of you to keep it."

A frown creased his brow. "You sayin' I can't come back to Fairhaven?"

"Not if you leave before the work day is finished. And what is more, I will tell every other planter on the Waccamaw that you are not a man of your word."

Trim pressed his lips together, clearly torn, but he finally turned on his heel and headed back up the path to the potato patch.

She let out a shaky breath. Perhaps she had prevailed in this battle of wills, at least for today. "One more thing," she called after him. "I want to know who owns that calf I saw being led through the woods just now."

Trim spoke without turning around. "I ain't the law."

He disappeared into the trees as a horse and rig came down the road, the wheels churning sand in its wake. The driver halted the buggy, opened the front gate, and jogged up the avenue.

"I'm looking for two little girls, about so tall." He held out one hand waist-high. "One is about—"

"They're here," Charlotte said. "Hungry and a bit untidy, but safe and sound."

"Thank God." His voice caught, and she saw how scared he'd been. "I shouldn't have left them at home alone, but their governess quit last week, and I haven't been able to find anyone suitable. Most of the good ones are employed in Charleston and have no wish for a life in the country." He stopped suddenly and bowed slightly from the waist. "Forgive me. I haven't introduced myself. Nicholas Betancourt."

She blushed as he took in her disheveled appearance and the toes of her father's boots peeking from beneath the damp hem of her old calico skirt. An amused but not unkind smile played on his lips. His eyes were direct— friendly—yet she couldn't help feeling there was something hidden in their moss-green depths. She smoothed her wrinkled skirts. "Charlotte Fraser. Please come in."

She led him up the newly installed steps to the parlor.

"Papa!" Mr. Betancourt's daughters rushed in from the kitchen and launched themselves at his legs.

"Papa, we were coming to surprise you, and we nearly drowned," Anne-Louise said.

"Oh, we did not." Marie-Claire tossed her head. "It's true the boat turned over and we couldn't set it to rights because of the current, but we were close to shore and waded out."

Their father frowned at them. "You disobeyed

me, and I am very disappointed. Especially in you, Marie-Claire. You're the oldest. You should have known better."

"But—"

"No excuses. Please go play in the yard for a moment."

"Yes, Papa."

Charlotte watched them go. "Don't be too hard on them, Mr. Betancourt. Their motives were pure."

"Perhaps, but I worry about Marie-Claire. She's developed a defiant streak since their mother died."

"I'm sorry." Perhaps that accounted for the girls' lack of manners. Now she regretted her unkind assessment of them. "I'm sure it can't be easy, bringing them up by yourself."

He leaned against the door frame, his long legs crossed at the ankles. "I've had some very good governesses since my wife's death, but none of them stayed very long. And now that we've moved to Willowood, it's proven even more difficult."

He watched his small daughters playing near the piazza, his eyes alight with paternal love, and her heart stirred. "Would you like some tea, Mr. Betancourt?"

"I don't want to trouble you any further. I appreciate your looking after my girls."

"It was no trouble, truly. I'm afraid I had little

to offer except bread and butter. Much to Anne-Louise's dismay."

He laughed and she noticed how attractive he was. "She is too fond of cake, I'm afraid."

They went inside. Charlotte poured tea.

"I couldn't help noticing your fields as I drove in," he said. "Would it be unforgivably impolite to ask how many acres you've planted?"

"Only twenty-five—a fraction of what we planted when my father was alive." She sipped her tea. "But now, with labor so scarce, even twenty-five seems too many."

He stirred milk into his tea. "I suppose you heard Theo Frost went bankrupt last year."

"Yes. Everyone is having labor problems, especially with the Federals overseeing the contracts. I'm having a hard time keeping my men on the job, though they're due a share of the profits." She couldn't quite keep the bitterness from her voice. "Thanks to the Yankees, nobody and nothing seems to count for anything."

He wrapped both hands around his cup. "Perhaps things will improve for all of us next year. I'm eager to get my land under cultivation. As soon as I can get my inheritance sorted out."

"You must be the one Josie Clifton told me about."

"You know Miss Clifton?"

"We met aboard the *Resolute* last month, and

she mentioned that an heir to Willowood had turned up."

"That's me." He finished his tea and stood. "I should collect my children and go. We've overstayed our welcome as it is."

"Not at all. I'm happy to have helped."

"Perhaps I'll see you in church on Sunday. I believe Mr. Glennie will be there."

On more than one occasion, Lettice had encouraged Charlotte to resume attending church, but Charlotte had been too caught up with getting her rice planted on time to do more than read in her Psalter. She had even missed last Sunday's Easter service, but it couldn't be helped.

"I've been busy getting settled, but I plan to attend services this week. Mrs. Hadley says everyone enjoys Mr. Glennie's sermons."

Charlotte followed Mr. Betancourt to the door and waved as he drove out of the yard with his daughters.

Nicholas Betancourt was certainly an intriguing gentleman—and a rice planter like herself. It would be a comfort to have a neighbor to talk to, someone who shared her dream of reclaiming the life she had once enjoyed on the river. Especially now, when her home was in disrepair, her workers unreliable, and the blessings of the past too far away to be remembered.

Four

Church bells pealed as Charlotte arrived for services. A soft morning breeze beckoned her through the wrought-iron side gate and across a yard shaded by moss-draped oaks and cedar trees.

How long had it been since she had worshiped here with Papa? He had so admired the imposing brick edifice with its graceful pediment, tall porch columns, and generously sized windows.

"Charlotte, there you are." Lettice Hadley hurried across the yard to greet her. "I wondered whether I'd see you today. I brought you some of the first strawberries from my garden. Remind me to get them from the rig after the service."

"Thank you. I arrived here too late to plant any this year." She glanced around for Mr. Hadley, but he was nowhere to be seen. "I'm happy to see you. I know it's a long trip from Alder Hill, and it's difficult for you to leave Mr. Hadley for very long."

"He was feeling better this morning and encouraged me to come. I miss having our own minister every week, and Charles knows how much I enjoy hearing Mr. Glennie's sermons."

She linked her arm through Charlotte's. "I brought you a proper teakettle too. It's a bit dented, I'm afraid, but it will do in a pinch. Tell me, is there any news as to when your household furnishings might arrive?"

"Soon, I hope. Augusta Milton was kind enough to store them for us after Papa sold the house. The lawyer is arranging for someone to bring them up on the *Resolute* as soon as Captain Arthur has room for everything. Not that there's very much left."

"I'm sure it will be a comfort to have your mother's things around you again."

Another horse and rig arrived, and Lettice turned. "There's Josie Clifton."

The young woman Charlotte had met aboard the *Resolute* tethered her horse and crossed the yard, her pale blue skirt trailing across the grass, her hat aflutter in the spring breeze. She waved to Lettice, who responded with a deep frown.

"I thought you were in mourning," Lettice said.

"Grandmother has been gone a year come May, and since Mr. Glennie will be here today, I decided to end my mourning early. I don't think she will mind."

"Perhaps, but propriety demands—"

"Oh, Lettice, forgive me, but these days no one cares one whit about propriety." Josie smiled at

Charlotte. "At least I don't. Hello, Miss Fraser. Oh, there's Mr. Glennie."

The minister, dignified in his worn black suit and clerical collar, greeted the small group of worshipers before hurrying inside.

"We should go in," Lettice said.

Charlotte followed Lettice inside. When her eyes adjusted to the light, she saw Theo Frost seated in the first pew and her heart squeezed. The Frosts and the Allstons, whose plantations lay along the Pee Dee River, were among Papa's oldest friends. For most of her childhood, Mr. Allston had been president of the Winyah Indigo Society, a charitable organization that he and Papa supported for the education of the poor. On the day the society opened its meeting hall, she and Papa joined the procession to the Georgetown Masonic Hall to listen to a celebratory address. Children from the school gathered at the corner of Prince and Common Streets, where Mr. Frost handed out scholarships along with notebooks and peppermint candies. Now, like so many others, he moved beneath a shroud of loss, barely able to meet his own needs.

Behind her someone giggled, and she turned her head to see Mr. Betancourt enter the church, holding his daughters by the hand. Marie-Claire, her hair in a thick braid adorned with a white ribbon that sat slightly askew, stared straight ahead, her expression sullen, but Anne-Louise grinned and waved to Charlotte as their father ushered them into a pew. He saw Charlotte then and bowed. She dipped her head in greeting as the opening hymn began.

The minister, now robed in a white alb and stole, stood and pronounced the opening sentences, his rich voice reverberating in the space. "The Lord is in his holy temple . . ."

Charlotte closed her eyes and relaxed into the familiar rhythm of the prayers, responses, and readings.

"The psalm appointed for this day is Psalm 95."

Charlotte opened her Psalter to follow along. But her thoughts returned to a verse she'd read earlier in the week. She turned to it instead:

O what great troubles and adversities has thou showed me! and yet didst thou turn and refresh me; yea, and broughtest me from the deep of the earth again.

It was a powerful thought. She glanced around at the sea of somber faces and the many worshipers still dressed in mourning clothes. Surely everyone in the Lowcountry must be hoping for deliverance from the travails the war had thrust upon them.

The air inside the church grew warm. Lettice and Josie took out their fans as the readings ended and the homily began.

Charlotte dabbed at her forehead with her handkerchief. So much was at stake, and so much remained to be done. Easter had passed almost without her marking it. But by Christmas, if her meager furnishings arrived soon and if the rice crop was successful, Fairhaven might look like a real home again. Perhaps she'd place lighted candles in every window and cedar boughs above the door as her mother had done. Invite the neighbors for mulled cider and sweets. In her mind, she flipped the calendar forward to the day when her troubles would be over and she could laugh again.

At last Mr. Glennie pronounced his blessing and led them in a final hymn, the notes lingering in the close, humid air. Charlotte rose and followed Lettice and Josie outside. While everyone waited to greet the minister, Charlotte excused herself to speak to Mr. Frost.

His eyes, so pale a blue they seemed colorless, misted at the sight of her. "Dear Miss Fraser. I am deeply aggrieved at the loss of your father."

"Thank you. I miss him terribly, but I could not wish him back. His last months were unbearably painful."

"I'm sorry for that, and sorry I missed the funeral. I was in Washington and heard of his passing on my return." He studied her intently. "What are you doing here? I assumed you'd take up residence in Charleston."

"I promised Papa I'd try to keep Fairhaven going. It meant more to him than anything. Besides, it's all I have left, except for the summer house on Pawley's."

Mr. Frost shook his head. "Noble sentiments, to be sure, but I must advise against it. I'm sure it's no secret that I myself have lost nearly everything, and Ben Allston is not far behind. Stolen blind by those who once depended on us and decimated by last year's storm, not to mention that prices have dropped to a disastrous level." He shook his head. "How do you suppose a woman alone with no resources can hope to succeed when experi-enced men have not?"

"I'm not completely inexperienced. I've worked alongside Papa all my life."

"Admirable, but not the same as being in charge on your own."

"Perhaps I will fail, but I must try."

He jammed his hat onto his head. "Stubborn as a mule, just like your father."

"I'll take that as a compliment, Mr. Frost."

With a curt nod, he headed for his rig and climbed inside. Lettice hurried over carrying a teakettle, a basket of strawberries, and a jar of cream. "Here you are."

"Cream? I can't remember the last time I had any." Charlotte popped a berry into her mouth and savored the explosion of sweetness on her tongue. "Oh, how I wish I could afford a cow."

"We have only one, but she produces more milk than Charles and I can use. You're welcome to more if you can use it."

"Thank you, Lettice. I don't know what I'd do without your kindness."

"It's nothing. Now, I must speak to Mr. Glennie before I go."

"I suppose I should pay my respects as well." Charlotte joined Lettice and Josie and a few others and took her turn greeting the minister.

Mr. Betancourt emerged from the church, his daughters rushing along in front of him. "Miss Fraser." He smiled down at her in a way that made her heart lurch. With his thick shock of dark hair and strong, even features, he was attractive as could be, but now was not the time to be distracted by sentimental feelings. Not when her future and the future of her plantation hung in the balance.

"Mr. Betancourt. How are your daughters? No more close calls in the river, I hope."

"None. We recovered my boat, I'm happy to say, but I have forbidden Marie-Claire to take it out again until further notice. A restriction she finds most grievous, I'm afraid."

She watched Marie-Claire and Anne-Louise playing tag beneath the trees. "They must miss their mother."

An imperceptible nod of his head and then:

"I was hoping to see you today. I have a great favor to ask."

"Oh?"

"Perhaps it's presumptuous of me, since we've only just met, but I'm in a most difficult situation, and I have no one else to turn to."

Josie Clifton hurried over, the satin ribbons on her hat dancing in the wind. "Mr. Betancourt." She curtsied and offered her hand for a kiss. "How perfectly lovely to see you."

"Miss Clifton. You're well, I trust."

"Just fine, sir. And better than ever to know we have such a dashing new neighbor on the Waccamaw. My mother says you must come to dinner very soon."

He flushed beneath his tan. "I'll look forward to it."

"Are those your children?" Josie asked. "I mean, they must be, since they were sitting with you during the service. Aren't they just the most darling little things?"

He laughed. "Well, yes, to me they are. But I suppose all fathers think their children are a cut above the rest."

"Well, they are darling. Simply darling."

Josie stood rooted to the spot and looked expectantly at the two of them. "Oh dear, I've intruded upon your conversation."

"Actually, I do have something to discuss with Miss Fraser. If you will excuse us?"

"Oh. Well, certainly." Josie smiled at Charlotte. "Will I see you at the Ladies' Society meeting on Wednesday, Miss Fraser?"

The prospect made Charlotte's head pound. She'd never felt at home among the women who flitted like gilded butterflies from one social engagement to the next. Reared mostly among men, she'd never been much good at the small talk that was the lifeblood of such gatherings—who was engaged to whom, whose coconut pie was the most delicious, what so-and-so had worn to town last Saturday. "I'm not sure I can get away."

"Well, come if you can." With a sweep of her new skirt, Josie turned and hurried to rejoin her mother.

The minister left in his rig, and soon the churchyard was deserted. Mr. Betancourt eyed the basket of berries. "Those look good."

"Mrs. Hadley brought them. Would you like one?"

"Don't mind if I do." He plucked a berry from the basket and ate it. "As I was saying, Miss Fraser, I am in a bit of a fix."

"I can well believe it. All of the Lowcountry is in trouble these days."

"I'm not speaking of Willowood, although my lands are as much in disarray as any." He inclined his head toward the children who had abandoned their game of tag and were picking violets growing beside the gate. "It's Marie-Claire and Anne-Louise that are of most concern to me."

"I see."

"Despite my best efforts, I have not been able to find anyone to teach them."

"Perhaps you should write to Mrs. Allston in Charleston. I understand she engaged a new French teacher for her school last year. Mademoiselle Le Prince. Girls from some of the best families in the city attend Mrs. Allston's. I'm sure your daughters would get on well."

"No doubt. However, the tuition and boarding fees are quite steep, and Anne-Louise, especially, still mourns their mother. I'd rather they stay with me if possible." He paused. "I was hoping you might tutor them. I can't pay as much as I'd have to pay Mrs. Allston, but—"

"I'm not a teacher, Mr. Betancourt, either by temperament or by training. I wouldn't know where to begin."

"But you are well educated and well read, judging by the books I noticed in your library the other day. And you treated the girls with great kindness when they appeared at your gate."

"I was happy to help. But I've a plantation of my own to run, and I know you're aware of the many difficulties one faces these days in doing so."

He let out a long breath. "Then your answer is no."

"I'm afraid it must be." The basket of berries and cream and the teapot grew heavy. She shifted the basket to her other arm. "Have you tried placing a notice in the *Charleston Mercury*?"

"Twice. But nobody suitable applied."

"I'm sorry."

"So am I." He looked around. "I don't see your rig."

"I haven't one. I walked."

"Then you must allow me to drive you home."

"You are kind, but I don't mind the walk, really." She smiled. "Walking has a most salutary effect upon my constitution."

"I'll say good day then." Moving with the power and grace of a thoroughbred, he crossed the yard and collected his children. She popped another strawberry into her mouth and stepped through the churchyard gate in time to see his rig disappearing around the bend.

To be certain, Nicholas Betancourt had his troubles, and she was not unsympathetic to his plight. Perhaps she should have tried harder to help him. But she was too beset by troubles of her own.

Five

Leaning heavily on her hoe handle, Charlotte pushed her bonnet to the back of her head and wiped her brow on a sleeve. All morning the sun had beaten down steady and hot. Now clouds were gathering over the sea, and the pleasant April breeze had turned to humid gusts. She shaded her eyes and looked toward the house, shining white in the distance, and to the empty road beyond. Trim had promised to come this morning with half a dozen men to help with the hoeing of the upland garden, but so far no one had appeared.

She finished hoeing around the corn and went down to her rice field, her heart lifting at the sight of twenty-five acres of moist, dark brown soil dotted with shoots of tender green. Balancing her hoe on her shoulder, she jumped the quarter drains and crossed the narrow plank bridge over the deep ditch that encircled the perimeter of the field. If only reliable workers could be found, she could plant a second field, mill half the crop, and cure the rest for seed.

She retraced her steps and followed the path to

the house, her head pounding from the heat and humidity. Her empty stomach groaned.

"Miss Cha'lotte." Two young Negro boys, bare-chested and barefoot, pounded along the path, each of them carrying a string of perch. "You want to buy some fish? Make you a fine dinner."

"Yes, they would, but I'm afraid I can't afford them. I suppose I must catch my own."

The taller of the two nodded. "Perch is bitin' real good on the other side o' the bridge—in that shady spot where that big tree went down last winter. All you got to do is throw your line in the water."

The creak of wagon wheels and the muted drumming of horses' hooves on the sandy road drew her attention. "Perhaps I will. But for now I must see who is coming along the road."

The boys sprinted away, and she hurried along the path to the house.

"Whoa." A thin man in a threadbare wool suit, a felt hat pulled low across his face, halted a loaded wagon at the front gate.

Charlotte ran down the avenue toward the road. Drawing closer to the wagon, she blinked and clapped a hand to her throat. "Alexander? Is that you?"

"In the flesh." He jumped lightly to the ground and took off his hat. "How are you, Cousin?"

"Absolutely stunned at the moment. And terribly happy to see you. We've had not a single word

74

from you since we heard you were missing at Gettysburg. We thought the worst." Her voice wobbled. "After all this time, we'd given up on ever seeing your face again."

"There were times I felt like giving up too." Her cousin leaned against the wagon. "After Gettysburg, I was held in the Yankee prison camp at Ft. Delaware."

"Ft. Delaware? I'm sure Uncle Harding must have inquired after you there."

"Maybe. It was a madhouse, especially when a sickness of one kind or another paid us a visit. Of course we all wrote letters home, but who knows whether any attempt was made to deliver—Easy there, girl."

Alexander reached out to calm his restless horse, a pretty cinnamon-colored mare with a white patch on her muzzle. "By the time I got out, the war had ended—and then I read in the newspapers about the ferry accident." He shook his head. "During those last months at Ft. Delaware, it was the dream of seeing Ma and Pa again that kept me going. And they were already dead."

. "We tried to find you, to let you know what had happened, but we never heard a word. And our letter to Fanny went unanswered as well."

"I should have come home then, but I—"

"Yes, you should have." Unexpected tears clogged her throat. "It wasn't fair to let us think the worst. Where on earth have you been?"

"After I located my sister in Philadelphia, I moved in with her and tried working at a factory there. But I couldn't get used to the winters . . . or the attitude toward Southerners. Fanny is married to a Yankee from Ohio now and—"

"My word! Why didn't she let us know you were alive?"

He shrugged. "She has put the past and everyone in it out of her mind. It's no excuse, I know, but that's the truth. I should have written to you myself. I don't know why I didn't. I . . . maybe I was trying to run from the past as well."

"But if you do that," she said softly, "you leave yourself behind."

"That's what brought me home at last. I got to Charleston a few weeks ago and went to see the family lawyer. He told me Uncle Francis had died and you'd returned to the Waccamaw."

"Yes. Dear Mr. Crowley." She leaned her hoe against the fence.

"I was hoping something was left of Father's holdings, but he died with hardly a dime to his name." Alexander shook his head. "Mother tried to warn him against buying Aunt Emma's place and her slaves, but he felt duty-bound to help her. Then the war came and he lost it all. But why am I telling you this? You know it well enough."

"Yes. Papa told me." She stroked the horse and was rewarded with a soft snuffle. "At least I have the beach cottage. And Fairhaven . . . for the time being."

He frowned. "Did Uncle Francis leave you debt-ridden too?"

"No, but Mr. Crowley can't find any proof that we own Fairhaven."

"That's ridiculous. Of course this land is yours. It's been Fraser land forever."

"But I need papers that prove it. Do you suppose Uncle Harding left any records behind? Mr. Crowley said even a letter might do."

"I don't think so, Charlotte. By the time I got home, the bank had taken everything to settle Father's debts. All that was left was my mother's wedding ring and a silver tea service."

"I see." She let out a gusty sigh. "Perhaps it doesn't matter. Without enough workers, this place may soon prove to be more than I can handle anyway. And Mr. Frost and Mr. Crowley are just waiting to say I told you so."

"At least you'll be more comfortable in the meantime." He swept a hand toward the loaded wagon. "I brought your things from Charleston. Mrs. Milton sends her regards."

"Oh, I am delighted. I've been making do with odds and ends, camping here with the barest of necessities and relying upon Mrs. Hadley for milk and cream." She peered into the wagon. "I don't suppose you've a cow in there?"

"Afraid not. But there are rugs and bedding and

winter curtains, plus your mother's walnut dresser and a few chairs."

"And Mama's china? I don't expect I'll be giving any fancy parties anytime soon, but I want it just the same."

"It's all here, assuming it didn't get broken on the trip. We hit some rough water just before we reached Winyah." He cast an eye to the lowering clouds and climbed onto the wagon. "We'd better get all this inside."

She opened the gate and Alexander drove up the long avenue to the house. While Charlotte rummaged in her pantry for something to eat, he unloaded trunks and crates and dish barrels.

She served tea and bread with honey and a few slices of bacon Mrs. Hadley had brought. Alexander buttered a slice of bread and drizzled it with honey. "Mr. Crowley said you are writing articles for some Yankee newspaper."

"Yes. The *New York Enterprise*. It doesn't pay much, but I hope it will help retire my debt to the bank this winter. Next year I'll have enough seed of my own and won't have the expense of buying it."

"But you'll still have the expense of hiring workers."

"True."

He ate a piece of bacon and sipped his tea. "Is there anyone you can rely upon?"

"Sadly, no—unless you'd like to stay. Perhaps

the workers will more readily respond to a man overseeing them than they do to me."

"I can't stay."

"Why not? I think it's a wonderful idea. You need a home, and I need help. And there's still time to plant more rice."

"Are the floodgates in repair?" He helped himself to another cup of tea.

"Only the trunks in the field I've already planted. But Thomas—"

"Even if we could get them fixed in time, there's still the plowing and raking out to be done. We couldn't possibly plant until the end of May, and then what would be the point? The maybirds would eat it all before it had a chance to mature."

She brushed away the hot tears stinging her eyes. "I see. You don't want to help me."

"Charlotte." He set down his cup. "I will admit I made a mess of the situation by keeping silent for so long and letting you think I was dead. But I brought your things, didn't I? And at my own expense too."

"Thank you. I don't intend to seem ungrateful." She stirred her tea and watched it swirl in the cup. "I didn't think it would be this difficult. I thought the Negroes would be happy to work here, especially those who belonged to Papa. Before the war they seemed to take such pride in their work. But now it seems there is little I can count on."

Alexander nodded and munched another slice of bacon.

"Remember how Papa gave prizes every year for the best hoe hand and the best plough man, the best thresher?"

"I do."

"Trim was nearly always declared the best hoe hand. But now he comes and goes like the wind. He readily acknowledges that he signed a contract, but he always finds reasons not to honor it."

"There is no shame in admitting that you made a mistake in coming back here." Alexander pushed away his empty plate and swatted at a fly buzzing about his head. "Mr. Crowley says anyone who tries to grow rice these days is a fool."

"Yes. He said as much to me as well. But I promised Papa. I can't quit now. It would feel like the worst kind of betrayal."

"I know, but Uncle Francis couldn't have known what it would be like. Maybe the lawyer is right and you should close up this house and move back to Charleston."

"And do what? Take in sewing? Work in a shop?"

"There are worse fates."

"Name one."

"Wasting your beauty and youth on some vanished dream. Your father wouldn't want that, no matter how much he loved this place."

"I made a promise."

He sighed and got to his feet. "You're just like Uncle Francis."

"You're the second person to tell me that." She rose and cleared the table. "Mr. Frost said the same thing at church a couple of weeks ago. He seemed almost angry with me for even trying to restore this place."

Alexander leaned over and kissed her cheek. "I'm leaving you the wagon and the horse, if you'll drive me back to Georgetown."

"Of course I will, but won't you need them yourself?"

"I'm leaving next week for Atlanta, for a job in a bank there. I'm taking a room in town. A horse and wagon would be an extra expense I can ill afford."

"I see. I wish I could afford to pay you for them, but—"

"It's all right. The fellow who sold them to me in Georgetown this morning gave me a good price. He's giving up on farming himself and heading back to civilization." He glanced out the window. "I should get going."

"So soon?" Charlotte came to stand beside him at the window. The sun had disappeared behind a thick cloud that cast a dark shadow over the garden.

"I'm afraid so. Captain Arthur is expecting heavy seas and wants to get underway as soon as possible in the morning."

"Wait while I change my dress."

Half an hour later, with Alexander at the reins, they set off for Georgetown. As the horse trotted down the shady road, Alexander kept up a steady stream of conversation about his new position, the new buildings going up all over Atlanta, and a certain young woman he had been introduced to upon his first visit. All too soon they reached Georgetown and the landing where the *Resolute* waited.

Alexander pressed his calling card into her hand. "Do write to me, Cousin, and tell me how you are getting on."

"I will." She caught his face in her hands. "I still can't believe you're alive and well. If only your parents—"

His brown eyes went bright with tears. "Yes. I wish they knew I came through the war all right."

He reached inside his pocket for his ticket. "I should go aboard. For what it's worth, I do hope you succeed. Uncle Francis always said you could be the best planter on the Waccamaw—besides himself, of course."

She clasped his hand. "Come to Pawley's this summer. I'll be there by early June. It'll be like old times when we were children."

"I can't promise. We'll see." He started up the gangplank, then turned back. "Oh. I found your daddy's old pistol in the bottom of one of the packing crates. I hid it in the woodbox behind the stove, in case you need it."

Papa had taught her to handle a pistol, setting up targets on an old log across the river. But she couldn't imagine ever actually having to use it.

The wind picked up, ruffling the water. Alexander clamped his hat to his head. "You'd better go on home before the storm hits. Write to me, Charlotte."

With a final wave, he hurried onto the *Resolute*. Feeling more alone than ever, she glanced at the darkening sky and turned her new horse and wagon toward home.

Yesterday a dear cousin I assumed was lost in the war came to Fairhaven bearing the pitiful, long-hidden remains of my father's household: a few pictures and rugs, my mother's curtains stowed in muslin bags, some odds and ends of furniture, and china meant for dinner parties I will never give. Still it is a comfort to have those few possessions that by clever concealment survived the Union army's destruction.

On the way home from the steamboat landing in Georgetown, driving the unwieldy wagon hitched to an unfamiliar little mare I have named Cinnamon, I raced against a storm that was both frightening and thrilling. Passing a friend's house, I saw several cattle standing in the road, their heads bowed against the rain, and the loose limbs of trees flying past. At the ferry that would take me across the Waccamaw, the horse shied as the flatboat dipped and slid against the current. For a moment I feared she would bolt, but one of the boatmen stood close by her as we were propelled from the river-bank, and she quieted.

By the time I reached home, the sky was black as pitch and the wind was rattling every door and window in this old house. About midnight, with the storm still raging, I lit a lamp and went up to bed, but the roar of wind through the trees, the sound of breaking branches sharp as rifle fire, and my worry about my rice field rendered sleep elusive.

Now it is afternoon. The sky is gloomy and dark, and trees are down across the avenue. This morning I ventured out to check on my new horse. Lacking a proper barn for her, I had left her in the leaky shed that stands behind the remains of the smokehouse. She seemed none the worse, but I rubbed her dry and led her down to the old pasture, where she seemed quite content to crop the new grass.

I took a walk about Fairhaven to assess the damage: some uprooted trees, a twisted section of fence. Loose shutters at the windows along the piazza. The tender shoots of my corn crop are torn and tangled. I hadn't the heart to check on my rice field. I fear the worst.

Charlotte blotted the pages and set them aside for mailing to the *New York Enterprise*. When the teakettle shrieked, she went out to the kitchen, spooned tea leaves into the pot, and added the boiling water. While the tea brewed, she sliced a pear Alexander had brought and rummaged in the pantry for bread and honey, her thoughts swirling like the river current. She needed hay and oats and a proper barn for the horse. Nails for repairing the shutters and the fence. Sugar and salt. A couple of chickens and a cow—she couldn't depend upon Lettice's generosity forever. And all of it would cost money. Perhaps all the naysayers were right and she had taken on more than she could manage.

Something tapped against the windowpane. She looked up to find a bedraggled peacock pecking at his reflection in the glass. Inexplicably tears stung her eyes. She willed them away. When faced with the impossible, of what use were tears?

Six

The wagon rattled along the rutted avenue leading to Willowood. The redbrick Georgian-style house sat nestled in a grove of pine trees that cast ever-changing patterns of light across the gray slate roof. Approaching the front entrance, Charlotte noticed cracked windows and peeling paint, burned-out storage buildings and neglected gardens. A rain-soaked rag doll lay in the muddy yard. Clearly Mr. Betancourt's plantation had fared no better than hers.

A dog barked, and Marie-Claire appeared from the side yard, a basket of clothes balanced on one hip. The wary expression in her eyes made her seem far older than her years.

Charlotte reined in, climbed down from the wagon seat, and straightened her hat. "Good morning, Marie-Claire. Is your father home?"

"He's in the library, but I wouldn't disturb him if I were you. He's cross as an old bear."

"Oh? And why is that?"

The child shrugged. "Every time he gets a letter from New Orleans, he's grumpy for days."

"That's too bad. May I go in?"

"Suit yourself. He told me and Anne-Louise not to make any noise because he's too busy trying to think. So we're doing the wash." She shifted her basket to her other hip. "Tamar was supposed to do it, but she isn't here yet."

"Perhaps she couldn't get here because of the storm. Quite a few trees blew down, and the road is still blocked in places. I had quite a time of it my—"

"Marie-Claire, where have you been?" Anne-Louise pounded across the yard, a scowl on her face. "I've been waiting for hours."

Charlotte bent down to the younger girl. "Hello. Do you remember me?"

The child nodded. "Papa said he wanted you to teach us but you wouldn't."

The door opened and Mr. Betancourt, the sleeves of his white shirt rolled to his elbows, emerged onto the piazza. "Miss Fraser. What a pleasant surprise."

"I told her you were busy," Marie-Claire said to her father. "Don't blame me."

The sisters hurried away, the laundry basket bumping between them.

He smiled. "I apologize for my daughter's behavior. She's cross these days, but then so am I."

"I've come at a bad time. Perhaps I should go."

"Not at all. I'm in the middle of some correspondence, but it can wait. May I offer you something to drink? Tea perhaps?"

"Tea would be lovely if it's no trouble."

"I'd welcome a distraction."

He ushered her into a wide foyer with polished pine floors and an elaborate crystal chandelier and then into a book-lined parlor furnished with delicate chairs, needlepoint footstools, and mahogany side tables. On the floor beneath the window, a violin rested in an open case. A pair of silver candlesticks graced the fireplace mantel, above which hung a portrait of a dark-haired woman wearing a crimson gown and an ermine wrap. Charlotte took it all in, feeling that somehow she had stepped back in time. How had such lovely things escaped the marauding Yankees' notice?

As if reading her thoughts he said, "I shipped these here from New Orleans after Christmas. If there was anything good about being occupied so early in the war, it's that people came out of it with most of their possessions intact." He indicated the portrait above the mantel. "My wife, Gabrielle. This was painted in New Orleans the year we were married. It was her wedding gift to me."

"She's lovely."

"Yes. She was quite a beauty." His voice as he studied the portrait was laced with pain that reminded her of her own wrenching loss.

The moment passed. He indicated a chair by the window. "Please make yourself comfortable.

I'm without any help today. Mrs. Hadley recommended Tamar, who appeared eager for steady work, but it seems she's often delayed of late."

"I remember her," Charlotte said. "When I was young and visiting Mrs. Hadley with my mother, Tamar occasionally accompanied her mistress to Alder Hill. Tamar was beautiful in those days. I thought she was brave too."

His brows went up. "How so?"

"She made no secret of her wish to hire out as a seamstress in Georgetown in order to save enough to purchase her freedom and that of her infant son. I'm sure a lot of slaves dreamed that same dream, but I doubt many of them were bold enough to say so."

"And was she successful?"

"I don't know. After my mother died, I was mostly away at school or with my father. But at any rate, she's free now."

"Yes, and she's a wonderful housekeeper—when she's here." He turned toward the kitchen. "Luckily I do know how to boil water. I won't be long."

She picked up a slender volume of poetry lying on the side table and thumbed the pages, reading random passages. A gentle breeze, fragrant with spring, drifted through the open window and ruffled the pages.

Soon Mr. Betancourt returned carrying a tray laden with pink china cups, a matching teapot, and a plate of crackers, each one topped with a strawberry and a dollop of cream. He set down the tray and dropped into the chair next to hers, his long legs stretched out in front of him. "Tamar brought a few strawberries yesterday. I believe you're fond of them."

Charlotte found herself reveling in the moment. For years she had nursed her father, kept their house, and wrestled with their accounts. Before that she had labored on Aunt Lavinia's farm. She couldn't recall the last time someone had taken care of her. "How kind of you to remember."

"I remember everything about you, Miss Fraser."

Her cheeks warmed beneath his approving smile. "Did you enjoy living in New Orleans, Mr. Betancourt?"

He poured tea and handed her a cup. "For a time. It is a volatile place now." He regarded her over the top of his cup. "Have you ever been there?"

"Once, just before we had to abandon the Waccamaw. A business trip with my father."

She remembered the city as a place of strange beauty and mystery that left her feeling unnerved. From the wrought-iron balcony of their hotel on St. Charles Avenue, she'd watched the changing drama in the street below. Dark-haired Creole girls hawked baskets of tomatoes. Nattily dressed cotton and rice brokers hurried toward the distant quay. A copper-skinned woman dressed in pink satin sold pralines and bonbons from a painted wooden cart.

On an afternoon carriage ride with her father, she drank in the beauty of magnolias and oleanders and rattling palms growing in secret gated gardens. She remembered a pair of nuns standing in the dim interior of a church and the faint scents of wine and incense wafting from the open doorway. The crowded wharves shifting and creaking beneath the weight of cargo, men, and horses. The odors of fish, tobacco, and burning sugar. At night the soft laughter of olive-skinned women promenading along the banquette rose into the humid air.

Even at seventeen she had sensed that beneath the city's genteel surface ran a current of tension that left her feeling on edge. No doubt the city was even more unsettling these days, with the Federals in charge.

Mr. Betancourt set down his cup and relaxed into his chair. "What brings you to Willowood?"

She liked his directness. She'd rehearsed her answer, but as she looked into his eyes, memory deserted her. She set down her cup. "Simply put, I lost my corn crop in the storm, and the sea tide ruined half my rice field."

"I see. Can you replant?"

"Perhaps. But to be perfectly frank, Mr. Betancourt, I have taxes to pay and a bank loan coming due this autumn, and replanting will mean more labor costs as well. I need more money than I can possibly earn writing for the newspaper."

"You've come for a loan, then." He poured more tea.

"A—oh no, I wouldn't presume to ask such a favor. I came to ask whether the position as tutor for your daughters is still open."

"But you were quite clear that it was not a job for which you feel qualified."

"That's true. I don't. But I have written out a proposed curriculum that I am willing to try on Tuesdays and Thursdays, and if it proves satisfactory . . ." She handed him a sheet of paper from her reticule.

He studied it briefly and set it aside. "I'm quite sure you will get on splendidly. And in any case, the situation is temporary. As soon as my affairs are sorted out, I'll enroll the girls in a proper boarding school, just as you recommended."

"Are you saying yes?"

"If I can afford your services. Would ten dollars a month be agreeable?"

"Ten dollars a—"

"It isn't nearly what you're worth, but as you said the other day, hard times have befallen us all."

"I was about to say that ten dollars is perfectly agreeable. More than I dared hope for, really. I'm grateful for your kindness."

"I am learning that poverty is a true test of

civility," he said. For a long moment their eyes met, understanding sparking between them. At last he smiled. "Perhaps it can also be a cornerstone of friendship."

He picked up his violin and began polishing the wood with a bit of red flannel. "My wife couldn't bear the hardships of the war. She missed her fashions and her entertainments. I am fortunate that my own favorite pastimes are without cost. My music, for instance."

He lifted the bow and drew it across the strings, filling the parlor with lush, sweet notes that pierced her heart. She closed her eyes as the music, blended with the birdsong coming through the window, poured out.

He finished on a rich, low note that lingered in the air and left her wishing for another respite from her many troubles. "That was lovely."

"I'm hardly more than an amateur, but the girls enjoy hearing me play."

The mention of his daughters brought her back to reality. Suppose her efforts to teach them failed? Perhaps she had too readily agreed to his plan. Perhaps she should reconsider.

"I know they will be delighted to return to their lessons. When can you start?" He returned his violin to its case and fixed her with his calm, expectant gaze. Clearly it was too late to withdraw from their agreement.

"I'll need a week or so to order some books

from Charleston, but we can start without them. What about this coming Tuesday?"

"Excellent."

They rose, and she offered her hand. "Thank you, Mr. Betancourt. I shall try my best to be a good teacher."

"I've no doubt of that. And I'm grateful to you for taking us on. My daughters need the steadying presence of a woman in their lives."

She glanced at the magnificent portrait above the mantel. "I lost my own mother at an early age. I know how your daughters must miss her, and how dearly she must have loved them."

Something flickered in his eyes. "My wife had many lovely qualities my children were too young to fully appreciate."

He walked her out and boosted her onto the wagon seat. "We'll see you soon."

Charlotte turned the wagon onto the sandy road. Now that her mission had proved successful, she was assailed with doubt. What on earth had possessed her to suggest such a scheme? What did she know about teaching? Her own schooling was a distant memory of endless days of ciphering, writing essays, and reciting poetry in halting French beneath Madame Giraud's unforgiving eye. An indifferent student, she had cared more for planting rice, riding her father's blooded horses, and reading her own cache of books.

At a bend in the road she came upon a couple of Negro men working to clear the fallen trees still littering the landscape. She acknowledged their doffed hats with a slight nod, rounded a final bend, and drove up the long avenue to Fairhaven. She unhitched Cinnamon and tethered her to an old laurel tree in the yard. It was not yet noon. Perhaps there was time to write out her order for books and take it into Georgetown for delivery to Charleston.

A rig rattled up the avenue from the road and came to a stop in the yard. Charles Hadley peered out. "Miss Fraser. Good morning."

"Mr. Hadley. What brings you out this way?"

He climbed out of the rig and lifted a basket from the seat. "Lettice sent you some eggs. And more strawberries."

"How kind, but you didn't have to make a special trip." She studied the man from beneath her hat brim. He seemed perfectly fine this morning—his brown beard neatly trimmed, a fresh linen shirt tucked into a pair of woolen trousers. Perhaps the demons that plagued him had been vanquished after all. What a blessing that would be for him and for his long-suffering wife. "I plan to buy a couple of chickens soon and save you the trouble."

"No trouble, I assure you. I was coming this way anyhow—to talk to John Clifton and to that fellow up at Willowood."

"Mr. Betancourt?"

"That's him. The contracts the Federals are making with the Negroes aren't worth the paper they're written on, so I've hired a foreman to gather up a crew and help oversee an early June planting. It's a risk, of course, planting later in the season, but if we have a long summer we might be all right. I thought Clifton and Betancourt might want to get in on it."

She shifted the egg basket to her other arm. Ideally, planting was finished by early May. But perhaps Mr. Hadley was right and a delayed crop was worth the risk. "I can't speak for them, but I myself am interested. I'm down to half a corn crop and half a rice field at present, but if I had dependable workers, I might be able to sow another field."

Hands on hips, he studied her face. "I don't mean to pry, but begging your pardon, how do you plan on paying them? Lettice said you're writing up little pieces for some Yankee newspaper to bring in extra cash."

"That's true. But I'm tutoring the Betancourt girls as well, and I have money from my bank loan still available. I've lived as frugally as possible." She indicated the egg basket. "And your generosity is most appreciated."

Mr. Hadley took off his hat and blotted his face with a large, starched handkerchief. "If you want my opinion, you ought to give up on this place and go on back to Charleston. Half the planters in the county have already set off to California and such. I hear Ben Allston is thinking of going to Texas." He shrugged. "You're smart and just as deter-mined as your daddy was, and they are fine qualities. But the Lowcountry will never be what it was."

"Thank you for your opinion. Will you allow me to participate in the hiring of the men or not?"

"If Clifton and Betancourt don't object, I don't reckon I will either." He sent her a half smile. "Besides, my wife would have my hide if I tried to stop you. She thought the world of your mama."

He settled himself in his rig. "The missus says to tell you she's planning a dinner for next Friday evening. Six o'clock. It's her birthday. We know you're still in mourning, but it seems the old customs don't count for much anymore."

Charlotte thought of Josie Clifton's showing up at church in a new spring frock before her year of mourning was up. Mr. Hadley was right. The old rules meant little in this strange new world.

"Lettice has invited everybody on the Waccamaw and the Pee Dee too," Mr. Hadley continued. "Leastways it seems so."

Charlotte nodded slowly. She'd spent the last two years of her father's life watching his slow decline and mourning his approaching death. Weeks ago the prospect of dressing up and attending a party would have filled her with overwhelming guilt, but she was beginning to see things differently. Perhaps attending a small private gathering of her oldest friends was something she could do for Papa, to prove she was capable of the task he'd set for her. "A birthday celebration sounds lovely. It's too quiet around here these days."

Mr. Hadley stuffed his handkerchief into his shirt pocket and gazed toward the river, seemingly lost in thought. "She thinks she can turn back time and make things like they used to be."

"I suppose we all long for happier days, Mr. Hadley. But perhaps we should indeed take up a social life again now that we're through with the war."

"We may be finished with the war, but it isn't finished with me."

She recalled the darkened rooms at Alder Hill, Lettice's anxious face and descriptions of her husband's lightning-quick shifts in mood. "My father often said that even adversity is not without its comforts and hopes."

"Huh." He picked up the reins. "The foreman's name is Jeremiah Finch. Got here the day before yesterday—walked all the way from North Carolina. I'll send him on by here to talk to you directly."

"Thank you. And, Mr. Hadley, would it be too much trouble to stop by here on your way back from Willowood? I've need of some books from Charleston. Perhaps you'd be kind enough to deliver my letter to Georgetown for posting?"

"No trouble. I'll be back in a couple of hours."

"And please tell Lettice I'm looking forward to seeing her on Friday evening."

"I'll tell her." He clicked his tongue to the horse and drove away.

Seven

"Look, Ma'm'selle, I did it." Anne-Louise crossed the shady piazza and thrust a damp paper into Charlotte's hands. "I figured out how many pints in a quart—all by myself."

Charlotte set down her pen and studied the paper. "That's very good. I'm proud of you."

The little girl beamed. "May I please play in the water tub a while longer?"

"I suppose so—until your sister finishes her sums." Charlotte glanced toward the open French doors at the opposite end of the piazza, where Marie-Claire had repaired with her book and papers. "But please try not to get your skirts any more soaked than they already are."

Anne-Louise returned to the wooden tub Charlotte had filled with water this morning. She had provided the girl with a set of measuring cups purchased in Georgetown and left her to discover on her own the relationship of cups to pints and quarts. She hoped her approach would prove more enjoyable to both girls than rote memorization and improve the older one's attitude. But so far neither the water tub experiments nor the walk they had taken to sketch the herons on the creek had had the desired effect on Marie-Claire. The girl seemed determined to remain unhappy.

A breeze sent her papers fluttering to the floor, and Anne-Louise ran over to help her collect them. "Is it time for tea?" the child asked. "I'm hungry."

"In a minute. I want to finish this piece before—"

"Hello?" A wagon had halted down at the gate. A thin, wiry man stood beside it, staring up at the house.

"Who's that?" Anne-Louise slipped her hand into Charlotte's.

"I don't know. Wait here with your sister."

Charlotte went down the steps and hurried down the avenue to the gate.

The man spat and wiped his mouth with the back of his hand. "Miz Fraser?"

"Yes?"

"Name's Jeremiah Finch. I reckon Mr. Hadley over at Alder Hill mighta told you 'bout me."

"He did, and I'm interested in speaking with you about planting another of my rice fields. But I'm afraid you've come at an inopportune time." She swept a hand toward the piazza. "My pupils are here until two o'clock. Would it be possible for you to call again later this afternoon?"

"Listen, ma'am, I walked here clear from North

Carolina to get work, and I spent the last week workin' on Mr. Hadley's place and tryin' to round up a decent number of workers I can count on. That in itself is no small job."

"Yes, Mr. Hadley told me. He says—"

"And then that high and mighty Yankee who has appointed himself the king of Georgetown come by this morning to tell me I can't make a contract with the blacks without his say-so." He pushed his hat to the back of his head. "On top of that, from what I hear, most of the plantin' season is actually gone. I don't have time to be makin' extra trips on account of you bein' too busy to talk to me."

She sighed. "Very well. Wait while I fetch the children, and I'll show you the field I have in mind."

He nodded and spat another stream of tobacco juice.

She returned to the house for her hat and gloves, rounded up the girls, and met Mr. Finch at the gate. They walked the short distance to the dock where her small rowboat was tethered. They climbed inside, and Mr. Finch took the oars. "Which way, ma'am?"

She pointed. "Three miles downriver."

He steered the boat into the middle of the river. Anne-Louise kept up a constant stream of chatter, asking the names of every bird and plant they passed, but Marie-Claire crossed her arms and stared into the water, refusing to speak despite Charlotte's efforts to engage her in the conversation.

At a bend in the tree-shaded river, Charlotte directed Mr. Finch to put ashore, and they walked up a slight rise to the field. He took off his hat and surveyed the fallow ground and the broken trunks. "I admit I ain't got much of a background in rice plantin', but I already know from my work on the Hadleys' place that this right here represents a heap of work."

"I'm aware of that. But I know an excellent carpenter who can fix the trunks. Thomas once belonged to my father. He repaired the ones in my other field. I'm sure he can do it in time for another planting. The question is whether or not you have enough workers to prepare the ground."

"Mebbe. I got a couple of men from Georgetown who have their own oxen. Rounded up a few field hands from over on the Pee Dee too." He wiped his brow with his sleeve. "Reckon I'm willin' to try if the price is right."

"Ma'm'selle, look!" Anne-Louise ran over, cradling a small turtle in her hands. "May I keep him?"

Marie-Claire shook her head. "You are not keeping that disgusting creature in our house."

"Papa won't care. Besides, I'll make a house for him outside. I won't let him into your room."

"You'd better not."

Mr. Finch cleared his throat. "Well, ma'am, do we have a deal or don't we?"

"How much?"

"Thirty dollars. But that don't include the seeds or fixing the trunks. Reckon I'll leave that to you."

"Thirty dollars!"

He shrugged. "I got a wife and four young'uns back home. I got to make a profit."

"I suppose so." She made a quick calculation. She could afford it—barely. And if the harvest proved successful, she'd recover her investment and perhaps earn a small profit. "All right, Mr. Finch. When may I expect you to begin work?"

"Friday, if this good weather holds and that uppity Yankee approves the paperwork. I'll fetch you to take a look once we get the field ready for plantin'." For the first time, the man smiled, revealing tobacco-stained teeth. "I want you to be happy with my work."

"I'm sure I will be."

They returned to the boat, Anne-Louise carrying her turtle.

"One more thing," Jeremiah Finch said, turning the boat upriver. "I have my own way of doin' things." The boat creaked as he pulled the oars. "Long as you remember that, I expect we'll get on just fine."

The air in the room was thick and warm, and dust motes swirled like snowflakes in the morning light. Kneeling beside the larger of the trunks Alexander had delivered, Charlotte lifted a pale pink dress from its muslin nest and held it up to the window. She studied the dress as one might study a painting, noting the voluminous sleeves that were several seasons out of fashion, a bit of lace trim missing from the bodice. The flounced skirt was flattened and wrinkled from years in storage. But the dress would have to do.

Before the war, her clothes press had bulged with dresses for every occasion—morning dresses, riding costumes, costumes for walking about and paying social calls upon her neighbors, and elaborately adorned and pleated evening dresses for the theater, all of them sewn from yards and yards of the finest silks and satins. No more. Since returning to Fairhaven she'd worn her black crepe mourning dress to church and to town. Here at home she wore dresses in dark blue, gray, or brown over serviceable undergarments that allowed her to move freely about the fields.

Not that she had much choice. Years of the Federal blockade had reduced everyone's wardrobe to tattered homespun.

The pink gown, created at a fancy store in Paris and carefully hidden in a friend's house in Charleston for the duration of the war, had been the delight of Charlotte's twentieth birthday, a bright spot of luxury amidst the deprivation. Now it seemed unfamiliar, a silk penitentiary requiring more layers of undergarments than she ever wore these days. She draped it across her bed and returned to the trunk for her crinoline and heavy petticoats. Had she ever actually looked forward to wearing such torturous garments?

Perhaps years of hardship had turned her into someone more untamed, less feminine than she ought to be. Less concerned with her appearance. During her later years at Madame Giraud's, she'd had her share of Charleston beaux. She was not unattractive. Her skin had been smooth and fashionably pale, her dark hair thick and glossy, her figure trim. But when she looked into the mirror now, she took little note of her complexion or her small waist or her expressive eyes. What she saw was a young woman unafraid to tackle a hard task. A woman who made choices and saw them through. In her own eyes, intelligence and determination were her most attractive assets.

In the yard below someone shouted, and she went to the window. Jeremiah Finch and his crew, which included Lambert and Moses, two of Papa's men, headed up the path to the rice field. The morning was still new, but judging from the workers' muddy dungarees, they had already checked on her second field downriver. She spotted Trim and Thomas, Papa's favorite carpenter who had repaired the trunks in her main field. Thomas seemed much older since the end of the war. His hair was now a snow-white cap cut close to his scalp, and his steps behind the heavy wagon were labored and slow. He was really too old for the backbreaking task of field work, but apparently he had signed on with Mr. Finch.

Jeremiah Finch shouted again. Thomas flinched and fell hard against the slow-moving wagon. Charlotte clattered down the stairs and into the yard, her unbound hair flying behind her. "Mr. Finch."

The wagon halted. The foreman broke off his tirade and frowned at her. "What do you want?"

"Is it necessary to shout at this man? He's—"

"Lazy and insolent, like the rest of this bunch." Finch spat a stream of tobacco into the dirt. Lambert and Moses, hats pulled low over their faces, regarded him and Charlotte with wary eyes.

"He most certainly is not lazy. My father thought highly of his industry—and his competence. I won't have him mistreated."

Thomas turned his rheumy gaze on her. "It's all right, young miss. You best go on back yonder to the house and stay outta the way."

"For once you're making sense, Thomas." Finch took out a stained handkerchief to wipe his face, and Charlotte caught a glimpse of a thin book of poems tucked into his breast pocket. This hard, uncouth man was a reader of poetry?

"I told you from the beginning not to interfere," Finch said to her. "Either you want your fields cultivated, or you don't. It don't matter to me one way or the other. But if you expect me to see to them, then you hold up your end of the bargain and stay clear of me and my men."

"You're forgetting something, Mr. Finch. These men are now free to decide whether or not to work for you. If they all quit, you lose your chance to provide for your family."

"And they lose the chance to provide for theirs." He grasped her arm and propelled her across the yard. "Don't tell me you're sidin' with them."

"I'm merely asking you to be kinder to a man of Thomas's years. Now let go of me."

"Now you listen," Finch said, his voice low. "You're a lady, and you think these men oughta be treated with respect. I understand that."

"So did my father." Charlotte wrenched her arm free and jammed her fists into her pockets. She glared at Jeremiah Finch. "If he were alive he'd—"

"But he ain't alive, and that's the rub." The overseer's voice softened. "Y'ask me, rice farming ain't a fit occupation for womenfolk. But as you are bound and determined to try it, you need me more'n I need you. So don't get on my bad side, or *I'll* walk away and leave it all to you."

Anger and a fierce disgust for him burned in her bones. But Finch was right. Without his men to hoe the tender plants and fill and drain the fields, to say nothing of attending to the harvesting and threshing, she had no hope of succeeding.

Finch raised his chin toward the men in the waiting wagon. "Since emancipation, they think they've got the upper hand, and the Yankees make it worse, feedin' 'em all kinds of lies. If you ain't firm with 'em, they'll take advantage. So you'd best just leave me free to take care of things the way I see fit."

Finch called to the young Negro man driving the wagon, and the men hurried up the path and out of sight. Still fuming, Charlotte watched them disappear before turning sharply on her heel and heading back inside.

In the kitchen, she put the kettle on to boil and set her heavy iron on the stove to heat, determined to put the unpleasant exchange behind her. This morning she had washed her hair and polished her best pair of shoes. She hadn't much experience with an iron, but her dress was wrinkled from long years in the trunk, and there was no one else to see to it.

Lettice's birthday party this evening promised to be quite an affair. Last Monday Charlotte had driven her wagon into Georgetown to pick up supplies and send a new article to the *New York Enterprise*. Coming out of the postal office, she'd met Josie Clifton and her aunt, Mrs. Thornhill, who was president of the Ladies' Society. Standing on the boardwalk outside the postal office, Mrs. Thornhill had enumerated Lettice's guest list on her fingers: the Cliftons, the Frosts, the Allstons, the Bankses. Herself, of course. And Nicholas Betancourt.

The teakettle shrieked. Charlotte measured tea leaves into the pot and poured the water in. Had Mr. Betancourt untangled his legal problems by now? She had scarcely seen him since she'd begun teaching his daughters. Yesterday the girls had walked from Willowood, appearing at her gate promptly at ten. On Tuesday it had rained, and Mr. Betancourt had delivered them in his smart little rig. But he'd offered her only the briefest of waves before disappearing into the mist, leaving her oddly disappointed.

She checked to see that her iron was hot, finished her tea, and spread the dress on the table. She touched the iron to the hem. Instantly the delicate fabric curled and browned in a puff of smoke.

"Drat, drat, and drat!" She set the iron aside and inspected the damage, a triangular spot as wide as her palm. She couldn't attend a fancy dinner party in a burned dress or one of her worn old work dresses. Her other fancy dress, a blue satin with out-of-fashion pagoda sleeves, had a badly torn hem, a rip in one sleeve, and needed a good airing. There wasn't time to make it presentable even if she had the skills to do so. And appearing in her mourning clothes would defeat the entire purpose of the evening. Disappointing as it might be, there was nothing to do but send word to Lettice that she couldn't attend the party after all.

She glanced at the clock. Trim and Thomas and the rest of Mr. Finch's crew would soon stop work for their midday meal. Perhaps Trim could take Cinnamon and deliver a note to Alder Hill. Mr. Finch wouldn't like it, but he worked for her, after all. He would simply have to manage without Trim for a couple of hours.

Leaving her ruined dress on the table, she went to the library to scribble a hasty note to Lettice, then gathered her hat and looked around for her keys. Before the war, keeping the house under lock and key would not have been necessary. But just last week, according to Lettice, Mrs. Banks had returned from Charleston to find her former servants, Dab and Chloe, making off with the parlor rug and her best china.

"Ma'm'selle?"

Charlotte looked up to see Marie-Claire, her dark hair in a terrible tangle, cradling a gray cat in her arms. She opened the kitchen door. Girl and cat came inside.

"What are you doing here today?" Charlotte bent to stroke the cat, but it drew its ears back and hissed.

"I found her beside the road. She's not mean. She's scared because she's lost."

"Does your father know where you are?"

"Yes, ma'm'selle. He sent you a note. Here, hold Mathilde."

"You've named her?" Charlotte had to seize the animal by the scruff of the neck to keep her from squirming away.

"Yes, and I'm keeping her no matter what anyone says." Marie-Claire produced a crisp white envelope from her pocket and handed it to Charlotte. "Papa says I am to wait for your reply."

Charlotte returned the cat to the child and it calmed down. She picked up her dress and they returned to the main house. She opened the envelope and scanned the brief note.

"I know what it says," Marie-Claire declared. "He wants to take you to that fancy party tonight." She nuzzled the cat, who snuggled against her chest.

"How did you guess?"

"He talks about you all the time, when he thinks Anne-Louise and I aren't listening. Just yesterday he told Tamar that you are a woman of substance."

"Did he?" Charlotte's cheeks warmed at the secondhand praise. To hide her feelings, she returned to the library for pen and paper. Marie-Claire and the cat followed.

"What does that mean, exactly—a woman of substance?" Marie-Claire asked. "I asked Tamar, but she told me it's none of my business. But it is my business if my papa wants to get me a new mother, is it not?"

"A new mother? Heavens. I doubt that's what he has in mind."

"But I'll wager you will go with him to Mrs. Hadley's birthday party."

"Ladies do not wager, Marie-Claire."

"Tamar does. She and Trim and Simon pitch pennies every afternoon when Papa is away."

"Nevertheless. Do you want to grow up to be like Tamar? Or like your mother?"

The girl's features darkened. "I want to be as pretty as *Maman*, but nicer."

"Your mother was lovely. I saw her portrait when I visited your house."

"Yes, but she didn't like us. She liked only Papa."

Charlotte hid her surprise. What kind of mother would leave her child with such an impression? Who could resist that sweet face and those wide blue eyes? True, Marie-Claire could be difficult, but she was also smart and hard-working. "I'm sure that isn't—"

"Holy cats." Marie-Claire seemed to have just noticed the garment draped across Charlotte's arm. "What happened to your dress?"

"I burned it with the iron, so I won't be going to the party after all. I have nothing to wear."

"You could sew a ruffle on the bottom. Then nobody would know."

Charlotte thought of her ruffled petticoat lying on the bed upstairs. "Maybe. But a cotton ruffle on a silk dress might look strange. Besides I'm not

113

very clever with a needle and thread. In the old days, my seamstress would have taken care of it."

"You could sew a matching ruffle onto the neckline, and then it wouldn't look so strange." Marie-Claire pointed. "There's some lace missing anyway. Did you know that?"

"I noticed. I was planning to wear my mother's cameo to cover it up."

"A ruffle would look much better."

Charlotte studied the girl. "You may be right. How do you know so much about ladies' fashion?"

"*Maman* loved fashion. She spent hours with her magazines and with Madame du Pont. She was *Maman*'s dressmaker. Very famous. Sometimes *Maman* would let me stay in her room and watch her fittings. If I promised not to talk."

The girl dropped her gaze and stroked the cat, who had fallen asleep, both front paws draped over Marie-Claire's arm. "*Maman* said my voice gave her a headache."

"Well, I think you have a very pretty voice. And I won't be a bit surprised if you grow up to be as famous a dressmaker as Madame du Pont."

Marie-Claire shook her head. "I want to be a rice planter, like you and Papa."

Charlotte looked past the girl's shoulder to the shaded avenue and the path leading to her rice fields. Unless conditions improved dramatically, Marie-Claire would need a different occupation. But why spoil a young girl's dream?

Eight

Candlelight trembled on the peach-colored walls, illuminating the faces of the party guests seated around the Hadleys' dining table. Mismatched dishes, chipped glassware, and a soup tureen missing one handle were arranged with military precision on a pressed white tablecloth. A crystal vase of pale pink roses gave off a faint fragrance that mixed with the spring air coming through the open windows. Despite her misgivings about her hastily repaired frock, Charlotte was glad she had come. The Allstons had not come after all, but the Frosts and the Bankses, who were among her family's oldest friends, had greeted her warmly, reminding her of how much she missed the alliances that had been such a part of her old life.

The trip from the Pee Dee ferry to Alder Hill, sitting next to Nicholas Betancourt as his elegant gray trotted smartly along the road, had been pleasant too. He had regaled her with stories of his boyhood adventures on the Mississippi River, his years at school, his efforts to teach his daughters to waltz. The one thing he seemed to want to avoid was any talk of Willowood.

"Dinner is ready, Miz Hadley." Dressed in a parrot-green silk gown and a matching turban, Florinda moved from kitchen to table, delivering platters of poached fish and stewed root vegetables.

Mr. Hadley lifted his glass. "To my wife, Lettice. Many happy returns."

Lettice, wearing a simple peach-colored gown several seasons out of fashion, patted the mountain of curls atop her head and smiled at her husband across the table.

"Hear, hear," Nicholas Betancourt said. "We toast your birthday, Mrs. Hadley, and thank you for your hospitality."

Charlotte caught his eye and lifted her glass, happy to be in his company. Handsome, smart, and with an infectious smile, Nicholas Betancourt charmed everyone at the table.

Lettice blushed as the guests clapped and lifted their glasses. "I am so glad you all came. Things have been entirely too quiet around here this spring. And I hope you enjoy our supper, though of course it isn't the same as in the old days."

Charlotte heard the sadness in her friend's voice. She smiled at Lettice across the candlelit table, in awe of the older woman's courage. Few could accept poverty with such quiet dignity.

"Nothing is like it was in the old days." Mr. Frost speared a carrot with his fork. He chewed and swallowed and eyed Charlotte across the table. "I understand you've hired Jeremiah Finch to help with your rice crop."

"Yes." Charlotte took a bite of the poached fish. "He seems to be competent enough, but I wish he wouldn't be so harsh with the workers. I realize one must be firm but—"

"Sometimes a firm hand is necessary," Mr. Banks said from the far end of the table.

"My father never raised a hand to his men. One can be firm without resorting to—"

"William," Mrs. Banks said with a slight shake of her head. "Perhaps we should change the subject?"

"Of course." He set down his glass. "Forgive me, Miss Fraser. Tell me, how are you getting on at Fairhaven?"

"My cousin gave me a horse and wagon, and I hired Trim and Thomas to make a few repairs around the place. Like you, though, I'm mostly occupied with my rice crop. I lost some in the storm, but I have hopes for a field downriver—if I can get it planted in time."

"And she's busy with teaching my daughters," Mr. Betancourt said, smiling at her across the table.

"Truly?" Josie Clifton set down her fork and turned her wide eyes on Mr. Betancourt. "I had no idea you were in need of a tutor, sir, or I would have offered my services. I am quite proficient in singing and embroidery. I know a little French.

And I think your children are simply darling."

Mr. Betancourt nodded. "So you've said. And I'm grateful for your willingness to help. But my daughters are in need of a solid grounding in mathematics, orthography, and literature. And in comportment, I must admit. Miss Fraser fills the bill quite admirably."

"Oh." Josie pursed her lips in a mock pout. "I'm afraid mathematics is not my strong suit. I try, but somehow numbers just fly right out of my head."

"Never mind, my dear," her aunt, Mrs. Thornhill, said. "A girl as pretty as you need never fret about such things. Don't you agree, Mr. Betancourt?"

Just then Florinda bustled in with a large tray and began clearing the dishes. "Is your comp'ny ready for cake and coffee, missus?"

"We are," Lettice said. "I've been looking forward to cake all day."

As the guests lingered over slices of warm spice cake and cups of strong coffee, the talk turned once again to the difficulties of planting rice, the recent drop in prices, and the necessity of moving away from the river during the sickly season.

"I suppose we will spend the summer with my mother's people in North Carolina," Mrs. Clifton said.

"Oh, Mother, must we?" Josie fussed with the ruffle on her dress. "Why can't I stay with the

Russells in Charleston? At least in town I might have a prayer of meeting some people my own age."

"Perhaps you'll visit us on Pawley's," Mrs. Banks said.

"Oh, that would be lovely," Josie said. "Much more pleasant than sitting around listening to Aunt Fern complain about the heat." Her eyes flashed. "I heard that Benjamin Cousins and his family are already back on the island for the season. I'd adore seeing him again. It's been ages and ages."

"We'll discuss it later," Mrs. Clifton said. "This cake is delicious, Lettice. I wonder if you might share your recipe?"

Lettice smiled. "I'm afraid you'll have to ask Florinda about that."

Mrs. Banks set down her cup and smiled at Charlotte. "I understand you'll be coming to Pawley's this summer."

"Yes. I'm looking forward to it. I've always loved the island, but my father was too ill to travel last year."

"I'm delighted to know we can look forward to your company. And I'm sure the Reverend Mr. Peabody will be glad too. Despite his short tenure at Litchfield, he's already pressing the Ladies' Mission Society to raise money to purchase blankets for an orphans' home in China."

"But won't that be awfully expensive?" Mrs.

Thornhill asked. "I don't see how he can hope to achieve such a lofty goal."

"He plans to make and sell ice cream. Or rather, he hopes the ladies will take it on," Mrs. Banks said. "I think he's counting on our little island's attracting more visitors now that the war is over."

Mrs. Thornhill shook her head. "I do hope the Tuckers won't come to regret allowing him the use of their chapel. He seems a bit too ambitious if you ask me."

Mr. Hadley finished his cake and stood. "I hate to say so, but I find that I am not feeling well."

"What is the matter, my dear?" Lettice got to her feet. The men at the table rose with her.

Mr. Hadley shook his head. "It's this blasted headache. I'm afraid I must lie down."

"Of course, old boy," Mr. Frost said. "Think nothing of it." He bowed to Lettice. "A fine supper, my dear. One to sharpen the mind and soften the heart, as they say."

"Thank you, Theo." Lettice waved a hand to her guests. "Please, gentlemen, be seated. Everyone enjoy your cake while I see to my husband. I won't be long." She wrapped an arm around Mr. Hadley's waist and they went up the stairs.

"What happened to him?" Josie asked. "During the war, I mean."

Mrs. Thornhill frowned. "Josephine Clifton, you know better than to pry."

"Well, nobody ever tells me anything. I'm not exactly a child, you know."

"It's common knowledge he had a bad time of it," Mr. Frost said, settling once again into his chair. "Best leave it at that, Miss Clifton. Poor Charles is a different man than he was before the war."

"We were all different men before the war," Nicholas Betancourt said quietly.

Florinda returned to pour more coffee. "Any of you ladies and gent'men want more cake?"

"I do." Josie handed Florinda her empty plate.

"No more for her, Florinda," Mrs. Clifton said, frowning at her daughter. "Keep eating like that, Josie, and you'll soon be too stout to fit into that fancy new dress of yours."

Josie pulled a face. "Oh, all right." She leaned closer to Charlotte. "What a tiresome evening this has turned out to be."

"Wait until the Frosts leave," her aunt murmured, brows raised. "There will be much to discuss then."

Josie brightened at the prospect of new gossip, though it seemed to Charlotte the dignified older couple could hardly be the subject of anything scandalous. Perhaps the Frosts' financial situation had grown even more precarious, but financial hardship was hardly news these days. Perhaps Josie's aunt meant only to pacify a young girl who had grown weary of the proceedings.

"Why don't we adjourn to the parlor?" Mrs. Banks said. "I'm sure Lettice will be returning soon."

"I could use some fresh air," Mr. Frost said. "Would you gentlemen care to join me for a cheroot on the piazza?"

Mr. Clifton and Mr. Banks followed Mr. Frost to the door. He turned, one hand resting on the rusty doorknob. "Coming, Mr. Betancourt?"

"In a moment. When I arrived this evening, I saw a painting in the hall that seems familiar. I was hoping for another look at it."

The men left, and Mr. Betancourt offered Charlotte his arm. "Shall we?"

He took up a flickering taper, and they crossed the wide entry hall to an alcove opposite the parlor. The space was empty except for a large, gilt-framed painting. Mr. Betancourt lifted the candle. "Of course it's hard to tell in this poor light, but I think it might be a Signorelli. It's similar to one that hung in my grandfather's dining room in Languedoc. He was convinced that his painting was one of a pair, though there was never any proof that the artist repeated himself."

"I don't think it's a Signorelli," Charlotte said.

"What makes you so sure?"

"For one thing, the brush strokes are slightly different. Signorelli tended to paint in very short strokes." She indicated a patch of deep green in the bottom left corner. "The colors on this one are more muted. And Signorelli was known for placing a small still life in the larger picture, but I don't see one here."

"Granted. But the darker coloring may mean only that the painting needs a good cleaning. If it is a Signorelli, it's more than three hundred years old." He moved the guttering taper. "I don't see a signature."

Above them a door opened and closed, and Lettice descended the staircase. Charlotte was about to ask her about the painting, but the pained look on her old friend's face stopped her words.

Mr. Betancourt, too, sensed that this was the wrong time to satisfy his curiosity. He returned the candle to the table, bowed to the ladies, and went out the front door, letting in the scents of tobacco smoke and jessamine.

"Is Mr. Hadley all right, my dear?" Mrs. Banks asked, her brown eyes full of compassion.

Tears brightened Lettice's eyes but she nodded. "As well as he will ever be, I suppose. He is plagued with nightmares that only strong drink seems to cure. His doctors in Charleston told us the drink is responsible for the headaches, but Charles is not willing to give it up."

"We will pray for him," Mrs. Clifton said. "And for you too, my dear."

Lettice's expression hardened. "If prayer could heal my husband, he would have been rid of his demons long ago."

Mrs. Banks glanced at the parlor clock. "Goodness, I didn't realize it was so late. We must go."

Lettice didn't protest as the ladies rose with a rustling of skirts.

"We must say good night as well." Mrs. Clifton clasped Lettice's hands. "I do hope you enjoyed your birthday, despite your dear husband's difficulties."

"I was happy to see you," Lettice said. "We must not wait for a birthday to plan another social evening."

"And we shan't." Mrs. Frost headed for the door. "I will see you soon, I hope."

Lettice stood on the porch while her guests took their leave. Mr. Betancourt handed Charlotte into his rig, and they followed the other conveyances down the darkened road toward the ferry landing.

"May I ask you something?" he asked as they neared the Pee Dee landing.

"Of course." Charlotte watched the ferrymen's lantern light winking through the dark trees.

"How do you know so much about Signorelli? Grandfather said he became fairly obscure in his later years and lacked a pupil of any note to keep his reputation alive. Certainly he is not very well known these days. But you seem to know his work well."

A girlhood memory rose in her mind, bringing with it a pang of sweet sadness. "It's a long story."

"I would like to hear it," he said, his voice soft in her ear.

A shrill whistle sounded. The Cliftons' rig, traveling just in front of theirs, rumbled across the short bridge and drew up at the ferry landing. A couple of ferrymen hauled on the heavy ropes and drew the flatboat near the riverbank.

The Frosts' carriage eased onto the ferry, followed by the Bankses' rig, but Mr. Clifton's horse balked. He snapped his whip. The horse shied and whinnied. One of the ferrymen rushed over and grabbed at the harness, but the rig rolled backward, its wheels catching on the edge of the flatboat.

One of the ferrymen ran to the rig and attempted to rescue the tilting buggy, but lost his footing and tumbled into the dark river.

"Help!" the other ferryman yelled. "He in the water and he can't swim a lick."

"Wait here." Mr. Betancourt jumped from his rig and ran to the riverbank just as Mr. Banks dove into the water. Charlotte gathered her skirts and hurried to the landing. Everyone on the ferry had left their rigs and huddled together, eyes anxiously scanning the water.

Mr. Banks surfaced, the ferryman in tow. "He's bleeding. Must have hit his head."

Mr. Betancourt waded into the water and helped bring the injured man to the riverbank. "Hand me that lantern," he called to the other ferryman.

He set the lantern near the injured man's head, wrapped his hands in his handkerchief, and probed the wound. The ferryman roused and moaned.

"Be still a moment." Mr. Betancourt called up to the waiting crowd, "Anybody have a cloth? A clean handkerchief will do."

Josie Clifton ran toward him holding the skirt of her bright-yellow frock, as showy and self-conscious as an early-blooming daffodil. "You are most welcome to my petticoat, sir."

He didn't look up. "Thank you. Be quick about it."

A ripping sound was followed by another moan from the injured man. A few moments later Mr. Betancourt rose. "That's all I can do for now."

"How bad's it, sir?" the other ferryman asked.

"The wound needs cleaning, and he will need a fresh bandage. Something for pain if you have it. But in a few days' time he should be recovered." Mr. Betancourt tucked his soiled handkerchief into the pocket of his dove-gray waistcoat.

"I been knowing his fambly all my life," the ferryman said. "I'll carry him on home soon's I get you folks acrost this river."

Mr. Betancourt and the other men righted the Cliftons' buggy, and soon they were underway. The other passengers remained in their rigs for the brief crossing, but Charlotte joined Mr.

Betancourt at the rear of the flatboat. All was quiet save the rushing of the water past the boat and the murmured conversations of the ferrymen. A soft breeze ruffled her hair. Starlight glittered on the dark river.

"That man was very lucky you were here to tend him," she said at last.

"It was nothing. Mr. Banks deserves all the credit for rescuing him." Hands in his pockets, he nodded toward the starry sky. "Beautiful, isn't it?"

"Yes." In the lambent light, Charlotte studied his face. "You seemed very much at ease tending his wound. Are you a physician, Mr. Betancourt? I don't believe I have ever heard you say precisely what your occupation is."

"I'm a rice planter, same as you. Or I will be when everything is settled."

"I see. But—"

"I was a physician once. But not now."

She was full of questions, but asking them would presume on their short and mostly professional acquaintance. "Forgive me. I didn't mean to pry."

He shrugged. "It was a reasonable question."

The ferryman blew his whistle, swung his lantern wide, and tossed the ropes to two men waiting on the landing. One by one the rigs rolled onto the road and on toward the Waccamaw.

Mr. Betancourt seemed disinclined to talk, so Charlotte closed her eyes and let the scented night air and the rhythmic sound of the horse's hooves soothe her.

"Almost home," Mr. Betancourt said when they reached the Waccamaw ferry landing. This crossing proved uneventful, and soon they arrived at the entrance to Fairhaven. Mr. Betancourt got out, wet shoes squishing, and opened the gate. They drove up the long avenue to the darkened house.

He walked her up the steps to the door. "Quite an evening."

She took her key from her reticule and fitted it into the lock. "Indeed. I feel sorry for Lettice. She tries hard to carry on as if nothing has changed."

"Sometimes that's the only way one can survive." He paused. "Will you be all right? Shall I wait while you light your lamp?"

"No need. But thank you. And thank you for escorting me this evening. I quite enjoyed myself, despite the accident at the ferry landing." She glanced at his wet trousers and shoes. "Too bad about your shoes."

He gave a rueful laugh. "And these are my best pair. My only pair, in fact, not counting my riding boots."

"I'm glad you can laugh about it."

"What good would it do to complain?" He spoke with the cheerful air of someone who expected that circumstances, no matter how dire, must one day come right again. "Besides, there's nothing like a near disaster to add a little spice to the proceedings. I'm glad the man is all right." He tipped his hat. "Good night, Miss Fraser. Pleasant dreams."

"Good night."

She went inside, lit the lamp, and watched him turn his rig for home.

Even though the ferryman's accident was a minor one, Mr. Betancourt's calm and competent manner and his concern for the injured man made it clear that he was a gifted physician.

Why then had he renounced his calling?

Nine

My neighbor at Alder Hill owns a painting that takes me back to my school days in Charleston. After our lessons and before evening prayers we were permitted to read or stroll in the secret garden behind Madame Giraud's house on Meeting Street. As I was the youngest girl in the school, I often tagged after my cousin Della and her friends, who usually treated me with a certain benign affection that was both an annoyance and a comfort. But one afternoon Della was in a cross mood and spoke to me so harshly that I burst into tears. I ran through the garden to the back gate, scaled it, and dropped onto the busy street.

A black-and-tan hound, nose to the ground, hurried along the street, and I decided to follow him. He led me down Meeting, past Queen Street, past St. Michael's Church, and then along Tradd Street, toward the river. At last he paused before a gate standing half open and barked.

An old man emerged from a narrow house situated on an alley and spoke to the dog. He raised a hand in greeting when he saw me. He was small, not much taller than I, with a wrinkled face the color of an acorn and thick white hair that fell about his shoulders like a shawl. Lively brown eyes regarded the hem of my blue frock, which was black with dirt from the street.

"Signorina, you are lost?"

"I know my way home."

"But you do not wish to go there."

"My cousin Della is mean as a snake. I hate her."

"I see. Perhaps some tea and a piece of cake would sweeten your mood."

The hound jumped up to lick my face.

"Come," the man said.

Madame Giraud forbade us to visit anyone without a proper chaperone, but I was angry with the world, feeling defiant, and I followed him inside. The room was dim and narrow and furnished with nothing but a bed and a table covered with rags and tubes of paint. On an easel opposite the window, a small painting—

A rig turned in at the gate and rolled up the avenue, interrupting the flow of words. Paper in hand, Charlotte rose and went to the door.

"Miss Fraser."

She smiled at the sight of her visitor, who stood before her wearing patched trousers, a loose-fitting shirt, and a tattered straw hat. His leather shoes seemed none the worse for their time in the river. "Mr. Betancourt. I wasn't expecting you."

"I know, and I'm sorry if I've arrived at an inopportune time."

"I'm working on an article for the paper, but it can wait."

"I'm glad to hear that, as I've come to propose an outing."

"Oh?"

"With me and the girls. They're playing on your little beach. I hope you don't mind."

"Of course not, but—"

"Splendid. Get your hat and let's go."

She glanced at the clock on the mantel. "I'm expecting Mr. Finch at four."

"We'll be back by then."

She thought of several good reasons to decline the invitation. For one thing, Mr. Betancourt was her employer. It was best to keep things on a professional basis. For another, she had summoned her overseer for a talk about the bill he had left on her porch yesterday. Several items seemed overpriced, and she was determined to get an accounting. But Mr. Betancourt looked so boyish and hopeful that she found herself agreeing.

She donned her hat, locked the doors, and settled herself into his rig. He clicked his tongue to the horse, and they set off for the narrow strip of sand at the river's edge. Shaded by tall trees, the little beach sloped gently to the swiftly running current. As they rolled to a stop, Charlotte was glad she'd come. This secluded spot had been her favorite escape since childhood, and yet she had spent little time here since her return to the Waccamaw. Mr. Betancourt took a basket and his violin from the rig.

"Ma'm'selle, I caught a fish." Anne-Louise, her skirt tucked up around her knees, hurried over to show Charlotte a small perch glistening silver in the dappled sunlight. "He's too little to eat, though."

Her father agreed. "Might as well let him go, *ma petite*. Maybe you'll catch him again when he's got more meat on his bones."

"All right." She regarded the fish dangling at the end of her line, seeming reluctant to relinquish her prize. "Marie-Claire hasn't caught anything."

"Who cares?" The older girl perched on a fallen log, her bright yellow skirt pooling at her feet. Her father called to her, and she looked up and gave Charlotte a halfhearted wave.

"What's the matter with her?" Charlotte asked.

133

"She seemed in a much better mood yesterday."

"That stray cat she took in has apparently run away," Mr. Betancourt said. "She's feeling a bit rejected, I suppose." He motioned her to a seat on the sand. "I forgot to bring a blanket."

"Papa," Anne-Louise called. "It is time to eat yet? I am about to perish." She tossed her catch into the stream.

He laughed. "Come on then. You too, Marie-Claire."

"I'm not hungry."

"Moping won't bring that cat back."

"Her name is Mathilde."

"In any case, you must eat something," her father said. "Tamar packed all your favorites."

Marie-Claire heaved a sigh and plodded over to join the others.

"I'm so sorry about Mathilde," Charlotte said. "Cats are an independent sort, I'm afraid. Perhaps she'll come back. You never know."

Marie-Claire plopped onto the sand, took the sandwich her father offered, and bit into it. "She can starve for all I care."

"She can look after herself. There are plenty of field mice around." Charlotte bit into one of Tamar's deviled eggs and closed her eyes. Perfection.

Anne Louise went straight for the cake. "Papa, play us a tune," she said between bites. "Maybe a song will cheer Marie-Claire."

"Your wish is my command, *ma petite*." He wiped his hands and took his violin from its case. "What would you like to hear, Marie-Claire?"

She shrugged. "I don't care."

"Play 'Buffalo Gals.'" Anne-Louise licked frosting from her fingers. "Or 'Pop Goes the Weasel.'"

"How about this one?" He settled his violin beneath his chin and began to play "Jeannie with the Light Brown Hair."

"I know who wrote that one," Anne-Louise said. "Stephen Foster."

"It's too hot out here," Marie-Claire said when the final notes died into the silence. "I want to go home."

"Can we go in the water, Papa?" Anne-Louise asked. "Just for a little while?"

"I suppose so." He put away his violin and offered Charlotte his hand. "Why don't we all go? We'll go downstream a ways where the current is not as strong."

Even Marie-Claire brightened at the prospect of her teacher's joining in. She ran along the bank to a place where the current slowed. The two girls tucked up their skirts and raced to the water, squealing as the cold water hit their skin.

"Shall we?" Mr. Betancourt squeezed Charlotte's hand, and she felt heat creeping into her cheeks. Once upon a time she had owned a proper swimming costume, a royal-blue wool complete with pantalettes that gathered at the ankles and a matching overdress. What had happened to it? Perhaps it was still tucked away somewhere in the Pawley's Island cottage. She glanced at her brown skirt. "I'm hardly dressed for bathing."

"Nor am I, but I'm not going to let that stop me." Sunlight filtered through the trees and shone on his face, revealing fine lines at the corners of his eyes. He took off his shoes and rolled up the legs of his patched trousers. "Let's go."

Anne-Louise splashed in the shallows. "Hurry up, Ma'm'selle. The water feels so delicious."

Charlotte took off her shoes and tucked her skirt into the sash at her waist. Soon the four of them were splashing and laughing like old friends. Charlotte grinned. Anne-Louise was right. The cold water did indeed feel wonderful. How had she forgotten such simple pleasures?

Later, while her damp hair dried and the girls played along the riverbank, she sat on a log with Mr. Betancourt, enjoying the river-cooled air and the sounds of birdsong.

He shaded his eyes and watched Marie-Claire weave a crown of trumpet vines for her younger sister for their improvised game of kings and queens. Anne-Louise waved a stick as if it were a scepter. Marie-Claire curtsied, and both sisters collapsed in laughter.

"I'm grateful to you," Mr. Betancourt said, "for taking on their schooling."

She leaned back and turned her face to the sun. "Anne-Louise has nearly finished the books I gave her, and the ones I have ordered have not yet arrived. She's clamoring to borrow my book of Peter Parley's tales instead." She smiled. "I can't fault her for that; it is still a favorite of mine too. I'll see if I can find more of my childhood books for her."

"Mr. Frost mentioned that you spent much of your childhood in the city."

"The two of you discussed my upbringing?"

"Only in the most complimentary of terms. At the Hadleys' dinner party, I mentioned that my Uncle Clayton had contributed to the Winyah Society. Mr. Frost said that your father was one of its most ardent supporters. That he believed in a well-rounded education and made sure you were sent to a fine school."

"He did. Though in truth I have little need of much of that fine education—apart from teaching your girls, of course. On the other hand, his lessons in growing rice are proving most useful." She smiled. "If Madame Giraud could see me now, she would be quite distressed, but not greatly surprised. I was not the most conscientious of students."

Marie-Claire had ventured too far down the riverbank. Her father whistled to gain her attention and motioned her to return. "You seem to have absorbed a lot of knowledge about art, though. Most people I meet have never heard of Signorelli. But you seem sure the Hadleys' painting is not one of his."

"Most of what I know about art I learned outside the hallowed halls of Madame Giraud's." She paused, remembering. "One day in a fit of pique I left school against all the rules and wound up at the door of an old Italian gentleman who lived just off Tradd Street. He was a painter—not a very successful one, as he was the first to admit. He made his living restoring paintings belonging to the wealthiest families in Charleston.

"That first afternoon he gave me tea and cake and showed me the painting he was working on—a scene of the holy family on their flight to Egypt. He told me the entire story of the painting, and when I showed an interest he allowed me to borrow his art books. I smuggled them into my room at Madame Giraud's and read them by candlelight when I should have been learning the many forms of French verbs."

Mr. Betancourt smiled. "I'm fascinated. Please go on."

"There isn't much more to tell. After that first day, I slipped away from school as often as I could to watch him work. It was a painstaking affair—stripping away two hundred years' worth of soot and grime an inch at a time. But the result was beautiful. He died only a year after my mother did."

His eyes held hers. "Too much loss for one so

young." He dropped his gaze. "So much sadness for us all."

"Papa?" Anne-Louise trotted over and deposited a handful of smooth river pebbles into his hand. "Aren't these pretty? I want to take them home and put them in a jar."

Mr. Betancourt nodded and consulted his pocket watch. "Speaking of home, I suppose we ought to go."

"Can't we stay longer? I want to look for more pebbles."

"Afraid not, my sweet. Miss Fraser has an appointment in a little while, and I must attend to some correspondence for tomorrow's mail. Go get your sister, please."

Anne-Louise hurried down the narrow beach, calling for Marie-Claire. Mr. Betancourt helped Charlotte to her feet, and together they packed up the remnants of their picnic. He gave the horse a leftover piece of carrot and stowed the basket and his violin case in the rig. "I'm glad you came with us today. I quite enjoyed myself."

"I did too. It was a welcome diversion from worrying about my business with Mr. Finch. I hope this afternoon's meeting doesn't turn unpleasant."

"He's a strange one. The day he came to Willowood, he spent half an hour talking politics. Despite his crude manners, he seems to be better educated than I expected."

"He reads poetry too—when he isn't busy berating his workers. I do understand the need to maintain discipline, but I wish he would be kinder about it."

The girls ambled toward them, their shoes tied together by the laces and tossed over their shoulders, their arms full of blooming vines. Mud clung to the hems of their dresses and to their tangled hair. They looked so innocent and carefree that Charlotte laughed.

He joined in. "You see the challenge I have before me in turning them into proper ladies—and why I am ever in your debt for your efforts."

"Marie-Claire reminds me very much of myself at that age. Independent, always testing the rules. She told me the other day that she wants to be a rice planter like you."

His eyes darkened. "It seems all our fortunes on that score are in jeopardy."

She studied his face. What was the nature of his problem with his plantation? She didn't know him well enough to question any of the mysteries —his departed wife, his abandoned profession— surrounding him. "Your difficulties regarding Willowood are not resolved, then?"

"Not yet. I'm going to Washington tomorrow."

She brushed away a cloud of gnats that had swarmed in from the river. "I can imagine how eager you are to get your fields into cultivation."

"I've nearly given up for this year. But if things

work out quickly enough, I might yet be able to plant a small crop. If Mr. Finch can keep his crew together."

She released a gusty sigh. His concern was well founded. But for better or worse, Jeremiah Finch and his crew were their only option.

"Tamar has promised to stay with the children while I'm away," Mr. Betancourt went on. "They will appear for their lessons as usual, and I'll be back on Friday. Late."

The girls reached the rig and piled inside, elbowing each other and giggling. Charlotte squeezed in beside Mr. Betancourt.

When they reached her yard, he helped her down, then placed one hand on her arm. "I have a favor to ask."

"Yes?"

"I don't know about you, but I feel as if we are old friends. I wonder if we might call each other by our Christian names."

"I'd like that."

He smiled and touched one finger to the brim of his hat. "Good-bye then, Charlotte."

"Good-bye, Nicholas. I hope your trip proves fruitful."

Ten

Charlotte tossed another armload of ruined papers into the trash barrel she had wrestled into her father's study. Though the sight of his plantation ledgers and stacks of torn correspondence rendered in his neat hand filled her with sadness and longing, holding on to a mountain of trash would not bring him back. And truth to tell, every small step toward restoring the house brought her a growing sense of peace, despite her ever-present concerns.

She pressed her fingers to her temples and briefly closed her eyes. Mr. Finch would expect a payment soon, and the *New York Enterprise* had not yet paid her for her last two articles. Yesterday she'd hitched Cinnamon to the wagon and made the trip to Georgetown to pick up supplies and check for mail. Nothing from New York. But a letter from Alexander in Atlanta had lifted her spirits.

In between teaching the Betancourt girls and keeping an eye on Mr. Finch, she had scrubbed, polished, and waxed the remaining woodwork until it gleamed. After a good airing, the summer linens and quilts her cousin had brought now graced her bed, adding a welcome spot of color in the whitewashed room. Her mother's china cups and teapots lined the shelves in the kitchen, and the front parlor, though devoid of its intricate mahogany woodwork, looked better now that her mother's blue and gold rug covered the cypress floor.

She had decided to convert the library into a classroom. With its generous proportions and tall windows facing the golden marshlands, it was a lovely place for her and her charges to pass the Lowcountry spring. Perhaps by the time she returned to Fairhaven for the winter, she could hire a chimney sweep to clean the fireplace. A crackling fire on a cool winter's evening would be just the thing.

She dusted the books that had survived the Yankees and stacked a few of them with the ones she had ordered on a plain pine table Lettice had provided. The girls could sit there to attend to their lessons while she sat at her mother's walnut desk.

She moved to dump more papers into the barrel, and her foot hit something that skittered across the wood floor. The key to her father's strongbox. She bent to pick it up.

For as long as she could remember, Papa had kept that key in the bottom drawer of his desk. But the desk was long gone. Perhaps it now graced some Yankee officer's home along with her stolen piano. Perhaps it had been used for kindling or for the making of a Yankee coffin. In any case she would never see the desk or the strongbox again.

She tucked the key into her pocket and finished sweeping the floor. Then she pumped clean water into her bucket and tackled the dirt-streaked windows, her mind filling with plans for the girls' next lessons. They needed more books already. Anne-Louise had finished the Peter Parley book. Marie-Claire had shown an aptitude for English composition and a talent for drawing. Soon Charlotte's small cache of reading material would no longer suffice.

She finished one window and moved to the next. Too bad she hadn't kept her copy of Oliendorff's grammar with her notes about French verbs scribbled in the margins. She wished she were more proficient in the language. Thinking of the times she had tried to bluff her way through Madame Giraud's lessons by randomly adding *vous* onto English words filled her with regret. Madame had not been fooled. She'd muttered and rolled her eyes and tapped her pointer on the chalkboard, her disapproving frown magnifying all of her pupil's shortcomings.

But perhaps now Charlotte's lack of proficiency with French wouldn't matter. Her arrangement with Mr. Betancourt—Nicholas—was only temporary, and he was well able to correct the girls' French himself.

Charlotte wrung out her rag and tackled another dirty window, still thinking of that long-ago classroom. Perhaps her dogged determination to prove everyone wrong and make Fairhaven profitable again was the result of feeling like such a failure at school.

With the windows finished, Charlotte emptied her bucket, spread her cleaning rags out to dry, and hurried upstairs to change her dress. The girls were due at ten.

She attended to hygiene, brushed and pinned her hair, and changed into a navy dress. It was too heavy by half for the warmth of this morning, but her budget didn't yet allow for new frocks—not when there still was so much to do to restore Fairhaven. Home was her first priority.

She heard a shout at the gate. The girls turned up the avenue, swinging their lunch buckets and laughing with a boy who walked between them. Thin as a rake, he moved with a loose-limbed gait, his eyes cast downward. Bony wrists protruded from the sleeves of a worn homespun shirt. His bare feet were brown and as hard-looking as tanned leather. Charlotte hurried outside just as the trio reached the veranda.

"Miss Fraser," Marie-Claire said. "This is Daniel Graves. He lives upriver from us—nearly all the way to Richmond Hill."

"Daniel." Charlotte offered a polite smile and inclined her head in greeting. She was uncomfortable with the notion of a strange boy accompanying two young girls and annoyed that he had inter-rupted her plans for the morning, which included a walk to the beach to sketch the wildlife along the river. But behaving rudely toward this waif would set a bad example for her charges.

"Ma'am." The boy stood straight and spoke respectfully. That was something.

"I'm glad to have made your acquaintance, Daniel, but now I must ask you to excuse us. The girls have much to learn today."

"Yes'm. That's why I come with 'em. Marie-Claire said you're the best teacher in the whole Lowcountry. And I am a boy in dire need of an education."

She couldn't help smiling at his forthright manner. "I see. What about the school near Sandy Creek?"

"Teacher quit back in January 'cause they's no money to pay 'im, and Pa can't afford to send me away to school. B'sides, the Yankees busted up the schoolhouse and took everything that wasn't nailed down."

"Perhaps a new teacher—"

"No, ma'am. I don't reckon no other teacher for fifty miles wants to take us on. And anyway, there ain't hardly any of us left since the blacks moved in and the rich folks left these parts. But me and Pa, we're stayin' put. We ain't rich, but we've got big plans. Soon as I get some schoolin'.'"

Marie-Claire plopped her lunch bucket onto the bottom step. "At least let him stay for today, Ma'm'selle. He walked an awful long way to get here. Think how you'd feel to come so far for something you wanted real bad, only to be disappointed."

"I won't be any trouble," Daniel said. "I don't expect to have books of my own or nothin'. And you don't have to pay me no mind. I just want to listen. No harm in that, is there?"

The earnest, hopeful look on the boy's face, his absolute faith that an education would bring an end to all his troubles, overcame her objections. "Very well. You may stay for today. But I'm afraid that's all I can promise."

He looked away and scrubbed at the ground with his bare toe.

"Come inside."

Abandoning her plan of taking them down to the river, she settled the girls at the pine table in the library and sent Daniel to the kitchen for another chair. As was her custom, she read from the book of Psalms to begin the day, then set the girls to their various assignments—an arithmetic exercise for Anne-Louise and an essay for Marie-Claire. As the younger girl recited the multiplication tables aloud, Charlotte noticed Daniel mouthing the

147

answers along with her. Never had she seen a boy so obsessed with learning. She gave Anne-Louise a handwriting lesson and set her to copying a verse from Proverbs, then she turned her attention to the boy. Was there any book on her father's shelf that might occupy him for the next four hours?

"Tell me, Daniel. What are your interests? What do you hope to accomplish with your schooling?"

"Me and Pa aim to buy us a riverboat and start a passenger service. Pa says now that the war is over, people will start travelin' again, and they will pay for a nice accommodation. But boats cost money, so that's why I got to learn and get a job soon as I can. I reckon it'll take a good long while to save up enough to get us a boat."

"An admirable plan. But jobs are scarce in these parts nowadays."

"I know that. Me and Pa aim to head north soon as I'm ready."

She pulled a tattered copy of *Two Years Before the Mast* from the shelf. "Perhaps you would enjoy this."

"Yes'm. I enjoy just about any book you can name."

He flopped into his chair, graceless as a puppet with broken strings, and opened the book. The room fell silent as the lessons progressed. At noon the girls shared their food with the boy, and afterward Charlotte began a grammar lesson.

At ten minutes before two, a horse and rig

turned up the long avenue. Anne-Louise ran to the window and peered out. "Papa's here."

Marie-Claire tossed her writing pen aside and looked heavenward. "Thank you, dear Lord. Now maybe Tamar will make a real dinner for a change."

Charlotte frowned. "She hasn't been giving you proper meals?"

Marie-Claire shook her head. "Cornpone and beans all week long, though Papa left eggs and bacon and a pound of rice." She waved one hand. "And I forget what else. Tamar said her son is sick and she didn't have time to cook things that won't keep. But she promised to make tea cakes when Papa comes home. Papa loves tea cakes."

Charlotte frowned. She didn't like the idea of the children having only makeshift meals. But perhaps Tamar's son soon would be well.

Anne-Louise opened the door. Nicholas Betancourt came in, swept his youngest daughter off her feet, and twirled her around. He took off his hat and set it on her head. "How's my fairy child?"

"I am very well, Papa. And how are you?"

He laughed and set her on her feet. "I see that Miss Fraser has succeeded in teaching you some of the social pleasantries." He smiled at Charlotte over the little girl's head.

She crossed the room to greet him. "I didn't expect you back until tomorrow."

"I didn't get much satisfaction from the folks in Washington. There wasn't any point in lingering."

"Would you like some tea?"

"I would," Anne-Louise said, "if there's any cake to go with it." She handed her father his hat and scampered away.

"Tea sounds lovely, but I came to fetch the girls. I promised to take them berry picking, and I think tomorrow we might have rain." He looked past her shoulder into the library. "Who's he?"

"Daniel Graves. He lives upriver. Walked down with the girls this morning."

Nicholas frowned. "And you let him stay?"

"Marie-Claire asked me not to send him away. I've told him he cannot come back."

"I should think not."

"He's very keen to learn."

"I'm all for that. But he does seem older than the girls, and we know nothing of his family. I worry about my daughters."

"As any father would. I do feel sorry, though, that the children around here lack a proper school."

"That boy is not the only one. When I first got here last winter, I rowed upriver past Litchfield, nearly to Brookgreen, looking for boundary markers. Didn't find a single one, but I saw plenty of people just barely scraping by."

"Perhaps their lot will improve as rice production does." She motioned to the girls to finish their lessons. "You were looking for the markers for your property?"

"Yes. Ever since I decided to settle here, I've been working on claiming legal title to my plantation. As I understand it, Willowood, Oatland, even this place were part of a barony going back to the early 1700s. My Huguenot ancestors were the original owners."

"Of Fairhaven?" She shook her head. "I'm sure you're mistaken about that. Our family has been in possession of this property for nearly a hundred years."

"I don't doubt it. But possession and ownership are not precisely the same. I assume you have a deed, or papers of some sort, to back up your claim."

Her stomach clenched. "You are standing in my parlor, telling me that you own my land?"

"Papa?" Books in hand, Marie-Claire came into the hallway and gave him a paper. "Look what I did today. An essay . . . and a poem for you."

He smoothed her hair and slipped the folded paper into his pocket. "I'll read it at home when I have time to appreciate it properly. For now, you and your sister will kindly wait for me in the yard."

Her eyes widened. "Are you fighting with Ma'm'selle?"

"Not at all. I'll be there in a moment." He

pointed a finger at her. "I do want to talk to you about that strange boy."

"He isn't so strange," Marie-Claire said. "He knows just about every song that has ever been written, and he knows more arithmetic than I do. And aren't you always telling us we should be kind to others less fortunate?" She dropped her voice to a whisper. "He walked all the way from Richmond Hill, and he hasn't any shoes."

She threw her father a stern glance before hurrying outside.

Nicholas turned his hat in his hands. "Forgive me if I've upset you. You may be right about your land. Other baronies in these parts were divided into parcels and sold. Perhaps mine was as well. But without any documents, we'll never know. I wouldn't want to invest in planting rice, only to discover it's on someone else's property. I doubt you would either."

"Of course not." She tried to keep the fear from her voice. He didn't know she lacked a deed for Fairhaven. Perhaps one could be found before he—

"There must be a record of my property somewhere. If I cannot find it here, I'm going back to New Orleans. General Longstreet has settled there. Our families were friends, and I served under him during the war."

"As a physician?"

He gave a quick nod but didn't elaborate. "I'm

counting on his hospitality for a few days while I look into the matter there."

"My father said boundary disputes were quite common when he was a young man. And were often quite unpleasant."

"I have no wish to cause trouble, but I do need to settle the matter. I've written to a distant cousin in Languedoc. Eugenie must be past seventy now, but perhaps she knows where the records are."

She saw him to the door, determined to remain calm. What good would it do to get upset? Besides, he had no proof of his claim either. "Enjoy your berry picking."

"It's early for blackberries, but the girls have their hearts set on an outing. If we find any, I'll save you some."

He climbed into the rig and drove away. She returned to the library to find Daniel still immersed in his book.

"School's over," she said.

He looked up and blinked. "Already?"

"Yes, it's almost three, and you have a long walk home."

He handed her the book. "Sure is a good story. Can I come back tomorrow and finish it?"

"I'm afraid not. And I must warn you not to go near the Betancourts' place again."

He shrugged. "I don't have to cross their land. I can get here in my rowboat. They don't own the river. Besides, bein' poor don't make you a bad character."

"You're right. It doesn't. You're a smart boy, Daniel. I hope one day you get a fine education as well as the boat you're dreaming about. But I can't take you on as a pupil."

"Because he can pay you and my pa can't."

"That's part of it, yes. But I plan to teach only until Mr. Betancourt can send his daughters to boarding school. I'm not really trained for it, and I have my plantation to run."

"You won't have it if he finds that land grant."

"Daniel, it isn't polite to eavesdrop."

"I couldn't help it." He rose. "Guess I ought to go."

He headed for the door, his shoulders drooping.

"Wait." She caught up to him and handed him the book. "Keep it. It's yours."

"But—"

"It's old and worn out. I doubt I'll ever read it again. You may as well have it."

"I appreciate it."

"You're welcome."

She closed the door behind him and leaned against it, gathering her scattered thoughts. Turning away such an eager pupil had left her feeling unexpectedly unsettled and disappointed, but Nicholas Betancourt's startling claim brought bewilderment and terror.

Nothing in her father's will proved their ownership of Fairhaven. For more than a hundred years, her family's right to it had never been questioned. But suppose Nicholas was right and his French cousin proved his claim?

Suppose Fairhaven was not hers after all?

Eleven

Hat in hand, Jeremiah Finch leaned against the door frame and waited while Charlotte wrote a check for his services. She blotted the document and handed it to him.

He glanced at it before tucking it into his breast pocket. "Much obliged, Miss Fraser. I trust you're pleased with my work."

Through the library windows she studied the greening rice field in the distance. "I haven't been to the field downriver this week. How is it faring?"

"Drained it yesterday. We'll start the first hoeing as soon as it's dry." He scratched his head. "Gabe and Peter went home sick. Reckon I might have to find somebody to replace them to keep everything on schedule."

"At church on Sunday Mrs. Clifton mentioned that one of Trim's nephews has returned from upstate. Perhaps you could ask Trim about it."

"Trim already told me." The foreman shrugged. "The boy may show up, or he may not. There's no telling these days. Everything's all ajumble."

"I wonder if you would consider hiring a young

white boy. His name is Daniel Graves. He's keen on getting an education, but he wants to earn money too. To buy a boat. He came here once with my pupils, and I—"

"Afraid not. I hired a couple of white men from Calais Plantation when I first got here, but it didn't take long to figure out that blacks and whites can't work together. Too many resentments and too many arguments. I spent all my time trying to keep 'em from each other's throats. Wasn't worth the aggravation."

"I see."

He frowned. "You worried about the boy?"

"I would like to help him if I can."

"You say he wants education. Maybe you ought to expand that little school you've got going." He indicated the pine table piled high with textbooks, maps, and the Betancourt girls' latest artwork.

She shook her head. "I'm only helping out Mr. Betancourt temporarily."

"Lambert said that Tamar told him Mr. Betancourt has left town again. Off on some business errand."

"Yes." The thread of fear that had wound itself around her heart since Nicholas Betancourt's departure for New Orleans tied itself into a hard knot. He should have been back on Saturday. According to Marie-Claire, no one had heard from him. And the time was fast approaching

157

when planters would pack up and leave for the seashore until the threat of yellow fever was past.

Just last night she had begun making a list of what she would take to the Pawley's Island cottage and what would be left behind, at the mercy of thieves and the elements. Someone would have to look after dear Cinnamon. Charlotte hated the thought of leaving the little mare behind, but there was no shelter for her on the island.

Mr. Finch fished a paper from his pocket and thrust it into her hands. "Almost forgot. I need some supplies to get my men through the season."

Charlotte scanned the paper: a dozen bottles of sarsaparilla, two bottles of paregoric, three pounds of Epsom salts, two packages of German vermifuge, two ounces each of laudanum and quinine, three gallons of castor oil and coal tar. Below that list was another: broadaxes, hoes, handsaws, chisels, hatchets, and a hundred pounds of tobacco.

She looked up at him. "All this will cost a fortune."

"Yes, ma'am, I reckon it will. But I can't keep the men healthy and fix your broken equipment and bring in your crops without the right tools and supplies." He shook his head. "I know it don't seem right, you having to concern yourself with their welfare, providing medicines and such, when they don't belong to you anymore. But those Yankees have the final say on the contracts, and they—"

"I understand." She opened her bank book and wrote out a draft to Kaminski's store.

"The tobacco is my idea. Keeps them happy, I reckon." He tucked the bank draft into his pocket but made no move to leave.

She looked up. "Is there anything else?"

"I was wondering if I could ask you a favor." He gestured toward the library shelves. "You've got a book of Byron's poems over there, and I'm kinda partial to him. Would you consider lending it to me?"

"I noticed you carry a book of verse in your pocket."

He blushed. "Walt Whitman. A present from my wife before I left North Carolina. She's not much of a reader herself, but she figured I'd enjoy it."

"Some people have said Mr. Whitman is a bit too—"

"Too frank?" He shrugged. "Maybe. But I like how he puts words together. Mary Susan said the poems might keep me from being so homesick, but I can't say I've enjoyed any benefits in that regard."

"I understand. I waited out two years of the war separated from my father. I missed him terribly."

"Sometimes when I get to studyin' on my wife

159

and young'uns, it's all I can do not to tuck tail and run."

She took the book of poems from the shelf. "I hope this proves a good distraction. I'd be very upset if you went home before my rice is harvested, and I'm certain Mr. Hadley and Mr. Clifton feel the same way."

He tucked the book under his arm and headed for the door. "One more thing. I feel like I ought to apologize for the way I spoke to you when I first got here. You've been fair with me, and I can appreciate how hard you're working to make a go of it."

"Thank you, Mr. Finch. Even though everything is different now, I still feel protective toward my father's old bondsmen. Thomas especially."

He nodded. "Well, I wanted to say I'm sorry. And I am sorry. I'll do my best to see you through, but it's a powerful long time till winter."

Dear Miss Fraser,
  I regret to inform you that due to a decline in subscriptions, the Enterprise has temporarily suspended publication. Enclosed please find a check in the amount of twenty dollars for the two reports of yours that we were pleased to publish. The others are being returned to you with regret and with

160

our sincere hope that we might resume publishing them when our situation improves.

Sincerely,
Edwin Sawyer, editor

Fighting disappointment, Charlotte tucked the letter into her reticule and left the postal office. It had taken longer than she expected to post her letter to Mr. Betancourt in care of General Longstreet, and now she was in a hurry to finish her shopping before Mr. Kaminski closed the store. She would have to figure out what to do about this latest news from Mr. Sawyer, but the noisy, smelly bustle of Georgetown was not conducive to rational thought.

Fishing boats creaked and bobbed at anchor on the Sampit River, filling the air with the smells of salt, seaweed, and the day's catch. Groups of Negro men, several of them barefoot, unloaded lumber, barrel staves, and bolts of fabric on the wharf while their children jostled each other and played tag among the row of wagons waiting in the street. The blacksmith's hammer rang. Bells tinkled as shoppers came and went from the bakery and the shoe repair shop.

According to the notice posted near the ferry landing, the *Resolute* was due to arrive in an hour. Already a line of buggies waited to meet the arriving passengers. Charlotte glanced at the clock tower and hurried along the boardwalk to Kaminski's Mercantile.

"Miss Fraser." Josie Clifton waved and crossed the street, hiking her skirts to avoid the dirt and horse droppings.

Charlotte was in no mood for socializing, but she forced a smile. "Good morning."

"I saw you coming out of the postal office. I'm so glad I caught you," Josie said. "There's something I've wanted to ask you, and I didn't see you at church last week." Josie snapped open her fan, stirring the thick, humid air. "Do you think we might find shade somewhere and something cool to drink? I can't believe how warm it's been, and June is not yet upon us."

"I'm afraid I'm in a hurry," Charlotte said. "I must collect some more supplies for my pupils, and Mr. Kaminski closes in—"

"Mr. Betancourt's daughters," Josie said. "Exactly why I wanted to speak to you."

"Oh?"

"It seems that you and Mr. Betancourt are quite close," Josie said. "Judging from the way he looked at you the night he escorted you to Mrs. Hadley's birthday party. Why, he scarcely took his eyes off you all evening. And don't bother telling me you didn't notice. A woman always notices the attentions of an attractive man. And Mr. Betancourt is quite attractive."

"Yes, he is. But—"

"I want him," Josie said.

"What?"

"I want to marry him. I know you saw him first. And you have the advantage, being his daughters' teacher and all, but you can't imagine the pressure my father is putting on me to find a suitable match. It's even worse now than it was before the war, and there's hardly anyone left to marry."

"That's true enough." Josie's plight was very real. Spinsterhood meant social death to those who cared about such things. But it amused Charlotte that Josie gave her credit for far more influence than she actually wielded.

She took out her handkerchief and blotted her face. "Well, Josie, I imagine that Mr. Betancourt will decide whom he will marry. I won't have a single thing to say about it."

She swallowed a sudden pang. Heavens above, was she jealous? Of the man who was trying to wrest ownership of her land? Absurd.

"Then you don't mind if I flirt with him in church on Sundays?"

"I have no claim upon his affections. But you might encounter resistance from Marie-Claire. She's quite possessive of her father. Anne-Louise, on the other hand, is desperate for a mother."

Josie's eyes widened. "But you mentioned that he plans to send them to school in Charleston soon. I don't imagine they'll be in the way for long."

163

Charlotte frowned. "In the way?"

"Don't misunderstand," Josie said in a rush. "They're all right as children go, but you must admit that even the most charming children are an impediment to courtship. And when we're married, we'll want some time alone. Perhaps Nicholas and I will take a trip to Europe. Spend a whole summer." She sighed and fanned her face. "His family is French, after all, and I've always dreamed of seeing Paris. Father promised me a trip, but then the war ruined everything."

The clock in the bell tower pealed the half hour. Charlotte shaded her eyes and looked toward the landing where a crew of men uncoiled a large rope to receive the *Resolute*, now a white speck on the horizon. The hot sun beat down, shimmering on the river. The bad news from the newspaper editor weighed heavily on her mind. She needed to collect her supplies and return home. And she was in no mood to discuss Nicholas Betancourt with anyone. "I really must go."

"Wait a minute." Josie's eyes, clear and hard as Venetian glass, sought hers. "You aren't cross with me, are you?"

"Of course not. I simply have too much to do today and too little time."

"I was hoping you might recommend me to Mr. Betancourt."

"Recommend you?"

"You know. Just casually remind him that I'm from a good family. And that I am not averse to his attentions."

The *Resolute*'s whistle sounded. Charlotte tucked away her handkerchief. "I'm running late. You must excuse me."

Josie huffed and flounced away. Charlotte completed her shopping just before Mr. Kaminski locked the door. Then she climbed in her wagon and guided Cinnamon along the river road, her thoughts jumbled. The conversation with Josie had rekindled her fears about Nicholas Betancourt's search for his land grant and what it might mean for her own future. Why could she find no record of her own claim? Papa had kept meticulous records of everything he owned at Fairhaven—from slaves to oxen to buttons. How could he have been so careless in preserving the documents that proved the plantation was theirs?

"Come aboard, miss!" The ferryman who had fallen into the water the night of Lettice's party, now working the Waccamaw crossing, seemed fully recovered. Grasping Cinnamon's bridle, he guided the wagon onto the ferry. Two women in a black buggy followed. The ferrymen pulled on the heavy ropes and the ferry entered the river.

Charlotte watched the fish jumping in the water, her mind once again filled with worry. She owed it to Papa to write to his lawyer once again and inquire whether news had surfaced. Fairhaven was her father's legacy. She had made a solemn promise not to let anyone deprive her of her last link to the world she once knew. Not even someone as appealing as Nicholas Betancourt.

The ferry nudged the dock, and Charlotte drove onto the road. Deep inside her mind, something important lurked, waiting to surface, if only she could remember it in time.

Twelve

Charlotte led Cinnamon into the yard and freed her from the wagon. The mare snuffled and flicked her tail, eager for her bucket of oats and molasses and a well-deserved rest. Charlotte gave her a perfunctory brushing and checked the water tub. After a day away from home—church in the morning, then a visit with the Hadleys—she looked forward to a good long rest and wished mightily for a long soak in a big tub. But she had yet to replace the zinc tub the Yankees had stolen. Yet another quick sponge bath would have to do.

In the gathering darkness she crossed the yard and went up the steps and along the piazza to the door. Inside, she lit her lamp and looked around the room. Finding everything in order, she pumped fresh water into a wooden bucket and climbed the stairs to her room. She bathed quickly, changed into her nightdress, and unpinned her hair.

The window was open to the sultry spring breeze. She stood for a moment drinking in the particular smells of the Lowcountry—the damp, loamy scent of the rice fields, wild jessamine, the smells of fish and mud rising from the serpentine creeks winding toward the sea. Watching the moon rise over the broad sweep of the river, she felt a surge of love for the land that brought the sting of tears to her eyes.

Down in the slave street, a pinprick of light glimmered. Charlotte leaned out the window, her eyes straining against the darkness, her ears attuned to the smallest sound. Certainly no one lived there now. Yet the light continued to burn, shining through the dark trees. Her heart sped up. Perhaps Yankees were on the prowl. Perhaps thieves were about, though there was precious little left to steal.

She turned from the window, slipped into her dressing gown, and shoved her feet into her shoes. Downstairs, she retrieved Papa's old pistol from its hiding place in the woodbox and silently thanked Alexander for his prescience. The gun probably wouldn't fire, even if she could find some ammunition, but perhaps the sight of it would be deterrent enough. She lit a lantern and crossed the darkened piazza, the gun at her side. Keeping close to the line of trees along the avenue, she hurried toward the slave street, her gown whispering in the new grass, the lantern light swaying across the darkened path.

The first three cabins on the left side of the street were dark. In the fourth, a light wavered and caught. The smell of sulfur filled her nostrils.

She doused her lantern and crouched between the cabins, her hands shaking, the pistol propped on her knees.

A slight figure appeared in the open doorway. Charlotte held her breath.

"The coast is clear." A boy's voice, urgent and low.

"I'm scared," a girl whispered back.

"Well, you were the one that was dumb enough to follow me. Now come on, if you're comin'."

"Promise you won't look."

The girl emerged from the doorway, ran down the dusty path, and disappeared into the woods. The boy followed, a guttering lantern held high. Charlotte frowned. Something about him seemed oddly familiar.

Soon the pair returned, heads bent low, the lantern flame trembling in the sudden breeze wafting in from the sea.

Recognition dawned. She got to her feet and stepped into the street. "Daniel Graves."

He stopped, the lantern slipping from his grasp. "Don't shoot."

She retrieved his lantern and held it high, illuminating two young faces tight with fear. "What on earth are you doing here?"

"Nothing." Daniel shuffled his feet and looked away.

She turned to the girl. "Who are you?"

"Lucy Wainwright. But I don't aim to cause

Daniel no trouble, ma'am. I'm the one came looking for him. It ain't his fault."

"It's his fault for trespassing on my land."

Daniel made a sound in his throat. "You gonna turn me in?"

"I don't know. It depends upon your explanation, which I have no intention of listening to out here in the dark. You'd best come up to the house."

He inched toward the cabin. "Got to get my possessions."

"What possessions?"

"He lives here now," Lucy said. "All by himself. I thought he was telling me a whopper, so I came to see for myself. Only it was a lot farther here than I thought. It was almost dark when I got here, and then it was too late to go home, and then I had to use the privy, and I guess that's when you saw the light, and now we are in trouble and it's my fault."

Charlotte stared at the pair, stunned into momentary silence. At last she said, "Daniel, is this true? Have you been living here in my slave street?"

"Yes'm."

"May I ask why?"

He shrugged. "Pa left."

"Where has he gone? When will he be back?"

"I don't know where he is, but he ain't coming back. He took everything with him 'cept for my

170

straw mattress and some dishes and such. Reckon he got tired of waitin' on me to make good."

Charlotte went inside the cabin and surveyed it by lantern light. A crumpled blanket lay atop the mattress in the corner. An upside-down metal bucket held a cup and a tin plate. On the dirt floor was a stack of books.

"I borrowed 'em from your library," Daniel said from behind her. "I been careful with 'em—was gonna bring 'em back."

"From my—How did you get inside my house?"

Another shrug. "Dinin' room window. Lock's broken."

Charlotte sighed, suddenly overcome with weariness. What to do with two runaways in the middle of the night? "All right. Collect your things and come up to the house."

Daniel gathered his belongings. Charlotte retrieved her own lantern, and they returned to the house. She lit the lamps and sat them down at the table in the library. "I imagine you're hungry."

"Yes'm." Daniel pushed his hair off his face. "Fish wasn't bitin' too good today—only caught one. And Lucy here was about to faint, so I let her have it."

"Very gentlemanly of you." Charlotte retrieved bread and butter and a few slices of ham from the kitchen house and brought them to the children. "Now, Lucy, where is your family? Won't your mother be worried about you?"

"Lucy's got eleven brothers and sisters," Daniel said, eyeing the ham.

"I'm number nine. Sometimes Ma loses count." Lucy bit into the slice of bread Charlotte had put on her plate. "Last fall my brother Quinn— he's number ten—was lost for two days 'fore we noticed he was missin'."

"Well, we'll get you home first thing in the morning," Charlotte said.

In the parlor the clock chimed. Both children ate in silence, their eyes drooping.

"What about Daniel?" Lucy asked a few minutes later as Charlotte led her up the stairs to her bedroom. "Where will he sleep?"

"I can sleep on my mattress in the library," he said. "I don't mind a bit."

Charlotte helped the girl wash up and undress. Lucy fell asleep immediately, one fist curled beneath her chin. Charlotte lay awake, listening to the old house creaking and settling as if it, too, longed for rest.

She closed her eyes and tried to empty her mind, but sleep eluded her. Having Daniel sleeping in her library, knowing he had come inside and helped himself to her books, made her uneasy. And yet she couldn't help feeling sorry for the boy. Times were terribly hard, but what sort of father left a child to fend for himself?

Lucy whimpered and flopped over in the bed, dragging the counterpane with her. Charlotte smoothed the child's hair. At least Lucy had a family to return to. But what would become of Daniel?

At last Charlotte slept fitfully and woke to pale sunlight streaming through the high window. While the children slept she made biscuits, then went outside to hitch Cinnamon to the wagon. Out in the road a wagon creaked and a couple of men shouted to one another. Mr. Finch and his crew, no doubt, on their way to her rice fields. She had hoped to take her rowboat down to the second field this afternoon. Perhaps there still would be time after Lucy and Daniel were safely delivered.

She slipped the harness over the mare's neck. Cinnamon snorted and blew out a long breath in protest.

"Steady, girl. I'm not looking forward to this trip either."

"Ma'am?" Daniel said from behind her.

She turned. "You startled me."

"Sorry. I come to see if I could help you with the wagon."

"I'd appreciate it. I wish I had a rig. The wagon is so cumbersome. Cinnamon doesn't like it either."

"I saw a cart down by the slave street the other day," Daniel said. "Weeds is all growed up around it, but it didn't look broke. I can go get it if you want."

"Would you?"

"Yes'm. Won't take me but a minute."

Charlotte stepped outside the shed and looked toward the river. The Waccamaw glittered in the spring sunlight as the tide came in, sending the snowy egrets and ospreys to higher ground. A fish flopped. A baby wood duck flapped his way across the surface. Charlotte inhaled the scent of water and sun-warmed mud. This land, this river, was in her blood. This was where she belonged. Nobody, not even someone as charming as Nicholas Betancourt, would take it from her.

Daniel appeared, pulling hard against the weight of the pony cart. Years of neglect had taken their toll; the wood had bleached to a soft gray, and a rusty nail protruded from one end of the seat. The wheels wobbled and creaked, but perhaps they would hold up for this one trip.

"You got any axle grease?" Daniel wiped his forehead. "Else that squeak is going to get awful monotonous."

"I'm afraid not," Charlotte said.

She watched as Daniel expertly hitched the horse to the cart. Lucy stumbled across the piazza and into the yard, her cheeks still rosy from sleep. "I'm hungry."

"I've packed us something to eat. We must be going."

Charlotte returned to the house for the food basket and her bag and keys. She locked the door, climbed onto the cart with the children, and shook the reins. The ancient cart lurched down the sun-dappled avenue.

"Now, Lucy, where do you live?" she asked when they reached the sandy road.

The girl pointed. "Down by Fairfield plantation. They's a shortcut between there and Oak Hill, but you can't get through excepting at low tide. Mama says we ought not to play down there anyway because of alligators, but I ain't never seen one."

"We'll stick to the road."

"Can we eat now?"

"I suppose so."

Daniel reached behind the seat for the basket, and the children fell upon the food like prisoners at a last meal. Charlotte left it to them, though she was beginning to feel hungry herself.

The morning grew hotter as they drove south past Hagley and Crowfield and then the thousand fallow acres of Fairfield that stretched along both sides of the river. Memories of bright spring days on Fairfield's wide green lawn, feeding the tame geese and ducks in the pond while her father talked business with Mr. William Alston, crowded in.

It seemed impossible that this plantation had once produced a million pounds of rice a year. Charlotte thought of the families she had known all her life, growing up along this river—the Wards, the Middletons, the Westons, and the two branches of the Alstons. Like her own family, they had enjoyed fine clothes and furnishings, blooded horses, and trips to Europe. The best of everything. Now they were as desperate for money as she.

"You can stop here, ma'am." Lucy brushed crumbs from her fingers. "I left my rowboat tied up in that cut over there."

"Are you sure?"

"Yes'm." Lucy jumped off the cart. "I'd best be going before Mama finds out I'm gone. It's my turn to help number three with the washing, and she'll be awful mad if it don't get done."

She disappeared into the trees, her bare feet stirring clouds of fine white dust.

Charlotte turned to Daniel. "Now, what about you?"

He shrugged, a gesture she was beginning to know well. "One place is good as another, I reckon." He gave her a sideways glance. "But I left my things at your house. I'll have to go on back with you to fetch 'em."

She eyed the boy. Every time she began to feel sorry for him, he reminded her of his cunning. On the other hand, there would hardly have been room on the small cart for the three of them and all of Daniel's possessions.

She was tempted to leave him to his own devices, but the hard sunlight on the river hurt her eyes. Hunger gnawed at her insides. The drive back home would take another two hours, the cart wheels screeching with every turn. She was in no mood to argue. Wordlessly she turned the cart in the road.

"Here, let me drive," Daniel said, reaching for the reins. "You look plumb wore out, and it's barely noon."

He braced one foot against the front of the cart and flicked the reins. Cinnamon trotted along the road. Charlotte shifted on the hard wooden seat to avoid the protruding nail, relieved to have Daniel at the reins. If only she had remembered her parasol.

She closed her eyes, and when she opened them again, they were nearly home. Daniel jumped down to open the gate and drove the cart through. He stopped in the yard and helped her from the cart.

"Go on inside, ma'am. I'll look after Cinnamon."

She didn't argue. In the parlor, she removed her hat and gloves and opened the windows. The afternoon breeze cooled her skin and rustled the papers she'd left lying on the pine table. Tomorrow the Betancourt girls would appear for school, and she was not nearly ready. Marie-Claire continued to show a talent for drawing and lately had taken more of an interest in the natural world. Anne-Louise had fallen in love with books and loved to show off her skills by reading aloud.

How best to encourage their natural tendencies whilst improving their knowledge and skills was a challenge that often kept her awake at night. Their father seemed pleased with their academic progress. But soon Marie-Claire must learn to waltz and to master the art of mindless conversation, the latter a skill Charlotte felt inadequate to teach. She herself had never felt comfortable gossiping with the other girls at school about who had a new dress or a new beau, whose marks were likeliest to be highest, or who had nearly gotten caught sneaking over the wrought-iron fence after curfew. She much preferred talking rice production with her father or listening as he discussed politics with other men around their dining table.

The door opened and slammed shut. Daniel came into the parlor. "The mare is all taken care of, ma'am."

"Thank you. And thank you for bringing the cart up from the slave street." She smiled. "It was much more pleasant to drive than my wagon, despite the noisy wheel."

"All you need is some axle grease."

"I'll get some on my next trip to town."

"You ought to build yourself a real barn before next winter."

She set her papers aside. "I know, but I haven't the materials at present, and I can't afford any until after my rice is harvested this fall."

"There's plenty of good lumber in the slave cabins—mostly cypress, which my pa says lasts forever. The way I figure it, you might as well use it for something."

"Maybe you're right. I'll think about it."

He nodded. "In the meantime, can I stay on down there?"

"Oh, Daniel, that cabin is not fit for human habitation."

"It keeps the rain off, and I ain't got nowhere else to go. I sorta like it down there too. It's so quiet of an evening I can hear the birds rustling in the trees and the river running past. Soothes me better'n anything. Besides which, you need somebody to help you with chores around here. And I promise not to take any more of your books without permission."

She pinched the bridge of her nose and willed her headache away. She had too much responsibility already. Still, for all of his bravado, Daniel was just a boy. A child in need of a home. How could she turn him away?

"I leave for the beach at the end of the month. You may stay in the cabin until then, and after that we'll see. But you will take your meals here in the house—no more foraging like a wild Indian. And no more campfires. I can't have you burning the place down."

A wide grin split his sun-browned face. "Much obliged, ma'am. You won't be sorry, not one bit."

"I hope not. Now please excuse me. My pupils will be here in the morning, and I must be prepared."

Daniel glanced out the window. "Looks like they're early. Here they come now."

Frowning, Charlotte rose and went out to the piazza. Marie-Claire and Anne-Louise made their way up the avenue. Each carried a pail and a small valise. Behind them stood Tamar.

The older woman looked much as she had on her infrequent visits to Alder Hill all those years ago. She was still of regal bearing, still willow thin, her hair long and straight and hanging past her waist in a thick plait. Despite years of hard work, she moved up the avenue with a dancer's fluid grace, the hem of her frayed yellow calico dress trailing in the dust.

Charlotte met them in the yard. Tamar placed a hand on Marie-Claire's shoulder and regarded Charlotte with a studied calm. "You Miss Fraser?"

"Yes." Clearly Tamar didn't recognize her. Why would she? The two of them had never spoken directly, and Tamar could hardly be expected to remember a white girl she had only glimpsed years before.

"You they teacher?"

"For now, yes. What's the trouble?"

"Mr. Betancourt promised to be back befo' now, but promisin' talk don't cook rice. I waited as long as I can, but I can't wait no more. I got to leave these babies with you."

Anne-Louise stifled a sob. Marie-Claire, too, seemed near tears.

"Of course they're welcome to stay the night. When will you be back?"

"I can't come back, miss. Not for a long while anyways. My man gone down to Charleston to work for Mr. Middleton. My boy, Mathias, got the consumption, and they's nobody else to look after him." Tamar's eyes filled. "Been sick all spring. Won't be 'roun' much longer, I 'spect." She clasped her hands at her waist. "Death is one ditch nobody can jump. But I got to take care of my chil' till the angels carry him home."

"Of course you must look after him," Charlotte said automatically. "I'm very sorry."

Tamar shrugged. "When trouble fall, it ain't gon' fall on the groun'. Gon' fall on somebody, and we gotta take it as it comes."

Marie-Claire sent Charlotte an accusing look. "We came here on Sunday, but you wouldn't answer the door."

"I was away all day, didn't get home until dark. I'm sorry I wasn't here when you came calling."

"Please say we can stay with you, Ma'm'selle," Anne-Louise pleaded. "Just until our papa gets home."

Charlotte closed her eyes. Of course there was no choice but to take the girls under her wing, at least until a better solution could be worked out.

But she had the plantation to run. She hadn't spoken to Mr. Finch in days. It wouldn't do not to keep an eye on his progress.

Marie-Claire dropped her valise into the dirt. "I don't think Papa is coming back."

Given all the problems on the river these days, Charlotte could hardly blame the man for writing off his disputed plantation as a lost cause. Ongoing labor problems, too much rain, the predations of the ricebirds were enough to give anyone pause. And he certainly was long overdue. But surely he would not willingly abandon his children.

She patted Marie-Claire's thin shoulder. "Of course he's coming back. He's simply been delayed for some reason. I expect he'll return any moment."

"Why can't he at least send a letter?" Anne-Louise set down her valise too. "Tamar said he would write to us if he couldn't come home."

Tamar confirmed this with a nod. "I ain't been knowin' they daddy too long, but I know he sets a lot o' store by these chillun. Don't make no sense why he ain't sent a letter."

"Perhaps it's on the way now. Tomorrow we'll ask at the postal office."

Tamar knelt in the dirt and took each girl by the hand. "You 'member you manners now, and don't be talkin' back to the teacher, y'hear?"

Both girls nodded.

"Don't forget to say you prayers ever' night. Ask the Lord to watch over your daddy wherever he go."

"We will," Anne-Louise said.

"An' if you think of it, say a prayer for Tamar too, and her boy."

Tamar rose, nodded again to Charlotte, and walked back down the avenue, her bare feet slapping on the hard ground.

Charlotte motioned to the girls, and they picked up their things and followed her inside.

"Daniel?" Marie-Claire's eyes widened. "What are you doing here?"

"Staying for a while. Helping out Miss Fraser." He folded his arms across his chest. "You weren't s'posed to come till tomorrow."

"And you aren't s'posed to be here at all."

"All right, that's quite enough." Charlotte rested a hand on Marie-Claire's shoulder. "Young ladies. Kindly remove yourselves to the kitchen and pump some water for washing up. You both look a fright."

After a hastily concocted lunch, Charlotte settled the girls at the table in the library. Daniel chose a book from the shelf and headed outside to the piazza. Charlotte drew her chair nearer to the open window and sipped her tea. What was taking Nicholas so long? Was he sick or injured? Or had he planned all along to win her good opinion before abandoning his children to her care? He had given up his medical practice; perhaps nothing mattered to him.

It was an uncharitable thought and one that perhaps was unwarranted. But if his motives were pure, why the long silence? Had he found proof of his claim? Charlotte finished her tea and picked up her book, but the words blurred on the page. Waiting for news of her fate was worse than knowing. Whatever the outcome, she wished it to arrive soon.

Thirteen

"Careful, ma'am." Jeremiah Finch reached for Charlotte's hand as she entered the boat and settled herself near the stern. The Betancourt girls squeezed in next to wooden crates containing dishes and kitchen utensils, bedding, her desk, a large tin tub for washing, and books—the essentials they'd need to begin the summer on Pawley's Island. Charlotte had delayed her departure for as long as she dared, hoping for their father's return, but mosquito season had arrived with no word from him. Yesterday she'd made the trip to Willowood to gather the girls' belongings and leave a letter for Nicholas. Now she set her picnic basket at her feet and opened her parasol.

"How long will it take to get there?" Marie-Claire shaded her eyes and looked across the river.

"Not long. We'll be there by suppertime." The overseer unfastened the ropes and, with an oar, pushed the long, narrow rice boat away from the dock. It wasn't in the best repair, but Charlotte felt lucky to have found it at all. She prayed it wouldn't spring a leak before they reached the island. And she hoped Mr. Finch was skilled enough on the water to get them there without mishap. Trim had gone upcountry and Thomas was ailing. There was no one else she trusted. The boat swayed and settled on the calm water as he turned it and headed upstream.

Anne-Louise turned her troubled gaze on Charlotte. "Are you sure Papa will know where to find us?"

Marie-Claire frowned. "You ninny. Papa isn't coming back."

"He is too. He promised."

"He hates us, just like *Maman* did."

Anne-Louise burst into tears.

Charlotte sent Marie-Claire a stern look and reached around a crate of dishes to clasp the younger girl's hand. "Don't cry. I'm sure your papa loves you very much and will be home as soon as he can."

"If he loves us, why hasn't he at least written to us?" Marie-Claire asked.

Charlotte wondered the same thing herself. On every trip to Georgetown, she had checked the postal office, anxious for news, but so far Nicholas Betancourt remained silent. "I don't know. But I'm sure he has a good reason."

"Even if he does come back, we won't be there," Anne-Louise said. "He'll think we ran away."

Charlotte smiled. "I left a letter for him at your house and one at the postal office too. When he gets back, he'll know we're at the beach."

"I've never been to the beach before," Anne-Louise said.

"You'll adore it," Charlotte said. "I spent every summer there when I was a girl. My papa taught me to fish there. I made a collection of seashells. I read magazines all day long. And at night I slept in a hammock on the piazza so I could listen to the ocean singing me to sleep."

"May I sleep on the piazza?"

"Possibly. We'll see whether the hammock is still there."

Mr. Finch guided the boat into Schooner Creek, a deep stream bordered on each side by tall stands of marsh grass intertwined with water lilies, wild roses, and scarlet lobelia. Charlotte pointed out an alligator that slipped from the marsh reeds into the stream, a row of little turtles sunning themselves, an osprey watching their progress from his massive nest.

Memories of childhood summers came back to her, sharp as a sea breeze. Before the war, moving to the beach each summer had involved loading furniture, bedding, trunks, provisions, even horses and cows, onto large flatboats that left Fairhaven at dawn for the eleven-mile journey along the meandering waterways. Her family had followed in a rowboat, the Negro oarsmen, Cuffy and Abraham, singing the whole way. She still remembered Abraham's favorite, still could hear his deep rolling voice in her head.

I believe I'll count the angel.
I do believe I'll count the angel.
How many angels in the band?

After her father's final summer on Pawley's Island, he had purchased a few pieces of furniture for the cottage—a simple pine dining table and chairs, a settee and chair for the parlor, a bed for Charlotte's room—thinking ahead to the time when she would make this journey alone and sparing her the necessity of a complicated move. If only he'd taken such care with the deed to her land.

Marie-Claire shifted on her makeshift seat. "How much longer, Ma'm'selle? I'm hungry."

"A few more miles, but we can eat now if you like." Charlotte opened a basket and handed each girl a sandwich and bowl of blackberries. "Mrs. Hadley sent these before she left for the city. Wasn't that thoughtful of her?"

Anne-Louise chewed her sandwich and nodded. "I like strawberries better."

Charlotte thought of her first day at Willowood, when Mr. Betancourt had served strawberries. She smiled at Anne-Louise. "Me too."

At last the boat emerged into an inlet. Charlotte strained her eyes, looking for the long wooden boardwalk her father had built years before. "There it is, Mr. Finch. Thank goodness the Yankees didn't destroy it. At least I won't have any trouble coming and going from Fairhaven."

The overseer guided the boat to the boardwalk and nudged it alongside. Steadying himself with one oar, he jumped onto the dock and drew the boat alongside. "No need for you to be traveling back and forth, ma'am. The rice fields are doing just fine, and besides, Mr. Hadley and Mr. Clifton are at the Cliftons' place up in the pinelands, keeping an eye on their gardens and such. One of us will let you know if anything goes awry."

"My father traveled back and forth from here every day, tending the rice. I imagine I can manage a trip or two each week. I don't doubt your skill or your diligence, Mr. Finch, but I feel uneasy that there is no one to guard my house while I'm away."

He shrugged. "Suit yourself. But there hasn't been as much stealing lately. I reckon the thieves have just about took all that's fit for taking."

"Even though I've agreed to let Daniel stay on, I'm concerned about my mare."

"I'll keep an eye on her, and he will look after her when I'm not around. She'll be all right." He lifted the girls out of the boat and set them on the dock, then helped Charlotte out. "Take the children on up to the house. I'll bring your things."

The cottage roof peeked from tall sand dunes where sea oats waved in the steady ocean breeze. The girls ran ahead, their shoes sounding hollow on the sun-bleached boardwalk. Charlotte took her first intoxicating draft of ocean air. She walked to the end of the boardwalk, skirted the dunes, and stopped dead still at her first sight of the rolling waves, the brilliant blue expanse of ocean. The sea mirrored the sun, splintering the light into tiny fires that flared and waned with the ocean's breath.

"Is that your house?" Anne-Louise pointed.

"Yes. Pelican Cottage. I spent much of my childhood here." She gestured toward a high corner window. "That's my room. It has windows on three sides so I can see the marshes and the ocean all at once."

"Which will be mine?" Anne-Louise asked.

"Come along, I'll show you."

Together they followed the sandy path to the house and went inside.

Marie-Claire wrinkled her nose. "It stinks in here."

Charlotte threw open the parlor windows to air out the house and led the girls across an open breezeway to the corner room her mother had kept for visitors. Furnished with a mahogany bed, a rocking chair, and a small dresser left over from her childhood, it too faced the sea. Before the war a parade of aunts, friends, and cousins had passed many a languid summer here. No one had slept here since.

Charlotte opened the window, letting in a freshening breeze that billowed the thin white curtains. "The two of you will share this room."

"I don't want to share," Marie-Claire said. "I'm practically grown-up. I want a room of my own."

"I'm afraid you have no choice—unless you wish to sleep on the floor. The other bedrooms except for mine are empty."

"Why?"

"Because for several years only my father and I summered here. We had no use for so many rooms. Besides, I'd rather spend my time swimming and fishing and reading books than dusting and polishing furniture. Wouldn't you?"

"I suppose. But, Ma'm'selle, why can't I have your father's room? I bet he didn't sleep on the floor."

"When he became very ill and we moved to the city to be near his doctor, we took his bed with us. It brought him comfort in his final months of life. He said it smelled like the sea."

"Oh."

Anne-Louise bounced on the bed. "I'm taking this side. I want—"

"Miss Fraser?" Mr. Finch loomed in the doorway. "Where do you want these boxes?"

"Just leave it all in the front hall. We'll sort it out later."

"This is the last of it. I put your dishes and provisions in the kitchen and left your washtub out back. Oh, and I brought you some drinking water from the well."

"Thank you."

He nodded. "I'll get the Graves boy to come with me tomorrow. We'll bring your rowboat and take the rice boat back to the plantation."

"I appreciate your taking him under your wing. I was hoping the Hadleys would look after him but—"

"Some days that man can't take care of himself," Mr. Finch said, "much less look after a young'un. Like I said, I don't want the boy working with my Negroes, but I can keep him busy with the garden and such. That is, if he can keep his nose outta the books long enough."

"You have the key I gave you?"

He nodded. "Not that a locked door will keep out anyone bent on thieving."

"Let Daniel read whatever he wants from the library, so long as it doesn't interfere with his work."

He glanced out the window. "Looks like a storm may be brewing. Old Thomas says storms break when the tide changes. Reckon I'd better be going."

Charlotte and the girls saw him off at the dock. When the boat disappeared into the inlet, she clapped her hands. "Who wants to go shelling?"

"Me!" Anne-Louise plopped onto the sand, unbuttoned her shoes, and yanked off her stockings. Charlotte and Marie-Claire followed suit. They tucked their skirts into their sashes and raced to the shore. Marie-Claire yelped when the water lapped over her bare feet. "It's cold."

"It won't feel cold once you get used to it." Charlotte bent to retrieve a tiny white shell and gently blew away the sand inside. She showed it to the girls. "This one is called angel wing."

"It's pretty." Marie-Claire slipped it into her pocket.

"Here's another one." Anne-Louise scooped it from the sand. "It's broken, though."

Thunder rumbled, and Charlotte glanced toward the horizon. "I think Mr. Finch might be right about the storm. We should go inside."

"But, Ma'm'selle, we just got here," Anne-Louise said.

"We'll look for more shells later." Charlotte extended her hand, and the little girl took it.

They retrieved their shoes and returned to the house. From the shelter of the elevated piazza, they watched a curtain of rain move onshore. When the rain blew in, they went inside. Charlotte closed the window, made a fire in the cookstove, and set the teakettle on to boil. They ate a cold supper at the pine table and watched the waves crashing onto the beach. When the gray light leached out of the leaden sky, she read from the Psalms, led the girls in prayers for their absent father, and put them to bed.

In her room, she set the key to her father's strongbox on the table and readied herself for bed. She brushed her hair, listening to the girls' whispered laughter, and was surprised at how happy she was for their company. Without them, she would be alone with her memories. As it was, thoughts of what she had lost and what yet might be in store kept her awake long after the storm had passed, leaving in its wake a sliver of moon and a froth of silvery stars.

"Halloo! Is anyone home?"

Charlotte rose from her desk in the parlor and peered out the window. The tide was coming in, turning the wide beach into a narrow strip of sand littered with bits of storm-churned driftwood. A flock of brown pelicans glided overhead. A pair of skimmers darted along the shore, inspecting the mustard-colored seaweed. And just outside the door stood Augusta Milton, whose cottage sat farther down the beach and closer to the marshes.

"Augusta. Hello." Charlotte embraced her old friend. "I wondered whether you'd arrived yet."

"Hello, my dear." With a swish of her skirts, Augusta crossed the bare floor and plopped down on the settee. "Got here last Saturday—just me and the milk cow. I saw Mrs. Weston last evening, and she told me she'd seen you arriving yesterday." Her thick gray brows went up. "With children in tow?"

"My pupils. Marie-Claire and Anne-Louise

Betancourt. I haven't had time to write to you about them. Their father went away on business and has not yet returned. I couldn't leave them alone."

"Of course not." Augusta folded her hands in her lap. "Where is their mother?"

"Deceased. For some years now."

"Oh, what a shame. But then, you were hardly more than an infant when your own dear mother passed, and you turned out just fine."

"I was twelve. Not quite an infant. But still, it wasn't easy."

Augusta smiled. "When a person gets to be my age, everyone in the world is an infant. Be that as it may, your dear father did right by you."

"Yes." Charlotte paused, remembering happier times and her father's habitual kindness. Would she ever stop missing the gleam in his eyes, the sound of his laughter? "The girls aren't awake yet. They're worn out from our journey yesterday. I was about to make tea. Would you like some?"

"Thank you, but I can't stay. The Seabrooks arrived last week, and I promised to stop by there this morning to help organize the summer mission drive. A new minister has arrived at the Litchfield chapel. The Reverend Mr. Peabody. He's quite keen on good works."

"So I heard."

"It seems we're going to make ice cream and sell it to the Northern tourists." Augusta's face darkened. "They can well afford it. And the proceeds will buy blankets for foreign orphanages."

"Does the minister think our little island will actually draw that many visitors?"

"He says they're coming here for fishing expeditions. And this fall there will be hunting parties on the Waccamaw and the Pee Dee. By the time fever season is over, we should have collected a tidy sum." Augusta rose. "We can depend upon your help, I trust."

"I'll do what I can, but I cannot neglect my teaching duties. I lost half of my first planting to a storm back in the spring. I need the income from teaching to pay the bills while I restore my house and fields."

Augusta shook her head. "I was saying to Mrs. Weston just the other day that it's admirable what you've taken on, but too daunting a task for anyone."

"I promised my father."

"He wouldn't hold you to it, Charlotte. I knew him all his life, and all he ever wanted was your happiness."

"But bringing Fairhaven back to life does make me happy. Without it, I have no idea what would become of me."

"Well, I imagine you'd carry on somehow. People always do." Augusta rose and patted Charlotte's arm. "You must come to dinner soon and bring your young charges along. In the meantime, I trust we'll see you in church on Sunday? Mr. Peabody hopes we islanders will come to services at the chapel for the summer. Reckon I'll give it a try."

"Then I will too. I must confess I'm curious about this Mr. Peabody."

"Oh, he's full of notions. In fact, he's already talking about establishing a medical clinic. There's no telling what he might suggest next. But I suppose we'll find out soon enough. In the meantime I must go. Good-bye, my dear."

Charlotte watched as Augusta hiked her skirts, picked her way along the beach, and disappeared into the dunes. It was true that people could survive more than they imagined was possible. The war had proven that. But if Nicholas Betancourt's claim to her land turned out to be legitimate, could she bear to forfeit the only thing in her life that really mattered?

Fourteen

Charlotte sat on the piazza of Pelican Cottage, a book open on her lap and a pitcher of water nearby. The balmy days of early June had given way to a scorching heat that even the ocean breeze could not completely mitigate. Not that Marie-Claire and Anne-Louise seemed to notice. Up at dawn nearly every day, they spent all day playing on the beach or crabbing in the creeks. Their shell collections now spilled from glass jars and seagrass baskets onto tabletops and along the piazza. Every day brought new discoveries—a whelk, a starfish, a flotilla of pelicans fishing for food just offshore. Seeing the island through the girls' eyes was another pleasure Charlotte hadn't anticipated when she brought them here.

School was still in session, although she had relaxed the hours since their arrival. Their abbreviated lessons took place late in the day, when the freshening breeze blew though the tall windows, rustling the papers spread on the pine table. Thanks to Augusta she'd obtained back issues of *Robert Merry's Museum*. Both girls delighted in the stories and poems, and reading aloud after supper had become a favored part of the daily routine. Less popular were the comportment lessons. She had taught them to make and pour tea, to write a proper thank-you letter, and to remark upon the weather with humor and grace.

On Mondays they walked to the north end of the island, where they purchased milk and vegetables brought from Georgetown. On her first trip to town, she'd returned to the island with a box of books she'd ordered from Boston and a letter from Cousin Alexander. He was engaged to be married at the end of the summer and hoped Charlotte could come for the wedding. If only she could. Here on the island there was little to do apart from attending church, tutoring the girls, and working on the missions committee. But a trip to Atlanta was a luxury she could scarcely afford. So much depended upon the success of her rice crop.

Twice since arriving on the island, she had sent for a boat and left the girls with Augusta while she made a trip to the plantation. Each time Mr. Finch had seemed none too happy to see her, but he'd given her a tour of both fields before riding with her to the upland to check the progress of her gardens. Daniel, seeming taller and even more sun-browned, had come out to show her what he was growing, and on her second visit he'd surprised her with the beginnings of a barn for Cinnamon. "When you come back after the black frost, it'll be ready," he'd said, unable to contain his pride.

She made a mental note to order some books for him as a present—as soon as she could afford it. With Nicholas Betancourt still absent, her much-needed teaching income was absent as well.

"Ma'm'selle, look." Anne-Louise pounded along the sand and onto the piazza. Opening her hand, she spilled half a dozen pieces of sea glass into Charlotte's lap. "I've never found so much of it together before. I bet someone lost their collection."

"Most likely." She admired the deep green color that reminded her of Nicholas Betancourt's eyes. Why hadn't he written? She would never admit to his daughters her fear that he had abandoned the three of them. "Leave it on the table and we'll find a jar for it."

"Tide's coming in," Anne-Louise said. "May we go crabbing this afternoon?"

"Not today. The minister from Litchfield Plantation is coming to visit."

Anne-Louise wrinkled her nose. "Do we have to wear shoes and serve tea?"

"No, but you'll need to play quietly in your room while he's here. Perhaps you can look through our books and choose what to read next."

"I already did. I want to read *Countess Kate*. I think it would be lovely to be a countess, don't you, Ma'm'selle?"

Charlotte grinned. "Oh, I don't know. I expect if one were a countess, one could never go barefoot and spend all day crabbing. A countess might have to wear a dozen stiff petticoats and very tight shoes and dine every night with stuffy old men who smell of camphor and hair tonic."

Anne-Louise giggled. "I wouldn't like that. But I still want to read the book."

"And you shall. But now please find Marie-Claire. It's time for lunch, and I've much to do before Mr. Peabody arrives."

"All right." Anne-Louise started down the steps, then turned suddenly and wrapped both arms around Charlotte's knees. "I wish you were my mother."

Before Charlotte could reply she raced down to the beach, calling for her sister.

An hour later the girls were fed and in their room. Charlotte took a sponge bath, pinned up her hair, and changed her dress. She had planned to spend this afternoon writing to Lettice Hadley and to Alexander, but after church on Sunday the minister had caught up with her in the yard and requested this visit. According to Augusta, his plans for the medical clinic were progressing; perhaps he had some new scheme for funding it. The ice cream sales were modest but steady, and there still was plenty of the summer left. Most of the plantation families would remain here until the first killing frosts in November. The Northern tourists arrived each week in a steady stream, taking up residence in the small inn at the northern tip of the island.

After a final check of the mirror, she went out to the kitchen to make tea and arrange short-breads on a chipped porcelain tray. Through the window she saw the minister arrive on horseback, his black frock coat flapping in the stiff breeze rising off the Atlantic. He tethered the horse to the ancient hitching post in the side yard.

Charlotte met him at the door. "Please come in."

He removed his hat and stepped inside. "Thank you for seeing me. I'm sure you must stay busy with two such lively girls about."

His kind brown eyes crinkled at the corners when he smiled, and Charlotte found herself smiling back. "It's a challenge to keep them constructively occupied when the beach is calling to them, but I confess I enjoy teaching more than I expected."

"Oh?"

"I'm not trained for it, and I've always felt inadequate for the task. But I can see real progress in both girls, and I do find that quite gratifying."

"I imagine so. Not unlike the satisfaction of seeing a sinner restored to the Father as a result of a well-delivered homily." He smiled again.

She motioned him to a seat on the embroidered settee, poured tea, and offered the shortbread, which he declined with a shake of his head.

She regarded him over the top of her cup. He sipped his tea and gazed out to the sea, seeming in no hurry to state his business. For one anxious moment she imagined he had come to deliver dire news about Nicholas. But then he set down his cup, his eyes on hers.

"I'm very glad indeed to hear that you enjoy teaching so, for I find that I am in need of a teacher."

"Oh?"

"I learned just last week that my widowed sister has died, leaving behind four children—two boys and two girls—who must be taken in. Perhaps you knew her. Esther Demere? She lived in Charleston before the war."

"I don't believe I ever met her. I'm very sorry to learn of her passing."

He cleared his throat. "My wife and I of course are willing to take them, but they will need some order to their days, and frankly Ruth is not up to the task."

"Mrs. Milton told me Mrs. Peabody has a weak heart. I am sorry to hear it."

He nodded. "She tires easily, and her work for the mission society takes what little strength she possesses. I'm busy with raising money for the Chinese orphanage and the medical clinic, and I fear the children will too often be left to their own devices at a time when what they need most is stability and a sense of purpose."

Charlotte remembered the months following her mother's death, when she stumbled through each day in a grief-induced fog, barely able to think or eat. The routine at Madame Giraud's, the daily lessons and recitations and essays, and the diversions provided by her schoolmates had kept her from dwelling too much on the awful reality she was powerless to change. Still, she was not prepared to provide such a routine for these children.

"I realize you will be returning to your plantation in the autumn," the minister continued, "but I hoped you might be willing for these next few months. I am prepared to offer you a small remuneration, of course, if you would—"

"What about the schoolmaster at Litchfield?"

"He won't be back until October at the earliest."

"Mr. Peabody, I sympathize with your situation. But even if I were qualified to take on such a task, I have only a few books." She waved one hand. "I have no chalkboard, nor proper desks and chairs, nor—"

"I've thought of that. You could move into the plantation schoolroom. There's a separate house for the schoolmaster, adequately furnished, and the schoolroom has everything you might require. I'm certain Dr. Tucker will be agreeable."

Papa's friend, Dr. Henry Tucker, had inherited Litchfield just before the war. It was said that rice planting was his life's sole passion and that he cared little for books. If that was so, perhaps he wouldn't object to her temporarily occupying the plantation schoolroom. Not that the idea held any appeal for her.

"My young charges have lost their mother too," she said. "Their father left a month ago on a matter of some importance, and we've had no word of him. They seem happy here, and I am reluctant to uproot them when their future is so uncertain. Perhaps a female relative, an aunt or a cousin, might come for the summer and take charge of the children. Or someone from the congregation?"

He sighed. "If that were possible, I wouldn't be here. There is no one else."

"I'm sorry."

He stared into his empty cup as if the answer to his dilemma might be hiding there. "What if I moved the school down here?"

"I beg your pardon?"

"What if I brought everything here? Your two girls could remain here and you'd have the desks and chairs and other things you need." He glanced around the parlor to the room beyond. "Your dining room would easily serve the purpose."

She walked to the window and looked out at the sea, fighting the fury building inside her. How dare he barge in and commandeer her home for his own purposes? It was too vivid a reminder of what the Northern carpetbaggers had been about for the past three years, raising taxes to astronomical levels and then taking property when the owners couldn't pay. And promising the Negroes the moon in exchange for loyalty at the polls.

Of course she was sorry that Mr. Peabody's nieces and nephews had lost their mother. Now, with the plantations in ruins, education for a different kind of life was more important than ever. But her own insecurities haunted her. And she hadn't spent much time around boys; she wouldn't know where to begin teaching Mr. Peabody's nephews. She had so many worries of her own. And now it seemed she was permanently in charge of Nicholas Betancourt's daughters too.

Tamping down her anger, she turned to the minister and forced a polite smile. "Again, I'm afraid I must decline."

He rose, a frown creasing his high forehead. "I see. May I ask one favor of you?"

"Of course."

"The children won't arrive until next week. In the interim, will you seek divine guidance on this matter?"

She nodded. "As I do in all things."

"That's all I ask." He retrieved his hat and made for the door. "Perhaps we can talk again on Sunday."

She watched him mount his horse and ride away, the horse's hooves kicking up sand.

Marie-Claire bounded barefoot into the room, her dark hair flying. "May we go to the beach now? I want to look for more angel wings."

Charlotte smiled, her irritation at the minister forgotten. Both girls had adapted quickly to island life. Sturdy and browned from endless hours on the beach, they had learned to appreciate the rhythms of the sea and the beauty and the wonder of her random gifts. They knew the names of the birds stalking the muddy shores of the tidal creeks, the grasses and flowers growing wild in the inlet behind the house.

Charlotte brushed a hand over Marie-Claire's unruly locks. "I suppose so. Get your hat and your sister and meet me on the piazza."

Ten minutes later they headed north, the girls chasing the receding waves. Here and there mothers reclined on blankets in the shade of the dunes, chatting or reading while their children splashed in the shallow surf.

"Ma'm'selle." Anne-Louise held up the remains of a horseshoe crab. "An arthropod."

"Very good, you remembered."

The child bobbed her head. "It's easy to remember things the way you teach them to us. Marie-Claire thinks so too, only she's too stubborn to say so."

She fell into step alongside Charlotte. "Marie-Claire thinks Papa is dead. Is he?"

"Of course not." Charlotte knelt on the wet

sand until their eyes were level. "I'm sure he is perfectly fine. Any day now he'll get my letter and he'll know just where to find us when he gets back. You mustn't worry about it."

She looked up to see Augusta Milton and Emily Weston coming along the beach, each carrying a picnic basket. Augusta waved as they drew near.

"Lovely day," Augusta sang out.

"It is." Charlotte got to her feet and sent Anne-Louise to join Marie-Claire. "Hello, Mrs. Weston."

Mrs. Weston nodded. "Lovely to see you at last. I've been looking for you ever since we arrived." She smiled at Anne-Louise's retreating form. "I heard you were looking after Mr. Betancourt's children." She glanced toward the two girls who were on their knees, digging in the sand. "I do hope he has not abandoned them. It has happened far too often since the war."

"Nicholas—Mr. Betancourt would never willingly abandon his daughters. I confess that I am worried, though. I expected his return long before now."

"And yet you don't seem too eager to have him back," Augusta said. "Is anything the matter?"

Charlotte shook her head. Part of her wanted to share the burden of her worries about Fairhaven. But for all their fine qualities, Augusta Milton and Emily Weston were not above gossip, and the last thing she needed was for Mr. Finch and her creditors at the bank to get wind of a possible property dispute. "I'm uneasy about leaving Mr. Finch, the overseer, in charge of everything. I don't know him very well, and he's looking after the Hadleys' fields and the Cliftons' too. I—"

"Speaking of the Cliftons." Emily shifted her basket to her other arm. "Just after you left to come here, I saw Josie Clifton and her mother coming out of the postal office in Georgetown. Up from Charleston for a couple of days, though for what purpose she didn't say. They send their regards."

Two young boys with a kite raced past, kicking up a shower of damp sand. Charlotte brushed at her skirt and placed a hand on Augusta's arm. "I'm glad for this chance meeting. I was about to say that I hope you can look after the girls for me on Friday. I want to see how my fields are faring. I'll leave early and be back before dark."

"They're welcome to stay," Augusta said. "Such bright minds. I'm sure I wasn't half as clever when I was their age." She patted Charlotte's hand. "All due to your unorthodox teaching methods, no doubt."

Mrs. Weston's dark brows rose. "Unorthodox?"

"Charlotte doesn't believe in rote memorization," Augusta said, "or in a set course of study. She lets the girls study whatever interests them."

"How intriguing." Mrs. Weston smiled at

Charlotte. "But tell me, then, how is a child to learn arithmetic if she has no interest in it?"

"Marie-Claire already knew the fundamentals when I began teaching her, and Anne-Louise as well, though to a lesser extent, so I can't be sure my method would work with pupils who have no basic knowledge." Charlotte shaded her eyes and scanned the beach for her young charges, who had abandoned their sand castle and were now helping the boys with the kite. "My arrangement with their father was for the short term, and there's a scarcity of books since the war, so I thought it just as well to adopt a more relaxed approach to the curriculum. Once they are sent to boarding school, there will be time enough for drills and exercises and endless memorization of useless information."

Mrs. Weston laughed. "It seems you have a talent for teaching. I wonder whether you know what a rare gift it is."

"Thank you, but I'm afraid my methods are the product of too little skill, too few books, and too much worrying over whether I'm doing enough to engage my pupils."

"Well, your methods certainly seem to agree with them," Mrs. Weston said. "But I should be getting home. My husband will wonder what has become of me."

Augusta nodded. "I must go too. But I'm happy to have the girls visit on Friday."

The two friends went on down the beach, their wide-brimmed hats blowing in the late-afternoon breeze. The air had cooled, but there was still plenty of light, and the girls were absorbed in getting the kite airborne. Charlotte settled herself on the warm sand, her back resting against the dune, and watched the sea, remembering a late-summer day with her father. She had been waiting for him near the salt works when he arrived late from his inspection of the fields on the Waccamaw. Together they walked back to Pelican Cottage to leave his things before heading to the beach for their customary walk. For weeks she'd waited with growing impatience for a set of books to arrive from Boston. Learning that they had not yet arrived at the postal office in Georgetown had put her in a disagreeable mood. She allowed that perhaps the order had not even been sent.

"Watch the sea, daughter." He halted her steps with a hand on her shoulder and directed her attention to the incoming tide, each wave folding in upon itself before sliding onto the sand as foam.

"Oh, Papa, it looks precisely the same as it did yesterday and the day before."

"Exactly. The sea never hurries and never falters. We expect it to be there each morning to usher in a new day and it never disappoints. Patience and faith are what the sea teaches us." His dark eyes shone with paternal affection. "You could use more of both, Charlotte."

Patience and faith. Today she felt woefully short of both. Perhaps she shouldn't have felt so angry toward Mr. Peabody, who only wanted the best for his sister's orphaned children. But it seemed that life presented her with an ever-lengthening list of things to do. On Friday she would visit her rice fields, settle up with the overseer, and check on Daniel Graves. She smiled, imagining him curled up beneath a tree, one of her books open on his knees.

If there was time, she might visit Willowood to reassure herself that Nicholas had not returned and somehow missed her letter. But if that had happened, wouldn't he know to ask Mr. Finch for her whereabouts or to look for her on Pawley's?

High-pitched squeals rose above the sound of the outgoing tide. Charlotte looked up to see that one of the kite boys had filled a bucket of water and was chasing Anne-Louise down the beach. Charlotte got to her feet just as Marie-Claire tackled him from behind. The two sprawled on the wet sand.

Charlotte hurried across the beach, arriving just as Marie-Claire jumped up, her face the picture of triumph for having saved her sister from a certain drenching.

"All right. Time to go."

"But I've hardly collected any shells," Marie-Claire said.

"You shouldn't have spent so much time with

those boys and their kite." Charlotte motioned for Anne-Louise.

Marie-Claire sighed. "I suppose the shells will be here tomorrow."

Charlotte let the girls go ahead of her up the beach, their arms wrapped around each other's waists, their dark heads touching, and she felt a rush of affection for them. Was she doing enough to prepare their minds for the rigors of a formal education?

Late-afternoon sunlight glinted on the water. A flock of brown pelicans flapped their way south as the first streaks of pink appeared in the sky. She removed her straw hat and filled her lungs with the warm salt air. This time of day on the ocean never failed to remind her of just how small human beings were when measured against the infinite.

"Will you seek divine guidance in this matter?" Mr. Peabody's words seemed to ride the ocean breeze.

"Hurry up, Ma'm'selle. We're exceedingly hungry." Hat in hand, Anne-Louise motioned to Charlotte.

She shepherded the girls inside and set about making a meal. They ate on the piazza, watching the first stars appear. Soon Anne-Louise yawned and drifted off, her head falling onto her sister's shoulder. Charlotte got them inside and into bed.

In her own room, she drew her chair to the open window. The curtains billowed and twisted in the steady sea breeze. Beneath a full moon, the dunes and the sea seemed soft and ephemeral, turning light and dark with the shifting shadows.

Her thoughts returned to Mr. Peabody's visit, and her conscience pricked at her. Declaring that it was their duty to turn necessity into virtue, Papa had never refused to help others when asked. But he'd had far more resources than she did now. She wondered whether he was watching over her from heaven and whether he would understand her refusal of the minister's request.

Summer lightning flashed on the horizon, followed by a rumble of thunder. A gust of wind caught the door and slammed it shut. Normally she enjoyed a storm over the sea, but tonight the brewing weather felt ominous. She closed the windows against the first rush of rain and doused the light.

Fifteen

At the far end of the inlet a boat appeared. Charlotte waved and hurried to the end of the dock. As the boat neared, she saw that it was not Mr. Finch manning the oars but Trim.

He maneuvered the boat alongside the dock and held it fast. "Mornin', Miss Cha'lotte, and ain't it a fine day?"

"Good morning, Trim." She handed him her food basket, her parasol, her walking boots and gloves, then stepped into the boat. Evidently Trim had done some fishing on the way upriver; a basket of perch sat in the stern. "Where's Mr. Finch?"

With one oar he pushed the boat away from the dock, then set the oar in the lock and began to row. "He ain't here no mo', miss."

Her stomach dropped. "What do you mean he isn't here? Where has he gone?"

"Back home, far as we can tell."

"To North Carolina?"

"I reckon so. For a while now, he been feelin' lonesome for his kin. Said he couldn't get used to this swamp country. Needed to see him some hills, I 'spect."

"So he simply left without telling anyone?"

Trim shrugged. "He tol' Mr. Clifton, I reckon, because Mr. Clifton come on down the day before yesterday and took charge of things. Sent Lambert and me upland to hoe the crops. Then this mornin' he tol' me to fetch you from this island. He said Mr. Finch tol' him your boat done sprung a leak."

"Yes. I'm afraid so." She much preferred rowing herself, but several boards had rotted out on her rowboat, and fixing it was one more expense she couldn't bear just now. "What about my rice fields?"

"Can't say, miss. Ain't been down there in a coupla weeks." Trim guided the boat through a narrow cut where a family of turtles had lumbered onto a log to enjoy the warmth of the sun. "I wouldn't worry none, though. We've had tolerable good weather, no more bad freshets to wash away the rice. Leastways not yet. But Mr. Hadley come back from Georgetown yesterday and tol' Mr. Clifton the steamboat cap'n says they's a storm comin' in."

Sunlight glimmered in the trees, dappling the tea-colored water. Charlotte unfurled her parasol and considered Trim's warning. Should she turn back now? If a bad storm came ashore, she might well be trapped at Fairhaven for days with no way to reach Augusta and the girls. But sometimes storms blew themselves out at sea and caused no real damage. And now that Mr.

216

Finch had quit the Lowcountry without a moment's warning, she was more anxious than ever to check on things and to see whether any word from Nicholas awaited her.

They entered the river. Trim rowed smoothly, his concentration focused on his task. They passed neighboring plantations, some showing signs of occupation, others clearly abandoned. Seeing the overgrown properties filled her with worry. Perhaps she would be the next planter to lose everything.

She watched the curve of the river, eager for a glimpse of home. As they neared the dock, she saw splashes of color through the trees and her heart lifted. In her absence, her mother's old azaleas and the banksia roses had burst into riotous bloom.

The gate flew open and Daniel Graves raced down to the dock. He was as thin and shaggy-haired as ever, but he had grown taller and more muscular. His pants were too short by several inches, and his biceps strained the fabric of his threadbare shirt. "Miss Charlotte. Come and see what I did."

From her seat in the boat she smiled up at him. "Hello, Daniel." She handed him her walking boots and her parasol.

Trim held the boat steady while she disembarked. "Will you be needin' me this afternoon, miss?"

"Not until I'm ready to return to the beach. I

can row myself down to the new field after I've seen to things here."

He tied the boat to the dock. "I'll be back when the tide turns. Get you home befo' good dark."

"Thank you, Trim."

Daniel grabbed her hand. "Come on, Miss Charlotte. Wait'll you see."

She followed along the avenue toward the house. Daniel pointed. "Finished your barn while you was gone."

She stared at the small, neat building nestled among a grove of trees. "You built this all by yourself?"

"No, ma'am. Mr. Finch helped me some 'fore he lit out for home. But I finished it. Come and see."

She followed him across the yard and into the barn to find Cinnamon waiting. "Hello, my sweet." She nuzzled the little mare's face. "I missed you."

Daniel grinned. "I told her you were coming. I think she misses you too. There's a storm on the way, so I brought her up from the pasture this morning. Didn't want to take a chance of her gettin' caught in it."

"I'm so grateful you're looking after her. And the barn is wonderful."

"You like it?"

"Daniel, I'm amazed. I had no idea you knew how to build things."

"Well, Mr. Finch and Thomas showed me how

to frame it up, but I learned a lot outta them books in your library. I've read nearly ever' book you've got." He pointed. "I fixed your cart so's you don't have to take the wagon all the time. Me and Trim fixed the squeaky wheel too."

"Well, I can't thank you enough. I'll pay you for your labors."

"No, ma'am. You gave me a place to stay and books to read, and I reckon that's plenty."

"I hope you're finding the house more comfortable than the slave street."

"Yes'm. But there ain't much left of the slave street. Me and Mr. Finch used most all the lumber outta the cabins to build the barn. But I reckon I'll be moving on pretty soon anyway. The county is planning to hire a new teacher for the school up by Sandy Island come next term, and I aim to take advantage of it."

"Where will you live?"

"Haven't figgered out that part yet. But I've been saving the wages Mr. Finch paid me. I reckon I can rent me a room if I have to."

Charlotte smiled. Daniel might be rough around the edges, but his mind and his ambition were first rate. "If you need help, you mustn't hesitate to ask me. I'll do whatever I can to see that you get the education you want."

The boy blushed and ducked his head. "Clouds are buildin' up. If you're going down to your rice fields, I reckon you best get going."

Sixteen

Four pairs of brown eyes followed Charlotte as she moved to the head of the dining table. She jammed her hands into her pockets and forced a smile. Her plans had not included teaching Mr. Peabody's nieces and nephews. But the events of the past week had reminded her of just how little control she actually exerted over anything.

The evening of her last trip to Fairhaven, the storm Trim predicted had arrived with a vengeance, flooding the sugarcane field and upland gardens and claiming most of her rice crop. The morning after the storm she'd tied up her skirts and waded into the ruined field where broken tree limbs, bits of trash, and clumps of marsh grasses floated atop the tender shoots. A single oar swirled past before getting caught in the trunk.

Even now, she could feel the despair of that moment lodged deep in her heart. She had surveyed it all, sick at heart but dry-eyed, until the bloated carcass of a drowned fawn washed up onto the flooded road. Then exhaustion, coupled with the oppressive humid air and the bright sunlight falling across her ruined world, broke her, and the tears came.

Since her father's death she'd lived on little more than hope and courage. Standing knee-deep in the warm muck, heartbroken and helpless, she'd felt both slipping away. For the first time since returning to the Waccamaw, she'd questioned whether it was possible to go on.

But what other choice did she have?

Upon her return to the island, she'd sent word to Mr. Peabody that she was willing to teach his young charges twice a week for the rest of the summer. She dreaded the prospect of teaching more children, but the added responsibility would leave her less time to mourn her loss, less time to worry about her future. Besides, with her rice crop gone, she needed every penny.

She handed out books and papers the minister had provided and, for the sake of the children, attempted to maintain a cheerful countenance. She wrote the day and date on the chalkboard and a list of words gleaned from the books the minister had sent. Behind her, papers rustled as the four little Demeres took up pencils to practice their penmanship. She moved from one child to another, offering encouragement and quiet correction, but her thoughts were of the ruinous situation on the Waccamaw. Her fields weren't the only casualties, of course. Mr. Hadley and Mr. Clifton had suffered similar losses.

She reached into her pocket for the brass key she'd carried since the day she'd found it amid the detritus in her father's library. Perhaps it was foolish to hold on to something so useless, but somehow the feel of the cool metal in her hand brought her some small comfort, as if somehow the missing strongbox would turn up and inside would be the answer to her dilemma.

"Teacher, when are we going to start our reading lessons?" Five-year-old Susan Demere, the youngest of the quartet, looked up from the bench the minister had delivered after services on Sunday—along with two pine tables, the chalkboard, two wooden bookcases, an atlas, and some tattered books. He and a couple of men from Litchfield had carried it all inside, arranging the tables and benches beneath the tall windows that looked out onto the shady piazza and to the glittering sea beyond.

Charlotte smiled at the little girl and strove to inject a note of cheerfulness into her voice. "As soon as the Betancourt girls return from Miss Augusta's."

Augusta had been feeling poorly the past several days. This morning Charlotte had sent Marie-Claire and Anne-Louise across the dunes with jars of crab soup and tea. It was the least she could do to repay her friend for looking after the girls in her absence.

She took her seat at the front of the room and

reread the report from the children's previous teacher. Apparently Bess, age thirteen, excelled in arithmetic and geography but needed help with orthography and penmanship. The two boys, eleven-year-old John and eight-year-old Lucas, were average in reading and arithmetic and less proficient in everything else. Susan knew her alphabet and how to count to a hundred.

Charlotte's head pounded. What on earth had she done? It was one thing to tutor Nicholas Betancourt's daughters a couple of days a week, letting them take the lead in this brief time before they began boarding school. Teaching an entire family was quite another matter. She looked at their freckled, upturned faces, scrubbed clean and somber with grief, and felt all of her old insecurities rising up. They needed so much more than she could possibly provide.

The steady sea breeze billowed the curtains and ruffled the pages of the Bible lying open atop her writing desk. *Will you seek divine guidance?*

Well, she had sought guidance during her evening prayers, listening for some still, small voice, and this is where it had led. To a dining room filled with motherless children in need of every gift she could give them—mental, emotional, spiritual—at a time when she felt she had nothing left to give.

She recalled the summer her mother had died, here in this very house while she was banished to the care of friends in Charleston. How she had wept and prayed that her mother's life might be spared, only to have it slip away. In the face of her most recent losses, it was hard to believe either in divine providence or in the efficacy of one's own efforts.

Anne-Louise and Marie-Claire raced across the piazza and into the dining room. They took their seats without speaking and folded their hands atop the table, their eyes seeking hers. She felt a wave of sympathy for them. The first meeting with the Demere children had been strained. Anne-Louise in particular had been possessive of Charlotte and reluctant to share anything with the newcomers. Marie-Claire, clearly unhappy at no longer being the oldest, had retreated behind her books, refusing to speak unless spoken to.

Charlotte nodded to them and was rewarded with a wink from Anne-Louise. She led the children in a few songs and, after a reading lesson, set them to work on a set of arithmetic problems.

Lucas, the younger boy, began to cry, silent tears sliding down his freckled cheek. She knelt beside him, one hand on his thin shoulder. "What's the matter? Are you all right?"

He sniffed and pressed his pencil to a clean sheet of foolscap.

"We can work on arithmetic later. Would you like to choose a book to read instead?"

He shook his head.

"He'll be fine, miss," Bess said, finishing her own copying. "It isn't your fault. Luc cries all the time. Uncle James says we must let him cry it out."

Remembering her own grief at the loss of her mother, Charlotte nodded to Bess and patted the boy's shoulder. She glanced at Bess's paper, then checked on John. He had crammed the word list into one corner and filled the rest of the page with a fanciful drawing of gulls and dolphins. He hunched over the page as if to hide it from her eyes.

She smiled down at him. "It's all right. Your drawings are beautiful."

The boy's hand stilled and he looked up. "Pa always said drawing is a waste of time. He said I ought to be learning something useful."

"Perhaps your father never heard of John James Audubon. His book of bird drawings is considered the best in the world. I think it's one of the most beautiful books ever."

The boy brightened and looked around the makeshift schoolroom. "You got a copy?"

"I'm afraid not. Not anymore. But perhaps you'll find one in a library someday."

"Oh." He picked up his pencil and added more shading to his picture.

"Later we're going to the beach. Maybe you'll see some real specimens to copy."

He looked up at her, his expression a mixture

of interest and wariness. "I never heard of going to the beach during school time."

"Well, here at my school, I believe that studying the things we find most interesting helps us learn the things we most need to practice. From now on you will be our official journal keeper. I want you to make drawings of everything we see. Later we'll look them up in our dictionary, and that will help us with our reading and spelling."

She continued around the table, assigning each child a specific task before settling them on the piazza for a story from *Robert Merry's Museum*. A new magazine subscription was a luxury she could ill afford. But in addition to tales of adventure and articles about nature, it contained thinly veiled lessons on the importance of citizenship, good manners, honesty, and courage. Stories of brave children making sacrifices for the good of others were more likely to impress her charges than any lesson she might deliver.

The children ate their lunches before gathering their things and setting off for the beach, Charlotte in the lead. Marie-Claire, eager to reestablish her position within the group, ran to the front of the line, then turned to face the rest while she walked backward across the hot sand. "Miss Fraser says right here is where the Gray Man walks when there's going to be a hurricane." She pointed toward the tall dunes. "He's a ghost, and he comes to warn people to get off the island. If you don't, you might get swallowed by an enormous wave."

Susan slipped her hand into Charlotte's. "Miss Fraser, are ghosts real?"

"I've never seen one," Charlotte said. "I think ghost tales and such are meant to entertain us rather than to make us afraid."

"Like 'The Legend of Sleepy Hollow,' " Lucas reminded his little sister. "Remember when Mama used to read us that—"

"Look," Anne-Louise interrupted. "A dolphin."

A hundred yards offshore, one dolphin, then two, arced above the waves.

"John, where is your paper?" Charlotte asked. But the boy was already on his knees in the sand, his hand moving quickly across the page. Susan let go of Charlotte's hand and ran to the water's edge, oblivious to the surging waves gathering just a few yards away.

Charlotte shouted to the girl and motioned her toward the shore, but the dolphins claimed the child's attention and she turned away just as a wave knocked her off her feet. Charlotte ran over and plucked her from the surf. "Are you all right?"

The little girl let out a deep gurgling laugh and wriggled free. "That was the most fun ever."

"I'm glad you're having fun, but the first rule of living by the sea is never to turn your back on the water. You can be swept away before you know it. You must obey me right away when we're down here, or you shan't be allowed to come with us again. Do you understand?"

Susan nodded.

"Very well. Now let's see what treasures you can discover on the beach."

Twenty minutes later Charlotte clapped her hands to get the children's attention and they went back to the cottage, where they spent the rest of the afternoon at their assigned projects. Marie-Claire retreated behind her poetry book. The two boys finished their arithmetic assignment. Bess quietly finished her own work and helped Susan look up the names of the shells she'd collected, then showed the younger girl how to write each one. Presently the minister arrived with his wagon to take them home. The children helped tidy the room, shouted a good-bye, and raced outside.

"Whew, I'm glad that's over." Marie-Claire collapsed onto the hard bench and cradled her chin in her hands. "I liked it much better when it was just the three of us."

"Me too," Anne-Louise said. "Those boys are exhausting."

Charlotte laughed. "At least they aren't rowdy, like some of the boys in the county school."

"I guess John and Luke are too sad to misbehave," Marie-Claire said, her sweet face suddenly clouded. "They miss their parents, like we miss ours." She looked up at Charlotte. "Tell me the truth. Is Papa dead?"

"I have had no such news, and we must not even think that. New Orleans is a very busy place these days." She caught the girl's chin in her hand and spoke the words she prayed were true. "He will be home as soon as he can. You'll see."

"That's what you said last week and the week before that." Anne-Louise heaved a sigh. "I wish he would hurry up. I've mostly forgot what our house looks like."

"Me too," her sister said. "But just the same, I like it here at the beach. Don't you, Ma'm'selle?"

"I've always loved this island and Pelican Cottage. But I love Fairhaven too." She gazed out at the sea and her fingers closed over the brass key in her pocket.

"Yoo-hoo! Hello! Is anyone home?" A woman's voice drifted across the dunes.

"Somebody's coming." Marie-Claire rose from the bench and ran to the door.

"I hope it's Miss Augusta," Anne-Louise said. "She promised to help me make a rag doll as soon as she feels better."

At the door, Marie-Claire curtsied to the visitor and said, "Good afternoon. Welcome to Pelican Cottage. Won't you please come inside?"

Charlotte nodded her approval of the girl's perfect manners but couldn't stop herself from blurting a very unladylike, "Josie Clifton? What are you doing here?"

Josie swished inside and turned in a circle,

taking in the makeshift classroom and the sparsely furnished parlor. Without waiting for an invitation, she plopped onto the settee and took out her fan. "What's going on here?"

Briefly Charlotte explained the situation.

"Well, I suppose you may as well become a schoolmarm now that the storm has nearly wiped all of us off the map. Poor Father is ready to give up. He's the one who insisted we occupy Oakwood Hall, to keep it out of the Yankees' hands, but I heard him tell Mr. Hadley he's thinking of going out west. To Colorado, maybe— or all the way to California."

Charlotte caught Marie-Claire's eye. "Perhaps you and your sister would like to play on the beach for a bit. Just don't go too far."

"We won't," the girls answered in unison. They ran outside, pulling the door closed behind them.

"I'm afraid I haven't any refreshments ready." Charlotte settled into the chair next to the window overlooking the salt marsh. "I wasn't expecting visitors."

"Oh, I don't mind. I can't stay long. Mother and I had one of Father's men row us over because Mother wanted to visit Mrs. Banks, but she isn't at home. So Mother is paying a call on Mrs. Weston instead, and she is so dreadfully stuffy that I decided to visit you." Josie smoothed her skirt. "Not that I wasn't dying to see you too. But everyone else around here is old as Methuselah, and all they want to talk about is how things were in the old days." She patted her ringlets and sighed. "It's all so tiresome I could cry."

"What about your friends the Kirks? I believe you said Mr. Kirk's niece is about your age."

"Yes, but all Patsy Kirk wants to talk about is marrying Nathaniel Venable. She never wants to talk about *my* romantic prospects."

Charlotte smiled. "How are things in Charleston?"

Josie snapped open her fan. "We stayed there for a while, but then Mother insisted we visit our cousins in North Carolina. Now that the storm has ruined the rice, though, we're closing up the house, and Mother insisted on coming back to supervise things."

The girls burst through the door, the hems of their skirts damp and covered with sand, their hair tangled and windblown. Anne-Louise carried a clump of seaweed that dripped salt water onto the floor. "Ma'm'selle, we found a poor little skimmer. Look."

She showed Charlotte the lifeless body of the bird caught in the seaweed, then turned to show it to Josie. "See, his beak is broken. Maybe he couldn't eat anything, and that's why he died."

Josie wrinkled her nose and pushed the child away. "Get that slimy thing away from me. It's disgusting."

"No it isn't. It's beautiful." Marie-Claire stroked

231

the bird's feathers. "And sad. I wish we could have saved the dear little thing."

"We're going to give him a proper funeral," Anne-Louise said, her expression solemn. "On the beach at sunset. You must come, Ma'm'selle." She turned to Josie. "And you too, miss."

Charlotte patted the child's arm. "I wouldn't miss it for anything. Now, please excuse me while I visit with Miss Clifton."

Anne-Louise planted an impulsive kiss on Charlotte's cheek and the girls returned to the beach.

"My heavens." Josie frowned. "Those two are like wild Indians. I understood that Mr. Betancourt hired you to turn them into ladies." She fanned her face and laughed. "Forgive me, Charlotte, but it doesn't seem you've quite succeeded."

Charlotte tamped down her irritation. "Marie-Claire greeted you perfectly when you arrived. I sent them out to play because I know you aren't fond of children. It's hard to walk the beach without getting dirty."

"Well, if I were in charge, I would have sent them to their rooms."

"No doubt." Charlotte watched the sunlight playing across the marsh grasses. "You were saying?"

"That we're quitting the Waccamaw for greener pastures. Or so Father thinks."

"Will you be going out west with your parents?"

Josie shook her head. "My father wants me to, of course. He thinks my marriage prospects might be better out there, but I am not about to wed some roughshod rancher. Or, heaven forbid, a grizzled old gold prospector."

Charlotte hid a smile. Josie was only seven years her junior, but sometimes she seemed more like a child than a young woman of nearly seventeen. "From what I hear, the gold prospecting days are past. I think it might be exciting to see someplace new."

"I don't care. I still have my hopes for Mr. Betancourt—if he ever returns from looking for his land grant in New Orleans."

Charlotte froze. She had never mentioned Nicholas's trip to the girl. But perhaps he himself had shared his plans with Mr. Clifton.

"How did you know Mr. Betancourt is in New Orleans?"

Josie blushed. Her fan stilled. "Why . . . I suppose you must have mentioned it that day in Georgetown."

Charlotte waited as her flustered guest continued to fidget, first with her fan and then with the satin ribbons on her hat.

Finally Josie said, "Oh, wait. Now I remember. Mrs. Hadley told me about it at church, shortly after her birthday party."

"But Mr. Betancourt made his plans much later than that. And Mrs. Hadley left Alder Hill quite

233

early this summer to look after her sister's family."

"Oh, all right." Josie got to her feet, sending her reticule and fan sliding onto the floor. "If you must know, I . . . I took the letter you posted to him from Georgetown."

Charlotte gaped at her guest. "You stole my letter?"

"I didn't intend to. I happened to see it lying on the counter when I went to post a letter to my cousins and, well, you refused to press my case with Mr. Betancourt, and besides, I was curious, so I . . ."

She burst into tears.

"Oh, Josie."

"You don't know what it's like," Josie said between sobs. "You don't care one whit about marriage, but I do. And there is no one else as handsome and charming as Mr. Betancourt, even if he is older than I would wish and already a father."

"You're wrong about me," Charlotte said evenly. "I want very much to have a husband and a family." She retrieved Josie's reticule, opened it, and extracted a handkerchief. "Here."

Josie sniffed and wiped her eyes.

"You have done both Mr. Betancourt and me a grave disservice," Charlotte said. "You've purloined my private correspondence and prevented Mr.

234

Betancourt from knowing the whereabouts of his children."

Josie shrugged and blew her nose. "You can send him another letter."

"I certainly shall. As soon as possible."

"You won't tell him about . . . that I . . ."

"No. I'll leave that to you."

The young woman blushed and retrieved her fan. "I must be going. Mother will be waiting."

Holding her skirts above the incoming tide, Josie hurried along the beach.

Seventeen

In a small depression at the base of the dunes, Marie-Claire dug a hole. Anne-Louise carefully laid the dead skimmer inside.

"Ashes to ashes, and dust to dust," the older child intoned as both girls filled the hole with sand.

Charlotte looked down at her in surprise. "Where did you learn that?"

"Papa told us it's what the priest said when they buried *Maman*." With her bare foot Marie-Claire pushed more sand into the hole. "We always say 'ashes to ashes' when we play funeral."

Anne-Louise nodded, her eyes bright. "We used to play it a lot, but not so much since we have you, Ma'm'selle."

The little girl smiled and caught Charlotte's hand. Charlotte smiled back, but misgivings crowded her mind. Both girls seemed happy here—and happy to have someone dependable to look after their needs. Anne-Louise in particular. Charlotte felt a growing closeness with them too. What would happen when Nicholas returned to claim them?

The tide was in. A freshening breeze stirred the sea oats as the light faded into the golden edge of evening. Marie-Claire, her dark hair blowing about her small face, dusted off her hands. "The skimmer is properly buried, and I am about to perish. When can we eat, Ma'm'selle?"

Anne-Louise leaned against Charlotte. "I don't feel like eating."

Charlotte placed a hand on the girl's forehead. "Perhaps you got too much sun today. You'll feel better when you cool off. Let's go inside and—"

"Here comes Mr. Peabody." Marie-Claire pointed to a rider pounding along in the surf. She frowned. "He sure is in an awful hurry."

The minister reined in and dismounted. "Miss Fraser." He paused to catch his breath. "Have you seen Susan? She's gone missing."

"I haven't seen her, but surely she would not have come this far on her own." Charlotte spoke calmly, but her heart stuttered in her chest. A five-year-old girl unaccustomed to the capricious power of the ocean could be swept away in the blink of an eye. She shaded her eyes and looked out at the rolling surf.

"Merciful God," the minister said. "You don't think she's out there?"

"I pray not. The beach is well traveled this time of year, with many people coming and going. I'm sure someone would have seen her had she ventured so far." She brushed her hair from her eyes. "What happened?"

"She fell asleep in the wagon on the way home. I stopped just for a moment to call on Mrs. Newton, who has been ailing lately. Afterward I drove on back to the parsonage. When we got there, I realized Susan was missing."

"The other children didn't see where she went?"

He shook his head. "John and Lucas didn't want to wait while I called on my parishioner, so they asked whether they could go on ahead on foot. It wasn't far and I didn't see why not. Bess was riding up front with me, and I suppose it never occurred to her to turn around and check on her sister." His voice broke. "After everything those children have been through lately, I simply cannot . . ." His Adam's apple jerked up and down. "We must find her. She doesn't know anyone on the island except you. I'm guessing if she got lost, she'd try to come here."

"Of course. The girls and I will walk the beach and call on our neighbors. Maybe someone saw her. Perhaps you could check behind the house, along the marshes and the dock. You'll see the old salt works at the far end of the marsh. She might have gone into the shed there."

They separated, calling out for Susan as they went. The Westons' cottage was dark, but a light glowed in Augusta's window. Charlotte's knock was answered by a surprisingly hearty-looking

Augusta, who beamed to see them and invited them in, insisting that Charlotte's soup had worked wonders. But her smile disappeared when she learned the reason for the visit.

"I haven't seen her—been indoors all day," Augusta said. "But I'll look around. Sometimes children play beneath the piazzas. If I find the girl, I'll bring her to Pelican Cottage straightaway."

Half an hour later Charlotte and the girls returned to the cottage. No one had seen a small brown-eyed girl in the pink calico dress. Though darkness was approaching, the minister was still out searching.

Charlotte sent the girls to wash up and fed them a cold supper of cheese, bread, and figs. She settled them with their books. "I'm going to see whether Mr. Peabody has found Susan. I won't be long."

She left by the back door and crossed the porch that faced the salt marsh, praying that Susan had not become lost somewhere along the tidal creek. In addition to snakes, snapping turtles, and mosquitoes, the creek was home to alligators. June was nesting season, and the females were protective of their eggs. Anyone who happened to stumble upon a nesting female wouldn't stand a chance.

A faint sound came to her on the evening breeze. A whimper? A whisper? "Susan?"

"I'm up here, miss."

Charlotte spun around. "Up where?"

"On the roof."

Charlotte looked up to see Susan crouched on the slick tin roof, both hands splayed.

"Stay there. I'm coming up." Why hadn't she thought to look there sooner? At one end of the back porch, a narrow rudimentary stairway led to the attic, which in turn led to a wooden trapdoor that opened onto the roof. Those stairs had been irresistible in her childhood, beckoning her to a clear vista of the endless sea and the star-strewn sky.

She clambered up and found Susan, tired and tear-stained but otherwise unharmed. She sat down beside the child to catch her breath. Relief and anger warred inside her. "Do you know everyone is looking for you?"

"I didn't mean to cause trouble. I only wanted to see where the steps went to. And then when I got up here, everything looked so pretty."

Despite her irritation, Charlotte smiled. "I know. The view from here captivated me too when I was your age. But it isn't safe to go climbing on rooftops. My papa punished me more than once for coming up here after he told me not to."

"What's captivated?"

"Never mind. Why didn't you come down when you heard us calling for you?"

The child's thin shoulders moved up and down. "When Mama died, Uncle James told us

240

she went to heaven and got her crown of stars. I thought if I got closer to heaven I might could see her. But I didn't."

"No. When the people we love leave us, we can't see them anymore. But we can feel the love they left behind."

"I tried to get down when I saw Uncle James. But the roof was slippery, and I was afraid."

Charlotte placed an arm around the child's waist. "Hold on to me. Let's get you onto terra firma and find your uncle."

Pelican Cottage
Pawley's Island

June 29, 1868
Yesterday the Reverend Mr. Peabody apprised us of his new charitable endeavor. The sale of ice cream, which was undertaken at the start of the summer, has yielded respectable results, but the small church on Litchfield Plantation lacks enough volunteers to see the venture through to summer's end. I am fairly certain that more than a little ice cream wound up in the bellies of the island's children as free samples, though no one begrudges them this small luxury on the heels of so many years of hardship.

The new project involves the sewing of garments for distribution to the missionaries in China. To this end Mr. Peabody has secured a goodly amount of sturdy cotton fabric, which the ladies will sew into shirtwaists and skirts, shirts, and trousers. Having no live models, we must guess at the appropriate lengths of sleeves and hems. I received ten yards of blue calico and five yards of white cambric, which I shall endeavor to turn into passable garments.

As the fabric was being distributed, I was reminded of my early years at Fairhaven, when all of our bondsmen and their families came to the house to receive material for their new clothes.

On New Year's Day, rolls of white homespun, red flannel, calico, and a heavier material my mother called "plains" were laid out on the piazza along with a variety of buttons, needles, and thread. Each woman, when my mother read out her name, came forward to receive one roll of red flannel and two rolls each of white homespun, colored homespun, and calico. Each man received one red flannel, two white homespun, two rolls of a dark-colored cloth called jeans, and one white plains. I helped distribute the blankets. One year the men got new blankets; the next year, the women; the next, the children. In this way, each household had some new blankets every year.

On the day after New Year's, each child appeared before our seamstress, a tall, light-skinned woman named Welcome. The girls received homespun for the sewing of everyday clothes and calico for their Sunday frocks. With my mother, I watched as Welcome held the end of a roll of homespun on top of the child's head, brought the material down to the floor and up again. My mother told me this measure would make one full garment without any waste.

Once a year, my father gathered strips of wood, upon which every servant's foot had been measured, and sent them to a shoe factor in Charleston. The factor obtained the correct number of pair of each size and shipped them to Fairhaven for distribution on the third day after New Year's. I still remember the excitement in the slave street when word came that the new shoes had arrived.

My father at one time had under his care more than six hundred men, women, and children. Our present endeavors for the Reverend Mr. Peabody's missionaries are on a much smaller scale. This is fortunate for me, for despite my Aunt Livinia's tutoring during the war, I lack any real skill with needle and—

"Hello? Miss Fraser?"

Charlotte set down her pen and went to the door, which was open to the ocean breeze. "Daniel?"

He grinned. "Surprised to see me?"

"Yes, but always happy to have you visit."

He glanced at her papers. "I'm interruptin' your work."

"It doesn't matter. I'm writing another article in hopes the newspaper in New York might resume publication one of these days." She motioned him inside "What brings you here?"

He proffered a crate of tomatoes, corn, and beans. "Garden's coming in better'n we thought it would after that storm. We got lots of tomatoes. Trim was supposed to deliver 'em, but his wife is sick. Mr. Hadley sent me instead."

"Mr. Hadley is well, then?"

"Sometimes he is and sometimes he ain't. When he's feelin' poorly, me and Trim keep things going. Trim says Mr. Hadley won't ever be the same."

"I suppose not." Charlotte inhaled the aroma

of the freshly picked tomatoes. "Thank you for bringing these over."

"No trouble. Being out on the river is more fun than picking corn any day of the week." He dropped his worn haversack onto the floor and looked around, eyes bright with curiosity. "I always wondered what this place looked like."

"It isn't the same as in the years before the war, but I don't mind. Being so close to the sea more than compensates for the lack of niceties. Would you like some refreshment? I imagine you're tired after the long row."

"Yes'm, if it ain't too much trouble, I could use somethin' to wet my whistle."

She took the vegetables to the back porch, found a glass, and poured cool water for Daniel. "Let's sit on the piazza. The girls just finished their lessons and are trying their hand at kite building with some help from our neighbor."

"Is she the gray-haired lady wearing men's boots?"

"She is indeed. I don't know what I'd do without Augusta. She looks after the girls when I have to be away." Charlotte led the way outside, and they sat in the ancient rocking chairs. "Now, what news have you?"

"Well, Mr. Clifton and his missus have packed up and moved back to Charleston. Mr. Clifton wants to head out west, but I don't think his wife wants to go." Daniel took a long gulp of water.

"His daughter sure don't. I overheard her arguin' with her daddy that he was ruining her chances to marry Mr. Betancourt. I didn't even know they was courtin'."

Charlotte laughed. "I had no idea you were interested in such things."

He shrugged his now-familiar Daniel shrug. "Anyway, me and Mr. Hadley stopped at Fairhaven on Saturday, on the way back from Georgetown. We cleared away some broken tree limbs and fixed the trunk in the field downriver."

"I hope he's paying you for all your hard work."

"Yes'm. I'm savin' as much as I can. Anyway, Mr. Hadley says you'll likely harvest a few barrels of rice from that one. And he says you might be able to plant a late crop if you're willing to take a chance on it coming in before the frost."

She sighed. "Oh, Daniel, I think I'm through taking chances."

"Mr. Hadley says a small harvest is better than nothing. He's going to plant again." Daniel drained his glass and set it down beside his chair. "Haven't seen your old peacock in a while. Cinnamon had a touch of colic again, but I dosed her with the aconite, and now she's right as rain. And I fixed the latch on the barn door the other day."

"I appreciate everything you and Mr. Hadley have done. But I don't expect you to keep up the place in my absence."

"Well, I built that barn mostly by myself, so I sort of feel responsible for it."

She sent him an approving glance. What a fool his father was for abandoning a boy with such promise.

"I got a letter from my pa," he said.

"You did?" She stared at him, surprised. "When?"

Just then Anne-Louise gave a shout, and Charlotte looked out to see a red-and-white kite struggling to take flight. Marie-Claire laughed. Augusta stood between them, ankle-deep in sand, one hand clamped onto her hat.

"Couple of days after the storm," Daniel said. "Me and Mr. Clifton were in the potato field, and Lucy Wainwright's daddy come down on his mule and handed it to me."

Charlotte smiled at the memory of the girl she'd found hiding with Daniel in the slave street. "How is Lucy? Has she embarked upon any more spy missions lately?"

"Not that I know of. Anyway, Mr. Wainwright said a Yankee fellow named Mr. Kelley who works for the government gave him my letter. Turns out Pa got a job working at a boatyard up north, and he wants me to come and work there too."

"Daniel, that's wonderful. When do you leave?"

"That's just it, ma'am. I like working with Mr. Hadley and looking after Fairhaven. I've been helping out at the Kirks' place too, up in the pinelands. It's real pretty up there, and Mr. Hadley says a person could live there year-round because mosquitoes don't like it up there. Anyway, I'm figgerin' on staying around for a while. I like being on my own."

"But you're still so young. And perhaps working in the boatyard will help you achieve your dream of owning a passenger vessel some-day."

"Maybe. You never can tell with Pa. My mama always said he was born with a restless streak that makes it hard to set much store by what he says. What if I travel all that way and then he up and takes off again? I wouldn't know a soul for a hundred miles."

"I see your point. Still, you'd have a chance to attend a real school if you went. If you get an education, you won't be dependent upon your father's whims. You'll be equipped to make your own way in the world."

"I reckon." He paused. "Miss Fraser, could I ask you a favor?"

"Of course."

"Mr. Hadley said you've got a salt works some-where around here."

"Yes, down on the marsh. But it hasn't been in use since the war."

"Could you show me how it works?"

"I doubt it works now, but I can show it to you. Why are you interested?"

248

"I'm thinking about buildin' one. Mr. Kelley told Lucy's pa that if the rice planters start cultivating other crops, more people might be interested in moving south, and we might get a new railroad that would go from Charleston all the way up to Wilmington. I figure if I had me a salt works, I could ship salt to every town on the rail line."

"You are a wonder, Daniel Graves. I'm sure I do not know where all those ideas come from."

He laughed. "From all the books in your library."

"Let me get my hat and tell Augusta where we're going." Charlotte retrieved her straw hat and hurried down the beach to speak to Augusta. She led Daniel around to the back of the house and down to the salt marsh, where fiddler crabs and a pair of egrets foraged for food in the pungent pluff mud exposed by the ebbing tide and fish darted through the shallow water.

"There once was a scaffold right here," Charlotte said. "With a pump and a wooden trough to move the seawater to the boilers."

Daniel peered into an empty shed. "I don't see the boilers."

"They were in the forest, a few hundred yards down that way." She indicated the general direction. "They're probably completely rusted out by now—and the Federals shelled them pretty regularly during the war. My father's bondsmen were in charge of the salt works, so I don't know much more about it, except that Father said it was best to pump the water at flood tide."

"How come?"

"The water had more salt in it then and less of the seepage from the marsh. When I was about your age, men from all over the Lowcountry came here to buy salt or barter for it. It was a scarce commodity back then. One year we earned more than seven thousand dollars from the sale of it."

Daniel let out a low whistle. "Seven thousand? That's a lot of money." He brushed away a dragonfly that had landed on his sleeve. "Reckon I'd need something sturdy for the boilers to set on."

"Ours were mounted on bricks, with the furnace down below."

"Don't seem all that hard to build one. Thanks for showing me around." He swung his haversack onto his shoulder and glanced toward the dock, where his rowboat swayed and knocked against the gray wooden pier. "I oughta be getting back. Sun will be setting soon."

She followed Daniel to the dock. She barely knew the boy, but she felt responsible for him. "You will let me know whether you decide to join your father? I'll need to arrange for someone to take care of Cinnamon."

He jumped lightly into the rowboat. "Yes'm. I'm thinking I'll stay put, but if I change my mind

I'll make sure your mare is looked after. And anyway, I wouldn't leave without saying good-bye."

She nodded, thinking of her ruined rice fields and Mr. Hadley's suggestion to replant. She looked out over the marshland, torn between despair and hope. "Ask Mr. Hadley to plant my first rice field again if he can. I'll be over there soon to pay him for the seed and the workers' wages."

"That's the spirit, ma'am." Daniel grinned as he set the oars into the locks. "Oh, I nearly forgot. I picked up the newspaper when I was in town. I already read it, so I thought you might like to have it." He took it from his haversack and handed it up to her. Then he pushed off into the creek and was soon lost from view among the marsh grasses.

Charlotte headed back to the house, unfolding the paper as she went. The front page was taken up with news of the coming inauguration of the new governor, Mr. Scott, who had been swept into office on a strong Negro vote. The Republican takeover of the statehouse was only the latest outrage among the planters, the main topic of conversation these days.

She turned the page and went stock-still as she read the headline, her stomach plummeting, her heart knocking hard against her ribs.

Eighteen

Pelican Cottage
Pawley's Island, SC
June 30, 1868
General James Longstreet
New Orleans, Louisiana

General Longstreet,

I write to you on a matter of utmost urgency. My employer and your friend from the war, Nicholas Betancourt, departed Georgetown District, South Carolina, in mid-May, bound for your home in New Orleans. I have had no word from him since, and a letter I sent him in your care went unanswered.

The local newspaper of Thursday last brings news of the yellow-fever epidemic in your city. I pray for your health, General, for the health of all the citizens, and of course for that of Mr. Betancourt, whose two small daughters remain in my care and who are anxious for his safe return.

I'm writing in the hope that this letter will find its way to your door and to Mr. Betancourt. His children and I would be most grateful for any news of him.

Charlotte signed and sealed the letter and tucked it into her desk drawer just as Marie-Claire rushed inside, bare feet slapping against the wood floor. "Guess what, Ma'm'selle? Some men are fighting down on the beach."

"Fighting?" Charlotte rose from her chair. "Where's your sister?"

"Over at Miss Augusta's. They're making a rag doll." Marie-Claire raked a tangle of dark hair off her face. "Mrs. Banks says the men are fighting about Independence Day. She says Mr. Banks is angry about the election of that horrid Yankee, Mr. Scott, and that we ought not even celebrate Independence Day at all. But we are celebrating, aren't we, Ma'm'selle? Anne-Louise and I want to go fishing and make a bonfire and watch the fireworks. You said we could. You promised."

"I know I did." She sighed. Politics aside, the last thing she felt like doing was celebrating. Nicholas might be taken ill, or worse. An outbreak of the fever could decimate a city in a matter of days. She turned away so Marie-Claire wouldn't see the worry in her eyes. "We'll carry on with our plans regardless of what others choose to do."

Marie-Claire beamed.

"Now, please tell Anne-Louise it's time to make lunch."

She went out to the kitchen to prepare the vegetables Daniel had brought. After their meal she settled the girls at the table with their books and their needlework and began sewing a shirt for the missionaries. Her needle plied the cloth in slow, uncertain stitches, her thoughts rattling around in her head like marbles in a jar. If Nicholas was alive, he would have written by now. If he had fallen ill, or worse, surely General Longstreet or someone would have sent word. Perhaps Nicholas had written and even now the letter was waiting for her in Georgetown.

She finished off a sleeve, knotted the thread, and snipped it. Papa had counseled patience and faith. But as she watched the sun slipping down the summer sky, all she felt was fear.

"Here come the Demeres." Marie-Claire turned from the window and let the curtain fall back into place. "I hope Bess remembered to bring her birding book."

The first day of July had arrived clear and white-hot on a sultry breeze that stirred the curtains at the open windows. At ebb tide, the calm sea mirrored the sun-bleached sky. Charlotte closed her book, eager to begin her lessons before the heat became unbearable.

Mr. Peabody halted the wagon, and the children piled off like ants from an anthill. Charlotte went to the door to usher them inside. John and Lucas ran to the table, leaving Bess and Susan behind.

Charlotte waved to the minister. "May I speak to you for a moment?"

He dropped lightly to the ground. She hurried down the steps to meet him.

"Miss Fraser. Looks like we're in for a hot one today."

"Yes." From her pocket she extracted the letter she'd written the day before. "I must ask a favor."

"Anything. The missus and I couldn't manage the children and our work without your help."

She pressed the letter into his hand. "Please post this for me right away. It's important."

He glanced at the address. "General Longstreet?"

"I'm worried about Mr. Betancourt." Briefly she summarized the article about the yellow-fever outbreak and Nicholas's friendship with the general. "With the telegraph lines still so unreliable, I can't think of any other sure way to reach Mr. Betancourt. He should have returned many weeks ago. I fear the worst."

"Then we must pray." He bowed his head. She followed suit but found it hard to feel anything. Until the war came to her door, she had always believed God was watching over all of creation. Now she wasn't so sure. How could she trust a

God who would allow such pain and horror? Such unspeakable suffering and loss?

"Amen." The preacher set his hat on his head and tucked her letter into his pocket. "I'll see that your letter leaves Georgetown at once, even if I have to take it clear down there myself."

"Thank you."

He climbed onto the wagon. "It's the least I can do. I don't think I ever thanked you properly for rescuing Susan from your roof. I must say the child gave me quite a turn."

"I'm glad she was unharmed." She glanced toward the cottage, where Bess and Susan stood on the piazza watching a gaggle of shorebirds scurrying along the sand. "The experience seems not to have affected her enthusiasm for learning."

"John has certainly taken to his lessons too. He seemed to be in trouble quite a bit at his former school. Nowadays I have to tear him away from his books to do his chores."

"I believe he may have a future as an illustrator. He's nearly worn down his pencils and the charcoal I gave him. If he had some proper pens and ink . . ."

"I'll see to it the next time I'm in town." Mr. Peabody slapped the reins against the horse's rump. "Good day, Miss Fraser. Please try not to worry. Mr. Betancourt is in God's hands—as we all are."

She returned to the house to find Marie-Claire

and Anne-Louise reading together. Bess had taken her place at the table and was helping Lucas read a magazine story. John, predictably, was already bent over his paper, sketching the seascape beyond the window. Susan was in the parlor running her fingers over the embroidered stitches on the settee.

Charlotte knelt beside her. "Good morning, Susan."

"Hello, miss."

"I see you're admiring the flowers."

"I like the purple ones."

"Those are violets. And these pink ones are primroses." Charlotte stood and held out her hand. "Now take your chair, please."

"I don't want to."

Charlotte suppressed an impatient retort. "Sometimes we all must do things we don't like to do," she said evenly. "Come along now. We mustn't keep everyone waiting."

Susan let out a long sigh and followed Charlotte across the hall to the dining room. She climbed onto her chair and leaned her head against Charlotte's waist while Charlotte picked up her chalk and wrote the day's word list on the chalkboard.

"Good morning, everyone. Please put away your reading and take out your paper and pencils. As soon as everyone has copied this list, we're going outside."

John's eyes widened. "Before arithmetic?"

"Before arithmetic. Later on it will be too hot to be out of doors. Besides, the tide is going out. We should see what we can discover in the tidal pools."

Ten minutes later, armed with glass jars for collecting specimens and sticks for digging in the sand, the children raced across the dunes and onto the beach. Lucas and John dropped onto their knees near a shallow pool and began scooping water. The four girls, their skirts carefully hitched up, continued a few yards farther along the beach, stopping now and then to peer into the tidal pools.

Charlotte fastened her straw hat securely beneath her chin and sat among the dunes, a book open on her lap. In happier times she had spent entire afternoons reading and watching the play of sunlight upon the water. But today her thoughts were too troubled. She closed her eyes and tried to empty her mind.

"Charlotte?"

She jerked and looked up to find Augusta peering down at her.

"Hello, Augusta." She waved a hand toward her six charges. "We're studying marine life today."

"So I see." Augusta lowered her tall frame onto the sand and took a jar of tea and two cups from her wicker basket. "I saw the children running around and figured you'd be close by." She poured tea and handed Charlotte a cup, her faded-blue eyes full of concern. "I suppose you heard about the altercation that took place over at the Bankses' cottage."

Charlotte nodded. "Marie-Claire told me."

"Politics is absolutely ruining this summer," Augusta said. "Even Mrs. Banks has taken up the cause. It's all she wants to talk about these days."

"What cause?"

"Why, defeating the Yankees who are bound to run for Congress now that we've been granted representation again. Not to mention keeping Ulysses Grant from winning the presidency."

Charlotte's gaze swept the beach as she counted heads. Lucas and John were sitting on the sand, poring over their collection of seashells. The two Demere girls were digging in the sand next to the tidal pool, but Marie-Claire and Anne-Louise had abandoned their quest for specimens in favor of building a sand castle. They were completely absorbed in their task, their heads bent over their task, all pretense of learning abandoned. A moment later Marie-Claire got to her feet and disappeared into the dunes with her tin bucket.

"Surely you've heard that Congress is about to vote on amending the Constitution to grant citizenship to the Negroes."

"I read it in the paper. But I don't see the point of getting involved in politics since we women can't vote anyway."

Augusta frowned. "But all the same, it behooves

us to influence the men in whatever ways we can."

"I've been too busy to keep up." Charlotte sipped her tea. "Besides, even the newspaper editors seem to think it doesn't matter much what we Southerners want. They say we're a defeated people with little say in what happens."

Susan raced across the beach and dropped to her knees in the sand. "Miss Fraser, look what I found." She handed Charlotte a cluster of tiny bright-green leaves. "Aren't they pretty?"

"Very pretty."

"They're a present. For you."

The little girl leaned down and patted Charlotte's shoulder.

Anne-Louise hurried over and plopped down on Charlotte's other side. She tugged on Charlotte's arm. "Ma'm'selle, guess what? I just saw a pirate."

"You did? That's very interesting. Later you can tell me all about it. Right now I'm talking to Miss Augusta, and it isn't polite to interrupt when ladies are visiting."

"But he almost kidnapped me. I had to fight him off with my enchanted sword. I ran him off, and he swam out to his ship and sailed all the way to New Orleans. I'm probably going to get a medal for saving the whole island."

Charlotte frowned. It wasn't like Anne-Louise to tell such fanciful tales. She glanced at Augusta, who merely smiled and shrugged. "You have

260

quite an imagination today, Anne-Louise. Perhaps we should write down your story and submit it to Mr. Merry's magazine."

Anne-Louise shot to her feet, arms akimbo, her expression dark. "You don't believe me."

"Anne-Louise Betancourt, you know perfectly well you did not confront a pirate on this beach today."

The girl dropped her gaze and kicked at the sand.

"What on earth has gotten into you? I want you and Susan to join the other children while I visit with Miss Augusta. Later we will talk about the importance of truth telling."

"But—"

"Go. Both of you." Charlotte brushed sand from her skirts as the girls turned away. "I'm sorry, Augusta. I don't know what possessed Anne-Louise. She's not in the habit of lying."

Augusta watched as the two girls raced along the sand. "If I had to venture a guess, I'd put it down to pure old jealousy. Perhaps a bit of fear."

"Jealousy? Whatever for?"

"Right now you are all Anne-Louise and her sister have in the world. Perhaps she's afraid you'll care more for the Demere children than for them. Her pirate story was simply a way of getting your attention. I wouldn't make too much of it."

"I cannot allow her to become untruthful."

"Of course not. Just don't be too hard on her."

Augusta drained her cup and returned it to her basket. "I must go. I promised to stop by the Bankses' cottage this afternoon. Mary Banks's cousin, Mrs. Rutledge, is visiting from Charleston. Mrs. Banks says Mrs. Rutledge wishes to discuss the current political situation and what we might be able to do."

"I'm sure you'll enjoy visiting. But discussing politics is a waste of time." Charlotte got to her feet and brushed more sand from her skirts. "The newspaper editors are right. We are at the mercy of the Yankees. They will run things the way they want, regardless of our wishes." She shrugged. "All I want is to be left in peace to restore my plantation."

"Why, Charlotte Fraser, I'm surprised at you. I've known your family my entire life, and in all that time I have never known a Fraser to succumb to such a defeatist attitude. If your father were alive, he'd certainly be in the thick of things."

Charlotte blinked back sudden tears. How different her life would be if only he were still alive.

"Oh dear," Augusta said, getting to her feet. "I didn't mean to upset you. I only meant—"

"It's all right." Charlotte fumbled in her pocket for her handkerchief and blotted her eyes. "It isn't your fault. I'm so worried I can barely think."

"About your rice crop?" Augusta patted Charlotte's shoulder. "Every planter around here is in the same boat. Nobody on the Waccamaw can afford to plant as much rice anymore. But there's little to be gained by crying about it."

"It isn't the rice crop that concerns me just now. It's Mr. Betancourt. He's in New Orleans and we haven't heard from him, and I read in last week's paper about—"

Augusta pressed her lips into a grim line. "The epidemic. I learned of it myself just this morning from Mrs. Rutledge. She says people are dying by the dozens. Is there anything I can do to help?"

Charlotte took a long breath to compose herself. "I've posted a letter to General Longstreet. Mr. Betancourt was to have been visiting him. I can only hope the letter reaches the general and that they have not succumbed to the outbreak. I couldn't think of anything else to do."

A loud squeal erupted on the beach. Charlotte looked up in time to see the two Demere boys pouring water over their sisters' heads. "I must go while I have some reasonable hope of restoring order."

Augusta patted Charlotte's shoulder. "You're a born teacher, you know."

Charlotte tucked away her handkerchief. You're kind to say so. I'm hoping only to make a little progress before the children go away to a proper school."

"Speaking of proper schools, I understand our new state superintendent intends to establish free compulsory education before long." Augusta settled her basket into the crook of her arm, and they started along the beach to collect the children. "A good thing, if you ask me. Not every family can afford an expensive school. Especially these days."

Charlotte waved to catch Bess's attention and pointed toward the cottage. The girl began rounding up the younger children. Anne-Louise ran over to Augusta and tugged on her skirts. "Miss Augusta, can we fly our kite again?"

Augusta laughed. "Not today, my love. There's not enough breeze. Besides, I'm busy visiting and making tea cakes for the Independence Day celebration on Saturday." She pursed her lips. "Not that we have much to celebrate these days. But it's a good excuse for a party."

"We're going fishing on Saturday," Anne-Louise went on. "And we're having a bonfire on the beach, and we're staying awake for the fireworks. Ma'm'selle said so."

Augusta winked at Charlotte. "Well, if Ma'm'selle said so, then it's sure to happen."

The Demere children ran over, their hair plastered to their foreheads, faces pink from the sun. "We found a horseshoe crab." Lucas held it up for Charlotte's inspection. "John drew a picture of it."

"That's fine. Let's go inside before we all get sunburned."

They continued a short way up the beach. When they reached the path leading through the dunes to Augusta's cottage, Augusta leaned over and patted Charlotte's cheek. "Remember what I said about Anne-Louise. And try not to worry about Mr. Betancourt."

When they reached Pelican Cottage, Charlotte quickly counted heads. "Where's Marie-Claire?"

Bess and Susan shook their heads. The boys shrugged.

"She was here just a minute ago," Lucas said.

"Anne-Louise." Charlotte placed a hand on the girl's shoulder. "Where's your sister? And do not tell me a story about pirates."

The girl's eyes went wide. "I don't know, Ma'm'selle. I saw her by the dunes when you and Miss Augusta were having tea. I waited for her to come back and help me finish our sand castle, but she was gone for the longest time."

"I bet she's on the roof," Susan said.

"Maybe she's still on the beach," Bess said. "You want me to go look for her, miss?"

"Let's check inside first." Charlotte herded them onto the piazza. "Perhaps she got too warm and came back here ahead of us."

"I'm parched," John said.

"I'm parched too." Lucas collapsed onto his chair, his head thrown back, arms and legs outstretched.

"Bess, would you please fill the water pitcher

265

and get glasses for everyone? I must find Marie-Claire."

After a cursory glance into the parlor and the breezeway and a check of the back porch, Charlotte mounted the stairs. Marie-Claire was sitting against the wall in the hallway, her knees drawn up to her chest, her face hidden in her folded arms.

"Marie-Claire?" Charlotte knelt beside the girl. "Are you all right?"

A choked sob escaped the child's lips. "Go away and leave me alone."

"What's the matter? Did you get too much sun? Are you feeling unwell?"

"I hate you."

The venomous words pierced Charlotte's heart. "What on earth have I done to earn such scorn?"

Marie-Claire raised her tear-stained face at last. "You liar."

"What?"

"Every time I ask you about Papa, you say he's fine. But today I heard you tell Miss Augusta you're afraid he's dead. Because of the epidemic."

Charlotte sighed. "Please listen to me. When you asked about your father, I had no reason to believe he was not perfectly fine. Two days ago, when Daniel Graves came over and brought us the lovely vegetables—remember?—he also brought the newspaper. It was only then that I learned of the yellow-fever outbreak in New Orleans."

The girl twisted a damp tendril of hair around her finger and said nothing.

"This morning I sent a letter to New Orleans, to a very famous general who is your father's friend. I've asked him to find your father and let him know we're worried and anxious for news. But you must believe that I never lied to you, and I never will."

"Sorry," the girl muttered.

"Even if the news is dire, I will always tell you the truth. I promise."

"What if the general can't find Papa?"

"Then we'll have to think of something else. Now, go wash your face and brush your hair, then come back downstairs. It's time for your lessons."

Nineteen

"Ma'm'selle?"

Charlotte rolled over in her bed and opened one eye. At the foot of the bed stood Marie-Claire and Anne-Louise, each clutching a lunch pail and a straw hat.

"Wake up," Anne-Louise said. "It's Independence Day, and we don't want to miss anything."

Charlotte threw back the covers, padded across the floor, and looked out the open window. It was still early. A seam of golden light glimmered along the horizon, silhouetting the dunes and the sea oats that moved in the hot breeze. Gentle waves tumbled onto the sand. "There will be plenty of time after we've had breakfast."

"We already ate," Marie-Claire said. "We've been up for hours."

Her sister nodded. "We want to get going while the fish are still biting."

"Then please excuse me while I get ready." Charlotte poured water into her washbasin and took her towel from its hook beside the window. "Perhaps you could fetch our fishing poles from the back porch."

268

The girls scampered away. Charlotte washed and dressed and pinned up her hair. Nicholas's children deserved a day of fun, and she would try to see that they got it, but her constant thoughts were of his whereabouts and his safety . . . and her plantation. She trusted Mr. Hadley to look after things as best he could, given his infirmities, and Daniel's help had proved invaluable. But Papa had taught her there was no substitute for personal oversight. No one, not even a trusted friend, much less a boy she'd known only a few months, could care about a place as much as she did. And she cared desperately for every acre of Fairhaven. The ravaged house and gardens, the green-and-gold marshes, and the crooked tidal creeks pulled on her like the moon on the tides. It had always been her refuge. Soon she must go home to check on things.

Half an hour later, fortified with a cold biscuit and a cup of coffee and armed with a book, Charlotte led the girls out the back of the house and down to the tidal creek. Egrets stalked the creek banks beneath clouds of insects buzzing in the marsh grasses as the rising sun cast a pink-and-gold glow over the water.

They settled themselves on the dock and baited their hooks. Anne-Louise swung her feet and hummed softly, her eyes fixed on the brown waters of the creek. Charlotte cast a sideways glance at the girl who, so far, had not told any more tall tales. But then, Susan had not been around since Thursday to arouse her insecurities.

Marie-Claire slapped at an insect and nearly dropped her fishing pole. "Can we go in now? I'm burning up already, and the stupid fish are not biting anyway."

"They're not stupid," her sister said. "They're smart. That's why they won't let us catch 'em."

The older girl rolled her eyes. "Fish can't think, you ninny."

"You take that back. I am not a ninny."

"Young ladies." With one finger, Charlotte marked her place in her book. "If you can't be kind to one another, we'll go inside and spend the day doing sums."

Marie-Claire swatted at a persistent dragonfly. "Anything is better than this. Even stupid sums."

"Somebody's coming." Anne-Louise pointed to a rowboat rounding a curve in the creek.

"It's Daniel Graves," Marie-Claire said.

He raised an arm in greeting. In another few minutes, he drew his boat alongside the dock and tossed his line to Charlotte. He clambered out holding a string of fish, a wide grin on his face.

"I didn't expect to see you back here so soon." Charlotte bent to secure the rope.

"Didn't expect it either. Mrs. Hadley has come up for the holiday with the mister, and he gave me the day off. But don't worry. I went by

270

Fairhaven this morning and took care of Cinnamon. She said to tell you she misses you."

Charlotte grinned. "I miss her too. Is everything all right?"

"Far as I can tell. Me and Mr. Hadley took the boat down to your field yesterday. Your new crop is planted."

"That's a relief."

"Yes'm, I reckon so. The garden's getting kinda spindly, though. Wasn't much to bring you this time. We could use some rain."

"So long as it doesn't wash away my rice again."

"Daniel, look." Anne-Louise held up her fishing pole, from which a small fish dangled. "We're going to cook him on the beach tonight and watch the fireworks."

The boy grinned. "Sounds good to me. We can cook mine too."

Marie-Claire rolled her eyes. "This is boring as dirt. I'm going back inside."

"Fine," Charlotte said. "You can clean the fish Daniel brought."

The girl wrinkled her pert nose. "No thank you."

"I'll do it." Daniel headed toward the house.

Marie-Claire crossed her arms and watched him go. "Why did he have to show up and spoil everything?"

"I thought you liked Daniel. You were the one who begged me to let him stay when he showed up for school at my house."

"I felt sorry for him. That doesn't mean I like him. I hope he doesn't stay the entire day."

"Well, he's a very smart boy, and kindhearted as can be. You will be perfectly cordial toward him or else miss the fireworks."

"I don't care about the fireworks. I don't care about anything." Marie-Claire's breath hitched, and suddenly Charlotte understood.

She gathered the girl into her arms. "I know you're worried about your father," she whispered. "So am I. But you must be brave and not frighten your little sister. And try not to take your feelings out on poor Daniel."

She motioned for Anne-Louise. "Let's go inside and start a pudding for supper."

They returned to the house and set about assembling food for their beach picnic. While Daniel cleaned the fish and scoured the beach for stones and driftwood, Charlotte kept the girls busy cracking eggs and measuring sugar and milk for the pudding. She scrubbed potatoes and corn for roasting.

By late afternoon, everything was ready. She sent the girls upstairs to rest, but the thumps and muffled giggles from overhead told her they were too excited to sleep. Meanwhile, Daniel made himself at home in her makeshift school-room, studying John's drawings of shells and horseshoe crabs, thumbing through the world atlas and a stack of tattered magazines. He soon settled on a book and went out to the piazza to read.

Charlotte tried to return to her own book, but worry about Anne-Louise's fanciful story and Marie-Claire's barely controlled anger made it hard to concentrate. Their father's absence was taking its toll on all of them.

Through the window she saw Augusta, her distant neighbor, Mrs. Carver, and Mary Banks walking down the beach, a heavy wicker basket between them. A small, gray-haired woman wearing a burgundy frock hurried along behind them. Mrs. Rutledge of Charleston, no doubt. Behind her came a couple of men carrying metal tubs and a group of children carrying kites and balls and sticks.

Anne-Louise pounded down the stairs. "Is it time yet?"

"Almost. Go tidy your hair and find your shawl. And tell your sister to do the same."

"I don't need a shawl. It's hot outside."

"It is now, but it might be quite cool by fire-works time."

A few minutes later the girls came downstairs, ready to go. Charlotte packed their food into two baskets and set a folded blanket on top. Daniel carried it all down to the beach.

Charlotte chose a spot close to the water but still protected by the dunes and set down her baskets. The girls helped Daniel dig a pit for the fire. Soon dozens of fires burned along the beach as more families arrived for the celebration. While the adults gathered to share the latest news, children played and splashed in the surf or built castles in the sand.

Daniel sat atop a dune with his book, seemingly oblivious to the noise and motion going on around him. But when the fire had burned down to red-hot coals, he helped Charlotte place the fish, corn, and potatoes for roasting, then joined a group of boys casting a net into the surf.

Mary Banks and the woman in burgundy strolled over. Mary handed Charlotte a flyer still smelling of printer's ink. "Charlotte, this is my cousin Mrs. Rutledge, visiting from Charleston. Adele, this is Charlotte Fraser. She owns Fairhaven on the Waccamaw and Pelican Cottage, just up the beach from us."

Mrs. Rutledge acknowledged the introduction with an appraising glance. "How do you do? Mary tells me you're attempting to run a plantation by yourself."

"I have some help, but the decisions—and the worries—are all mine."

"My word. What a brave thing to do." She patted Charlotte's hand. "I wish I could introduce you to my nephew. If only Griffin would stand still long enough, he would enjoy knowing someone so pretty and so accomplished." She paused. "Augusta Milton tells me you aren't much interested in our cause."

Charlotte turned the paper toward the firelight to make out the words. "Citizenship for Negroes while white women beg for suffrage? We say no! Sign our petition now!"

"Surely you agree with us, Miss Fraser," Mary said. "Just how far does male dominance go? I'm tired of being told that I suffer from an error of belief simply because I want equality." She paused for breath, then plunged ahead as if giving a well-rehearsed speech. "Since the war we have had to shoulder burdens never meant for us. If women must pay taxes, manage their properties, and support their children single-handedly—as many have—then certainly they deserve a say in making the laws we're all forced to obey."

Charlotte tucked the paper into her pocket. She'd never imagined that Mrs. Banks, who by sheer good fortune had escaped the fate she'd just vividly described, felt so passionately about the issue. Perhaps Mrs. Rutledge had awakened the younger woman's political conscience.

Charlotte had never considered herself much of a crusader either, but she couldn't deny the woman's logic. The war had required of women a large measure of endurance and sacrifice, self-sufficiency, and inventiveness. Surely now the men could see that their old beliefs about female dependency were no longer true, that the war had not only set the Negroes free but freed women as well from the constraints of old roles and old expectations.

"We're not against citizenship for the Negroes," Mrs. Rutledge added. "We recognize that the old system is at an end, and perhaps it should be. We must move forward for the good of everyone, black and white, but at the appropriate time. We say first things first, and that means women need the vote. If we were granted suffrage, we might then have an opportunity to influence the formation of laws beneficial to all. The sooner we—"

"Mary, there you are," Augusta said, coming to a stop before them. "I should have known you'd be trying to convince Charlotte to join your merry band. Your husband is looking for you."

"All right. I'm coming." Mary Banks clasped Charlotte's hand. "At least take the flyer home and study it. I'll come by one day next week, and we can talk more then."

Mary and Mrs. Rutledge left. Charlotte sat down and patted the blanket. "Join me, Augusta?"

Augusta sat down, her dark green skirts spread at her feet. "I can't stay long. I promised the Chamberlains I'd sit with them and help Elizabeth with the baby. He's been sick off and on all summer, and the poor girl is run ragged. She's been looking forward to this outing for weeks."

Charlotte smiled up at her old friend. "Augusta

Milton, whatever would the people on this island do without you?"

"The better question is what would I do without them." Augusta paused and stared into the flickering fire. "You know, Charlotte, when I was your age, all I wanted was to live in Paris and paint. I needed no one and nothing except my art. Romance seemed frivolous, a home and family as appealing as a ball and chain. And for a while, I lived out my own glittering dream."

"I never knew that."

"Oh, yes. People said I had a good bit of talent. But deep down, I realized I'd never be more than a good copyist." She picked up a handful of sand and let it trickle through her fingers. "The Hadleys own one of my best efforts. A copy of an early Signorelli."

"Nicholas Betancourt admired it at Lettice's party last spring. We debated whether it was authentic."

"I brought it back with me when my star faded and my patrons moved on to others with more talent. The Hadleys paid me generously for it. Which was a blessing, since the young men in my circle had long since chosen wives." She brushed the sand off her fingers. "And here I am, rattling around by myself in that drafty old cottage."

"I'm sorry."

"Don't be. I'm not looking for sympathy. I took

the risk, made my choices. All in all, I am not unhappy here in the twilight of my years."

In the firelight the older woman's features softened, and Charlotte understood why she had been considered such a beauty in her day. Augusta patted Charlotte's hand. "I have many friends. Things to do that make me feel useful. Quiet pleasures that make me feel quite content."

A high-pitched whine, followed by a loud boom, signaled the start of the fireworks. Augusta rose. "Listen to me nattering on. Don't pay me any mind, my dear. Firelight always brings out the melancholy in me." She lifted her hand in a little wave. "I must get back to Elizabeth."

"And I must find Daniel and the girls. Our supper should be done by now."

Augusta left, picking her way carefully in the dark. Charlotte got to her feet and called for her charges. The three of them, their clothes damp and smelling of seawater, hauled themselves onto the sand.

"We're exhausted," Anne-Louise declared. "Mary Chamberlain has a kite that can fly all the way to the moon. We chased it almost as far as the causeway. It would have gotten lost, except I jumped about a hundred feet and grabbed the tail just in the nick of time."

Charlotte sent the girl a sharp look, a brow raised in question. "Truly?"

"Nah, she's just jokin'," Daniel said. "Right, Anne-Louise?"

Anne-Louise dropped her gaze and fussed with her sleeves. "Just jokin'."

"Remember when we talked about the boy who cried wolf?" Charlotte opened her basket and took out their plates and utensils.

The girl nodded. "Nobody believed him when he got into real trouble because he told too many stories that weren't true."

"Is the food done?" Marie-Claire asked. "I'm hungry enough to eat a horse." She grinned at Charlotte. "Not Cinnamon, of course."

Charlotte feigned relief. "Thank goodness for that."

Daniel helped remove the fish, potatoes, and corn from the glowing coals. Charlotte served their plates and spooned the pudding into their bowls. They ate and watched the fireworks exploding over the dark water. Far down the beach, someone began a chorus of "The Camptown Races." Daniel and the girls joined in.

Their sweet harmony sent a wave of sadness moving through her. Would she wind up like Augusta, belonging to no one? Even if she could bring Fairhaven back to its former glory, would the plantation by itself be enough to sustain her for the rest of her life?

The fireworks ended, and the night grew chilly

as a cool breeze arrived on the evening tide. People packed up and headed for home.

"Daniel?" Charlotte stacked their dishes into her basket and folded the blanket. "You're spending the night with us. It's too late to take the boat home."

"Oh, no, ma'am. I'm meeting Mr. Hadley's friend Mr. Ambrose down by the causeway. He's taking me to his house for the night so's I can help him fix his barn in the morning. He come up from Charleston the day before yesterday and brought the latest edition of the *Mercury* with him." Daniel fished in his pocket for the newspaper. "I brought it for you, but then I forgot all about it this morning. It's only a little bit damp."

"Thank you, Daniel. I'm always keen for news."

"Yes'm. I imagine so." He jerked a thumb. "Front page is all about General Longstreet. Mr. Ambrose says he was one of the best officers in the Confederate army and General Lee's right-hand man, even if they didn't always agree. Mr. Ambrose says it's a real shame the general is so sick."

"General Lee is ill?"

"No, ma'am. General Longstreet. Paper says he's in a bad way."

Charlotte went still.

"You all right, Miss Fraser?"

She took a steadying breath. "I'm fine, Daniel,

just shocked to learn of General Longstreet's illness. You'd best get going before it gets any later. I can handle our things."

He hurried away.

Numbed to her core, Charlotte managed to collect their belongings and get the girls home and into bed. Then she took the lamp into the parlor and read the newspaper account of the general's illness, her eyes racing down the page. Old war wound . . . complications . . . exhaustion. No mention of yellow fever. Perhaps he'd had a chance to speak to Nicholas before falling ill.

Unable to sleep, she took off her shoes and went out to the back porch. She climbed the narrow staircase to the attic, pushed open the trapdoor, and stepped onto the roof.

She inhaled the misty salt air and drank in the beauty of the rolling sea by moonlight, the dying remnants of cook fires glittering like a diamond necklace ringing the beach. She sat down, unmindful of the damp seeping into her skirts. Questions about Nicholas, about whether he had proof of his claim to the barony that included her land, whether he was even alive, demanded answers.

For whatever reason—illness, unwillingness, disappointment—he had gone silent. If he wouldn't—or couldn't—come to her, for the sake of the children if nothing else, she must go to him.

Such a journey was not without risk. The trip would be difficult and expensive. The thought of the yellow-fever epidemic was terrifying. But the current situation was not fair to her or to the children. Still, if life were fair, perhaps there would be no need for courage.

She watched the sparks from a dying fire spiraling into the darkness and hoped that when the time for this journey arrived, she would be brave enough to take it.

Twenty

New Orleans
24 July 1868

The train shuddered to a stop. Charlotte massaged the tight muscles in her back and peered out the soot-streaked window. The New Orleans station buzzed with noise and movement. Passengers crowded onto the platform to await their baggage, jostling a Negro man sitting cross-legged on a bench. Bearded businessmen in dapper gray suits and bowler hats dodged a gaggle of ragtag children and a one-legged man wearing a tattered Confederate uniform. Smoke from a huge factory across Basin Street billowed against the white-hot summer sky.

The other women in the passenger car gathered their fans, gloves, umbrellas, and reticules, preparing to leave the train. Caroline Mayhew, a fashionably dressed, olive-skinned woman with piercing brown eyes who had boarded the train south of Atlanta and promptly introduced herself to Charlotte, smiled wanly and brushed a speck of soot from her sleeve. "Are you as exhausted as I am?"

"I can't remember the last time I slept." The trip had involved a twelve-hour voyage aboard the *Resolute* from Georgetown to Charleston and a rail journey to Atlanta. Three days later she had boarded a car on the Southern Louisiana Passenger Railway bound for New Orleans. She was numb from the jostling ride on hard wooden seats and covered head to toe with soot and dust.

"I do hope you find your employer is well." Caroline fluffed the feathers on her hat, an oversized concoction of pink silk flowers, netting, and ribbons. "This is a dangerous time to be in the city."

Charlotte blotted her face with a wrinkled handkerchief. "Do you not fear for your own well-being?"

"Of course I try to be careful. But the fever seems not to spread directly from one person to another."

Charlotte nodded. Most people on the Waccamaw feared mosquitoes and bad air more than contact with fever victims.

"Besides, the fever mostly attacks newcomers," Caroline said. "Here, it's the immigrants who seem to have the worst time of it. The Irish especially. Local whites seem to be resistant— and the Negroes, of course."

Perhaps Nicholas was safe. But then why had there been no word, especially to his children?

"Is someone meeting you here?" Caroline

scrubbed at her face with a lavender-scented handkerchief.

Charlotte shook her head, arranged her hat, and drew on her blackened cotton gloves.

"Then you must allow me to take you to your hotel. My carriage and driver are waiting."

"I'm not sure where to stay. I haven't a reservation."

"I recommend the Orleans Palace on Prytania Street. The food is good, and the hotel is quite safe for a lady traveling alone."

Charlotte swallowed. The hotel sounded quite grand and no doubt it had prices to match. But she was too exhausted and too anxious for news of Nicholas to count the cost. "That sounds fine. Thank you."

Caroline gathered her voluminous skirt and hooked her bag over her arm. "Come on. Let's get out of here."

They joined a group of other passengers carrying satchels and cases and emerged onto the busy platform. A short time later they collected their luggage and settled into Caroline's waiting carriage. The Creole driver clicked his tongue to the horse and they pulled onto the busy street.

Through the open windows came the babble of voices speaking half a dozen languages, snatches of accordion music from shadowed doorways, and the calls of Italian street vendors hawking tomatoes and melons. In a shady courtyard, two

Federal soldiers leaned against a wall, talking. A burly black man scrubbed a shop window with a red rag, one arm hanging useless at his side. As the carriage made the turn onto St. Charles Street, Charlotte caught a glimpse of a funeral cortege just ahead. A feeling of dread unfurled in her chest.

"Here we are," Caroline said moments later. "Gustav Dubois is the hotel manager. Tell him I sent you. He'll look after you."

"I cannot thank you enough."

"My pleasure, Miss Fraser." Caroline squeezed Charlotte's arm. "I do wish you well in your search."

"I don't suppose you could tell me where I might find General Longstreet."

Caroline shook her head, a small frown creasing her smooth forehead. "I'm afraid not. I've been away all summer. But you don't want to associate with him anyway. From what I read in the papers, he hasn't exactly been a popular figure around here since he wrote those newspaper articles encouraging us to accept Yankee occupation." She lowered her voice. "Some have gone so far as to call him a traitor to the South."

The carriage driver opened her door and offered his hand as she stepped out. "Go on inside, miss. I'll bring your baggage."

Charlotte looked up at the hotel, taking in the pair of monolithic columns framing the elaborate wrought-iron balcony and windows tall enough to walk through. To one side was a brick and slate courtyard filled with clematis and trumpet vine, a pair of stone benches, and a burbling fountain.

She entered through a great, light-filled hall flanked by double parlors furnished with velvet settees and mahogany tables. In front of her rose a wide circular staircase.

A short, bald-pated gentleman wearing a black suit crossed the foyer and bowed. "I'm Mr. Dubois. May I help you?"

Before she could speak, Caroline Mayhew's driver entered, carrying Charlotte's bags.

"Andre!" The hotelier's face split into a wide grin. "I hope the sight of you means that Miss Mayhew has returned to our city."

"Yessir, she sho' has. I just now fetched her from the train station." Andre plunked down Charlotte's bags.

"Well, tell her I hope to see her soon. I'm eager for news of her adventures abroad."

Andre nodded and hurried out.

Charlotte explained her circumstances. "Miss Mayhew recommended your establishment."

"And how long will you be staying with us?"

"I'm not certain."

"That poses no difficulty whatsoever." Mr. Dubois led her to a desk tucked discreetly beneath the massive staircase. "We have plenty of space. Not too many visitors in July to begin

287

with; a goodly number of the locals go to their fish camps for the summer months. Now, with this outbreak, more people than usual have left the city. Including, I'm sorry to say, several of my staff."

He ran his finger down a printed list. "I think the Blue Room would do nicely. It has a private bath and a lovely sitting room overlooking the rear courtyard but, sadly, no lady's maid to attend to your needs."

"I'm accustomed to taking care of myself." She opened her reticule. "How much?"

"I wouldn't feel right charging you full price since I cannot provide you with full service. Would seven dollars be all right?"

It was a king's ransom, but she handed him a few bills, which he slid back across the desk. "You're a friend of Miss Mayhew's, and your plans are indefinite at present. Let's settle the bill upon your departure."

He tapped a small bell on his desk and a uniformed bellman appeared. "Please show our guest to the Blue Room."

An hour later Charlotte had bathed, washed her hair, and changed into a fresh dress. She unpacked her bags, settled into her chair at the small escritoire overlooking the courtyard, and opened her notebook. Where to begin looking for Nicholas? The first thing to do was find General Longstreet, despite Miss Mayhew's warnings. Unpopular though he might be, he was a friend of Nicholas and the only man of influence she knew of in the entire city. If Nicholas had already come and gone from the general's house, perhaps the general could tell her whom to contact, where to begin her search.

If he was still alive.

A knock sounded at the door and she rose to answer it.

A young Negro woman in a starched white apron over a blue dress came in bearing a silver tray. "Mr. Dubois sent you some supper, miss."

"Thank you. I am hungry."

"Yes'm. Folks from the Atlanta train always is, time they get here. Normally the dining room would be open, but with this sickness ever'where . . ." Her voice trailed away as she crossed the room and set down the tray.

"I understand." Charlotte closed her notebook. "Tell me, are most of the afflicted in a hospital somewhere?"

"Them without no fambly done been taken to the convent. Usin' it as a hospital, they say. Lots of folks are dyin' at home, I reckon. My man has been tendin' a lot of burials up at Lafayette Cemetery." She waved one hand. "Enjoy your supper, miss. You can jus' leave your tray outside the door. I'll be back for it directly."

In the morning, Charlotte woke to a discreet tap on the door. The serving woman had returned with a plate of fresh melon, a cinnamon-and-sugar-infused beignet, a pot of chicory-laced coffee, and a pitcher of cream.

"Mr. Dubois said to tell you he's sorry we don' have no eggs." She set the tray down. "They's a café just a block over on St. Charles if you need somethin' more substantial."

"This will be plenty. Please be sure to give Mr. Dubois my thanks."

When the woman withdrew, Charlotte devoured the meal and set the empty tray in the hallway. She pinned her hair, pinched some color into her cheeks, and descended the staircase just as a distant church bell tolled the hour.

Mr. Dubois stood in the entry hall, deep in conversation with a wiry, dark-skinned man. But he quickly concluded his conversation when he saw her. "Miss Fraser. I trust you slept well."

"I did, and I thank you for two delicious meals."

"I could do much more if my regular chef were here, but alas, he's decamped to Terrebonne Parish." He shrugged. "We do the best we can. How may I help you this morning?"

"I'm looking for General Longstreet. I believe he might have news of my employer, who has gone missing."

The hotelier's brows went up. "Indeed? The last I heard, the general was gravely ill and housebound. In any case I doubt much news of anything has come his way. Most people here have taken a dim view of his call to accept Northern rule."

Charlotte nodded. "So says Miss Mayhew, but I still must find him. He has not responded to my letters."

"And I doubt he will. He—" Mr. Dubois paused as a quartet of hotel guests came downstairs. "Please excuse me a moment."

He hurried over to the two ladies and planted kisses on their proffered hands. He spoke to their escorts, shook their hands, and summoned the bellman. "John, please find a carriage for these fine folks and see to their bags."

The taller man in the party smiled and pumped the hotelier's hand as the bellman hurried up the stairs. "That's what we love about staying here, Gustav," he said. "No detail escapes your notice."

"Ah. I'm glad you are pleased. How much more I could do for you if only I had the entire staff at my disposal."

While he attended to the other guests, Charlotte wandered to the window and looked out. Carriages and rigs rattled along the busy street. Women pushing carts and perambulators dodged knots of Federal soldiers and noisy children kicking a ball along the banquette. Down on the corner, a vegetable seller was opening up his cart as if this were a normal day and the city was not caught in the grip of a deadly epidemic. But perhaps this part of the city was unaffected. She recalled more than one such outbreak in Charleston when she was young when certain parts of town were decimated while others went unscathed.

The bellman came down laden with bags, hatboxes, and a trunk. The guests followed him onto the street and a carriage drew up at the door.

"Miss Fraser." Mr. Dubois joined her at the window. "Please forgive the interruption. The Morellis are regular guests when they are in town. Lovely people, but they do require special tending. Theater people are so temperamental, I find, and so easily offended." He motioned toward the parlor. "Would you care for more coffee?"

"No thank you. I'm anxious to get started—if only I knew where to start."

"Yes, well, as I was about to say, I heard that the general has left New Orleans. However, he isn't the only Confederate general in town."

"Oh?"

"This city has drawn them like bees to honey. General Hood is here. He had an insurance business for a while, but I'm not certain what he's doing now. General Early comes and goes. General Beauregard may be the one to see, though I hear he doesn't much care for strangers."

"General Beauregard?" Charlotte felt a flicker of hope.

"You know him?"

"Not really. I met him once, years ago."

"He isn't quite the same now." Mr. Dubois shook his head. "It's a shame, what the war did to so many fine men. Ruined them for anything but fighting and killing."

Charlotte thought then of Lettice Hadley's husband. Another walking casualty of the late Confederacy. But she couldn't dwell on that, not when Nicholas might be sick or dead. She opened her reticule and took out her notebook and pencil. "Where might I find General Beauregard?"

"Ah, *ma petite*, that's hard to say. He keeps an office at the railway company, and he owns a few properties here in town. But from what I hear, he's mostly in residence at his place on Chartres. I forget the address, but the carriage driver will know. If not, tell him to look for a house with big pillars and a curving double stair out front."

Mr. Dubois held out both arms, elbows bent, his hands curving inward in imitation of a staircase. Charlotte wrote it all down, but from what she had seen on the drive from the train station yesterday, the description fit half of the houses in New Orleans.

"Come," Mr. Dubois said. "I'll summon a carriage."

Twenty-One

The carriage rocked to a stop. The driver jumped down and opened the door. "This is it."

Charlotte left the carriage and studied the house. There were the pillars and the curving double staircase Mr. Dubois had described. Through the wrought-iron side gate, a colorful garden beckoned, in sharp contrast to the shuttered windows that offered no hint of welcome. Across the street, a pair of nuns and a gray-haired priest hurried toward the door of a neighborhood church.

"Shall I wait for you, miss?"

"Oh. No, I haven't any idea how long this might take." She handed him a couple of bills. "Could you call for me here in, say, an hour?"

"Mebbe. Depends on whether I'm busy." He pocketed his money, climbed up, and drove away.

Charlotte looked around, then ascended the staircase and rang the bell. A small dark-skinned man dressed entirely in white answered it. "Yes?"

"My name is Charlotte Fraser. I must speak to General Beauregard."

"You and half of the free world."

"Is he home?"

"He's here. But he's having his breakfast and not expecting any visitors."

"I apologize for arriving unannounced. But I've come all the way from Charleston to find someone who has gone missing. I'm hoping the general can help."

He drew himself up, blocking the doorway. "Somebody goes missing, you call the police."

She sighed. "Would you mind asking General Beauregard if he will spare ten minutes in the service of a Confederate lady?"

"War's over. Confederacy's dead." He made a move to close the door.

"Wait. Please." She fumbled with the clasp of her reticule. "If he won't see me, would you at least deliver a note to him?"

She scribbled on a wrinkled calling card and pressed it into his hands. The door slammed shut.

When the butler did not reappear, she descended the stairs and stood on the banquette, eyes narrowed against the bright sunlight. What should she do now? Wait to see whether the general would see her, whether the carriage driver would return? Walk back to the Orleans Palace? Or cross the street to the church and hope that someone there would help her?

"Miss. Over here."

Charlotte whirled around.

A thin girl in a ragged calico dress stood in the narrow alley next to the general's house, a small white dog tucked beneath one arm. She strolled over to Charlotte. "They wouldn't let you in, eh?" She grinned, revealing several missing teeth.

"I'm afraid not." Charlotte held her breath against the stench coming off the girl.

"He leaves home at ten sharp ever' morning."

"The servant?"

"No, you ninny. The general."

"I see." Charlotte sighed and consulted the small watch she wore on a chain around her neck. Not much past eight. She didn't relish a two-hour wait in the rising heat, but it might be her only chance to seek the general's help.

"Gon' get awful hot just standin' here till ten," the girl said. "Another hour and it'll be hot enough to stop a hummingbird's wings."

"Yes." Already beads of sweat were forming on her brow, and the bodice of her dress clung like a second skin.

"I can take you to my place. Ain't far."

"That's very kind, but I couldn't impose."

The girl frowned. "Ma'am?"

"I wouldn't want to inconvenience you."

The dog began to whine, and the girl jostled him to quiet him. "If you ain't the most impossible person I've ever met. Would you mind speaking in plain old English? I don't know any of them fancy words."

Despite the odor and the girl's unkempt appearance, Charlotte found it hard not to like her. "When someone offers to open her house to a lady, the polite thing to do is to ref—to say no thank you. It's what we call the rules of etiq—of proper behavior."

The girl threw back her head and laughed. The dog wiggled and did his best to lick her face. "Oh mercy me, fancy lady. Me and Cosette here don't have a house worth the name. When I said I'd take you to my place, I meant my cool spot down on the river. It's just a fallin'-down warehouse shack, but I got it fixed up real nice, and it keeps the sun and the rain off. We can sit a spell till it's time for you to come back here and waylay the general." She stared into Charlotte's face, her dark eyes lively with curiosity. "What you want with that Creole anyway?"

Charlotte shook her head. She was tired of explaining.

"Reckon it ain't none of my business," the girl said. "Forget I asked. Me and Cosette's goin' home. You coming or ain't you?"

The morning was heating rapidly, the humidity a tangible presence. The carriage driver was unlikely to return for her, and she didn't relish the prospect of a long, hot walk back to the hotel. Maybe it was foolish to follow the girl when an epidemic was raging, but if this urchin was telling the truth and she could actually speak to the general, perhaps it was a chance worth taking. "I'm coming. Thank you."

The girl laughed again. "Don't thank me till you seen the place. Ain't nothing to brag on, that's for sure. Come on."

Charlotte followed her through a maze of streets and alleyways, past Saturday crowds in the outdoor markets and a blur of faces in shades of white, brown, and black. All along the banquette, women in bright tignons tended their children, street vendors plied their wares, and pairs of nuns glided past, hands tucked inside their habits.

At last Charlotte and the girl emerged on the waterfront. "Jackson Square's up that way, past Chartres Street." She jerked a thumb. "Me and Cosette don't go up there too much. We like it down here."

She led the way along a creaking wharf that smelled of fish and horse droppings. Dead fish, rotten apples, and watermelon rinds floated in the placid, rust-colored water. They came to a row of shacks, the wood weathered to a silvery gray. The girl pushed open a door and waved her hand. "After you."

Charlotte crouched and entered a cramped space containing a thin, narrow mattress, a cast-iron skillet, a chamber pot, and a stack of old news-papers. In the corner stood a bamboo fishing pole and a metal bucket. A rusty stewpot gave off the odor of fish, potatoes, and onions. The only light came from cracks between the boards and the open doorway, which overlooked the river.

The girl plopped down on the mattress. "You don't like it. I can tell. I told you wasn't nothing."

"Do you live here alone?"

"Nope. I got Cosette here."

"But what about a parent, a relative? You seem young to be on your own."

The girl shrugged. "I'm nigh on fourteen. That's old enough."

Charlotte's heart went out to the girl. "What happened to your family?"

"Dead."

"Oh. From the fever?"

"Nah. Cholera got my mama when I was ten. Pa got shot one night in a brawl down at the lottery building."

"I'm so sorry."

"Don't need to be crying over neither one of 'em. My mama was what you call a lady of the evening. Kept comp'ny with fancy gentlemen. And Pa wouldn't be dead if he wasn't a gambling man."

"Still, someone should look after you."

"Oh Lord. Please tell me you don't aim to reform me. I swear, for a while there right after Pa met his maker, the church ladies was down here just about ever' week, trying to get me into an orphanage or a boardin' school or some such." She waved a hand toward the stack of papers. "I can read good as anybody, and count money so's I don't get cheated. I got me a place to sleep and the best dog that ever lived. I come and go when I feel like it. Don't know what else a body needs."

Charlotte bit her tongue to keep from speaking aloud. She could think of plenty of things. Proper food and a safe place to sleep. A dentist to remove those rotting teeth. Water and soap for bathing and someone to teach the girl how to get on in the world. "How do you manage to eat?"

"They's plenty of ways. Fishin' mostly. Sometimes I make a little money toting stuff off the quay for Mr. Collins. Most days me and Cosette go up to Royal Street where the fruit sellers work. Sometimes they throw away apples and plums and such at the end of the day. Perfectly good too. No sense wasting it."

"I suppose not."

"Last fall a cotton ship blew up and stuff scattered everywhere. Watermelons, cracker tins, jars of jelly, a good-sized ham hock. Me and Cosette picked up a wheelbarrow full of food. Ate real good for almost a month." The girl went to the cooking pot and used a wooden dipper to spoon stew into a cracked china bowl. She let the dog slurp some from the dipper and then held it out to Charlotte. "Want some?"

Charlotte swallowed. "No thank you. I just had breakfast."

"Suit yourself." The girl drank the concoction

straight from the bowl, wiping the dribble from her chin with her sleeve. The dog jumped into her lap, tail thumping, and she plucked a bit of potato from the bowl and fed it to the dog.

Charlotte blotted her face with her handkerchief and surreptitiously covered her nose as she breathed. Her heart ached for this lost child. No one should have to live in such squalor, even if she claimed to like it.

Presently a red-and-white steamboat chugged into view, its wheels churning the muddy water, lively banjo music spilling from the open deck. Women in brightly colored dresses leaned against the rail.

"That's the *Mary Eileen*," the girl said. "Comes this way ever' Saturday, docks just up the quay at ten o'clock sharp." She picked up the dog. "Reckon you best be getting back on over to Chartres if you want to catch that general."

They went outside. Charlotte looked around at the unfamiliar surroundings. How on earth had she gotten here? And how would she find her way back?

The girl grinned. "Completely lost, fancy lady?"

"I'm afraid so."

"Come on. Me and Cosette'll walk you back."

A few minutes later they emerged once more onto a street. "This is Chartres," the girl said. "The general's house is just down that way. Try not to get lost between here and there."

Charlotte couldn't help smiling. "You've been an excellent guide. I want to pay you for your services and for your hospitality."

"Well, if you want to, I won't say no."

Charlotte opened her bag and pressed a bill into the girl's hand. "Thank you, Miss . . . I'm afraid I haven't asked your name."

"Solange." The girl wadded the bill and stuffed it into her pocket. She peered down the street, shading her eyes with her hand. "Here comes General Beauregard, right on time. Just like one of his trains."

Charlotte hurried to meet him, reaching his house just as he descended the curving staircase, one hand resting lightly on the black wrought-iron railing. Even in civilian clothes he stood ramrod straight, shoulders back, every inch the military officer he once had been.

She stood on the banquette clutching her reticule, her heart hammering. "General Beauregard."

"Yes?" He studied her, one hand still resting on the railing, his expression one of polite curiosity.

"Please forgive this intrusion. My name is Charlotte Fraser. I left a message with your butler this morning."

His dark brows went up. "I received no such message."

"Perhaps he forgot or hasn't yet had time yet to deliver it. I was here only a couple of hours ago, but he would not admit me."

He waited, calm and unmoving.

"I met you once years ago, when you were posted to Charleston. My father and I were dining at the Mills House when you and your adjutant came in. You and Father spoke about our rice plantation and about Ft. Sumter and the defense of Charleston harbor."

"I'm certain you're right. I met dozens of local citizens during my time there. But I can't be expected to recognize them now." At last, he smiled. "Especially one who could not have been much more than a child at the time."

"Of course not. I wanted only to remind you of our meeting in hopes it might induce you to help me."

He sighed. "Permit me a guess. You or your cousin or your father needs a job. Or a political favor. Or a loan of cash."

"None of that. My father died last winter."

"I'm sorry. I shouldn't have spoken out of turn."

A horse and rig clattered past, and he took her elbow to draw her away from the street.

"I've come in search of my employer." Once again, she shared the details of Nicholas's long absence and her pressing need to find him.

"Come," he said. "Let's sit in the garden. It's cooler out here than inside this time of the morning." The general led her through a small gate to a little garden overflowing with bright flowers. Clipped boxwood hedges formed a low green border around a concrete fountain. A pair of benches sat beneath a palmetto tree, its fronds rattling in the sultry breeze.

General Beauregard motioned Charlotte to sit and then chose the opposite bench. "I regret that you came so far to see Longstreet. He decamped the city for New England a week ago. He's in a bad way himself, not really fit to travel, but he was worried about his family getting the fever and insisted upon removing them to safer climes."

"Then I'm too late." She slumped against the bench.

"Looking for anyone these days is like crawling through a meadow, searching for a four-leaf clover. Finding your employer amidst the present chaos will be a matter of great good luck, I'm afraid."

"But if he's . . . if he's no longer alive . . . surely records are being kept."

The general shook his head. "My dear Miss Fraser, in the areas of this city where the fever is prevalent, upwards of twenty people are dying every day. There's little time for record keeping or for proper burials. If your employer has succumbed without anyone to claim him, more than likely he's buried in a mass grave somewhere."

Tears blurred Charlotte's vision. Nicholas in a mass grave, with no one to mourn him or to mark his resting place? The prospect was too distressing to contemplate. "What about the convent? I heard that some of the sick are being cared for there."

"At Ursuline, yes. You can ask, I suppose. Father Alphonse is doing the best he can."

She rose and began to pace. "Surely there is some way to find Mr. Betancourt."

General Beauregard sighed. "Do you know how many people reside in New Orleans?"

Before she could venture a guess, he answered his own question. "Close to two hundred thousand. You've said you have no idea where he lived when he was here before the war. No known relatives we might contact." He pressed his fingers to his eyes. "It's quite impossible. Nevertheless, I will ask around town and see whether I can discover any news. You said he served the Confederacy?"

"Yes, with General Longstreet. I'm grateful for any inquiries you can make on Mr. Betancourt's behalf."

"If I discover any news, I'll send word. Where may I find you?"

"The Orleans Palace."

"Your friend has one thing in his favor," General Beauregard said. "Those of us who grew up here have developed a certain resistance to the fever, as have natives of our other Southern port cities—or so I'm given to understand. But all

305

the same, you ought not to stay here any longer than necessary."

Charlotte felt a bit better. Perhaps she wasn't in as much danger as she first thought. And perhaps Nicholas was not only well, but had already left the city and was on his way back to South Carolina, their letters having crossed somewhere along the way.

The general consulted his pocket watch. "I'm sorry to rush off, but I am late to the railway office."

"I apologize for having detained you."

"Not at all. I wish I could have been more helpful. Come with me."

He crossed the courtyard and knocked on a door tucked beneath the rear staircase. A young man of perhaps twenty, with olive skin and black curls, stepped out. "Yessir?"

"Pierre, this is Miss Fraser. I want you to drive her back to her hotel."

"General Beauregard?" Charlotte said. "I hope you won't think it too much of an imposition if I ask to be driven to the convent hospital instead. I'd like to speak to Father Alphonse as soon as possible."

"I can't advise it," the general said. "The situation there is terribly distressing. I suggest sending the priest a note instead."

"But I want to know right away whether Father Alphonse can help me find Mr. Betancourt."

"Very well." The general raised both his hands, palms out. "The convent, Pierre. And then the Orleans Palace."

Pierre smiled at Charlotte and touched one finger to his forehead in a kind of salute. "It won't take a moment to fetch the horse and rig."

The general offered her his arm and they returned to the street. "Try not to worry. Yellow fever is deadly, no question, yet many who are stricken do survive. For all we know, the good doctor is recovering somewhere and waiting only until he feels strong enough to travel."

Moments later Pierre drew up in a smart black buggy, and General Beauregard helped Charlotte inside. "Give the priest my regards. Tell him I sent you."

"I will. And thank you."

Pierre rattled the reins and they set off, the heat of the morning close and still. Charlotte suppressed worries about her dwindling bank account and the nightmarish scene awaiting her at the convent. She focused her thoughts on Marie-Claire and Anne-Louise, the way they had clung to her as she prepared to leave the island, their dear little faces so full of worry and hope.

Finding Nicholas Betancourt would be worth any price she had to pay.

Twenty-Two

On Dauphine Street, Pierre brought the rig to a stop outside a low white building just as bells tolled the hour. A cobbled walkway stretched from the banquette to the front door, which was flanked by white marble statues of saints at prayer. Dark-painted shutters framed tall windows open to catch any passing breeze. In the side yard, cypress and banana trees shaded a wagon draped in black. A yellow flag hung unmoving in the thick heat, warning of the pestilence inside.

"Are you sure you want to go in there, miss?" Pierre's dark eyes were full of concern. "It isn't too late to change your mind. I can speak to Father Alphonse, if you'd rather."

She shook her head, avoiding the sight of the makeshift hearse waiting in the yard. "I'm ready."

He helped her out of the rig. "Take your time. I'll be right here when you're ready to leave."

She walked up to the door, lifted the heavy brass knocker, and let it fall. Footsteps sounded and then the door opened. A tiny, gray-eyed nun, her face pleated with wrinkles, peered up at her. "Yes?"

"I've come to see Father Alphonse. General Beauregard sent me."

Wordlessly the nun stood aside and motioned her into a dimly lit vestibule. Charlotte had a fleeting impression of soaring colored windows, fountains, carvings, and a sea of flickering candles giving off a sweet scent.

"Wait here." The nun glided away and returned presently with a tall, barrel-chested priest, a florid man with a shock of white hair and a red mark on either side of his nose from where spectacles had pressed into his flesh. Sunlight streamed through the stained-glass window, casting ribbons of purple and green onto his close-fitting cassock.

"Father Alphonse?"

He nodded, as if the effort of speech was too costly.

"I'm searching for someone." By now the story of her employer's long absence, her worries for his safety, and her long journey to find him had become so rote she barely realized she'd spoken.

When she finished, the priest sighed. "You're asking the impossible." He waved one mottled hand toward a set of doors off the vestibule. "I've got forty people in there in various stages of distress. Before that, there were forty others, and before that—"

"I understand. Would you mind if I took a look,

to see whether Mr. Betancourt might be among them? I promise not to disturb anyone."

"I can save you the trouble. Of the unfortunates here today, only five are men, and none of them could possibly be the man you described."

"I see." Heat, worry, fear, and crushing disappointment crumbled her resolve. She opened her reticule, took out her handkerchief, and pressed it to her eyes.

The doors opened and a young nun hurried out, the hem of her black habit whispering on the marble floor. "Father? It's Mrs. Mahoney. She's fading fast and asking for you."

"I'm coming." He sent Charlotte a curt nod. "I'm sorry you came here for naught. Excuse me."

He spun away, the young nun running ahead of him. The older nun placed a hand on Charlotte's arm. "I'm sorry Father Alphonse wasn't of more help and that he seemed so abrupt. Even a man of his great faith finds himself tested when death is a daily companion."

Charlotte turned toward the door, a fierce headache blooming behind her eyes. The general was right. She shouldn't have come. New Orleans was awash in pestilence and chaos, and the chances of finding Nicholas in the midst of it were practically nil. There was nothing more to do but admit defeat and return to Pawley's Island.

"You might ask in the Faubourg Marigny," the nun said. "Just yesterday Sister Marguerite returned from looking after the German and Irish families down there. A makeshift infirmary has been established in a white stone house, she said, close by the railway station."

"I suppose it's worth a try."

The nun patted Charlotte's arm. "You mustn't give up hope. In times such as these, we must all look to God for strength."

A moment later Charlotte returned to the waiting rig. Pierre helped her inside, then settled himself and picked up the reins. "That didn't take long. Any luck?"

"I'm afraid Father Alphonse wasn't any help. But one of the nuns told me to try in the Faubourg Marigny. Do you know where that is?"

Pierre nodded. "It's a neighborhood—not far from here, but not exactly the best part of the city. Mostly Negroes and immigrants live there. The yellow fever has been rampant down there all summer."

Charlotte gave him the nun's description of the house, and they set off through streets choked with people, wagons, carts, and horses. As they turned the corner, they came upon a group of Negro men, voices and fists raised in anger.

Charlotte turned around in her seat. "What is that disturbance all about?"

"Reconstruction," Pierre said. "It's at the heart

of all our troubles these days. Ever since the Federals took over, blacks and whites have been at each other's throats. Some people think the Northerners are stirring up tensions on purpose, merely to add insult to injury."

He stopped to let a young mother carrying a baby cross the street. "General Beauregard is beside himself these days because the Federals have outlawed teaching French in the schools."

"Outlawed it? Why?"

The rig rolled on down the street. "They don't need a reason. They do whatever they choose. Rubbing our noses in our defeat, if you ask me. Ah, here we are."

He slowed the rig as they approached an area of long, narrow cottages with gray slate roofs set along a series of crooked streets. Distant church spires pierced the white-hot sky. In a large square facing the railway station, a few families came and went, stepping around piles of half-burned timbers that gave off an acrid odor. Heat shimmered above the street. A shaft of light refracted from the windows of buildings on the square.

"This is Washington Square," Pierre said. "The general calls it the heartbeat of the Marigny." He pointed to a group of houses situated across the river. "Some years ago the rich Creole men kept their second families hidden there. Wasn't much of a secret, though."

The rig jostled across the railroad track. Charlotte spotted a stone house with two rows of tall windows, a steep slate roof, and a yellow flag tacked above the front door. "This must be the house the nun told me about."

Pierre halted the rig. He took out a red bandana and wiped his face. "I'm happy to help you out, miss, but I surely hope this is the last stop for today. I'm awful thirsty."

"I won't be long. You've been very patient, and I am grateful."

She hurried up the walk and knocked at the door. Soon it was opened by a girl of no more than fourteen with pale blue eyes and stringy blond hair lying lank across her thin shoulders. "We haf no more room for sick people," she said in a thick German accent. "You'll haf to go somewhere else."

"I'm not sick. I'm only looking for someone. May I come in?"

The girl shrugged and stepped aside.

Charlotte went in and blanched at the horrific scene before her. Every inch of the floor was covered with mattresses and piles of blankets, upon which rested a dozen victims of the fever. Despite the open windows, the room reeked of human waste, vomit, and decaying flesh. In one corner lay a fly-covered pile of linens stained with blood and urine. In another, a small wooden stand held pitchers of water, a stack of towels, and a few white enameled basins. Beneath the front window sat a low carved wooden table and two chairs. An endless cacophony of moans, curses, and screams filled the air as patients clawed at their skin or shivered with convulsions.

Charlotte's stomach rolled. She pressed her handkerchief to her mouth and averted her gaze, concentrating on the small landscape painting hanging crookedly on the wall and then on the brown curve of river visible through the window. Anything to keep from looking at the misery surrounding her.

Two nuns moved serenely among the afflicted, pausing to wipe drool and vomit from slack mouths, speaking a word here and there, touching fevered foreheads, and doling out medicine. As the young German girl passed among them with her pitcher and compresses, the patients begged for water, for laudanum, for death.

Charlotte felt lightheaded. So this was how her own mother had died—writhing in agony, begging for death's sweet release. All her life her father had refused to supply even the barest details of her mother's last days. She had resented his sending her away from her mother's sickbed, resented the stubborn silence that had seemed his way of keeping her mother all for himself. Now she realized not knowing had been a blessing. She silently thanked her father for his wisdom and prayed that the general was right and there was little risk to her own health.

She breathed through her mouth and prayed not to lose consciousness—or the remnants of her long-ago breakfast. She moved through the cramped room and forced herself to look into each tortured face, going weak-kneed with relief when she realized none of them was Nicholas.

"Miss?" Charlotte put out a hand to stay the German girl on her rounds. "Who is in charge here?"

"Nurse?" The woman on the mattress nearest Charlotte lifted her arm and caught Charlotte's hand in a weak grip. "Help me."

Before Charlotte could move or summon one of the nuns, the woman vomited a thick mass, black and grainy as coffee grounds. The overpowering stench of it wafted through the room.

"Frau Hiller." The girl knelt beside the woman to bathe her face. "You lie still now—I clean you up." She tossed Charlotte a towel. "Doctor says vee must clean up ze vaste at once."

Charlotte blotted the spittle from her skirts and then mopped up the foul-smelling vomit from the floor. She tossed the soiled towel onto the growing pile in the corner and rinsed her hands in a basin of brown-tinged water. "Is the doctor here?"

Just then a young woman entered from the side yard, her arms laden with stacks of towels. A battered leather medical bag hung from her shoulder. She set down the towels, opened the leather bag, and turned around, both hands full of brown medicine bottles.

Charlotte stilled. The chaos around her receded. She blinked. "Josie Clifton?"

Josie blanched as white as the starched apron pinned to the front of her dress. For a moment the two of them stared at each other, speechless. "My stars," Josie blurted at last. "Charlotte Fraser. What are you doing here?"

"I might ask you the same thing. The last time we spoke, you were headed west with your family."

Josie shook her head and handed the medicines to one of the nuns. "I said my father was going west. That was never my plan."

Nicholas. Nicholas had always been her plan. And the letter Josie had stolen from the postal office in Georgetown had told her just where to find him. "Where is—"

The taller of the two nuns stepped between them, a deep frown creasing her face. "Ladies," she said in a fierce whisper, "if you have nothing better to do than to stand here gossiping while people are dying at your feet, then you can both get out."

"But—" Josie began.

"Out!" the nun shouted just as the door flew open.

A man stepped inside, his sweat-stained shirt hanging loose over blood-spattered trousers that seemed too big for his thin frame. Thick, dark hair fell nearly to his shoulders and he desperately needed a shave. He was frowning too, no doubt displeased at the disturbance. "Sister Beatrice? What's the trouble?"

Twenty-Three

"Nicholas."

Until he turned to look at her, Charlotte could not be certain she had spoken his name aloud. Her throat tightened at the sight of him. She moved toward him as if in a dream.

"Charlotte?" Stepping carefully around his patients, he crossed the room in three long strides and without a moment's hesitation embraced her. "Dear God in heaven."

For a moment they clung together, an island of calm amid the death and chaos surrounding them. She leaned into the circle of his arms, trying desperately not to cry. At last he drew back to look at her. "How are you? And my children? Did you receive my letters? And the money I sent?"

"No." She looked up at him in complete surprise. "I've heard nothing since you left in May. Your daughters are well, but we were worried even before we learned of the epidemic."

"The fever has been fierce this year."

"We had to know whether you were all right. It seemed the only way to find out was to come here. I arrived yesterday and have spent this entire day seeking word of you." Tears clogged her throat. "I feared you were dead. You should have written, Nicholas."

"I just told you. I did write. More than once. I sent money to pay for your tutoring and for Tamar and the girls. I was in over my head here, and Miss Clifton offered to post the letters for me. I was wondering—"

Josie's smile faded like a satin ribbon left in the rain. "Well, I'm tired. I must be going."

"Just a minute." Nicholas stopped her with a look and motioned her toward the door. "Outside."

The three of them went into the yard. Charlotte glanced toward Washington Square, deserted now in the brutal heat. Pierre had parked the rig under a tree and had fallen asleep, one hand still grasping the reins, oblivious to the rattle and shriek of the train just pulling into the station.

Nicholas rounded on Josie, his eyes blazing. "You told me Miss Fraser begged you to come here and assist me with the fever patients while she took the girls to Pawley's Island for the summer. Is that true?"

Josie paled. "Well, maybe not exactly. She did take them to Pawley's. But there she was tied down to that dreadful little school of hers, just beside herself with worry and responsibility, and there I was with loads of time on my hands.

So I just decided to come and look after you."

"And how on earth did you know I was in New Orleans?"

"Yes, Josie." Charlotte fought the anger burning through her veins. "Why don't you tell Mr. Betancourt how you learned of his whereabouts?"

A group of young girls in straw hats and frilly dresses ran pell-mell through the silent square. Nicholas pulled Josie and Charlotte into the shade of the building. "What's this all about, Miss Clifton?"

"Oh, so now that Charlotte is here, it's 'Miss Clifton,' is it?"

"Please answer my question."

Josie dropped her gaze. "I . . . I took the letter she'd written you from the postal office in Georgetown. And I . . . I didn't post the letters you wrote to her."

"I was working day and night to save lives, and I trusted you with a simple errand." Nicholas folded his arms across his chest. "What happened to the checks?"

Josie shrugged. "For goodness' sake, it wasn't all that much—but enough to buy food and rent a cheap room." Her eyes filled. "It's awful living there, but anything is better than being forced to go out west and marry some smelly old cowboy."

"One dollar or a million, stealing is stealing." Nicholas shook his head. "It takes quite a lot of nerve to purloin other people's mail and forge a signature on a check. I don't know whether to admire your audacity or have you arrested. Though the more I think about it, the more I'm inclined toward the latter."

Josie's lips trembled. "Don't do that, Nicholas. I'll pay you back."

"How?"

"I don't know. Somehow." She took a pair of ruby earbobs from her pocket and held them out to him in her open palm. "I take these with me everywhere I go. I don't dare leave them in my room. They'd be stolen in an instant. They're bound to be worth something."

"I don't want them," Nicholas said. "All I want is for you to stay away from me and from my patients."

"But, Nicholas, you care for me, deep down. I know you do. Last week when we went walking you said—"

Charlotte felt an unexpected stab of jealousy. Seeing Nicholas today had made her realize just how much she cared for him. Were he and Josie courting?

"I know what I said." Nicholas took out a handkerchief and wiped his face. "I am grateful for your help with the fever patients. And I care for you as any person ought to care for the well-being of another. But that's all there is to it, Josie. I'm sorry if you thought otherwise."

She burst into tears. "Oh, you are hateful—both

of you. I never want to see either of you again. I . . . oh!" Josie went pale and swayed on her feet.

Nicholas steadied her with a hand on her shoulder. "Are you all right?"

"What do you care?" She shook him off. "I'm sick of all this filth and death. I'm going home. My head hurts."

She hurried across the square and disappeared down a side street.

Nicholas watched her retreat, a frown creasing his brow. "I hope she's all right."

"You're practicing medicine again."

"Unintentionally. I came here to find my land grant and got caught up in this epidemic."

At his mention of the disputed barony, Charlotte felt a jolt of fear. For weeks she'd been too busy with her school and too concerned about Nicholas to think much about her ownership of the plantation. Now apprehension lodged in her midsection, sharp as a thorn. When Nicholas returned to the Waccamaw and reclaimed his children, growing rice would be her only source of income. If she lost Fairhaven, what would become of her?

"Did you find your land grant?"

"Yes."

Her heart thudded. Heat pressed onto her head until she too felt faint.

"And?"

A wagon carrying two bodies wrapped in sheets turned the corner and rattled across the railroad tracks.

"We'll discuss it later. You look pale, Charlotte. Are you all right?"

Whatever the news, she wanted it now. But he was right. This was not the time or place to discuss such a weighty matter. She indicated her soiled skirts. "I'm fine. I need to get cleaned up."

"Me too. Where are you staying?"

"The Orleans Palace."

He whistled. "Pretty fancy."

"I suppose. I haven't seen much of it. I arrived only yesterday and left soon after breakfast this morning in search of you." Briefly, she described her efforts to locate him and nodded toward the still-sleeping Pierre. "General Beauregard was kind enough to lend me his driver. It's high time I returned him."

"May we have dinner this evening? I want to hear about my daughters and about everything going on at home."

"All right."

"I'll check on my patients, clean up, and come to your hotel. Will six o'clock be too early?"

"Six is fine."

He walked her to the rig. She woke the driver and introduced Nicholas.

"So you found him." Pierre grinned at her.

"Then it was worth riding around all day in this heat."

"I'm sorry it was so much trouble. Please let the general know Dr. Betancourt has been found and thank him for me." Charlotte clasped Nicholas's hand as he handed her into the rig.

"Thank him for me too." Nicholas leaned into the buggy, his eyes warm with affection. "I'll see you at six."

Pierre clicked his tongue to the horse and turned the buggy. Charlotte released a pent-up sigh and watched Nicholas striding back into the makeshift infirmary. This trip had been a costly one in more than one sense, but finding Nicholas was worth it all.

The young driver seemed disinclined to talk on the way back to her hotel. Perhaps he was as spent as she. Lulled by the motion of the rig and the press of the afternoon heat, Charlotte struggled to keep her eyes open as the horse clopped toward Prytania Street.

"Here we are, miss." Pierre halted the rig at the banquette and jumped out to assist her.

"Thank you." Charlotte stepped out of the rig. "I'm grateful for your help."

"Glad it turned out so well," he said. "These days we're getting more than our share of unhappy endings." He fished a watch from his pocket and snapped it open. "The general will be home from the railway office soon. I should be getting on back before he sends out someone to look for me."

He refused the tip she offered and climbed into the rig and drove away. Charlotte hurried into the hotel. Mr. Dubois was absent from his small desk in the reception area, but the parlors were filled with ladies taking tea, reading the newspapers, and chatting quietly. Caroline Mayhew looked up from her teacup, stood, and crossed the parlor to the foyer, her russet silk skirts swishing on the carpets. "Hello. I wondered whether I'd see you today." She gestured toward the group seated in the parlor. "My book discussion group—what's left of it—meets here every Saturday afternoon."

"You've lost members to this epidemic?"

"Indirectly. Several of our number went north as soon as word of the fever got out. They are all well as far as I know." She fanned her face. "We had quite a lively conversation this afternoon about Mr. Alger's book on the friendships of women. But it isn't the same when so many are absent."

"No, I suppose not."

Caroline eyed Charlotte's stained skirts, and Charlotte blushed. "I'm afraid I look a fright, and smell even worse." She indicated her soiled clothing. "But at least I found my employer."

"And he's well?"

"Yes. Taking care of the sick in the Faubourg

Marigny—one of whom cast up her accounts on my skirt."

"You poor dear. What you need is a nice warm bath and—" Caroline looked around the room. "Wait here."

She hurried away and soon returned with a female version of Pierre—a slight, olive-skinned girl with lively dark eyes and a mop of black curls pinned into a falling-down coil at the nape of her neck. "This is my lady's maid, Fabienne. She'll help you bathe and change. I must be away, but there's no hurry. Mr. Dubois will see that she gets home safely."

"Thank you, but I can manage."

Caroline shook her head. "You're dead on your feet. And besides, Fabienne is a genius at dressing hair."

"Come, Ma'm'selle," Fabienne said softly. "You will soon feel much better. I am sure of it."

With both hands, Caroline made a shooing motion. "Go along now. I'll find Mr. Dubois and have him send you up something to eat."

Too spent to protest any further, Charlotte took out her key and led the maid up the winding staircase to her room. Fabienne prepared a fragrant, steamy bath and then withdrew. Charlotte undressed, piled her soiled clothing in the corner, and sank gratefully into the warm soapy water, where she remained until the water cooled and her fingers began to wrinkle. When she had dried off, Fabienne came in, eyes averted, and handed her a stack of clean undergarments.

Minutes later Charlotte sat at the small white dressing table, watching Fabienne's nimble fingers as she brushed, twisted, and pinned her damp hair into a cascade of shining curls. At last the maid gave Charlotte's hair a final pat and smiled into the mirror. "Well, Ma'm'selle? Are you pleased?"

"I like it very much, though I'm afraid I could never duplicate such an elaborate style on my own."

The young woman smiled. "It is not so difficult. It only takes practice." She paused. "I hope you won't mind that I took a look in your wardrobe. Which dress will you wear this evening? The pink one with the ruffles or the blue silk?"

"The blue, please." Nicholas had already seen her in the pink gown at Lettice Hadley's birthday party at Alder Hill. Before her trip to New Orleans, she had sponged and aired the blue dress and repaired the torn sleeve and the ripped hem. Though the pagoda sleeves were out of style, the fitted bodice and scooped neckline showed off her shoulders and her small waist. She stopped herself. Nicholas Betancourt's opinion of her appearance had become much more important than was prudent. But she couldn't help hoping he would approve.

Fabienne helped her into the dress, her slim

brown fingers expertly working at the row of tiny mother-of-pearl buttons. She pinched the fabric. "This dress is loose on your bones. Shall I take it in for you?"

"Thank you, but there isn't time. My employer will—"

A knock at the door stopped her words. "Come in."

The young Negro woman who had delivered her dinner last evening came in with a tray of sherry and biscuits. "Mr. Dubois sent you some refreshment."

"I'll take care of it." Fabienne set the tray on the table by the window and waited until the serving woman withdrew. "Is there anything else I can do for you, Ma'm'selle?"

"No thank you." Charlotte took a bill from her bag and handed it to the girl. "I appreciate your help, Fabienne. Please thank Miss Mayhew again for me."

Fabienne left, closing the door softly behind her. Charlotte took a seat at the table and nibbled on a biscuit. She was ravenous, but too overwhelmed by the city's strange contradictions and too disturbed by the day's tumultuous events to eat very much. She couldn't stop thinking about Solange, so young and alone, scrounging for food and shelter on the waterfront. What would become of her and of the hundreds of children sure to be orphaned before this epidemic was past? Without someone to guide them, how would they get on in a world so different from the one they once knew?

Finding Nicholas was an answer to prayer, but the suffering at his infirmary had been almost unbearable. And then there was Josie Clifton. Despite the fact that the girl was a liar and a thief, Charlotte couldn't help feeling sorry for her. How terrible it must be to feel so pressured to marry. And where would Josie go, now that her family had gone west and Nicholas had banned her from the infirmary?

Charlotte poured sherry into a crystal glass and stared out the window, seeing nothing. Most pressing of all, what did Nicholas's discovery of his land grant mean for her own future?

Leaving the sherry untouched, she crossed the room and sat at the escritoire to compose a letter to Augusta. Marie-Claire and Anne-Louise would be delirious with happiness to know their father was safe. She finished the letter and addressed it for posting just as a church bell tolled the hour.

After one last glance into the mirror, she took a deep breath to quell her jangled nerves and went downstairs to meet Nicholas.

Twenty-Four

He stood at the foot of the curving staircase watching her descend. He had changed into a pair of fine wool trousers, a white shirt, and a jacket that emphasized the set of his shoulders. His thick dark hair was still damp and curling over his collar. A smile lit his face.

"Charlotte. You look lovely." He assumed a playful pose, one foot on the bottom stair, a hand clapped over his heart. An actor in a play. "Fairer than the evening air, clad in the beauty of a thousand stars."

"Thank you," she said, smiling into his eyes. "Marlowe, if I'm not mistaken."

"Yes. One of my favorites." He steered her toward the door. "I've booked a table at Pascal's. It isn't very fancy, but the food is good and it's close by. I hired a carriage, but . . . do you mind walking?"

"Not at all. A walk will feel wonderful after spending all day in General Beauregard's buggy."

Nicholas instructed the driver to wait for him, and they set off along Prytania. The sun was not yet down, but a slight cooling breeze wafted in from the river, bringing with it the scents of jessamine, burning sugar, and an acrid smell she couldn't name.

"They're burning tar in the squares again tonight," Nicholas said. "Some people believe it prevents the fever."

"Does it?" She lifted her hem as they skirted a couple of small boys playing marbles in an open doorway. Beyond an iron gate a patch of garden, heavy with the scent of magnolias, beckoned.

"I'm afraid not." He took her arm as they crossed the street and continued down St. Charles. "The entire South is plagued with it summer after summer. Yet no one has been able to isolate the cause. Or to find an effective treatment."

"I understand that's one reason General Longstreet left the city."

He glanced at her, a question in his eyes.

"I wrote to him, hoping you were still at his house or, failing that, that he would help me find you. But I had no answer, and when I arrived yesterday I learned he has gone north. To keep his family safe from the fever, I was told."

"And to keep himself safe from the volatile political situation." They met another couple on the street, and Nicholas inclined his head to the lady as they passed. "I don't mind telling you I will be glad to get out of here as well. I miss my children, and I'm weary of this town. Some parts of town have turned into a powder keg this summer."

"And yet the hotel manager told me that several generals of the Confederacy are living here now," Charlotte said. "I suppose they must believe it's worth the risk to build a new life."

A moment later they entered a cobblestoned alley lined with brightly painted buildings, each adorned with wrought-iron balconies and staircases. Nicholas stopped before a heavy mahogany door. "Here we are."

He led her into a small restaurant lit with candles and tiny oil lamps. Half a dozen round tables dressed in crisp white linen were scattered about the room.

A tall, gray-haired man of indeterminate years with a white apron tied about his waist hurried over to greet them. "Ah, my dear Mr. Betancourt, there you are, and with such a beautiful lady."

Nicholas grinned. "Good evening, Pascal."

"I saved the best table just for you."

Pascal led them to a table overlooking a rear courtyard and held Charlotte's chair. When they were seated he shook out her napkin and, with a flourish, placed it on her lap. "*Bon appétit*."

"What's on the menu tonight?" Nicholas asked.

"I have a very fine poached fish, peas with sweet basil, and for the soup course a shrimp stew. And my wife made a hazelnut torte."

"We're famished," Nicholas told him. "Please bring us everything."

The restaurateur hurried away. Nicholas moved

the flickering taper to the side of the table and gazed directly at Charlotte. "I'm so very happy to see you."

"And I'm happy to know you are still among the living." She looked around the room, which seemed to glow in the soft flickering light. "This is a lovely place. I hope I'm not taking you away from your patients."

He shook his head. "Dr. Werner lives just down the street from the infirmary. He and Sister Beatrice know where to find me. Though there is precious little I can do for the most serious cases."

She nodded. "My mother died of the fever when I was twelve. My father said then there was no cure."

"There still isn't. All I can do is try to relieve their suffering. Some recover on their own; others slip away."

"I read that some doctors are using tincture of iron and doses of mercury."

"Yes, but mercury poisoning is often as fatal as the disease." He toyed with his spoon. "During the war some doctors experimented with large doses of it and lost entire companies of soldiers. Thankfully, most have given up on it, and on blood-letting too. Salves for the skin, laudanum, and prayer are really all we have to fight the disease."

"Perhaps a cure will be found soon."

"I hope so. But research and experimentation require a great deal of time and money."

The door opened. A man came in and nodded to Nicholas, who returned the greeting before turning back to Charlotte. "There's so much to talk about, I scarcely know where to begin." His gaze sought hers. "You said my children are all right."

"They're doing very well, though they were upset when Tamar had to leave them with me."

He frowned. "What are you talking about?"

She described Tamar's plight and the move to Pawley's Island for the summer. His shock gave way to anguish as she described their fears for his safety. "It wasn't your fault, of course. If osie hadn't stolen our letters . . ."

"Where are the girls now?"

She reached over to lay a hand on his sleeve. "All is well. They're staying with my friend Augusta, whom they adore."

She told him about their days on the beach at Pawley's flying kites and collecting seashells, their studies, her work with the Demeres, and the Fourth of July celebration. Delaying the time when she must hear the news about his land grant. "They are happy, though of course they miss you terribly and worry about you. I've already written to Augusta to let them know you are well."

"I'll write to them too, and this time I won't trust anyone to post it."

"Poor Josie." Charlotte paused while the waiter brought a small basket of bread and served the soup, a fragrant mixture of shrimp, tomatoes, and okra. "Seeing her today gave me quite a start."

Nicholas spooned his soup. "She surprised me too, turning up unannounced. Of course her story didn't ring completely true, but the epidemic had spread, and I was too grateful for another pair of hands to question her motives." He buttered a piece of bread. "To her credit, she has worked tirelessly alongside Sister Beatrice and the others, with hardly a complaint."

"I'm surprised to find you practicing medicine again. The night of Lettice Hadley's party you seemed set against it."

"I was, but no physician worth his salt could turn away from such suffering." He shrugged. "Longstreet once told me that a general chooses his battles, but physicians find that the battles choose them."

"I suppose that's true."

"There is simply so much we don't know about how to prevent and treat illness, and when something new is discovered, we are often too slow to act." He scooped a fat shrimp from his soup bowl and ate it with apparent relish. "Cholera, for instance. We've known for years that it's transmitted by contaminated water, but so far we've done little to eradicate sources of contamination, and people continue to die needlessly.

It's hard to keep going in the face of so little progress."

"I suppose many doctors must have felt that way during the war."

He set aside his soup bowl. "If only we'd known about the importance of antiseptics back in sixty-five, so many more soldiers' lives could have been spared. If Dr. Lister had published his findings on the efficacy of carbolic acid just two years sooner—"

The waiter set another basket of warm bread on the table. Nicholas offered the basket to Charlotte, then took two slices and slathered them with butter. "Ah well. This isn't exactly an appropriate topic for dinner with a lady. Tell me, have you been back to the Waccamaw this summer?"

"Yes. Our overseer, Mr. Finch, has quit the Lowcountry and headed back home. Mr. Hadley and Mr. Clifton were looking after my rice fields, but since the Cliftons went west, it's only Mr. Hadley, a few hired men, and Daniel Graves."

"The boy who turned up at your house for tutoring?"

"Yes. He has been a godsend this summer. His father sent word for him to come north, but Daniel wants to stay and attend the new county school next term. He's determined to make a success of his life."

Pascal arrived with the fish and vegetables and collected their soup bowls.

"I suppose it's just as well I didn't plant rice this spring," Nicholas said, "since Finch has decamped and there are so few to tend it." He sampled the fish and nodded his approval. "Nobody makes a better poached fish than Pascal."

It smelled delicious, but his mention of their plantations knotted her stomach. She attempted a small bite and then set down her fork. "So you found your papers regarding the barony."

"Yes. Or more accurately, they found me. Just after Longstreet left town, Father Sebastian, my wife's former parish priest, came to see me. He told me his church burned down during the war, leaving nothing standing but the fireplace. When they sorted through the rubble, they discovered the church silver had been buried beneath the bricks in the hearth, most likely to keep it out of the hands of the Federals. My papers were stuffed inside a chalice along with some family letters."

She drew as deep a breath as possible given her tight corset, willing away the butterflies dancing in her midsection. "How did they get there?"

"He claims not to remember." Nicholas helped himself to another slice of bread. "Gabrielle must have given them to him for safekeeping when she fell ill, not realizing what they were. It isn't so unusual when you stop to think about it. The Polks of Tennessee hid their silver in one of their porch columns."

"I suppose you're right. Father hid a few of our things at the home of a friend in Charleston."

Nicholas nodded. "Anyway, Father Sebastian said he'd been looking for me through my distant cousin, Therese St. Clair. But she died years ago." Nicholas took another bite of fish. "I was surprised he didn't know. Her story was fairly well known in her day."

Despite her apprehension over what this discovery meant for her, Charlotte couldn't help being intrigued. "Go on."

"From what I understand, Therese was quite a beauty. She claimed kinship with Lafayette through the Marbourgs, but that may be only a rumor." He drained his glass. "Sometime in the thirties she came over from Paris and married a Carolina planter, but shortly afterward she was lost at sea. Anyway, Father Sebastian had been looking for me ever since the papers turned up. It wasn't an easy task since we've no family left on this side of the Atlantic. Therese was the only one he had to go on."

"How did he find you?"

"One of his parishioners, Mrs. Wimberly, looked after the girls for a time just before my wife died. I suppose Gabrielle told her that my ancestors had once been granted some land on the Waccamaw. Anyway, Father Sebastian was preparing to go to Willowood to look for me when we ran into each other down in the Marigny."

She took a ragged breath. The truth could be postponed no longer. "And?"

"It seems that Willowood and everything south, all the way down to Oak Hill, was part of a barony that John Carteret, one of the lords proprietors, granted to my family. It passed to my grandfather sometime around 1785 and then to my father almost fifty years ago."

"I see." Charlotte went numb. If his land extended that far south, then he owned Fairhaven too.

"I intend to have the papers properly recorded as soon as possible, for the sake of my daughters," Nicholas went on. "One day the land will be theirs, though who knows whether it will have any value by then."

She sipped water to dissolve the lump in her throat. But what else could she expect? Of course he wanted to protect what was his and secure his children's future. Any responsible father would do the same. Regardless of the consequences for others.

"This has come as a shock to you." Nicholas covered her hand with his.

"To say the least. If it's all yours, I don't understand why no one ever challenged my father's claim."

"According to my lawyer, the original grants

weren't always formally filed. Some of the papers were kept at home and passed from father to son. Sometimes the boundaries were disputed or changed or land was bought and sold and the deeds not officially recorded. It's possible that's what happened in your case." He sipped water from a cut-glass tumbler that caught and splintered the candlelight. "Most of the lords proprietors never even came to Carolina to inspect their property. They simply appointed lawyers to sell it. And during the war, of course, a great many records were destroyed."

Charlotte thought of the pile of papers the Federals had left torn and wadded on the floor of her father's study. "But miraculously, your records survived."

She couldn't keep the bitterness from her voice. She withdrew her hand from his and felt even more alone. This was the end of her dream of restoring her land and claiming her future. The end of her friendship with Nicholas and his daughters. The end of everything.

Pascal appeared with two slices of torte on thin china plates and a tray set with coffee cups and a silver pot. "Compliments of my Cecile," he said. "Enjoy."

But Charlotte's appetite had fled. "I'm afraid I can't eat another bite, Nicholas. And I'm very tired. Please take me home."

"Listen to me. I know this is upsetting, but you

must know that after everything you have done for Marie-Claire and Anne-Louise, I'm not about to displace you. Besides, a bill of sale or a deed to Fairhaven might still come to light."

She thought again of Papa's strongbox. The Federals must have taken it years ago. Otherwise she would have stumbled across it by now. But what if somehow it had survived and was waiting to be discovered? What if it contained proof of her right to Fairhaven? It was too much to hope for. She pushed her plate away.

"I've been through all my father's papers, everything that wasn't destroyed. And I've had his lawyer go through all the papers in his possession too. It isn't there."

"Please don't worry. We'll come to some accommodation—a yearly rental, a long-term lease. There are several ways to—"

"Thank you, but I don't want to live as a tenant on the very land my father worked so hard to improve." Tears threatened, and she blinked them away. "Especially not in the house where I grew up. It would be too painful. There must be some—"

The door banged open, and the young German girl from the infirmary burst into the room. Spying Nicholas, she rushed to the table, nearly upsetting Pascal's dessert tray. "Dr. Betancourt, Sister Beatrice asks that you come at once."

"What's the matter?" Nicholas was already

rising from his chair, pulling bills from his pocket.

"It's Miss Josie, Doctor. She's burning up with the fever and asking for you."

Nicholas jumped to his feet. "I'll be there as soon as I see Miss Fraser home."

Without waiting for him to hold her chair, Charlotte rose as well. "Josie seemed fine this afternoon. Just a headache from all the excitement. But surely that—"

"The fever strikes very quickly. I hoped her distress this afternoon was the result of the heat and her emotional state, but I'd better see to her."

"I'd like to come with you."

He looked into her face, one brow raised. "To the infirmary? You're sure?"

"Yes." Despite what she had just learned, she felt drawn to Nicholas, compelled to share his burden. Perhaps it made no sense to feel this way, but there it was.

Nicholas caught Pascal's eye and pointed to the money he'd left on the table. He offered her his arm, and they returned to his carriage. He handed the girl and Charlotte inside and called up to the driver, "Hurry!"

The driver spoke to the horse in its traces, and the carriage lurched along streets enveloped in a thick cloud of acrid smoke. Here and there fires flickered in deserted squares and on street corners. Long shadows danced against shops and cafés already shuttered for the night. Minutes later they drew up at the stone house across from Washington Square, quiet now in the summer darkness save for the trilling of insects. In the middle of the square a tar fire burned, sending up thick smoke that burned Charlotte's eyes. A single lantern illuminated the adjacent railway station and a horse-drawn hearse standing near the front door.

With instructions to the driver to wait, Nicholas helped Charlotte from the carriage. The girl jumped out and ran for the door.

"Liesl," Nicholas said, his voice low and commanding. "Please wait."

The girl's eyes darted toward the waiting hearse. "But, Doctor, someone has died. I haf to know."

"We'll know soon enough. Would you fetch my bag?"

The girl disappeared into the makeshift office in the side yard. Nicholas and Charlotte went inside.

Sister Beatrice glided toward them, a basin of pink-tinged water in one hand, a flickering lamp in the other, and indicated the far side of the room. "She's over there, Doctor."

Nicholas nodded. "Who have we lost tonight, Sister?"

"Mr. Becker, just after you left this afternoon, and poor Mrs. Hiller just moments ago. I'm afraid dear Liesl will be heartbroken."

When the girl came inside with Nicholas's bag, the nun gathered her into her arms and murmured the news. Liesl gave one loud sob and ran from the room, deliberately kicking over a washstand on her way out. Charlotte understood. When her mother died, she had rampaged through the house in a fury of grief, raking books from their shelves, throwing a crystal vase of wilted roses against the wall, slamming doors so hard they rattled in their wooden frames. As if such destruction could somehow numb her pain and bring her mother back.

"Mrs. Hiller was her teacher from their days in Germany," Nicholas said, setting the washstand to rights. "They were inseparable."

"What about Liesl's parents?"

"Her mother succumbed two weeks ago. Her father is still alive as far as I know. Come. Let's check on Josie."

They made their way among the sick and dying to Josie's side. Nicholas took his stethoscope from his bag and knelt beside her cot. He looked up at Charlotte. "Could you ask Sister Beatrice for a basin and some towels? And a lamp, please."

Charlotte hurried to comply and returned to his side. He propped Josie's shoulders onto a stained pillow and covered her with a thin blue quilt. "How long have you been sick?"

Josie gave a slight shrug and licked her lips.

"Two weeks. I felt awfully sick for a few days, but then I got better."

"And were you jaundiced?"

"I don't know. A little, I suppose. But you were helping at Dr. Werner's house, and we were all so busy you didn't notice."

"Why didn't you tell me?"

"I . . . wanted to be . . . with you. You would have sent me away."

"Foolish girl." Nicholas motioned for Charlotte to kneel beside him. "Roll her sleeves up, please."

"You aren't going to bleed her, are you?" In the yellow lamplight, the room spun before Charlotte's eyes. Bloodletting was an old-fashioned treatment for everything. Years ago her father's doctors had tried it as a way to restore his failing lungs, but she had never seen the procedure done. Now she regretted her decision to accompany Nicholas here, but it was too late to turn back. She inhaled a deep breath of fetid air, unbuttoned Josie's cuffs, and rolled up the girl's sleeves.

"Dr. Werner still believes in phlebotomy," Nicholas said. "But I've no reason to suppose it's worth the risk." He took a small tin container from his bag. He washed his hands, scooped a yellow salve with his fingers, and began massaging it firmly into Josie's fevered skin.

The girl moaned and her head rolled to one side.

"Wring out those towels and bathe her face," Nicholas instructed. "When one towel gets too warm, change to another. Keep her as cool as possible."

Charlotte focused on his hands as he bent to his task. She remembered that magical afternoon on the river last spring when he had played the violin for her, his long fingers grasping the bow. It seemed a lifetime ago.

Josie gasped as Charlotte applied the cool compresses that quickly warmed against the girl's fevered brow. Again and again Charlotte applied the compresses as Nicholas massaged the salve into Josie's skin. Despite the open windows, the air in the room was warm and still. Charlotte wiped her brow with her sleeve and tried to keep pace with Nicholas's sure movements.

"Miss?" Sister Beatrice stood behind Charlotte. "I've no right to ask, but I wonder whether you would help me with Mrs. Chamblin. She's wanting to turn onto her side, and I can't lift her."

"Of course." Leaving Nicholas to tend to Josie, Charlotte followed the nun to the woman's mattress. Together they managed to get Mrs. Chamblin onto her side. Then a young boy called for water. Wordlessly Sister Beatrice pressed a pitcher and a glass into Charlotte's hands before hurrying away to check on an old man who was calling for her. A younger nun, her face pale and round as a balloon, scurried along behind them, picking up soiled linens and depositing them into a wicker hamper.

As the putrid smells of disease and death wafted through the stuffy room, Charlotte was thankful she hadn't eaten much dinner. She was perilously close to losing the few bites she'd consumed before Nicholas's news stole her appetite. She poured water from the pitcher and held the boy's shoulders while he drank, then fluffed the sweaty pillow of the woman lying next to him.

Another hour passed. The front door opened and a black-clad undertaker came in, accompanied by two men carrying a stretcher. Sister Beatrice led them to the two bodies, which were quickly loaded onto the stretcher. Charlotte stood at the window, gulping the tar-scented air, wishing she hadn't been so quick to offer her help. How on earth could anyone bear such misery day after day?

"Charlotte?" Nicholas stood behind her, drying his hands on a white towel. "There's nothing more to be done for Josie tonight. Give me a moment to speak to Sister, and I'll see you home."

"I can go alone. It isn't that far, and it's obvious you're needed here."

He looked into her face, and she saw how utterly exhausted he was. "Dr. Werner will be here in a little while so that Sister can get some sleep. I'd really like to talk to you if you're up to it."

Despite the distressing news he'd delivered earlier in the evening, her heart turned over. "All right."

While Nicholas checked on the other patients, the younger nun appeared with a basin of clean water, soap, and towels. "I thought you might be wanting to freshen yourself, miss."

"Yes, thank you." Charlotte dipped the towel into the cool water and washed the sweat from her brow and the back of her neck. The elaborate hairstyle upon which Fabienne had lavished so much care was now matted, the pins falling onto her wrinkled skirt.

She looked down at the sleeping Josie, her resentment all but forgotten. The girl had helped others, even if her motivation for doing so had been less than altruistic. That counted for something.

"Ready?" Nicholas appeared at her side, and they left the infirmary.

Nicholas called up to the carriage driver, "Orleans Palace, please. Prytania Street."

As he handed her into the waiting carriage, a wagon clattered along the street and came to a stop at the infirmary door.

"More patients," Nicholas said, his voice tinged with fatigue. "Some days it seems this scourge will never end."

Charlotte tucked her skirts about her. "Will Josie be all right?"

"I don't know. Sometimes after an initial bout of the fever, patients recover. But based on what she told me, this is her second battle with it, and the second round is often fatal."

"Should we attempt to contact her family?"

He passed a hand over his tired eyes. "I suppose so."

"I haven't posted my letter to Augusta yet. I'll ask her to make some inquiries. I know Josie has relatives in North Carolina, but I don't know their names."

He nodded and stared out the open carriage window. Charlotte followed his gaze. Distant music and the smells of burning tar, stagnant water, and honeysuckle rode the hot breeze wafting through the carriage. "Do you ever worry that you might contract the fever?"

He shook his head. "I had it as a boy. I'm immune. Which obligates me to do all I can for others."

"You're wearing yourself out, Nicholas. I understand your desire to help. But you must think of your daughters. They need you too."

"I realize that. I've already spoken to Dr. Werner about finding a replacement for me. But doctors who are willing to step into the middle of an epidemic are scarce."

"Marie-Claire and Anne-Louise will be ecstatic to see you. How soon might you come home?"

"Perhaps in a week or two, if we don't have

many more cases coming in." He sent her a tired smile. "Now, of course, I must wait to see how Josie fares."

The carriage drew up at the hotel, the horse snorting and jingling his harness. Neither Charlotte nor Nicholas moved. Insects sang in the garden. At last she said, "What did you want to talk about?"

In the moonlight coming through the window, his profile was endearing. Familiar. He leaned over, and his hands—strong, warm, healing—enveloped hers. "So many things, but suddenly I am too tired to think."

The carriage driver jumped down and opened the door. "Here we are, sir. The Orleans Palace."

"Just a moment." Nicholas turned to her. "When you were here before with your father, did you go to Milneburg? On Lake Pontchartrain? It's a beautiful place, and there are all kinds of entertainments."

She shook her head. "We were here only a short time, and my father was always in meetings. There wasn't much time for sightseeing."

"Then come with me tomorrow. It's Dr. Werner's turn to take charge, and I promised to deliver some quinine to one of his patients in Milneburg. I'll check on my patients here first thing, then we can take the train to the lake. We'll spend the day and be back before dark."

"I don't know, Nicholas. I—"

He took her hand. "Please say yes. I cannot tell you how much I need a respite from the clinic, and I would love to spend the day with you."

Fatigue, worry, and the unrelenting humid heat gnawed at her. And in the wake of his news about the barony, she had much to sort out. But the prospect of an entire day of leisure beside a cooling lake was too tempting to refuse. "All right. I'd like that."

He helped her from the carriage and walked her to the door. "Thank you for your help tonight. You performed admirably."

"I'm only glad I don't have to do it every day. I can't imagine how any of you bear it."

"It does take its toll." He opened the door with a weary smile. "I'll call for you at ten tomorrow, if that isn't too early."

"Ten will be fine. Good night, Nicholas."

She watched through the doorway as the carriage rolled through the porte cochere and onto the street, headed for St. Charles Avenue. She went inside and up the stairs, bone tired but too enervated to sleep.

Twenty-Five

Filled to capacity with Sunday revelers, the train slid into Milneburg station and shuddered to a stop. Charlotte gathered her parasol and reticule and followed Nicholas off the train. The five-mile ride from Faubourg Marigny on the Ponchartrain Railroad had been too short and too noisy for much conversation. But now, as they joined a group of travelers headed toward the Washington Hotel, they finally had a chance to talk.

Nicholas had visited the infirmary early before calling for Charlotte at the hotel. On the carriage ride to the train station, he reported that no patients had died in the night. Josie appeared to be improving and was sleeping peacefully. He had left instructions with Sister Beatrice to give her another dose of laudanum if she needed it. And Dr. Werner had reported that new cases at Father Alphonse's convent clinic seemed to be slowing.

"Does that mean the worst of the epidemic is over?"

"Perhaps. I pray so. Though of course we won't

be completely out of danger until the black frost." Nicholas offered her his arm. "Are you hungry?"

"Not very. The hotel cook returned from the hinterlands last night, and this morning Mr. Dubois fed me as if I'm royalty. I think he's happy to have someone to look after."

"Then let's walk for a while. We'll deliver this quinine to Mr. Morgan's tobacco shop and take in the sights."

They reached a set of stairs attached to a network of wooden boardwalks that led past hotels, noisy saloons, bathhouses, and shops. All were built on wooden piers in the shallows of Lake Ponchartrain, giving pedestrians the illusion of walking on water. Charlotte waited in the shade of the building while Nicholas went inside the tobacco shop. Moments later he returned, and they continued down the long boardwalk.

"Is Dr. Werner's patient all right?" Charlotte asked.

"I believe so. He says he feels better today." Nicholas indicated the shimmering lake. "It's quite something, isn't it? I came here for the first time with my grandfather when I was a boy. Of course, there weren't nearly so many buildings here then. The lighthouse was just a rickety old wooden one."

He watched two young boys playing tag, a wistful look in his eyes. "Look at them. So full of possibility. When I was their age, I'd lie in my room for hours listening to the steamboats passing on the river. Dreaming of what would happen when I became a man."

She imagined Nicholas as he must have been as a boy—long-legged, green-eyed, full of hope and imagination, and she felt a sense of loss at not having known him when they were young and unburdened by grief and responsibility.

"It's like another world here, Nicholas. Hard to believe it's only five miles from the infirmary."

He nodded. "Gabrielle—my wife—and I came here often when we were first married. After a while it became routine for me, but she never tired of it. She always loved New Orleans more than I did."

They strolled past a shady park across from the train station where a courting couple sat on a bench, their heads bent to a conversation meant only for them. "You must miss her terribly," Charlotte said.

"Yes. Her death was quite a blow. I don't think anyone ever fully recovers from such a loss." He smiled into her eyes. "But I've made my peace with it. My children are a great comfort."

They continued to the end of the boardwalk, where an old Creole man in a faded red suit had set up a souvenir stand. Nicholas stopped to consider the man's wares: delicately carved miniature carousels, shiny wooden sailboats sporting tiny linen sails, porcelain dolls with painted faces.

"What shall I buy you for a souvenir?" Nicholas asked.

"That's kind of you, but not necessary."

"I know. But I want to." He selected a black lacquered box painted with pink and white camellias and opened the lid, releasing the tinkling notes of Brahms's lullaby. "What do you think of this?"

"It's lovely, but—"

"How much?" he asked the old man.

The vendor held up three fingers, and Nicholas handed over the money. "I want to get something for the girls too."

She watched as he considered each object, turning it over in his hands, lips pursed in concentration. Finally he chose one of the little sailboats and a gold-clad jumping jack wearing a purple jester's mask.

"What do you think of these?"

"They're wonderful."

"But?" He regarded her, brows raised in question.

"Anne-Louise fancies dolls these days. She asked Augusta to make one for her. And Marie-Claire considers herself much too grown-up for toys. She's become friends with one of the children I teach, an older girl. She won't admit it, but she idolizes Bess."

"I see." He set the toys aside, his smile replaced by a look of sadness. "It's one sorry day when a father has no inkling of such things."

"You mustn't blame yourself. You came here to secure their right to your property, and you've accomplished that."

"I suppose."

"And Josie stole the letter that would have given you news of their interests."

"Still, I never intended to stay away so long. Perhaps I've become too involved in caring for the fever victims."

"Father was fond of saying it's a sin to waste one's talents, but you have done your part." She handed him the music box. "This will be the perfect gift for Marie-Claire. Her first grown-up present. And she will never forget that it came from her father." She smiled. "I still have a gold locket my father gave me for my tenth birthday."

"But I wanted you to have it."

She ran her finger along the satiny wood of the little boat. "This suits me just as well. I'll treasure it as a reminder of today, and of all my journeys."

He paid for the boat and the doll and tucked the package under his arm. "Let's go. I want to show you the lighthouse."

She slipped the little boat into her reticule, and they joined others on a leisurely stroll along the long pier, past an oceangoing ship riding anchor and then to the brick lighthouse at the end of the pier. From beneath the shade of her parasol, Charlotte looked out over the glittering waters of the lake. Across from the network of board-walks, a steady stream of men and women in their Sunday best came and went from the bathhouse and the Washington Hotel. In the park several black-clad musicians hurried about setting up a bandstand, and a pair of redheaded boys in short pants and straw boaters struggled to launch a kite. Couples in rowboats drifted on the water, their voices snatched and released by the steady breeze.

Nicholas grinned down at her. "Are you hungry yet?"

She wasn't really all that ravenous, but Nicholas obviously was, and so she nodded. "Something cool to drink would be most welcome."

Half an hour later they were seated at a table in the hotel dining room enjoying a luncheon of chilled potato soup and grilled trout. Afterward they listened to the concert in the park and bought lemon tarts from the bakery just down the boardwalk from a crowded saloon.

When they heard the train nearing the station again, Nicholas consulted his pocket watch. "I hate for the day to end, but I suppose we ought to go soon. Dr. Werner asked me to stop by his house this evening, and I promised to have you home before dark."

Twenty-Six

Charlotte heard Nicholas's quick intake of breath. "Are you certain? Perhaps she's only sleeping. Sometimes the laudanum will—"

"She is not sleeping. Please come."

Nicholas and Charlotte followed Liesl into the stench and despair of the crowded infirmary. "Over there." The girl pointed to the pallet where Josie lay pale and still.

Nicholas made his way closer and reached down to check her pulse. Charlotte stood rooted to the spot, struggling to take air into her lungs. Usually death from the fever was far from instantaneous. How could Josie have succumbed so quickly?

Nicholas got to his feet, his face dark with anger, and strode over to Liesl. "Where is Dr. Werner?"

"He came here zis morning, but he has gone."

"As well he might be." Nicholas turned to Charlotte. "Josie Clifton bled to death."

"No."

"I'm certain of it. Dr. Werner had no right to bleed my patient. I left explicit instructions for her care."

Liesl began to cry. "Is not my fault."

359

"Of course it's not." Nicholas patted the girl's shoulder and surveyed the room. "Where is Sister Beatrice?"

"She did not come today." Lisle wiped her tears. "Sister Luke helped Dr. Verner *mit* Miss Clifton, but she left too. There is no one here but me. I am sorry."

Charlotte placed her arm around the girl's shoulder. "You mustn't cry. No one blames you."

Nicholas let out a long breath. "These patients need tending. Liesl, will you fetch my medical bag, then get the hamper and collect the dirty linens?"

"Yes, sir."

"And find the undertaker and send him along."

"Yes, sir."

He turned to Charlotte. "I need your help."

"Of course."

For the next two hours, while Liesl removed soiled bedclothes and brought clean ones off the clothesline out back, Charlotte bathed fevered brows, applied salve to cracked skin, offered fresh water to those able to drink. She mopped vomit and urine, changed filthy linens, emptied basin after basin of dirty water. Nicholas listened to failing hearts and feeble prayers and administered doses of laudanum.

The undertaker arrived for Josie's body just as darkness fell. Nicholas, his face suddenly haggard, spoke quietly with the undertaker, then lit a lamp and set it on the small table beneath the front window.

Charlotte rose from the bedside of a young child and massaged the burning muscles in her back. She rolled her neck and pressed her fingers to her tired eyes.

"I'm sorry," Nicholas said, his voice rough with fatigue. "You're exhausted. I had no right to ask you to stay."

Her eyes met his. "I wanted to help you."

"Let's get you home."

"You should rest too."

"I will. And tomorrow I intend to have a talk with Dr. Werner. With any luck he will have found that replacement he's promised. I'm not one to give up easily but—"

"You've done more than your share. And your daughters need you every bit as much as these patients do."

With a last look at his patients, Nicholas spoke quietly to Liesl, one hand resting on her shoulder, and then ushered Charlotte out into the humid twilight. Outside the train station a burly man lit a torch and set fire to the tar barrel. The flame flickered and caught. A puff of black smoke drifted across the square.

"Will Liesl be all right staying here alone?"

"Dr. Werner is due here within the hour. If Liesl needs help before then, she knows to call upon his neighbor, Mrs. Lapierre."

He found a carriage for hire, handed Charlotte up, and tossed his bag inside.

"Dr. Betancourt?" The moon-faced nun who had assisted Sister Beatrice stepped from the shadows.

"Sister Luke," Nicholas said. "I wondered what had become of you."

Sister Luke broke into a fit of weeping. "Sister Beatrice has contracted the fever."

Nicholas sighed and pinched the bridge of his nose, seemingly too exhausted for words.

"I tried to tell Dr. Werner about Miss Clifton," the nun said. "I told him you wanted only the sleeping medicine and the cool baths, but he insisted he knew best. He ordered me to assist him while he bled her."

"I understand."

"No, you don't, sir." The nun's breath hitched. "It was me that killed her."

"What?"

"I . . . I gave her the laudanum, like you said, and I never should have. Not after the amount of blood she lost."

Nicholas clenched his fists until they turned white. "Please go on."

"He said Miss Clifton was young and strong, and the loss of so much blood would help the fever go out of her more quickly. When he finished, he told me to bandage her arm and then he left." Sister Luke drew a balled handkerchief from the sleeve of her habit and wiped her eyes. "When I checked on her an hour or so later, she was burning up and begging for medicine, talking out of her head. I didn't know what to do. There was no one to ask. So I gave her the laudanum, and then she—"

"You mustn't blame yourself, Sister. Miss Clifton was in her second bout with the fever. We can't be certain she would have recovered even if Dr. Werner had not countermanded my instructions." His voice softened. "You eased her suffering. There is nothing wrong in that."

Sister Luke nodded, her brow still furrowed.

"Where is Sister Beatrice?"

"At the convent. They are looking after her there."

"Good. As soon as Dr. Werner arrives, I want you to go home and get some rest. Without Sister Beatrice, you're needed here more than ever."

"You aren't angry with me?"

"On the contrary. I'm grateful for the mercy you showed my patient."

A sad smile spread across the young nun's face. "Sister always says you are one of God's own angels, Dr. Betancourt."

He climbed into the carriage. "Good night, Sister."

Nicholas seemed to need silence. Charlotte folded her hands in her lap as the carriage rolled along in the darkness. When they reached Prytania

363

Street and the Orleans Palace, he got out first and helped her alight.

The theater troupe that had returned to the hotel early this morning was performing a human tableau for the enjoyment of a small group of people gathered near the main entrance. Illuminated by several large lanterns, two women draped in purple stood poised with bows and arrows, while the men hoisted a fake deer onto their shoulders. In the shadows stood Mr. Dubois and several men dressed in hotel livery.

Nicholas regarded the colorful scene, a small frown creasing his forehead. "What do you suppose they call this particular work of art?"

Charlotte shrugged, too exhausted by the day's events to give much thought to entertainments. "I'd love to go up to my room, but I don't wish to disrupt the performance."

"They can't hold that pose for very long," Nicholas said. "Perhaps we can wait in the courtyard."

They crossed the lawn and entered the walled garden. Light from lamps burning in the guest rooms above them cast a soft glow onto the flower beds and the fountain. Charlotte sank gratefully onto a wrought-iron bench and attempted to tidy her hair.

"May I join you?"

"Of course."

She made room for him on the bench. For

several moments they sat in silence, filled with the particular energy that comes from a shared experience.

At last Nicholas said, "Have I told you how much I appreciate your assistance?"

"You have. I'm glad I was able to help."

"You've a true woman's heart, Charlotte. Somehow you keep going despite adversity."

"Circumstances have given me little choice."

"Still, I don't know many women who would have done what you did tonight, let alone take on the task of restoring Fairhaven."

"My father often said the line between courage and folly is a thin one. Sometimes I wonder why I ever imagined I could succeed."

"The land means everything to you, doesn't it?"

"Yes, but now I realize there's nothing to be gained by wanting a life I can never have again."

They fell silent once more, listening to the whirring of crickets in the grass and the murmurs of the crowd watching the tableau.

"I feel terrible about Josie," Charlotte said. "Her family will be inconsolable when they get the news."

"Yes. I've arranged with the undertaker for burial tomorrow at Lafayette Cemetery."

"Someone should speak to the minister, choose a reading and a hymn. Perhaps I could—"

He stopped her with a shake of his head. "There won't be time. Every undertaker in the city and every coffin maker are struggling to keep up. Tonight when Mr. Trimble came for Josie, he told me he has four more burials scheduled for tomorrow and two for Tuesday. A quick interment is all we can expect."

"At least she won't be buried in a mass grave somewhere." She fought the tears welling in her eyes. "I feared that was your fate. I don't think I could have borne it."

"Dear Charlotte." His voice was a mere whisper on the breeze. He turned to her, and she realized he was about to kiss her.

"Nicholas—"

"If you intend to refuse me," he murmured, "now would be the time."

His kiss was warm, confident, and tasted slightly of lemon tart. Her arms went around his neck, and they clung together in the warm darkness.

Whistles and loud applause rippled across the lawn as they drew apart. Nicholas looked into her eyes, and she was overcome with confusion and longing, not knowing what to say that might prolong this perfect moment.

"Either the tableau just ended," he said, "or else they approve of our performance."

She was grateful for the darkness that hid the sudden heat in her face.

He gave a soft laugh, and her fatigue fell away. They walked to the door as the crowd dispersed. The performers were carrying their props inside.

"Good night, Charlotte," Nicholas said. "I have much to do tomorrow, but I want you to rest."

"I am tired, but I must write to Augusta again. Perhaps she will know how to reach Josie's family. They must be told, though of course they won't arrive in time for the burial."

"I'll be back tomorrow. As soon as I can."

She gave him a sideways glance. "That's what you said the day you left the Waccamaw."

He squeezed her hand and let her go.

She took her key from her reticule and hurried up the curving stair to the Blue Room. Someone had turned the covers down and replenished the water in the crystal carafe. She drank deeply before shucking off her soiled dress. She ran a bath, letting the warm water relax her knotted muscles and soothe her jumbled emotions.

Nicholas's kiss had caught her off guard and left her longing for more. Obviously he felt something for her. But how could they have a future when he owned the land that for all her life she'd thought was hers?

She dried off, slipped into her nightdress, and brushed her hair, her thoughts swirling. This entire journey—finding Nicholas, the trip to Milneburg, Josie's sudden death—seemed like a long and convoluted dream.

She touched her fingertips to her lips, exhilarated and unsettled by the memory of his kiss. Was this what falling in love felt like?

She dragged the brush through her hair with more force than was necessary. It would not do to fall in love with the man who intended to take Fairhaven from her. Even though in his shoes she would do exactly the same thing.

A shout in the street drew her to the window. In the courtyard below, several members of the theater troupe were milling about, singing loudly and slightly off key. She turned away and drew the curtains.

Nicholas was lucky to have recovered his documents from the burned-out church. How clever of his wife to have had them hidden in the—

Charlotte. The fire . . . the fire.

She went stock-still, her stomach clenching as understanding dawned.

She crossed the room to the escritoire and picked up her pen.

Dear Augusta,

It is my sad duty to tell you Josie Clifton has died of yellow fever and is to be interred here tomorrow, July 27th, at Lafayette Cemetery. I have no knowledge of precisely where her family has gone. Josie told me only that they were headed west. Perhaps the Hadleys will know how to reach them, although one almost wishes they could be spared such a wrenching loss, especially as the epidemic precludes any opportunity for a proper farewell. I wrote to you upon my arrival here on Friday the 24th of July, and Mr. Betancourt has written to Marie-Claire and Anne-Louise. I hope both letters reach you soon. No doubt he has told them that he is quite well, having been exposed to the fever in his childhood. The epidemic is no threat to him, except as it taxes his endurance in caring for others.

I am well and planning to return to Pelican Cottage as soon as travel can be arranged, for I must return as soon as possible to Fairhaven. I will write again to let you know when to expect me. Oh, Augusta, I believe that Papa may have left something important in the house, something critical to the future of Fairhaven. I must know at once whether my fondest hopes for my plantation may yet be realized. I will explain when I see you. In the meantime, kiss the girls for me and for their father. Pray that this scourge is over soon and that his own return home will be swift and safe.

Your Charlotte

Twenty-Seven

"You're certain you have everything?" Nicholas smiled down at Charlotte and placed a hand in the small of her back to guide her along the crowded platform. The train, belching cinders and smoke, waited on the siding. Passengers and draymen came and went from the station house, dodging Creole boys selling cigars, newspapers, and candies.

"I think so. I couldn't sleep last night. I had plenty of time to pack."

In the days since their kiss in the garden, they had seen little of each other. Nicholas's work at the infirmary and meetings with the doctor who had arrived to replace him had kept him too busy for socializing. But he had insisted on escorting her to the station.

He bought two bonbons from a skinny boy in bright yellow pants and handed her one. "You won't forget to give the girls their presents?"

The doll and the music box he had bought for them in Milneburg were safely tucked away in the bottom of her travel satchel, along with her little boat. "I won't forget. And in any case, I'm sure they've received your letter by now. They'll remind me."

He took a bite of candy. "I hope it won't be much longer before I can see them."

"When will you be home?" She nibbled on the sweet and tucked the rest away for later. This morning Mr. Dubois had sent up a breakfast of eggs, sausages, biscuits, and coffee along with a box lunch for the train. As eager as she was to return home, she would miss the dapper hotelier's excellent meals.

"A month or so, I think. Sister Luke told me yesterday that Sister Beatrice is recovering and plans to return to the infirmary. As soon as my replacement settles in, I'll be on my way." He popped the rest of the bonbon into his mouth and took out his handkerchief to wipe a bit of sugar off his fingers. "I just wish I could go with you right now. There's so much I need to do at home."

The joy she'd felt at spending these few moments with him dissipated, replaced by a familiar mix of disappointment and worry. Yet beneath it all a faint, rekindled flame of hope burned. Was it possible that Fairhaven might yet be saved?

She watched the sunlight playing on his face. She should resent him for the threat he posed to her future. But as she waited with the others preparing to board the train, she couldn't deny the undercurrent of attraction running between them, made stronger by everything they had shared, everything they had endured.

The train whistle shrieked. Passengers surged toward the cars carrying their satchels, whiny children, hatboxes, and birdcages.

"Good-bye, Charlotte. Safe journeys." Nicholas looked into her eyes and squeezed her hands.

"Good-bye." She boarded the train and chose a seat by the window.

Nicholas stood on the platform, a piercing sweetness in his haggard face. He lifted one hand in a little salute as the train rumbled to life and slid out of the station.

"Your husband, dear?" The woman seated opposite her straightened her straw hat and, with a rustling of skirts, settled in for the long journey.

"My . . . oh. No. My employer." But not for much longer. Somehow she must find a way to provide for herself when even the small salaries Nicholas and Mr. Peabody paid her were withdrawn.

"Humph." A gleam lit the woman's pale eyes. "Maybe for now, but I saw the way he looked at you. He let you go, but he didn't want to." She opened a box and took out an apple. "Want one?"

"No thank you." Charlotte took a book from her satchel and made a show of finding her place. The novel was not all that compelling, but she wasn't in the mood to discuss Nicholas Betancourt—or the myriad emotions warring inside her.

The woman ate her apple and lapsed into sleep, her head falling to one side as the train rounded a sharp bend.

After days of travel, the train from Atlanta finally arrived in Charleston. Charlotte waited wearily for her bags, then took a room at the Mills House to await the next departure of the *Resolute* for Georgetown. She paced her room and picked at her food, eager to get home and test her revelation. But as long as she was forced to wait here, it wouldn't hurt to speak to her lawyer once more. Perhaps Mr. Crowley had uncovered something during her absence— something more substantial than a vague intimation based on a deathbed utterance.

But the lawyer seemed irritated by her sudden appearance. He muttered and grumbled and lectured her all over again regarding the folly of her undertaking at Fairhaven. He allowed that perhaps Providence had intervened to save her from a fate even worse than losing her home. He reminded her that Pelican Cottage still was hers. It had a roof and a door to keep out the rain, which was more than could be said for some folks these days.

"I have done all I can do, child. Now go away and leave me alone." He consulted his watch and snapped it shut, putting an end to the conversation.

Now she was on the last leg of her long journey. The ferry from Georgetown approached the southern tip of Pawley's Island and jolted slightly as it nudged the short pier.

As Charlotte disembarked, the Reverend Mr. Peabody's horse and rig clattered down the sandy strip of road and rolled to a stop in front of her. Charlotte grinned. Augusta and the girls had come for her.

"Ma'm'selle, you're home." Anne-Louise tumbled from the rig and leapt into Charlotte's arms. "I thought you were never coming back. And you found our papa."

Behind her sister, Marie-Claire smiled shyly and waved. Charlotte set Anne-Louise on her feet and held out her arms to the older girl, an unexpected rush of love coursing through her. How she would miss them when Nicholas returned and sent them away to a real school.

Augusta climbed out of the borrowed rig and embraced Charlotte. "What a time you've had, my girl. I'm so glad Mr. Betancourt is well. And sorry as I can be about Miss Clifton."

"As am I." Charlotte looked out to sea. Despite her concerns, the waves rolling and shimmering in the early August heat worked their magic, infusing her with a sense of gratitude and peace. Mr. Crowley was right. Regardless of what happened to the plantation, Pelican Cottage and this magnificent beach would always be hers. And it would have to be enough.

"Papa's letter said he was sending us a present," Anne-Louise said. "Did you bring it?"

"I did. Right here in my bag." Charlotte opened her travel satchel and took out the doll and the music box. Marie-Claire opened the little lacquered box and listened to the tinkling notes, a pensive expression in her eyes. Anne-Louise squealed and clasped the doll to her chest. "She's beautiful, Ma'm'selle. What's her name?"

"I suppose that's for you to decide."

"I'm going to name her Gabrielle after *Maman*."

"I think that's a fine idea."

The ferryman plopped Charlotte's baggage at her feet. "Will that be all, miss?"

"Yes, thank you." Charlotte handed him a coin.

Augusta rubbed her hands together. "It'll be a tight fit, but I reckon we can figure out how to get all your paraphernalia into the rig."

A few minutes later, with Charlotte's belongings packed tightly about their feet and Anne-Louise perched on Charlotte's lap, they set off for home, the horse trotting confidently along the shady road.

"I'm glad you got my letter in time to meet me," Charlotte said. "I could hardly walk home with all this baggage."

Augusta grinned. "Mr. Peabody was more than

happy to lend me his horse and buggy. He thinks very highly of you."

"I was sorry to stop the Demeres' lessons so abruptly, but I had to know whether Mr. Betancourt was all right."

"Papa's letter said for us not to worry because he can't get the fever," Marie-Claire said. "He already got it when he was my age."

"That's right." Charlotte glanced at the girl and smiled. "But I didn't know that before I went to look for him." She patted Marie-Claire's hand. "Now tell me. What have you learned while I was gone? Did you finish reading your books?"

"Yes, Ma'm'selle."

"And, Anne-Louise, did you practice your handwriting the way I showed you?"

"Sort of."

Augusta laughed. "When she wasn't busy helping me make tea cakes, or fishing in the creek, or a thousand other more interesting things."

"I can't thank you enough for looking after them."

"It was no trouble. I had a lovely time. My old house will seem awfully empty tonight."

They reached the end of the road. The girls piled out and raced ahead and were soon lost in the dunes, leaving Charlotte and Augusta to follow with her bags, travel satchel, parasol, and reticule.

They piled everything in the cottage foyer. Charlotte removed her traveling hat and her cotton gloves, soiled from days of train travel.

"When I got the letter saying you were on the way home, I bought a few things at the store. Mary Banks brought by some tomatoes and corn. And I baked a cake. I figured you'd be too tired to fool with making a meal tonight."

"Thank you. I am exhausted." Charlotte plopped onto the settee. "You thought of everything."

"You're welcome. Now, tell me what's troubling you."

Charlotte released a gusty sigh. "Am I really so transparent?"

"I've known you all your life. I can tell when something's not right." Augusta's faded eyes bore into hers. "Out with it."

"Mr. Betancourt found the deed to his property. Apparently it also includes Fairhaven."

"Oh dear."

"Yes, but then I remembered something Papa told me right before he died. It may mean everything. Or nothing. But I won't know until I can get to Fairhaven." She brushed away her tears. "Oh, Augusta, I'm hopeful and scared to hope, all at the same time. If I'm right, I still may have a chance. If I'm wrong, I'll lose every acre of my land."

The older woman let out a low whistle. "That is indeed a kettle of fish. But as long as you have this place, you have a home."

"I suppose."

Augusta patted her hand. "Something tells me that Fairhaven is not your only concern."

Charlotte hesitated. "It's . . . Mr. Betancourt himself. Dr. Betancourt. I think most highly of him."

"You're in love with him, you mean."

"No, I—"

"Best call it what it is, girl. I can see how you feel about him just by the way you say his name." Augusta raised a brow. "Does he return your affections?"

"I think so. But—"

"Then everything will work out, somehow. Where love is concerned, it's important to have a little faith." Augusta rose. "Here come the girls. I'll see you later. I must return Mr. Peabody's rig."

"Please thank him for me, and tell him I'll be ready for the children on Monday."

Augusta snapped her fingers. "In all the excitement I forgot to tell you. The schoolmaster returned to Litchfield last week, much earlier than expected. The reverend said to tell you the Demere children will attend the plantation school beginning next week."

"I see. I suppose he'll expect the return of his globe and books and the other things he lent us."

"I reckon so. But the summer is winding down. The Betancourt girls will be off to school in

Charleston once their father gets home. Why not let them enjoy a few weeks free of lessons before then?"

Anne-Louise pounded along the piazza and burst through the door, her new doll tucked under her arm. "I heard that, Miss Augusta, and I think it's a stupendous idea."

Charlotte laughed. "I might grant you your freedom if you promise at least to practice your penmanship."

Anne-Louise wrinkled her nose. "Doesn't sound much like freedom to me." She made a place for her doll on the embroidered settee. "Is there anything to eat? Gabrielle and I are excruciatingly hungry."

Charlotte laughed. "Find your sister and we'll make supper."

At the door, Augusta turned. "I left some mail on the table from my last trip to town."

"Thank you."

The older woman pointed a gnarled finger at Charlotte. "Don't forget what I said about Mr. Betancourt."

Anne-Louise followed Augusta onto the piazza. Charlotte went to the kitchen and set about preparing a meal. The girls came back inside, and she sent them to wash up. Marie-Claire returned first and plopped down on the bottom stair, the very picture of dejection.

"What's the matter?" Charlotte carried a tray

to the dining room and opened the windows wider to draw in the cooling breeze.

Marie-Claire shrugged.

"Don't you like the present your father sent?"

"I like it. It's pretty."

"I thought so too. And very grown-up."

"I suppose so."

"Are you feeling unwell?"

"No, Ma'm'selle. I feel fine."

"Then why the long face? I should think you'd be very happy now that your father is coming home."

"I want to see Papa but—" The girl brushed away tears.

"Scoot over." Charlotte sat down on the stair beside her. "Tell me what's troubling you."

"When Papa gets home, he'll send us away to school. And I don't want to go. I like it here."

Anne-Louise clattered down the stairs and plopped down on the stair behind them. "Me too, Ma'm'selle. I don't want to go away to school. I don't see why you can't keep on teaching us."

Charlotte twisted around on the stair. "That's a lovely thing to say, but there are many reasons why you must go to school. For one thing, I simply don't know enough to teach you everything your papa wants you to learn."

"Like what?"

"Well, to begin with, French. I was the very worst student in my entire class, and since leaving school I've had few occasions to practice what little I do know. But a command of French is a requirement for every well-brought-up young lady. Along with drawing and needlework and literature and comportment and the many other things we've worked on this summer."

"Oh, is that all?" Marie-Claire's blue eyes flashed. "I already know French. Anne-Louise was too little, but I learned French from Papa and *Maman*. Listen: *Non. Oui. Merci. Au revoir*."

Charlotte hid a smile. "That's a fine start, but I'm afraid there is a bit more to it than that."

"I don't care," Marie-Claire said. "I'm going to be a rice planter like you and Papa. Who needs French?"

"I don't care about French either," Anne-Louise said. "I'd rather learn about turtles and birds and hermit crabs. And how to build kites and things. And read books like *Countess Kate* and *Little Women*."

"I'm sure your teachers in Charleston will make room for those things too." Charlotte rose and held out a hand to each girl. "Let's not worry about it today. The new term in Charleston won't begin until October. We've lots of time before then."

After their meal, the girls went outside to play. Charlotte looked through the mail Augusta had left. All of it was postmarked weeks before—a note from Lettice Hadley, a letter from Alexander,

381

and a thin envelope in a hand she didn't recognize.

"Hello?" A tall bewhiskered man in a white shirt and wool trousers stood at the door, one hand cupped to his eyes.

Frowning, the letter still in her hand, Charlotte went to the door. "Yes?"

"Miss Fraser?"

"Yes."

He doffed his hat. "Justus K. Jillson. I wrote to you last week. May I come in?"

She stood aside and ushered him into the parlor. "I've just returned from a long trip and have not yet had time to read the mail."

"Even better. I've often found it's more advantageous to plead one's case in person. May I sit down?"

"Please." She motioned him to the settee and took the chair opposite. "What's this about?"

"Well." He cleared his throat. "As you may know, the state of South Carolina intends to establish free public schools in every county. And the sooner, the better—wouldn't you agree?"

His salesman-like approach was irritating. Who wouldn't agree on the importance of schooling?

"Perhaps you'd best come to the point, Mr. Jillson."

"Quite right. I saw the Reverend Mr. Peabody during the Independence Day festivities last month, and he bent my ear for quite a while, singing your praises as a teacher. He said you've ignited such a thirst for knowledge in his young charges that he can scarcely keep up with their questions."

"That was kind of him."

"He says your methods are somewhat . . . unorthodox."

"Perhaps. I'm not trained as a teacher. I'm guided by instinct and by the children's own interests." She folded her hands in her lap. "They seem to learn more that way than through more formal recitations. I doubt the state of South Carolina would approve."

"You're correct in that assumption. There is much to be said for the tried and true." He leaned forward, pale hands on his knees. "Still, good teachers are scarce. And we all appreciate your late father's commitment to the welfare of the young people of our state. As commissioner of education, I'm prepared to offer you a position in the new school we're opening near Sandy Island next spring. Assuming you are willing to adhere to the more conventional methods of instruction. I'm certain the headmaster at Litchfield will be glad to show you the ropes."

He sat back in his chair and beamed at her as if he'd just offered her the keys to the kingdom. "What do you say?"

The prudent thing to do was to accept his offer. The salary, however modest, would be essential, especially if she failed to find proof of her ownership of Fairhaven. But memories of her own school days crowded in—the long hours spent copying out lessons, struggling with memorization, the daily tedium relieved only by her occasional secret forays to the artist's studio off Tradd Street. Her teachers at Madame Giraud's, well-meaning though they were, could scarcely conceal their own boredom and impatience. Even in her precarious situation, she couldn't trade her sense of well-being for money.

"Thank you for the offer, Mr. Jillson. I'm honored that you think so highly of me. But I have my plantation to run. I hope to finish restoring my house and to resume cultivation of Carolina Gold."

The commissioner shook his head. "I admire your tenacity, but you know as well as I do that those days are behind us now." He stared at her intently. "You won't even consider my offer?"

"I'm afraid not."

"If you don't mind my saying so, I think you're being rash, throwing away a solid offer of employment in favor of a plan that cannot possibly succeed." He stood and jammed his hat onto his head. "I can see myself out."

She watched him disappear among the dunes. As much as she disliked admitting it, the man had a point. Maybe she was chasing a dying dream.

But there was only one way to find out.

Twenty-Eight

The boat rocked on the tide-pulsed waters of the creek. Charlotte unfurled her parasol against the morning sun as Trim set the oars and pushed off through tall stands of yellowing marsh grasses that soon obscured the dunes and the cottage beyond.

This morning Marie-Claire and Anne-Louise had protested when she roused them from sleep for the short walk across the dunes to Augusta's cottage. The promise of a bonfire on the beach upon her return mollified them. Now she sat drinking in the quiet beauty of the morning, the ocean's muted roar, the fine silvery mist rising off the tidal creeks as the clear morning sky slowly gave way to gray clouds and a stiff breeze coming off the Atlantic.

"Gon' have ourselves a blow befo' this day is done." Trim squinted at the sky and guided the boat past an abandoned alligator's nest and into a narrow stretch of water carpeted with bright green lily pads.

She scanned the sky. "I hope it won't be too severe, this close to harvest time."

In another few weeks, her first crop, small though it was, would be cut, stacked, and dried, then threshed and put into barrels for shipping. As a girl she had often stood with her father at the landing while the schooners *Perseverance*, *Waccamaw*, and *Julius Pringle* plied the river, transporting barrels of Carolina Gold to her father's rice factors in Charleston. Those days were gone, but at least she would have something to show for all her hard work.

"Yes'm. We could've started cutting rice las' week, but the tide was too high. Banks was kinda leaky too."

Charlotte swatted at a cloud of flies. "How have the other crops fared this summer?"

"Since you was las' to home, the sugarcane done real fine. Mr. Hadley hired some women from town to help with the grindin'. We got a barrel of good molasses from it." He wiped his brow with a bright green bandana. "Lambert and Old Thomas been hoeing the peas and cuttin' wood for the thrashing machine. My wife, she come up from town now and then to look after the chickens."

"How is Florinda? Mrs. Hadley wrote that she was ill."

"She been ailing some, but I been doctoring her with mustard plasters. Reckon she's a little better these days."

They entered the whitecapped Waccamaw,

blue-gray now beneath the gathering clouds. Charlotte's heart constricted. She loved every inch of this river. To lose the right to live here would be like losing a limb.

Another half hour brought them within sight of the house. Daniel waited on the dock.

Trim let out a long sigh. "That Graves boy turn up here ever' day, reg'lar as a clock."

Charlotte had to smile. Trim might fancy himself a free businessman now, but he couldn't conceal his love for Fairhaven. Before the war, he had shown a certain possessiveness toward it, hastening to point out to her father or to the overseer a loose hinge, a broken trunk, a bit of falling plaster. It was clear he still felt proprietary about it, even as he strove to assert his independence.

Daniel waved and helped Trim secure the boat. As Charlotte closed her parasol, thunder rumbled in the distance, and a flash of lightning forked through the darkened sky, sending her hurrying for shelter. As eager as she was to check on her rice, it was foolish to risk a trip downriver with a storm rolling in. She crossed the yard to the house, the solitary peacock—returned from his wanderings—waddling along in front of her. Daniel and Trim brought up the rear.

"Reckon I'll be getting' on up to the Cliftons' place now, befo' the rain gets bad," Trim said. "I'll be back this afternoon to take you home."

Charlotte nodded and fished her key from her bag. "Daniel, you'd best come inside until the rain passes."

The boy followed her inside and headed for the library. "Trim said you were coming today, so I brought your mail up from Georgetown."

She quickly sorted through the pile, another letter from Lettice, a bill from her book supplier in Boston, two copies of the Georgetown paper. Nothing from Nicholas. Perhaps he was already on his way home. She went out to the kitchen, rummaged for her kettle, and opened the food basket she'd brought, one eye on the gathering storm.

She made tea and shared her meal with Daniel, who wolfed down two thick sandwiches, a wedge of cheese, and one of Augusta's berry tarts without looking up from his reading. By mid-afternoon, the sky had turned black. Thunder shook the bones of the old house and rattled the windowpanes. Wind soughed in the trees. Heavy rain lashed the windows.

Charlotte lit the lamps and sat in the library with Daniel, watching the rivulets coursing down the window panes. Daniel sat quietly, still absorbed in his book. Charlotte opened the newspaper to stories about the new government and the Freedman's Bureau, but new worry blurred the page.

The mature fields might well withstand a

downpour, but too much rain could ruin everything. And no matter what happened with the barony, she was determined to bring in one last rice crop. With luck, she would at least realize enough money to pay back her bank loan.

Another hour passed before a wagon turned in at the gate and lumbered up the muddy avenue to the house. Trim jumped out, a blanket over his arm, and raced for the front door. Charlotte let him in.

"Mr. Hadley sent me to fetch Daniel," Trim said. "One of the fences done blowed down, and they need him to help get the Cliftons' cows out of the corn patch befo' they trample it all to pieces."

"In this weather?"

"Yes'm. And you might as well plan on stayin' right here till morning. The river's risin' fast, an' water is nearly up over the road."

Trim tossed the blanket to Daniel. "Come on, boy. Let's go."

Daniel wrapped himself in the blanket, though it would be soggy and useless within minutes. He followed Trim out to the wagon. Soon they were lost in the curtain of rain.

Now Charlotte was alone. For a few moments she prowled the silent rooms, torn between fear and hope. Would her crop survive? And would she find what she came to look for?

The fire . . . the fire.

That night in New Orleans, thinking about the burned-out church where Nicholas's papers had been found, she'd been struck with the sudden thought that perhaps her father, with his final breath, was not remembering Charleston's great fire at all. What if he'd hidden something important in the fireplace in his study, just as he had hidden her birthday doll all those years ago?

As the storm raged on, she turned up the wick in the lamp and set it on the hearth. Crouching inside the wide fireplace opening, she ran her fingers along the far wall of the brick firebox and along the rough, raised ledge.

At first she felt nothing but soot and soft gray ash. Then her fingers closed over something solid and cold. She was aware of her every breath, of the crazed tripping of her heart as she crawled farther into the fireplace and lifted the lamp.

"Guess what, Ma'm'selle?" Anne-Louise caught Charlotte's hand the moment she stepped from the boat. "We had a storm, and Miss Augusta let us sleep in the attic in case the water got too high but it didn't. And me and Gabrielle weren't scared, but Marie-Claire was."

"I was not." Her sister took Charlotte's other hand. "I wasn't afraid at all."

"You were too. I heard you crying when it was dark. Guess what else, Ma'm'selle. This morning we found some treasures on the beach and Mrs. Carver brought us a pie and I ate two pieces."

The girl paused for breath as Charlotte turned to wave good-bye to Daniel. The storm had downed trees and ripped several shutters from their hinges. He and Trim would have plenty to do, making repairs.

There was nothing to be done about the rice. Torrential rains and fierce winds had left the fields in ruins.

Nicholas's daughters kept up a constant stream of chatter as they neared the house, their little faces turned to hers like sunflowers toward the sun. Augusta was waiting inside with a pot of tea and a platter of biscuits and jam. Charlotte's empty stomach groaned. She and Daniel had left the rain-swollen Waccamaw at first light, her father's long-missing strongbox on her lap.

She'd recognized the box the moment the lantern light fell upon it. She had stayed awake the rest of the night, unable to think of anything else, wishing she had remembered to bring the key with her. After carrying it in her pocket for so many months, why had she forgotten it now?

Perhaps the box held nothing more than a few family keepsakes. But if that were true, why had her father taken such pains to keep it out of the hands of the Yankees? And why would he have tried so hard to tell her about it in those final moments before his death?

After their meal, the girls ran down to the beach in search of more flotsam and jetsam from the storm. Augusta left for a meeting at Mrs. Banks's cottage. Mary's cousin, Mrs. Rutledge, was still on the island, helping the women of Pawley's Island push ahead with their plans to send a suffrage petition to the president.

According to the newspapers, that Yankee general Ulysses Grant was favored to win the November presidential election. Augusta reported that the ladies hoped that Mr. Johnson, a Southerner, would plead their case with the Congress before he finished his term of office. Though he hadn't sided with the Confederacy during the war, perhaps the ties of blood would render him more sympathetic to their request.

Charlotte washed the dishes, poured herself another cup of tea, and took her cup to the dining room. Through the open windows she could see the girls, hats askew, bent over the latest gifts from the sea. She set the small strongbox on the table, her heart thudding. Suspended between what she knew and what she hoped.

She inserted the key into the lock and the lid sprang open to reveal a stack of receipts, a faded newspaper clipping, and an old-fashioned wedding ring set with pearls. She swallowed a wave of disappointment. Well, what had she expected, really?

She held the narrow wedding band up to the

light. It was clearly an antique, judging from the setting, and one she had never seen. Her mother's ring, wider and set with diamonds and emeralds, had been lost the summer before she died and never recovered. Perhaps Father had purchased this one as a replacement and somehow forgot it. Perhaps her mother hadn't liked it or had secreted it in the box for safekeeping during her travels.

Charlotte returned the ring to the box and was about to close the lid when a tiny tear in the fabric lining caught her eye. She ran a fingernail beneath the seam, and the lining yielded readily. Beneath the fabric she felt a smoothly fitted bit of wood that formed a false bottom. With a bit of fiddling the wood insert came away to reveal a yellowed letter, brittle at the creases, atop a thicker document and another faded newspaper clipping.

"Tragedy at Sea: Ninety Passengers Lost as Ship Wrecks off North Carolina Coast." Charlotte read the account of the loss of the steamer *Home*, along with most of the passengers and crew. Papa had never spoken of it, but this disaster must have held some significance for him. Otherwise, why had he taken such pains to preserve the story?

She unfolded the letter, her stomach dropping at the opening words. The room, and the sound of the girls' laughter above the gentle roll and whisper of the sea outside her window, fell away.

New York
5 October 1837
Francis P. W. Fraser
Fairhaven Plantation
Georgetown District, South Carolina

My dear Francis,
The fault for our present discord is entirely mine. I never should have agreed to a marriage that has brought us only grief and unhappiness. When we met in Paris, I was so taken with you that I believed my deep affection would overcome my misgivings at beginning a life so far from all that is beloved and familiar to me. But I find that the life of a planter's wife, so fraught with uncertainly and isolation and so dependent upon forces beyond a mortal's control, is unbearable despite the high regard I have always had for you.

These few weeks apart have convicted me of my selfishness. You can no more give up your life than I can mine. I am returning my ring with my deepest apologies and with every hope that you will find someone whose temperament and aspirations more nearly match your own. I will of course sign the necessary legal papers before my return to Paris. In two days' time I leave for Charleston aboard the steamer Home. I should like to collect my personal belongings from Fairhaven before returning to Paris at the end of the month. I shall be honored to bid you farewell then if you so choose, but I won't think less of you should you decide not to come.

That God may bless you and grant you the light of his countenance is the earnest prayer of your affectionate wife—

Therese St. Clair

Every family has its secrets. Charlotte reread the letter and let it fall into her lap. All her life she had revered her father. Had thought him courageous, fair, and most of all honest. But now she saw him in a different light, her childhood perceptions peeling away like layers of paint from an old picture to reveal a clearer image beneath.

Papa had been married before, and to none other than Nicholas Betancourt's cousin Therese. Why had Papa never told her? Had her mother known?

She unfolded the other document, which was

also creased and brittle with age, her eyes traveling rapidly down the page. "John Carteret, Lord Proprietor . . . by royal grant . . . Fairhaven barony, South Carolina, being twelve thousand acres comprising the boundaries thus described . . ."

She sat back in her chair, relieved as a desert wanderer suddenly coming upon an oasis. Then the questions started. Why had Papa failed to properly file his claim to the barony? A simple oversight? Or was it somehow tied to his failed marriage and the tragedy that followed? She would never have all the answers.

News of Papa's first marriage was enough to set her mind whirling. But the land grant, apparently left unrecorded all these years, raised more troubling questions. Should she send the papers to Mr. Crowley? File her claim in Georgetown and hope Nicholas had not yet recorded his? As much as she wanted to keep Fairhaven, she couldn't hurt him. But she didn't want to give up her land either, even though the storm had left her with a debt she couldn't pay.

"We'll come to some accommodation." Perhaps Nicholas would agree to a division of the land— if he recognized her claim. Would he think it too coincidental that the grant had turned up just after he discovered his own? She could hardly blame him for such suspicions. It seemed entirely too convenient to be believed. And yet it had happened.

Two boys raced past the dining room window and plunged into the rolling surf. Automatically Charlotte lifted her head. Her two charges were no longer in sight.

No doubt they had gone on down the beach, looking for driftwood for the promised bonfire. She returned everything to the strongbox and locked it, then took her straw hat from the hall tree and stepped out onto the piazza.

Afternoon sun blazed across the water, silhouetting a flock of pelicans gliding just above the surface. Farther down the beach, a young couple strolled hand in hand in the direction of the causeway. Charlotte took off her shoes and walked along the broad curve of the beach toward the dunes where the girls often played. Moments later she spotted the pink of Anne-Louise's frock and her sister's green one, bright against the dun-colored dunes.

She called to them, but the girls didn't seem to hear. Moving closer, she saw a man's form prostrate on the sand, and her heart sped up. She prayed the girls had not come upon some local gentleman too far into his cups—or, worse, a drowning victim.

Anne-Louise turned toward her then and cupped her hands to her mouth. "Ma'm'selle! Come quick!"

Charlotte hiked her skirts and ran.

Twenty-Nine

Anne-Louise ran toward Charlotte, a huge smile on her face, her index finger pressed to her lips. "Shhh. Ma'm'selle, don't wake Papa. He's very tired."

"Don't wake . . . What on earth are you talking about?"

"Papa's home." Anne-Louise pointed down the beach. "He walked all the way from the causeway to surprise us. But we saw him first, and then he wanted to surprise you, but—" She paused, her sun-browned face the picture of seriousness. "You don't believe me. You think I'm telling tales like the wolf boy again, but I'm not."

Marie-Claire caught up to them and danced a little circle around Charlotte. "Ma'm'selle, Papa is home, and he's going to make the bonfire when it gets dark, and he said we could stay awake as long as we wanted. Then he sat down to rest his eyes and fell asleep."

The girls led her to the spot where Nicholas lay, his long legs stretched out on the sand, clear autumn sunlight falling across his face.

398

"See, Ma'm'selle?" Anne-Louise whispered. "I wasn't crying wolf. It's really him."

Nicholas opened one eye, then unfolded his legs and shot to his feet. His cheeks were pink from the sun, his thatch of dark hair tousled.

He had never looked more appealing. Charlotte couldn't stop the slow smile that spread across her face.

He bowed. "Miss Fraser. A pleasure to see you."

She laughed. "I wondered when you might arrive, but I didn't expect to find you lying on the beach like a bit of flotsam."

"I wanted to surprise you, but the girls were out here when I arrived." He indicated a few pieces of wood piled against the dune. "I agreed to help them build a bonfire, but I'm afraid the journey caught up with me and I drifted off."

"I'm glad you're home."

"Me too."

Anne-Louise leaned against his leg. He picked her up, and she patted both his cheeks and nuzzled his neck. Marie-Claire latched onto his hand.

"How are things in New Orleans?"

"Not as many new cases as when you were there. Dr. Werner and Dr. Fordyce have things under control. Sister Beatrice recovered and is back on the job."

"I'm glad of that." She looked around. "Have you been to Willowood?"

"Not yet. The *Resolute* got caught up in the storm, and we were late docking. I got here just this morning."

He set Anne-Louise on her feet. "It seems the storm was pretty bad here."

They started walking up the beach. "Bad enough to down some trees and wipe out my rice crop."

He frowned. "Both fields?"

"I'm afraid so. Not a single head of rice left above the seawater. That was my third planting and of course it's much too late to put in another."

"I am sorry."

She shrugged. "It's the planter's curse, I'm afraid. We can do everything right and still we are at the mercy of the weather."

The girls ran ahead, playing tag with the waves.

The wind tore at her hat, and she tied the ribbon more firmly beneath her chin. "Did you file your deed yet?"

"Yes. I figured the sooner the legal question was settled, the sooner I could move forward with my plans."

"I see."

He stopped and lifted her chin until their eyes met. "I told you before that we'll work out a satisfactory agreement—a mortgage on the acreage you want or a partnership of some sort.

I know how much the house means to you and how hard you've worked to restore it."

"Circumstances have changed, Nicholas." She jammed her hands into her pockets and continued along the wet sand.

"Oh?"

She hated to spoil the joy of his homecoming, but now that he had already filed his claim, nothing was to be gained by waiting. "It appears that John Carteret, or his lawyers, made a mistake. Fairhaven barony was granted to my grandfather. The paper was in my father's strongbox all along."

He stopped walking, a look of pure astonishment flooding his face. "You can't be serious."

"I know it seems unlikely, but it's true." She paused, dreading to tell him the rest. "It's dated 1784."

"A year earlier than mine."

"Yes."

"You might have told me that night in New Orleans when we discussed my claim."

"I didn't know. Papa hid the papers in a strongbox inside a fireplace at Fairhaven, on the brick ledge of the chimney. I thought the Federals had stolen the box along with his desk, where he usually kept it. But then when you told me about finding your papers beneath the fireplace hearth, I remembered something my father told me the night he died. I didn't say anything to you at the time because it was no more than a hunch. I found it only last night."

"Very convenient." He loped along the beach, head down, saying nothing.

She hurried to keep up with his angry strides. "I agree the timing seems suspect. But there's more. I also learned that my father was married before he wed my mother."

"That's not so unusual."

"No, it isn't. But my father was married to your cousin. Therese St. Clair."

"To . . ." He frowned. "What is all this, Charlotte? Some kind of devious plan to wrest my land from me?"

Devious? Was that what he thought of her? She spun away, fighting for control. "I thought you knew me better than that."

"I thought so too, but surely you can't expect me to believe we both have a claim to the same piece of ground. It's too coincidental."

"I'm as surprised as you are. But you yourself said that such mistakes happened often back then. And if two families had to have been granted the same barony, I am glad to share it with a . . . friend."

He didn't answer. They returned in strained silence to Pelican Cottage. The girls shook the powdery sand from their feet and ran upstairs. Charlotte led Nicholas into the dining room and handed him the documents.

He read the account of the shipwreck and the letter from Therese St. Clair, then picked up the land-grant document. She waited, trying without success to decipher the expression in his eyes. At last he set everything aside. "It seems authentic enough. I suppose I owe you an apology."

"You said if a deed turned up, you'd recognize my claim."

"Yes."

"I'm sure my father loved your cousin very much, and then he lost her in the shipwreck. Perhaps the land grant no longer seemed important to him then. Or perhaps he simply forgot as time passed and the matter never came up. Until now."

He sighed. "This certainly complicates my plans."

"And mine. I don't relish the thought of a dispute any more than you do."

The girls clattered down the stairs dressed in their flannel swimming costumes and carrying blankets, pails, and shovels. Nicholas opened his arms to them and planted kisses on their heads. He caught Charlotte's eye. "We've both had a shock. Let's enjoy the rest of the day and take up these serious matters later."

"What serious matters?" Marie-Claire asked. "I hope it isn't boarding school."

Nicholas laughed and shook his head. "Have you a swimming costume, Miss Fraser?"

"An old one. I found it when we first arrived here this summer. But it's terribly out of fashion."

"The fish won't care, and neither will I."

This morning's revelations and Nicholas's harsh words had left her in no mood for an outing. She marveled at how quickly he could dismiss their conversation and its implications. "I don't think—"

"Please, Ma'm'selle," Anne-Louise said. "The summer is over, and when Papa makes us go away to school, you're going to miss us terribly."

That much was true. She might be angry and disappointed in Nicholas, but it wasn't the children's fault. She ought not to spoil Nicholas's homecoming for them. She went upstairs and soon emerged in her old wool-flannel swimming dress and matching pantalettes. Her swimming boots and cap were long gone, but there was nothing to be done about it.

"Very fetching." Nicholas grinned as she descended the stairs.

She glanced away, unwilling to forgive him for his accusations. Unwilling for him to see that despite it all, his compliment had pleased her.

"Papa, can we please hurry?" Marie-Claire cocked one hip. "It'll be dark soon, and the water will be too chilly for swimming."

Charlotte took a blanket from the press in the hallway. They crossed the piazza and returned to the beach. While the girls retrieved the small pieces of wood they'd collected earlier in the day, Nicholas dug a pit in the damp sand. He piled the wood inside, then shucked his coat and kicked off his shoes. "Last one in is a rotten egg."

With loud whoops, father and daughters rushed into the gently rolling surf. Charlotte waded in slowly, inhaling sharply as a cold swell washed over her and lifted her off her feet. She squinted against the bright sunlight angling across the sea and treaded water, listening to Nicholas spinning a story of mermaids and pirates. His daughters dove and surfaced, their dark hair streaming behind them, their hands undulating like small white fish just below the surface. He caught her eye and smiled before he too dove beneath the waves. She closed her eyes and drifted, trying to empty her mind.

When the sunlight waned they swam to shore, where Nicholas lit the fire and they huddled beneath their blankets. As the fire crackled, sparks flying upward into the softening blue twilight, he entertained them with stories of his adventures in New Orleans and of the interesting people he'd encountered on his long journey home. The girls told him about the Demere orphans and the day Susan hid on the roof. They described Daniel's visit, the Independence Day fireworks, and the funeral for the dead skimmer.

"You sent him off in fine style," Nicholas said, his voice grave. He kissed Marie-Claire's head.

Anne-Louise snuggled against her father. "We love Pelican Cottage. But we missed you more than anything. Didn't we, Ma'm'selle?"

"You did indeed." Filled with the languid fatigue that follows a swim in the ocean, Charlotte wrapped the blanket more tightly around her shoulders and dug her toes into the sand.

"When are we going back to Willowood, Papa?" Marie-Claire raked her fingers through her damp curls. "I can barely remember what it looks like. And I want to see if Mathilde has come home."

"I'm going over in the morning to check on the storm damage." Nicholas caught Charlotte's eye. "Is there any chance you'll let me sleep on the back porch tonight?"

"The hammock has rotted away, and it's too chilly for sleeping outside anyway. The girls can share my room and you can have theirs."

"Thank you. I hesitate to prevail even more upon your hospitality, but I'm wondering whether you could possibly let them stay on here for another couple of days while I find out whether our house is habitable."

"All right."

On the sea the starlight broke and multiplied. The smell of salt and seaweed rode the sharpening September wind. Charlotte stared into the firelight. She wanted the question of

406

their dual claim settled. The sooner, the better. But would she see Nicholas at all after that? The fever epidemic had brought them close. Working side by side in the infirmary, they had developed an easy companionship on equal terms, something she had not expected when she set out to find him.

Now that the crisis was over, and a legal dispute loomed, perhaps their relationship was at an end as well.

Marie-Claire told her father a joke that made him laugh. How she would miss that sound if they became enemies. She studied his face in the flickering light and thought about how much more she stood to lose.

Thirty

While roof repairs were underway at Willowood, Nicholas and his daughters had gone to visit the Kirks in the pinelands. They'd been gone for more than a week. Without the girls' constant chatter and bright laughter, Pelican Cottage seemed devoid of life.

"If their absence is making you so unhappy, perhaps you should go over to Fairhaven." Augusta peered at Charlotte over the top of her spectacles. "There's nothing to keep you here. And you said you wanted to make some new curtains for the parlor."

Charlotte's needle stilled above her embroidery frame. None of the plans for the house that had so excited her upon her arrival last spring held much appeal these days. "I suppose."

Augusta patted her hand. "Cheer up, my dear. Lovesickness can be quite painful, but it's rarely fatal."

Charlotte resumed her stitching. Despite the contested barony, she couldn't deny her deep yearning to be with Nicholas every day. "I'm not lovesick."

Augusta glanced at her, a knowing smile on her

lips. "A woman can tell what another is thinking by the way she draws her thread."

Charlotte knotted a pale lavender thread and snipped the end with a pair of tiny silver scissors. "I will admit my tender feelings for Nicholas Betancourt. But I'm worried about how our claims can be resolved. It seems that in such a situation, there can be only one winner."

"You said he has already had his claim to the barony recorded?"

"Yes, but mine has the earlier date."

"Perhaps he intends to purchase your interest in Fairhaven."

"I doubt it. Even if the weather cooperates next year, the rice trade is dying. The chances it can ever be profitable again are practically nil, and he knows that as well as anyone." She set aside her needlework and bit into one of Augusta's warm, moist tea cakes. One more thing she would miss when the summer season ended. "On more than one occasion he has alluded to some sort of plan, but I have no idea what he has in mind."

"I know how much you love Fairhaven, but is that a good enough reason to hold on to it at any cost? Isn't it possible that in letting it go you will gain something even more valuable?"

"But I made a promise to my father, even if he wasn't the man I imagined him to be. And my land is—"

"My dear girl, an old house and ten thousand

acres of fallow land will be cold comfort in your later years. Whatever plan Mr. Betancourt has in mind deserves your serious consideration."

Charlotte watched a small boat beating against the incoming tide. As painful as it was to admit it, perhaps she too was struggling against the inevitable.

"Mr. Betancourt thinks very highly of you," Augusta said. "I can tell."

Charlotte thought for the thousandth time of their shared kiss. Had it meant anything to him, or was it nothing more than a brief release from the endless horrors of the infirmary? Every time she thought of it, her stomach went tight, but Nicholas gave no indication he remembered it at all. Perhaps his medical training had taught him to suppress his emotions.

She returned Augusta's steady gaze. "He has not declared his feelings."

"He will sooner or later. And his daughters clearly adore you. Even Mrs. Rutledge remarked upon it during the Independence Day celebration." Augusta rose from the rocking chair on the piazza. "And speaking of Mrs. Rutledge, I must go. I promised Mary to accompany them to Georgetown, and I can't be late."

"Thank you for the tea cakes. And the advice."

Augusta smiled. "Shall I send word to Fairhaven to have Trim row over for you in the morning?"

"I suppose I should go and check on things. Perhaps a change of scenery will clear my head."

When Augusta had gone, Charlotte cleared their tea things and answered a letter from Lettice. Then she took a walk on the beach, nodding to others as she passed. She collected a broken whelk and a handful of angel wings and set them carefully in the window ledge when she returned to the cottage. Anything to pass the empty hours.

She went to bed early, woke early, and went down to the dock to wait for Trim. Shortly after sunrise, his boat rounded the bend in the creek.

He lifted a hand in greeting. "Didn't expect to see you again so soon, miss." He steadied the boat while she entered. "It's a hot one today, but frost won't be long in coming this year. Las' week I saw a caterpillar already lookin' fat and fuzzy. Reckon we might have us a cold winter this year for sure. All the signs point to it, anyways."

Trim turned the boat and began to row. She opened her umbrella against the bright sun and looked out over the marshes. Patches of goldenrod and black-eyed Susans dotted the banks. The last of the red trumpet vines wept blossoms into the brown river.

"Boiled another gallon of molasses yesterday," Trim said. "Hens been layin' good too. I collected the eggs for you this mornin'."

"Thank you." She trailed her hand in the water, content to listen to Trim's report.

"Lef' you some ducks all dressed out on the back porch. They 'bout took over the fields lately. Lookin' for they own food, I reckon. The boy Dan'l, he been lookin' after your mare real good. Reckon she'll be in fine shape to take you visitin' when folks get home to the Waccamaw." The oars rattled in the locks as Trim shifted on the wooden seat. " 'Course, I don't reckon they's many left by now. Mast' Clifton done gone out west, Mast' Allston over on the Pee Dee give up on his place; he managin' somebody else's land now. And Mast' Hadley, he seemed some better for a good long while, like the work of lookin' after your plantation agree with him. But he ain't doin' no good these days a-tall."

Charlotte nodded. Lettice had said as much in her last letter.

Shortly after nine Trim guided the boat to the dock at Fairhaven and held it fast while she disembarked.

He studied the sky. "Gon' be a fine day on the river. No storms this day." He grinned. "Yes', sho is gon' be a fine day." He wiped his brow on his shirt sleeve. "Reckon I ought to finish diggin' the p'tatoes."

"Are they any good?"

He scratched his head. "Turned out tol'able well, what they is of 'em. Me and Florinda pulled a few beans yesterday. Mast' Hadley said we could have 'em. That was befo' we got word you wanted to come over today."

"It's all right, Trim." She headed up the path to the gate, closing her umbrella as she went. "I'm not very fond of beans anyway."

He laughed as he secured the boat and jumped nimbly onto the dock. "You just like you daddy was. Mast' Fraser liked his corn an' collards, but beans wasn't no excitement to him at all."

She reached the gate and pushed it open. "I should be ready to go by three or so. I want to be back on Pawley's before dark."

"Don't worry, Miss Cha'lotte. I'll come to carry you back." Trim circled the house and headed up to the potato patch.

Charlotte walked the long avenue to the house and let herself in. The air was close and warm. She threw open the windows and went from room to room, feeling restless and slightly out of sorts. Without fabric and her sewing supplies, she couldn't make curtains today even if she wanted to. And she had no desire to spend the morning roasting the duck Trim had brought. Why had she even come?

She went out to the barn. Daniel had evidently come and gone, bringing Cinnamon in from pasture. The mare had plenty of feed, the water trough was full, and the stall smelled of fresh straw. Charlotte spoke to her gently and, on a whim, decided to ride. She couldn't remember the last time she'd ridden just for the pleasure of it.

She found a bridle and bit and led the horse down the sun-dappled avenue to the gate. She boosted herself onto the bottom rung, then onto Cinnamon's back. Without a saddle, she couldn't go fast or far, but the minute she urged Cinnamon through the gate and onto the road, the sense of joy riding always brought her returned. Charlotte let the mare set her own pace, content to breathe the air and feel the late September sun on her face.

As they neared the road leading to Willowood, she saw something in the ditch up ahead and her breath hitched. Drawing closer, she saw a man in a torn and bloody suit lying facedown in the mud. She halted the horse and slid to the ground.

She knelt and felt for a pulse. "Sir?"

He moaned and turned his head to the side, revealing a swollen and bruised cheek.

"Good heavens. Mr. Hadley?"

Had he taken a tumble while riding? She looked around but saw no horse, wagon, or cart. "Mr. Hadley, it's Charlotte Fraser. Are you all right?"

He struggled to a sitting position and stared at her through bloodshot eyes. The smell of alcohol wafted from his soiled clothes. He waved one hand in her direction. "Leave me alone."

Pity and disgust warred inside her. Clearly the poor man still struggled with private demons she couldn't begin to understand. How in the world had Lettice lived with it for so long?

"You still here?" Mr. Hadley made a shooing motion. "I told you to get away from me."

She bent over him and fought to contain her anger. "Listen to me. Do you think you are the only one who has ever risen to a bleak morning? We've all suffered. And you, sir, are all Lettice has left in the world. She's trying to carry on, and you owe it to her to get on with life. Stop feeling sorry for yourself. Rebuild your plantation. Or move to town. But do something to make a life for her."

He shrugged and blinked at her like a sun-addled lizard.

"What happened?" she asked. "How did you get here?"

"Got robbed, if you must know. By a couple of workers off that fellow Betancourt's place. But don't go blabbing it to my wife. She'll be mad enough at me as it is."

"And I don't blame her. I realize you saw some terrible things during the war, and I am truly sorry. But there is no excuse for such shameful behavior."

He shrugged. "You don't know the first thing about watching people die."

"Oh, but I do. I've just come from an infirmary

in New Orleans where people died of the fever every day. Including Josie Clifton."

He frowned and scratched his chest. "Josie Clifton is dead?"

"Yes. And a thousand others too." She took her handkerchief from her pocket. "Wipe your face."

He complied as if he were a child. "Josie Clifton. My word. What the devil was she doing in New Orleans?"

"That isn't important now. Can you stand?"

"I'm not that drunk." He leaned on her, struggled to his feet, and climbed from the ditch onto the road. "Izzat your mare?"

"Yes." The strange look in his eye made her suddenly wary. She had known the Hadleys her whole life. For Lettice's sake she felt compelled to help him, and yet she couldn't help feeling uneasy.

He ran his hands over the mare's sleek sides. Cinnamon tossed her head and snorted as if she didn't trust him either. He cursed and yanked hard on the bit.

"Mr. Hadley, stop. You're hurting her."

"So now you know all about horses too." His lip curled into a sneer. "Is there anything you don't know, Charlotte Fraser?"

She stepped between him and her little mare. "Plenty. But my father taught me how to handle horses."

"Oh, that's right. Saint Fraser was a master of

everything. King of the Waccamaw. The most celebrated purveyor of Carolina Gold. The richest and smartest man in the entire Lowcountry. Except for one small thing." He leered at her, and she recoiled from the sickly sweet fumes wafting from his clothes. "Word has it the arrogant fool never recorded his title to Fairhaven barony, and now you stand to lose every acre of it to that quack who has laid claim to Willowood."

Tears burned her eyes, but she wouldn't give him the satisfaction of knowing he had hurt her. She wrenched the reins from his hand. "For Mrs. Hadley's sake, I was prepared to lend you my horse, but you seem perfectly capable of getting home under your own power."

He belched and raked his hair from his eyes. "Indeed I am." With exaggerated care he retrieved his hat from the ditch and set it onto his head. "Good day, Charlotte Fraser. Mistress of Fairhaven."

He ambled into the thick woods beside the road. Lacking any way to boost herself onto the horse's back, she led the mare down the sandy road at a brisk clip, anger churning inside her. What a disgraceful man. How had he learned of Nicholas's claim to the barony? Not that it mattered now.

Too shaken to examine her cane field or the potato patch, she returned home, looked after the mare, and went inside. Judging from the angle of the sun coming through the library windows, she still had several hours before Trim's return.

In the kitchen she set the teakettle on to boil and returned to the library just as Nicholas rode through the gate. Dismayed at her disheveled appearance, she fussed with her hairpins and shook the sand from her hem before going to the door.

Nicholas tethered the horse and ran lightly up the steps. "Good afternoon."

"Good afternoon." Despite her unsettling encounter with the drunken Mr. Hadley and her unresolved differences with Nicholas, she smiled. How good it was to see him. "How did you know I was here?"

"I was at Willowood today, checking on the roof repairs, and I ran into Hadley just down the road. He said you'd woken him from a nap." Nicholas looked skeptical. "He was in a nasty mood. I wanted to be sure you were all right."

"I'm fine. Angry with him." She stood aside and motioned him inside. "The Hadleys were my parents' friends for years. Lettice was my mother's closest friend. And Mr. Hadley's help was invaluable this summer, especially after Mr. Finch left. But the way he spoke of my father just now, disparaging everything Papa accomplished—it was awful. And I was only trying to help him."

He smiled into her eyes. "My grandmother had

a saying: 'Never catch a falling knife or a falling friend.' Old Hadley is a ruined man and deserves our sympathy despite his bad behavior."

"I suppose."

The teakettle whistled.

"I hope that means tea is forthcoming," he said. "I'm parched."

"I won't be a moment."

He settled into a chair in the library. She went out to the kitchen for the tea and brought it in on an old wooden tray. He sipped and set down his cup. "Just what I needed."

"How are the repairs coming?"

"Almost finished. My daughters will be happy to hear it. The Kirks have been fine hosts, but I'm afraid Miss Patsy is the nervous sort and not accustomed to the ways of children."

"Your girls are very well behaved. I'm sure Miss Kirk can have few complaints."

"Their good manners are a testament to your teaching. I'm ever in your debt."

"They were willing pupils, once Marie-Claire adjusted to the routine."

He smiled and picked up his cup again. "I'm afraid she gets her temper from my wife's side of the family. Although Gabrielle could be quite charming when she wasn't in high dudgeon."

"All children pass through such stages. My mother often despaired of making a lady of me."

"And yet she succeeded admirably." He smiled

in a way that made her heart stumble. "I'm glad you're here. I've missed you, Charlotte."

"I missed you too. And the girls, of course."

"I'm glad to hear it." He finished his tea. "Do you have time to talk?"

"About the barony."

"Yes. Even before I found my papers, I was working on a plan. I've been thinking about it ever since your copy turned up, and I realized that if you are willing, nothing has to change."

"What do you mean?"

"It's clear to both of us that no matter how much we might want to continue growing rice, those days are gone. Even if we have good luck with the weather next year, it's impossible to hire enough reliable labor to plant, hoe, and harvest all this acreage."

As much as she wished otherwise, he was right. It had taken six hundred slaves to keep all of Fairhaven under cultivation. Hiring such a large number of workers was an impossibility now. Most every other planter on the Waccamaw had already realized the futility of it and made peace with it in one way or another. How much more was she willing to risk to keep a promise that no longer mattered?

Her entire life she'd revered her father, never doubting his judgment or his affection. His love and approval were all she'd ever wanted. Now she understood that his willingness to let her tag along after him in muddied boots and faded dresses, his sanguine approach to her poor grades in school, had more to do with the fact that he was too busy to attend to her upbringing. His love of the land, his brooding secrets, his obsession with producing the best of the Carolina Gold had rendered him too preoccupied to attend to matters of her future.

Now she was on her own. She couldn't think any longer of promises.

She studied Nicholas over the rim of her teacup. "I suppose you're going to suggest growing cotton next year."

"No. The current price for cotton won't pay the taxes, let alone workers' wages and the cost of taking it downriver. I have a better plan." He proffered his empty cup. "Is there any more tea?"

She filled it and waited, her hands folded in her lap, while he drank half of it in one gulp.

"Your claim predates mine, and there's no purpose in fighting you in court. What I'm proposing is that we have new papers drawn up, giving us each our separate houses and some acreage for gardens and such. The rest we will own jointly for our lumber business."

"Lumber?"

"I've been reading about the scarcity of pine in the east. New York is importing it from Michigan these days. We have a lot of it around here, and it's worth much more than we can ever earn growing rice."

Even though her thoughts were unspooling faster than she could voice them, the sight of Nicholas, so excited about his plan, warmed her heart. His absolute faith in the soundness of his venture was contagious. And she cared too deeply for him and for his daughters to oppose him in court. She would find a fair solution no matter what. "Supposing I agreed. How would we get the lumber to market?"

"I've been thinking about that. If you're willing, we could convert the steam engine in your rice mill into a sawmill."

"But wouldn't that be terribly expensive?"

"About five hundred dollars for a fifteen-horsepower model. I can raise that amount without too much trouble. Anyway, I'm thinking we could lay down a timber track and use mules to haul the milled lumber to flatboats at a landing on the Waccamaw and from there to vessels headed north."

"It sounds complicated."

"I'm not saying it will be easy. But Henry Buck had a similar sawmill operation near here back in the twenties. I don't see why we can't have one too."

She couldn't help smiling at his boyish enthusiasm. "I suppose you've calculated our potential profit too."

"Yes, ma'am. Pine is going for up to sixty dollars per thousand feet in New York and Philadelphia. I figure every acre of our land is worth fifty dollars for the lumber alone. What do you say?"

She chewed her bottom lip, astonished at the thoroughness of his plan and weak-kneed with relief that he had kept his promise to recognize her claim to the barony. "It seems like the solution to all our difficulties, but it's a lot to take in all at once."

"I know it is. But I'm certain it will work if we act quickly, while the demand is still strong." He grinned. "All of Georgetown will be amazed at just how much two misfits can accomplish."

Were they misfits? Huguenot blood was considered an asset in these parts, but his abandoned medical practice and his unfamiliarity with rice cultivation had set him apart. Though welcomed by locals, he was still essentially a stranger in a tightly knit society that prized social and family ties above all else. And Charlotte herself had led an unconventional childhood, following her father about. She'd never really fit in with the other girls at school. And she had never enjoyed the usual feminine pastimes that occupied so many hours of a woman's daily life. She had always been driven by the need to accomplish something lasting. Something important.

She poured more tea into her cup and added

sugar. "I never imagined either of us as lumber barons."

"I have no desire to become a baron. All I need is my home, my children, and enough money to pursue my research."

She studied the calm light in his eyes, the determination in his handsome features. "You're going back into medicine, then."

"Not as a physician."

"It isn't any of my business, but I've always wondered why you gave it up when clearly you're so gifted."

He studied his hands. "I intended to resume a private practice after the war. For a long time I thought the memories might fade enough to allow me to do that one day. But some memories never fade."

Sensing that he wanted to say more, she folded her hands and waited.

Nicholas stared out the window, his fists resting on his knees, every muscle tensed. "That day at Gettysburg, General Longstreet argued with General Lee about strategy but wound up supervising Pickett's charge anyway. Against his better instincts. And it was a disaster."

"My father said that if Gettysburg had gone in our favor, we'd have won the war."

"Perhaps." He paused, remembering. "In the aftermath, my job was to sort the wounded. To decide which of the sick and injured should be placed on trains for transport to hospitals and which were too seriously wounded to survive. I stood there in the heat, knee-deep in blood and bloated corpses, watching hope leech out of the faces of the living when they realized they were being left to die. And there was no way to save them."

She shuddered. "It was war, Nicholas. You did what you had to do."

"True. But somehow that knowledge doesn't comfort me much." He turned back to her. "And then this summer in New Orleans I found myself having to make those same choices again. Who should get most of the nuns' attentions, the most laudanum. Who might survive the fever, and who was clearly beyond saving. Once again I found myself powerless to help them."

His pain was palpable. She reached over and took his hand. "I'm sorry."

"I want to follow up on Dr. Lister's work," Nicholas said. "To investigate whether better methods of fighting infections can be found. I want to find out why our Southern cities are plagued each year with malaria and yellow fever and half a dozen other deadly maladies. And I want to build you a school."

"A—"

"A school equipped with the best of everything. One where you can continue using the methods that have worked so well with my daughters."

She stilled. What on earth had given him such a notion? "I'm honored. But I'm not obsessed with teaching the way you are with medicine. It has its rewards, but the daily routine is too confining." She shrugged. "I suppose I spent too many years following my father around in the fields. I'm too restless. I cannot spend the rest of my life in a schoolroom."

"But think of Daniel Graves. And the Demeres. And the young orphan girl you met in New Orleans."

"Solange."

"Yes. She can't come to South Carolina, of course, but Lord knows there are plenty of children right here whose needs are just as great. And if you don't want to teach them yourself, we can hire bright young teachers willing to adopt your methods. You could write a book about your approach and travel to other schools to train others and give lectures."

She watched the sunlight moving across the floor. A lifetime of teaching was not for her. But he was right—the children did need someone to care. Someone to direct their futures and give them hope. She would never be a by-the-book sort of teacher, but perhaps by writing and lecturing she could make a difference. Besides, without her rice fields to look after, how would she fill her days? She had never been one for idleness.

She could feel his eyes on her as she considered this new vision of her future. At last he said, "Marie-Claire and Anne-Louise will be your first pupils."

"But I thought you planned to send them to Mrs. Allston's."

"I made some inquiries when I passed through Charleston. Mrs. Allston is very well respected, but it seems she's having a hard time keeping the doors open."

"There are others. Mrs. Mason Smith has a school. And Mrs. John Laurens. She's related to the Frosts, I think. You met them at Mrs. Hadley's party last spring."

"I remember."

"I'm sure the girls would do well at either of those establishments."

"No doubt. But since coming home I've realized how much I would miss them if they went away to school. I've already missed so much of their lives because of the war and its aftermath. They can be loud and messy and altogether exasperating. And yet when the house gets too quiet, I find myself going in search of them."

His eyes were so full of love for them that her heart turned over. "I did the same at the cottage this summer. They make for very good company. Most of the time."

He laughed. "I'm glad you agree."

A light breeze wafted through the window.

Bars of golden sunlight lit the distant river. Charlotte shifted in her chair and looked at her watch. "It's nearly three. Trim will be coming for me soon."

He rose. "I should go too. With any luck the roof will be finished, and the men will want to be paid."

At the door, he hesitated for a moment. "You'll think about the lumber mill?"

When he stood so close, he was impossible to deny. "Yes."

"And the school?"

"Yes."

"The girls are clamoring to visit Pelican Cottage. I must attend to some things here, but we could come over on Saturday if that's agreeable."

"That would be lovely."

"We'll be there on the morning tide." He tipped her face up to his and her breath caught. "I wish it were Saturday already."

Thirty-One

Charlotte heard their voices before they crossed the dunes—Marie-Claire's droll belly laugh, Anne-Louise's excited chatter, Nicholas's teasing response. And then they were finally there, three pairs of feet pounding along the piazza to the door, the girls hanging on to Nicholas's hands, a pair of windblown bookends.

"Ma'm'selle." Anne-Louise let go of her father and launched herself into Charlotte's arms. "I thought Saturday would never get here. I stayed awake all night last night."

"She isn't teasing." Nicholas set down his violin case and a large picnic basket. "She was afraid we'd miss the turning of the tide."

"I wasn't afraid," Marie-Claire said. "Because Papa already figured out the tides."

Charlotte smiled, thinking of how she'd believed in her own father all those years. She hoped the child's faith in Nicholas would never be misplaced. But perfection was too much to expect of mere mortals.

"We brought a thousand things to eat," Anne-

Louise said. "Are you hungry, Ma'm'selle? I am. It has been hours since breakfast."

"I'm not hungry just yet." Charlotte set the little girl on her feet and sniffed the basket. "But something smells heavenly."

"Papa cooked everything himself."

Charlotte folded her arms and cocked her head. "I didn't know you could cook, Dr. Betancourt."

"My dear Miss Fraser," he said with a grin, "I possess many talents yet to be revealed."

"Papa, may we play on the beach?" Marie-Claire asked.

"You may. If you can tell me the golden rule."

"Never turn your back on the ocean," the girls recited in unison.

"And don't go any farther than Miss Augusta's cottage. I don't want to spend half an hour looking for you when it's time to eat."

Nicholas watched them run pell-mell though the hall and out onto the sand before turning to Charlotte. "Would you like a walk?"

"I'll get my hat."

They crossed the piazza and stepped onto the beach. As they walked, Charlotte turned to watch their footprints disappear beneath the swirl and froth of the incoming tide. Sandpipers and skimmers scurried along in front of them, searching for food among the whelks, moon shells, and sand dollars bleaching in the clear

430

autumn sunlight. October had brought the first real release from the humid weight of summer. Now, in his company, Charlotte felt the weight of the past months lifting too.

They crested a dune that afforded a view of the bright expanse of ocean in one direction, the sweep of the river and the golden marsh in the other, a panorama that never failed to take her breath away. The breeze rippled the marsh grasses, bringing with it the smell of seaweed and salt.

"Look," Nicholas whispered.

She watched a great blue heron rise from the marsh to circle the tidal creek and thought of everything she had lost, of the thousand small griefs that pricked at her. Of the way dreams could get chipped away a little every day until it was impossible to remember them at all. She shaded her eyes, following the heron's unhurried flight. Perhaps the key to life was to accept as destiny the desire for what is forever denied. To make peace with the longing until it turns to joy and the two become indistinguishable one from the other.

The heron's dark shadow moved across the dunes. She thought again of days on this beach with Papa, of the lessons he'd tried to teach her. That life gives us loss and pain, and deep disappointments that often return as blessings. Maybe that was what it really meant to be restored. To move somehow from desperation to delight, from fear to faith.

"Have you come to a decision about the lumber mill?" Nicholas reached for her hand as they continued along the beach, their feet sinking into the soft sand.

"I've thought of little else. It's a sensible plan. And a generous one. You found your claim to the barony first. You could have made it difficult for me but you didn't."

"I had an ulterior motive."

She looked up at him, brows raised in question.

He cleared his throat. "It should come as no surprise that I am quite taken with you, Miss Fraser. And I would like permission to court you. If you are agreeable."

She searched his face. "We hardly know each other."

"A situation I'm eager to rectify." He clasped her hands and drew them to his chest. "All the time I was away, even among the sickness and sorrow, I couldn't stop thinking of you. I want you to share my world, Charlotte. To get to know you. To let you get to know me."

The look in his eyes, a mix of hope and uncertainty, cut through to her heart. She wanted to say yes. And yet . . . "I've had a lot of disappointments, Nicholas."

"I promise I won't be one of them." He drew her

into an embrace. "Can't you at least give me a chance?"

I wonder whether I shall ever again feel so lucky. It seemed a lifetime ago since she had penned that line aboard the *Resolute*. Now, standing in his arms, she knew the answer.

30 November 1869
Miss Charlotte Fraser
Fairhaven Plantation
Georgetown, South Carolina

Dear Miss Fraser,
  I am pleased to inform you that the Enterprise has resumed operations and I am once again able to offer to publish the account of your attempts to revive your rice-growing enterprise. If you are amenable, please send at your earliest convenience the fine pieces I was compelled to return to you last year, along with any others you may have completed in the interim.
  From time to time we are apprised of the many unsavory situations arising from Southern Reconstruction. I hasten to say that I hope you, dear lady, have been spared the worst of it.
                    Sincerely,
                    Edwin Sawyer, Editor

10 December 1869
Willowood Plantation
Georgetown District, South Carolina
Mr. Edwin Sawyer, Editor
The New York Enterprise

Dear Mr. Sawyer,

Yours of the 30 November received. I am most grateful for your kind good wishes and for your offer to publish my articles, which I am pleased to return herewith. Though they don't tell the whole story, I am happy for you to have them at the agreed-upon rate.

The cultivation of Carolina Gold is no longer a viable enterprise. Without adequate numbers of reliable workers and without the tools, equipment, and livestock that were stolen from us during the war, we can no longer continue the tradition that lasted for generations. The planter class is no more.

Lumber is the new hope for many in the Lowcountry, and I am happy to say that my business formed last year is flourishing. Fairhaven, my ancestral home, has been converted into a school employing two teachers for the education of twenty-six pupils.

Please forgive the brevity of this letter. I write in haste, for I leave tomorrow for a brief lecture tour before returning for Christmas preparations.

With all good wishes for the season and the new year, I remain,

Very truly yours,
Charlotte Fraser Betancourt

Author's Note

Dear Readers,

On my first visit to the beautiful South Carolina Lowcountry fifteen years ago, I discovered a book called *A Woman Rice Planter*, by Elizabeth Allston Pringle. Written under the pseudonym Patience Pennington, the book is a collection of pieces Mrs. Pringle wrote for the *New York Sun* in the years after the Civil War. The daughter of Robert F. W. Allston, a former South Carolina governor, Mrs. Pringle, who by that time was a widow, describes her difficulties in keeping workers, her changed relationships with her father's former slaves, the devastation of her crops from the storms she called "freshets," the decline in the price of rice that eventually led to the extinction of the rice culture. I fell in love with Elizabeth and with her story.

In the summer of 2012, I boarded a small motorboat in Georgetown in the company of my husband and Captain Rod Singleton, a native of the area and a student of Mrs. Pringle's life and work. We headed up the Sampit River to the Pee

Dee and her family's rice plantation, Chicora Wood. My first glimpse of it, glimmering white in the shade of ancient hardwood trees, brought tears to my eyes. Standing in the small boat, snapping away with my camera, I felt completely connected to Elizabeth. I could almost see her standing on the piazza, looking out toward the sea and worrying about an approaching storm. It was a moment I won't ever forget.

From Chicora Wood we headed to the Waccamaw River, where more than thirty rice plantations once produced millions of pounds of the superior strain of rice called Carolina Gold. For purposes of my story, I chose to set the novel at a fictional plantation on the Waccamaw. "Fairhaven" is modeled after Chicora Wood, though, and the difficulties my characters experience in the novel are inspired by the real-life experiences of planters on both rivers in the postbellum years. I adhered to the historical record whenever possible, but in a few instances I invented situations such as Mr. Peabody's use of the Litchfield chapel, and I placed ferry landings and causeways where they were necessary to tell my story.

A word about the name "Allston." Eagle-eyed readers will notice that I have spelled it with one *l* and with two. That's because the two branches of the family spelled the name differently. Governor Allston and his family used the double *l*, but William Alston, who is briefly mentioned in the story, used only one.

And a word about yellow fever. During the nineteenth century, yellow-fever outbreaks plagued America's port cities every summer. Charleston, Savannah, New Orleans, Mobile, Memphis, and others braced each year for the scourge. Families who could afford to leave for the summer went to the beach, to New England, or to Saratoga, New York. As one of the Allstons wrote, "to remain in the country during the summer would be Suicide."

In 1868, the year this story takes place, New Orleans escaped the worst of the fever, recording only a few cases. During the previous summer, however, thousands of people were affected. Though I bent the timeline a bit, the conditions, treatments, and other details of a yellow-fever outbreak are taken from the historical record, as are the details regarding the Confederate generals—Beauregard, Longstreet, Hood, and Early—who moved to New Orleans after the war.

Pawley's Island, where my character Charlotte spends the summer, was the traditional summer home of several of the Lowcountry planters, including the Allstons. They moved their entire households—furnishings, kitchen equipment, and even livestock—from their plantations to the beach in order to escape the "country fever." There they stayed until the "black frost," a heavy frost that killed the mosquitoes and made it safe to return home.

Mrs. Pringle was born near the family home on Pawley's Island on May 29, 1845. After the war she returned to Chicora Wood and remained there until her death on December 5, 1921. Her obituary noted that she died "at the scene of her life's labors in the beautiful home overlooking the river, quietly and peacefully" and that her passing would be "read with sorrow by hundreds who had been entertained and strengthened by her published works . . . and had come to look upon her as almost belonging to their circle of friends."

After spending so many years researching and writing the novel she inspired, I feel the same way.

San Antonio
February 25, 2013

Reading Group Guide

1. Early in the novel, Nicholas suggests to Charlotte that poverty can be the cornerstone of their friendship. In what ways does shared hardship affect relationships? How did hardship affect their relationship?

2. What was your initial impression of Charlotte? Of Nicholas? How did your impressions of them change over the course of the novel?

3. How did the war change the roles of Southern women? How were these changes shown in the story?

4. Charlotte and Mrs. Hadley take different approaches to dealing with their circumstances. Which do you think is more helpful? Why?

5. What are some of the difficulties Charlotte faces in dealing with her father's former bondsmen?

6. Charlotte muses that Southerners had no idea that Reconstruction would be a tragedy all its own. What are some of those tragedies portrayed in the novel? How do the characters deal with them?

7. Charlotte learns that her father was a different man than she had thought him to be. How did this discovery change her? Have you ever had a similar experience?

8. If you had to choose one word to describe Charlotte, Nicholas, Daniel, Trim, and Tamar, which words would you choose and why?

9. This novel takes place at the beginning of freedom for former slaves. What difficulties did they face and how did they attempt to deal with them?

10. The title of the novel refers to the exceptional strain of rice produced in the South Carolina Lowcountry prior to the war. What other meanings does Carolina Gold hold for the story?

Acknowledgments

This book is truly a team effort. I have many people to thank, beginning with my extraordinary team at HarperCollins/Thomas Nelson and my new publisher, Daisy Hutton. Thank you, Daisy, for your grace, care, and wisdom. My editorial team, Ami McConnell, Natalie Hanemann, Amanda Bostic, and Becky Monds, sat around the conference table in Nashville and asked the right questions about this story. My new primary editor on this book, Becky Philpott, provided insights and thoughtful commentary and the book is better as a result. It's so much fun working with you all.

I'm lucky to work with the world's most meticulous line editor, for whom no detail is too small to warrant scrutiny. Thank you, Anne Christian Buchanan, for your sense of story and your remarkably keen eye.

Kristen Vasgaard, thank you for yet another amazing book cover.

Books would not get anywhere without a marketing and publicity team and a great sales staff. Thank you, Katie Bond and Ruthie Dean, for your creativity and enthusiasm and for your willingness to listen to my wild and crazy ideas. Thanks, too, to our talented sales people who represent my books in the various channels.

A great group of people at Nelson work behind the scenes to make things run smoothly and I thank them: Jodi Hughes (a.k.a. my elf), Kerri Potts, and Laura Dickerson.

Thank you to my wise and caring agent, Natasha Kern.

Captain Rod Singleton of Georgetown, South Carolina, spent a day with me on the storied Pee Dee and Waccamaw Rivers and contributed his encyclopedic knowledge of the Carolina rice trade and of Mrs. Pringle's life and work. Thank you, Captain Rod.

Maryjo Fairchild at the South Carolina Historical Society in Charleston answered my questions about the photo of Mrs. Pringle as a young woman that graces this book and assisted in obtaining it for use here.

Jonathan Sanchez at Blue Bicycle Books in Charleston, the staff at Indigo Books on Kiawah Island, and the volunteers at the Georgetown Historical Society helped in locating books and other valuable research materials.

Reader Karen Carver of North Carolina suggested the name "Cinnamon" for Charlotte's little mare, and it fits perfectly. Thank you, Karen.

As always, I'm grateful to my family and friends and my writing community, especially my BFF, Leanna Ellis. Your encouragement keeps me focused when the words are flowing . . . and when they aren't. I love you all.

About the Author

A native of west Tennessee, Dorothy Love makes her home in the Texas hill country with her husband and their two golden retrievers. An accomplished author, Dorothy made her debut in Christian fiction with the Hickory Ridge novels.

Center Point Large Print

600 Brooks Road / PO Box 1
Thorndike, ME 04986-0001 USA

(207) 568-3717

US & Canada:
1 800 929-9108
www.centerpointlargeprint.com